HISTORY & MYTHOLOGY FOR KIDS

EXPLORE TIMELESS TALES, CHARACTERS, HISTORY, & LEGENDARY STORIES FROM AROUND THE WORLD – EGYPT, GREEK, NORSE & MORE

HISTORY BROUGHT ALIVE

FREE BONUS FROM HBA: EBOOK BUNDLE

Greetings!

First of all, thank you for reading our books. As fellow passionate readers of History and Mythology, we aim to create the very best books for our readers.

Now, we invite you to join our VIP list. As a welcome gift, we offer the History & Mythology Ebook Bundle below for free. Plus you can be the first to receive new books and exclusives! Remember it's 100% free to join.

Simply scan the QR code to join.

Keep up to date with us on:

YouTube: History Brought Alive

Facebook: History Brought Alive

www.historybroughtalive.com

CONTENTS

EGYPTIAN MYTHOLOGY FOR KIDS: DISCOVER
FASCINATING HISTORY, FACTS, GODS, GODDESSES,
BEDTIME STORIES, PHARAOHS, PYRAMIDS, MUMMIES &
MORE FROM ANCIENT EGYPT

EGYPTIAN MYTHOLOGY FOR KIDS

DISCOVER FASCINATING HISTORY, FACTS, GODS, GODDESSES, BEDTIME STORIES, PHARAOHS, PYRAMIDS, MUMMIES & MORE FROM ANCIENT EGYPT

HISTORY BROUGHT ALIVE

INTRODUCTION

Ancient Egypt. You might not know specific facts, but I am sure you have already heard about these: pyramids and mummies. Am I right? Well, surprise, these things are two of the most known characteristics of an old civilization called Ancient Egypt! Before it became the country it is today, in the North of the African continent, Egypt went through a lot of events, especially in the years known as "B.C.," which means Before Christ. That's right! These things happened way before the birth of Jesus, which was more than 2000 years ago. That is how old Egypt is.

You may not know a lot about Ancient Egypt, but this book is here to help you solve that problem—I have united all of the most important points of that period and will show you how awesome they were. Don't believe me? Well, let me tell you what you can expect from this book (let me go ahead and say: a little bit of everything).

You will learn about the Egyptian kingdoms and the pharaohs who ruled them. Did you know that a pharaoh is a name given for the queen or king of Ancient Egypt and that they wore some cool crowns that had the image of a snake on them? Well, they were the most powerful people in the kingdom, so I guess it was alright for them to wear whatever they wanted.

In this book, you will also read about what life was like in Ancient Egypt and what made it so special. I will give you a tip: it is related to the Nile River. The Nile is the longest river on earth, and it is home to hippopotami and crocodiles. Of course, the Egyptians were scared of them, but I will tell you more about it later.

And guess what: there are many stories that used to be told at the time and myths about gods and goddesses (and a particular surprise story, wait and see) that will help you understand everything they believed in. There is a small section on who the main gods were and what they represented. Ancient Egypt also had some mythical creatures, and they were really cool, too.

There is also a part in this book that talks about something that was very important to the Egyptians, which is death and what happened after you died. But do not be scared or worried, it was something that belonged to their culture, and we need to tell you about it so you understand them better. Just so you can see how important death and the afterlife were to them, it is related to the mummies, the pyramids, the temples, and writing. I know, it's crazy, right? How can people like death this much? It is not fun at all. Or maybe they thought it was; you have to read to find out.

Finally, there is a super special section of the significant inventions of the Egyptians. Can you believe that we still use some of them today? I will not tell you what they are right now, but could you try to guess? When you get there, you will be able to see if you got it right or not. You will see that the Egyptians were really smart people and that their inventions helped them and are still very useful to the present day.

Did I make you curious? I hope I did so you can read on! This book has answers to all of the questions about Ancient Egypt and more! Sit tight and enjoy the ride. You are in for some real fun! See you at the end!

CHAPTER 1
KINGDOMS

Ancient Egypt refers to the place that is known today as the country of Egypt, in the North of the African continent. The people who lived there were known as Egyptians, and they still are! Before it was one country, Egypt was divided into two: Upper (in the South, known as White Land) and Lower (in the North, known as Red Land) Egypt. However, a King came by around 3100 B.C. and decided that he would join both parts of the country so it would become one. When that happened, the period known as Ancient Egypt started.

Before King Menes, Egypt was in what historians know as the Predynastic Period. Predynastic means that it was before the dynasties, which is when the rulers' children became kings or queens after their parents. Ancient Egypt existed for more or less 3000 years, and it was huge! It had many ups and downs and kings and queens during this time. It existed until the Romans invaded the country and took power.

In this chapter, you will learn about the different kingdoms that existed in Ancient Egypt.

Predynastic Period (6000 B.C.–3100 B.C.)

During the Predynastic Period, something really important happened in Egypt. People stopped hunting animals and started growing their food by using the water of the second largest river in the world, the Nile. They also stopped hunting animals and started to domesticate them. This means they would not go out to look for their food, but they would have the animals controlled near them to provide what they needed. Because this was a very, very long time ago, there is very little information about this time. However, Egyptologists, which is the name of those who study Egypt, found objects and drawings that helped them understand what happened at the time.

Life in Upper Egypt

Like I said before, Egypt was divided into Lower and Upper Egypt. While excavating the area where this was, archaeologists were able to find lots of cool things that tell them the story of the place. For example, they know that the White Land (another name for Upper Egypt) was home to the Badarians and their main city was Nekhen. They were able to understand this through drawings that were made in rocks, which people did to tell stories. This is the beginning of the Egyptians' writing, known as hieroglyphics.

Something else that these drawings told the historians is that the people in Upper Egypt lived in tents! This is probably because they needed to move around, and it is easier to carry a tent than build their own house (it is also faster). However, they found out that the Egyptians changed from living in tents to living in homes made of bricks dried by the sun during this time. This probably happened because now they grew their own food and didn't need to move around as much.

Archaeologists in this area have also found some pretty neat objects from the time, like ceramic pottery, jewelry, and tools that the Egyptians used. Finally, they also discovered something that is very common today: the use of cemeteries. Before, when their loved ones died, they would be buried near their family's home. However, during this time, Egyptians started using cemeteries to bury those who died.

Life in Lower Egypt

Do you know how the Badarians lived in Upper Egypt? Well, the North of Egypt was home to another population: the Faiyum A. They lived near the delta of the Nile River, which is where the river finishes and sends its water to another body of water. Historians believe that since there was more water and more resources in this area, the people in Lower Egypt were more developed and had more money. It even had a capital named Memphis.

One cool thing to know is that it was in Lower Egypt that the first forms of government were developed. The land was divided into tribes, and each tribe had its leader. There was also one leader that was responsible for all of the other leaders. Archaeologists have discovered some exciting things about these people. Remember how I said that they started farming and growing their own food? Well, excavations have discovered that the people in this area built places to store their food, which is pretty advanced for them. Plus, these structures were both above and underground. Can you imagine? They also did ceramic work and made baskets.

Finally, it was in Lower Egypt that they discovered what type of animals the Egyptians were domesticating. Can you guess what they were? No? Well, don't worry. I will tell you: they were sheep and goats!

Early Dynastic Period (3100 B.C.–2686 B.C.)

Like I said before, King Menes unified Egypt and, with him, began what historians call the First Dynastic Period. King Menes was a really smart guy, and so when he saw that Lower Egypt was more developed than Upper Egypt, he decided to establish the new capital of the country there, near the Nile, of course. He gave it a really nice name: White Walls.

But something also happened in the religion of the country. People started believing that the king had superpowers and they could talk to the gods. They started thinking that the king was on Earth to be the interpreter for what the gods wanted. How do we know this? Well, during this time, the first hieroglyphics were written, and this has allowed historians to learn more about the time.

The Early Dynastic Period had three dynasties: the First, the Second, and the Third—all from related but different families. And that is a lot of people! For example, the First Dynasty lasted 260 years and had no less than six different kings.

There is also something really cool about this time. Something really important happened. I will give you a clue: there were great advances in culture, technology, and architecture. Can you guess what was so important that happened at this time?

Well, if you guessed that the first pyramid was built, you are right! The first pyramid was built during the Third Dynasty, near the end of the Early Dynastic Period. They also developed the calendar during this time, and their writing got more elaborate, allowing researchers to have more information about the time.

Old Kingdom (2575 B.C.–2130 B.C.)

After the Early Period, a new time started in Ancient Egypt. This period was known as the Old Kingdom, and it lasted for a long 445 years! During this time, Egypt had the Fourth, Fifth, and Sixth Dynasties, with more kings and queens. But the most important thing about this time was that it was when the most pyramids were built. For example, the Great Pyramid of Giza and the Sphinx were constructed during this time. Because of this, this period is known as "the period of pyramid builders." We will see a lot more about the pyramids further along in the book, so hold onto your horses, and we will get there!

Another thing that happened during this time, more specifically during the Fifth Dynasty, was that the Egyptians started worshiping a new god. The God of the sun, Amun-Ra. Because of this, the priests began having more power, although they still answered to the king. But it was not only the priests that had more power. The generals in the military and the nobles also started having more influence and government participation. Finally, when a king who was not so smart took power at the end of the sixth dynasty, the people saw that he was not very good, so they took him out of power. A new period started in Egypt, known as the First Intermediate Period.

The First Intermediate Period (2181 B.C.–2055 B.C.)

The First Intermediate Period had four dynasties—the Seventh, Eighth, Ninth, and 10th. There were many rulers during this time because there were a lot of wars in Egypt, so the kings and queens kept changing. What was once a territory with one king who had all the power now were separate territories with different governors, and one kept trying to invade the other. There was also a big problem with people from outside of Egypt trying to invade the country. All of this led to the economic and political weakness of the country.

The Middle Kingdom (2056 B.C.–1786 B.C.)

After all the mess that Egypt lived through during the first intermediate period, it was finally in the Middle Kingdom that a king finally reunited the country. This king belonged to the 11th dynasty, which lasted for only one king, who was later killed. A new king started to rule the country when that happened, and the 12th Dynasty began.

During this time, Egypt had a really strong military and started invading other countries. They wanted to get more goods and more money, so they tried to attack all of the kingdoms nearby that they thought had these things. However, by the 13th Dynasty, Egypt lost control of most of the territories it had conquered. There were also a lot of people arriving in the country, especially from Asia. With this loss of power, the country was weak again and separated into different territories, bringing what was known as the Second Intermediate Period.

The Second Intermediate Period (1786 B.C.– 1567 B.C.)

The first thing that happened during the Second Intermediate Period was a change in the capital of Egypt—it was transferred from Memphis to Thebes. Also, during this time, different dynasties existed at the same time since each one controlled a different territory. However, this made Egypt a weak country and allowed it to be invaded by a foreign civilization: the Hyksos, who got power but maintained most of the Egyptian cultures and traditions.

Everyone lived in peace until the leaders of Thebes decided it was time to reunite the country. They kicked the Hyksos out of Egypt and regained control of the country. They finally reunited the North and the South with the Middle land, which led to a new period in Egyptian history.

New Kingdom (1567 B.C.–1085 B.C.)

During the period of the New Kingdom, Egypt became an empire. This means that it controlled many territories, and these were from the northeast of Africa to other countries such as Syria, Babylonia, Palestine, and Assyria. It was also during this time that Egypt had some of its most famous kings—can you guess which ones they were? If you said Tutankhaum and Amenhotep, you are right! Because of the reach that the Egyptian empire had in other countries, trade went really well for them, and they were able to get many objects from different places in the world.

Something really curious happened during this time, which was the Ramesside period. It had this name because there were 11 kings named Ramses, one right after the other.

Although it has a curious name, this period was a good one for Egypt, since the kings gained more importance and religious messages were written on the walls of temples. These temples were huge—they had to be big and beautiful to honor the kings and the queens.

However, although this was a really positive time for Egypt, by the time that King Tutankhamun took power, it had lost most of the territories of its empire, which led to a Third Intermediate Period in the country's history.

The Third Intermediate Period (1085 B.C.– 664 B.C.)

Because of the challenges brought by the loss of territory, there were great changes in most aspects of Egypt's culture, society, and government. The government once again spread out and gave space for the 21st to the 26th Dynasty. Something different was going on, where one part of the territory was ruled by a king and another by priests.

It is known that there were kings from another country named Libya during this period and that Egypt had lost almost all of the territories it had conquered during the New Kingdom. Most of the Egyptian traditions were left aside by the different origins of the rulers. Syrians and other territories invaded Egypt and tried to force their culture onto the locals.

The Late Period (664 B.C.–332 B.C.)

Egypt was so weak that other countries kept invading them, particularly the Persians, who were quickly expanding their territory. They stayed in Egypt for more or less 100 years until the last of the native kings came to power, from the 28th to the 30th Dynasties. In trade, the Egyptians started trading more with the Greeks, who were close to them through the Mediterranean Sea, and because of this, many of them came to live in Egypt.

Since the Greeks were people who loved to write, something really interesting happened during this time: Several writers from Greece wrote down what they saw during their trips to Egypt. This is really cool because it provides us today with a lot of the information we have about the time.

The kings also started to do a lot for Egypt, focusing more on their own land rather than trying to expand. Because of more internal focus on the part of the kings, the economy and the culture started to revive. One of the main characteristics of the period is the increase in animal worship, which reached its peak during the Late Period.

Unfortunately, all that is good came to an end. This period lasted for only about 60 years when Persia once again invaded Egypt and was taken from power by Alexander the Great from Macedonia.

Macedonian and Ptolemaic Period (332 B.C.– 30 B.C.)

After the invasion of Alexander the Great, the military in Egypt was divided and, after his death, began the Ptolemaic rule, a family of nobles to whom Egypt was conceded after the division of the empire by his generals. Their descendants ruled Egypt until the death of Cleopatra in 30 B.C. The queen, who was known for being extremely capable and an ambitious ruler, stayed in power until the Roman invasion and is, still today, the most famous female ruler of Ancient Egypt.

CHAPTER 2
GEOGRAPHY

If I asked you to point out Egypt on a map, would you be able to do it? Egypt is located in the North of the continent of Africa, and it has three water sources: the Mediterranean Sea, the Red Sea, and the Nile River. To its left is Libya, and to the south is the country of Sudan. Today, the country's capital is Cairo, which is located very, very close to the Great Pyramids of Giza.

Egyptologists say that invading Ancient Egypt was hard because of its geography. On two of its sides are water bodies, and on the two others, there is the desert. No one was crazy enough to walk through the desert heat for days to attack them, so it provided the country with natural protection. To protect them even more, to the south of Egypt, there is a chain of mountains, which also help to protect the territory.

However, it would be impossible to talk about Ancient Egypt

without talking about the Nile. The river provided, and still provides, the Egyptians with everything they needed—from a water source for farming to a means of transportation. After the Nile flooded, it left the land just right to plant the seeds. The land that results from the Nile floods is called kemet, or black land. Meanwhile, the Egyptians also had a name for the hot, dry land of the desert: it was called a *desert*, or red land.

The Nile

Did you know that the Nile is the longest river in the world? Well, it is! It also has three branches and six waterfalls. These branches are called the White Nile, the Blue Nile, and the Atbara River. The three branches are important because they provided the Ancient Egyptians with water for farming, especially the Blue Nile with its floods. Because the water from the river gave them a way to grow their food, the Nile was seen as a symbol of life by the Egyptians, contrary to the desert that exists on the other side of the country. It is also the reason why many of the cities in Ancient Egypt developed near the river.

The Nile was so important to the people in Ancient Egypt that their calendar was built according to the cycle of the river—its floods and droughts. The Egyptians had specific names for each of the three phases that the river went through. They were named according to each possibility that the river presented: the inundation season, Akhet; the growing season, Peret; and the harvest season, Shemu. Although today there is a dam to prevent the Nile from flooding, back in Ancient Egypt, the river used to flood for no less than six months, at the same period year after year. And because they were really smart, the Egyptians built canals leading to their crops coming from the Nile, which meant that they had water throughout the whole year to irrigate their crops.

Here is a curiosity for you: it was not only the river that was important but also the papyrus plants that grew around it. Although some people might just look at them as normal water plants, the Egyptians used them for a very important reason: to make something called papyrus, just like the plant itself was called. And do you know what papyrus was used for? Well, to make baskets, sheets, ropes, perfumes, medicine, and shoes, among many other things. One of them will probably surprise you: to make paper! Yes! Papyrus is the paper the Ancient Egyptians used to write on. They made scrolls and other documents with this type of paper, and it contains much of the information that we know about Ancient Egypt today.

Due to its proximity to water, the Egyptians also became experienced boatbuilders. They used the river to transport their people and goods, and for funerary reasons. However, the most important characteristic was the trade routes that it allowed the Egyptians to have—the other lands that they could access to sell their food and buy products from others.

The Mountains

The mountains in the South of Egypt protected them from possible invaders. After all, can you imagine climbing a mountain to attack another country with swords, shields, animals, and everything else that war requires? Well, because of this, the mountain barrier is considered an essential factor of protection to the Egyptians and made it possible for them to develop without much worry of an invasion from that region.

The mountains also played an important part in the flooding

of the Nile. The reason for this is because every year when spring arrived, the snow that had fallen on the mountains would melt, and guess where all the water went to? You guessed right! The water would go to the Nile, and that would make the river flood.

The Desert

Egypt shares boundaries with two deserts: the Arabian and the Libyan deserts. Just like today, it was very rare to have people living there since there is almost no life—no animals to eat or hunt and little water to drink or to use to grow food. This is the main reason why Ancient Egypt developed near the Nile and not more centrally in the desert. It is estimated that more than 90% of Egypt is composed of deserts.

The Egyptian deserts are also known as the Western and the Eastern deserts, in reference to their location on the Nile River. In both, the climate is very hot and dry due to the lack of rain. There is almost no vegetation to be seen. However, they have caves, mountains, dunes, and bumpy areas.

Many historians say that the story of Egypt would have been entirely different if not for the desert. They believe that civilization would not have developed as it did. They also claim that the desert provided important things to the Egyptians, such as a specific type of sand they used to make glass. The constructions would also not be the same, as they would lack the primary resources to build them. Finally, history wouldn't be as preserved as it is today. This is because due to the lack of water and humidity, everything that was built a long time ago did not suffer too much decomposition and mostly remained intact. It would also be easier for invaders to access the country, increasing foreign influence.

The Mediterranean Sea

The Mediterranean Sea lies in the North of Egypt, which borders the country for almost 1000 kilometers. Some of the country's main cities are located along this coastline, and the same happened during the Ancient Egyptian civilization. Some of the country's main cities which still exist include Rosetta, Rafah, and Alexandria.

Although in the past, Egypt received goods from other countries that bordered the Mediterranean, a trade route was only established much later, near to the period in which Ancient Egypt existed. The participation of the Greeks was especially significant during this time. They traded products with the Egyptians and established a cultural trade. There are documents which tell about the visits of writers and researchers of the European country to the region, allowing a register of the period.

CHAPTER 3
LIFE IN ANCIENT EGYPT

Life in Ancient Egypt was very exciting. They always brought innovation from others and added new things to their culture. They had pets, art, agriculture, their own language, and way of writing. In this chapter, you will learn a little bit more about the aspects of the life of the Ancient Egyptians, and maybe you can find something that they did back then that you have now!

Government

Ancient Egypt had what historians call a theocratic monarch. This means that they had a king or queen and that they were both the leader of the country and the main religious leader at the same time. At that time, religion and government were one, even though the country's ruler was not a priest. However, the priests were appointed by the ruler to take care of the temples of the gods.

To best understand the structure of the government they had at the time, I will teach you a trick: if it was called a kingdom, then there was only one ruler for the unified territory; if it was called an intermediate period, this means that the government was not central and that the power was spread among territories. Finally, when I mention empire, this means that they had territories not only in Egypt, but in other countries, and even continents.

Society

Ancient Egyptian society was very defined—there were the upper, middle, and lower classes. The pharaoh, or king, was on top of the pyramid as the most important person in society. After he or she came to the vizier, who was responsible for helping the king or queen rule. The vizier supervised the collection of taxes and was the second most important person in Egyptian society. Next came the landowners, government officials, military officers in high posts, priests, and doctors. The Egyptian middle class consisted of soldiers, merchants, artisans, and scribes. Finally, the lower class was composed of farmers and slaves. The farmers were responsible for taking care of the land for the owners and growing and harvesting crops for food. The slaves were generally prisoners captured in wars.

One important piece of information that you should know is that there was a very good legal system in Ancient Egypt—even enslaved people had rights. The social classes were also not delimited: This means a person from a lower social class could go up and be part of another social class if they studied, for example. Finally, you should know that, even though the Ancient Egyptian society was dominated by men, women also had rights—they could inherit the land and even divorce their husbands if they wished to do so.

Agriculture

As mentioned in the previous chapter, agriculture was extremely important for the Ancient Egyptians. It was, in fact, the most important economic activity of the country during this time. With the help of the Nile, they used to grow their own food and were also able to store it for periods of time with the development of better construction techniques. But what kind of food did they grow? Can you guess?

If you guessed wheat, barley, fruits, and vegetables, you are correct! These are precisely the main types of food grown by the Egyptians. Now, are you able to tell me what they are used for? Can you imagine what kinds of fruit were grown? Well, let's start with the fruits. Historians have identified the remains of watermelons, grapes, apples, peaches, pears, and figs as a part of the Ancient Egyptians' diet. They have also identified that they used wheat to make bread and barley for beer as a part of their daily diet. Other crops grown by them were onion, garlic, and lettuce.

Agriculture was also used for other purposes aside from producing food, such as making makeup, growing plants for medicine, and making fibers for clothes and shoes.

Animals

Did you know that animals were very important for the people of Ancient Egypt? They were used for several reasons: as pets, for food, for transportation, for cooking grease, for clothing, to help in farming, and for representing their gods! And don't think that the only animals they had as pets were dogs and cats. Oh no! They had hippos, crocodiles, hawks, and even monkeys as their pets. We can know all of this because of the drawings that were made inside the pyramids and some other stone-carved documentation. Maybe we should look a little closer at each of these animals and know what they were used for? Come on, let's go!

Cats

The cat was probably the most important pet in Ancient Egypt. Not only were they used as a pet, but they also gave their god Bastet the form of the cat. Therefore, it is safe to say that the Egyptians loved their cats very much. Egyptologists believe that almost every house in the kingdom had a pet cat, and, mind you, they could be big or small. The pharaoh, for example, had cheetahs and lions as pets, which symbolized the power that he had. Cats were also useful, as they kept the house clean and free from rats and other animals.

Dogs

Did you know that the Ancient Egyptians also had dogs as pets, like you might have one? Although they were mainly used as protectors of the house against invasions and were less frequent than cats, some Egyptians had dogs as pets. They were used for many reasons we still have around today: for hunting, protecting, helping the police, and for company, of course. Many pharaohs have been depicted in their tomb drawings hunting with their dogs or simply in their company. These animals were so important to the people that the Ancient Egyptian god Anubis was represented as both a dog and a jackal.

Horses

Although the Egyptians did not have horses until the New Kingdom, they did have them, but not for the reason you are imagining. They did not ride the horses; they used them to help pull their chariots. The horses were used for war and hunting, but it was mostly the higher society that had them since they were expensive and complicated to look after. This means that there were very few horses in Ancient Egypt, but there were a significant number of mules, which were used to carry and transport materials.

Ibis

The ibis is a bird that was also used to symbolize an Egyptian god, Thoth. The Egyptians liked to observe birds in the wild but also raised them in captivity and used them as a way of making money.

Hippopotamus

Would you like to have a pet hippo? Well, let me tell you something—the Ancient Egyptians had hippos, but they were not nice at all! Hippopotami were not good pets because they were both scary and fascinating, especially when they were protecting their offspring. They are very aggressive animals who lived in the Nile and destroyed boats and attacked people who got near them. For this reason, it was not a good idea to have them as pets, although the Egyptians were so fond of them that they represented one of their gods in the form of a hippo—Taweret. In Pyramid drawings, the pharaohs are generally pictured fighting them. Today the hippopotami are extinct from Egypt and are considered the deadliest animal on the planet.

Crocodiles

Another animal that was very common in Ancient Egypt was the crocodile. Like the hippo, the crocodile was feared by the Egyptians. They were considered very aggressive and territorial and, therefore, more drawings of pharaohs fighting them can be seen in tomb drawings. The crocodile was also the representation of Sobek, a powerful god in Ancient Egypt known to take husbands away from wives.

Animals for Farming

Just like we have pigs, goats, and sheep today, the Ancient Egyptians also had them. They also had oxen for help with agriculture, chicken for their eggs, and cows for their milk. The skin of the sheep was used to make clothes, and the pigs were used for their fat. The Egyptians obtained meat and horns for decoration and artifacts from bulls and oxen, and they got their milk from cows and goats. Not very different from what we have today, isn't that true?

Writing

The language of Ancient Egypt is not very known, but have you ever seen their writing? You probably have, somewhere, since they are drawings that represent sounds and are called hieroglyphics, which means "sacred engravings" in Greek. This form of writing was used in tombs, temples, and pyramids, and written on stone and papyrus so that the Egyptians could spread a message, tell a story, or even reach the gods. Egyptologists have identified over 700 hieroglyphics, which can represent a sound, a situation, or a syllable—it is writing with a picture that is not a picture. Although the hieroglyphics are the most known form of writing in Ancient Egypt, they also had three other forms of writing: Hieratic, a form of cursive writing used by priests; Demotic, which was also cursive and used by people in general; and Coptic, the last stage of Egyptian writing adapted with Greek influence.

The Rosetta Stone

Have you wondered how historians know what was written in hieroglyphics if no one uses it anymore? I mean, take a look at an example of this writing and tell me what you can read... Absolutely nothing. However, a discovery made by the troops of Napoleon when they invaded Egypt has allowed this mystery to be deciphered. It is called the Rosetta Stone.

The Rosetta Stone was discovered in 1799 by French soldiers while they were repairing a fort in the city of Rosetta (thus, the name). The stone is a simple piece of rock that has some crucial information: It has the exact text in three languages— one of them is hieroglyphics, the other demotic, and the other ancient Greek. However, lucky for us, these historians were able to read ancient Greek, which made it much easier to know what was written in the other languages. Today, the stone is displayed in the British Museum in London and is available to be seen.

Architecture

When people think about Egypt, one of the first things that comes to mind is the great pyramids. Yes, the great pyramids are an extraordinary example of Ancient Egyptian architecture, but there is a lot more to know about what they built. Egyptians also built temples, monuments, gardens, tombs, and fortresses.

Because there is almost no wood in Egypt due to the existence of the desert, most of the constructions at the time were made from sun-dried bricks that came from the soils of the Nile River. They also used sand and gravel to complement the structures, as well as limestone for decoration.

Art

Arts and crafts were very important in Ancient Egypt. Although they did not have any precious metals such as gold and silver, they had a lot of clay to work with from the Nile, which made it its main type of art for some time. The pottery had a reddish-like color, and the Egyptians mastered its creation. However, they soon started using the clay for other purposes, such as building statues of the pharaohs, of the gods, and even in constructions. When they did these kinds of work, they paid a lot of attention so that everything would be proportional and symmetric, which means that all the sides had to be the same and that one thing was not a lot bigger or smaller than the other so that it didn't look strange.

The Ancient Egyptians also liked to paint. This can be seen in the drawings in the tombs, the palaces, and the temples. They used six colors: red, green, blue, yellow, white, and black. Every color had a meaning and was used to represent specific things, such as blue and green representing plants, the water and the sky, and gold representing the sun. Like the clay work, most of the paintings done by the Egyptians were related to religion and to the kings, who were generally pictured bigger than the other elements because of their importance. This was a general rule—the more important you were, the larger your drawing would be.

Finally, there are the relief carvings, which means you have a wall, for example, and you carve something on it so that a form or an image pops out. The Egyptians used this technique a lot, and it can also be seen in the temples, especially on the walls. Some kings had relief carvings on their walls, representing divinities or rulers. Other things that were carved were stones and ivory tusks.

CHAPTER 4
PHARAOHS

The pharaoh was the ruler of Egypt, known to be both the head of state and the religious leader of the people. A curiosity for you is that the word 'pharaoh' means "great house," but it was soon used as a synonym for the king or queen. Another interesting thing you should know is that although most people refer to all the kings and queens of Egypt as pharaohs, it was only during the New Kingdom that this title was used. To make things easier, we will adopt the popular term 'pharaoh' for all of the rulers of Ancient Egypt.

Ancient Egypt had many famous rulers, both men, and women, out of a total of approximately 300 rulers. They were usually sons, daughters, or declared heirs of the kings who came before, who inherited the throne after their parent's death. During this time, the kings wanted to keep their bloodline clean, so most of the kings married daughters of nobles or princesses. Sometimes, they also married their sisters or half-sisters.

The pharaoh is said to have two jobs—religious leader and head of state. As the religious leader of the people, he was supposed to be the intermediary between the gods and the population, interpreting what the gods wanted and appointing priests to take care of the divinities. As the head of the state, the pharaoh was supposed to rule the country and protect its borders from invaders while invading other countries to look for natural resources, goods, and riches that they did not have in Egypt. It was also the pharaoh's duty to collect taxes, lead the military, and care for the people.

Throughout the history of Ancient Egypt, the name 'pharaoh' gained importance until it reached its peak in the New Kingdom. However, these were also some of the most turbulent times that the Egyptians faced and, therefore, the name then lost its power. It once was a symbol of status and strength, but when the Persians and Alexander the Great invaded the country, it lost most of its status.

In this chapter, you will learn about some of the most famous Egyptian pharaohs. For many of them, very little information is known for many of them because of the destruction of tombs due to war and the lack of historical documents.

Menes (2930 B.C.-2900 B.C.)

King Menes was the first ruler of Ancient Egypt, known to have unified Upper and Lower Egypt. He established the First Dynasty and founded the country's first capital in Memphis. Other names attributed to him are Narmer and Aha, the first being more commonly heard.

Djoser (2686 B.C.-2649 B.C.)

King Djoser reigned during the Third Dynasty, and the most significant accomplishment attributed to him is the construction of the first pyramid—the Step Pyramid.

Khufu (2589 B.C.-2566 B.C.)

The main accomplishment of this king of the Fourth Dynasty was the construction of the Great Pyramid of Giza. The pyramid, which was known to be the tallest structure built by man for almost 4000 years, is still one of Egypt's main touristic points today and was built as the king's stairway to heaven. Little is known about his reign and what he looked like since only one statue of him was recovered. Pieces of others were found inside the constructions he built, but none is enough to give a clear picture.

Hatshepsut (1478 B.C.-1458 B.C.)

Hatshepsut was the second queen to assume control of the country. She is considered a successful ruler, keeping peace and establishing trade routes. She was said to have connections to divinity since she claimed that her mother was visited by the god Amun-Ra during her pregnancy. Although a woman, portraits of Hatshepsut show the image of a woman who dressed like a man and had a male's characteristics, such as a beard and shaved head. She had only one daughter, and once she gained power (which she stole from her stepson), she adopted a more feminine look. Some of her most considerable accomplishments are regarding construction—first of the temple of what would later become known as the Valley of Kings and later the temple of Karnak.

Amenhotep III (1388 B.C.-1351 B.C.)

Amenhotep III did not have much military trouble, as his reign was characterized by being peaceful and economically stable since he took power during one of the most prosperous periods in Egypt. One of the main things that were found from his time as a ruler are 200 stone scarabs (stone-carved beetles) that documented part of his reign. He also distributed stone tablets with messages throughout the kingdom, which left good documentation of the time. His temples were not preserved, leaving only two statues of him so that people could have an idea of what he looked like.

Akhenaten (1351 B.C.-1334 B.C.)

Pharaoh Akhenaten was the son of Amenhotep III. He was named Amenhotep IV, but he changed his name once he became king. One of his main characteristics, which differed from most of the Egyptians at the time, was that he was a monotheist, which means he believed in only one god. This god was the sun god Ra and it even led him to move the country's capital from Thebes to Amarna. At the same time, he was not saving any money and ordered that a new capital be built in an inhabited part of Egypt. His wishes for the country almost left it bankrupt, especially due to the radical changes he wanted to make—he wanted it to be a revolution in the country. Yes, maybe he was a little crazy.

This king was almost as known as his wife, Nefertiti, who played an important part when he was the ruler. She supported him during his decisions to change the religion in Egypt and his other plans. Nefertiti is known for a limestone bust made in honor, an object of art that is one of the most copied in the world of those belonging to Ancient Egypt. She is the mother of three of his daughters and the famous King Tutankhamun.

Tutankhamun (1332 B.C.-1323 B.C.)

The most famous pharaoh of Ancient Egypt, King Tutankhamun, was probably close to your age when he became king—he was just 9 or 10 years old. Can you imagine ruling a country while you are a kid? He was famous not because of anything he did but because his tomb was found practically untouched in 1922. Many museums around the world have pieces that were found in his tomb, and you can see them and have a taste of what it was like to be a king in Ancient Egypt. Commonly known as King Tut, he died when he was just 20 years old but denied his father's (Akhenaten) wishes of having a monotheist Egypt and brought back polytheism or the belief in many gods.

The Tomb of Tutankhamun

King Tut's tomb is the only tomb discovered to the present day which was left relatively untouched. It was found in 1922 by a British archaeologist named Howard Carter in the Valley of the Kings. Although there were signs that the tomb had been raided during Ancient Egyptian times, the main room of the tomb was left untouched. One of the characteristics of the tomb was that it was untidy. Still, historians are unsure if it is because of the robberies or because it had to be finished quickly since the king died at a very young age and the preparations were not ready.

Among the objects found inside the tomb were walking sticks (it is believed that he had a problem with his leg, so he needed help to walk), sculptures of gods, boats, and chariots, among other things. During the emptying of the tomb, over 5000 objects were counted by the archaeologists. Can you believe it? That is a lot! There were so many things inside King Tut's tomb that it took no less than eight years to empty them. Can you imagine having your room filled with so many things that it takes eight years to clean it all up?

In any case, the discovery of this tomb is one of the most important in modern history because it allows us to have a small glimpse of what the pharaoh's tombs looked like originally. Today the room can be visited by only a few people. However, due to the great demand of curious people and tourists who wanted to see what a tomb was like, a copy was made nearby so that the original art did not get ruined and the structure was not compromised with so many visitors. Today, most of the treasures found inside the tomb can be seen in the Cairo Museum in Cairo, Egypt.

Ramses The Great (1279 B.C.-1213 B.C.)

Ramses II, also known as Ramses the Great, was a great king. He was the father of no less than 96 children. Yes, you read that right. He had 96 children! He was also not afraid of spending money, which almost left Egypt without any. He built temples, cities, and monuments, especially since he thought he was a god, so he wanted the whole country to support him through his constructions. He also did some things that weren't very nice—he had slaves and also claimed he created some places that other kings had built.

Cleopatra (51 B.C.-30 B.C.)

Raise your hand if you have ever heard about Egypt's most famous queen: Cleopatra. If you haven't, no worries: I will tell you more about her. She was the last pharaoh of Ancient Egypt and is very famous. She even had many movies made about her and books written about her life. Cool, huh? Egyptologists claim that she was beautiful, had a calm voice, and spoke many languages. However, since there are so many stories about her, people have a hard time telling apart what is the truth and what is a myth.

She was born in Greece, and one of the main things she did was bring peace to Egypt. She is also known for having romantic relationships and children with two Romans, the ruler Julius Caesar and the general Marc Anthony, when the Romans invaded Egypt.

A curiosity about Cleopatra is that her tomb was never found. Archeologists keep looking for it to learn more about the famous Egyptian queen. Still, other than rumors, nothing has been found so far.

CHAPTER 5
GODS AND GODDESSES

Ancient Egypt's population was polytheist, meaning they worshiped more than one god. Egyptians believed that there was a god that represented different things in their life, such as the sun, the air, and death. Egyptologists have identified over 1500 deities, which is another name for gods, but there are many more that remain unidentified in the Egyptian pantheon. It is believed that the number can be well over 2000. Can you imagine? Two thousand gods to worship! How did they keep track of it all? I guess that remains a mystery.

Although Egyptians had temples for worshiping these gods, these were controlled by the priests named by the pharaohs and were not accessible to the public. Yes, you read it right. The temples were built for the gods but, unlike today, people could not go inside them. What happened was that during the specific day dedicated to the god, they would be brought out from the temple so that the people could celebrate them. Then they would be taken back inside until the next festival.

The temples were built to please the gods, as the people would do anything to be on their good side. This also means making offerings to them and holding festivals in their honor. The priests treated the statues, or representation of the gods as if they were real people, can you believe it? They would give their statues food and water, clothe them, decorate them with jewelry, and do their makeup.

When studying the Egyptian divinities, it is possible to see that they have animal characteristics or are represented by animals most of the time. It is believed that these gods were initially symbolized by animals but later, with the development of the culture, changed to the representation of humans with an animal head. Another curious fact is that some of the gods who are portrayed as humans are drawn with the thing they represent on top of their heads. For example, the god of the sun has a sun on top of his head. Due to the size of the Egyptian kingdom, it was not unusual for two gods to represent the same thing in different regions, leading to one shadowing the other on some occasions.

Because of the large number of worshiped gods (remember, over 2000!), their importance was constantly changing due to the season or a certain event. It was also common for one god to absorb characteristics of another throughout time or for two gods to become one, such as the example of Amun-Ra. Here are a few of the main Egyptian gods and their characteristics.

Nut and Geb

The Egyptians believed that all of the gods descended from the same family, which in this case were Nut, the sky goddess, and Geb, the god of the Earth. These gods were married, and Nut, who was the mother, gave birth to the five original gods: Osiris, Isis, Set, Nephthys, and Horus, the Elder. Nut is usually represented in human form, and it is said that each of her limbs represents a cardinal point—north, south, east, and west. Since she was the goddess of the sky, she is generally found in drawings on the ceilings of the tombs. Geb is associated with fertility and is considered to be the father of snakes. Myths in Ancient Egypt said that his laugh caused the earthquakes.

Osiris

Osiris was the god of the underworld, who symbolized death, resurrection, and the cycle of the Nile floods, which are associated with agricultural fertility. He was married to his sister Isis, who brought him back to life after being killed by his brother, Set. He is considered one of the most powerful gods, and because of that, the Egyptians wanted to be buried near his temple. He is usually portrayed as a mummy or as having green-blue skin, a color that is associated with the dead. He is the lord of death and, in the Egyptian Book of the Dead, he is the judge of those who comes into the afterlife.

Isis

Isis is considered one of the most important goddesses in Egyptian culture and represents a mother and wife's virtues. This is because of her dedication to resurrecting her husband. She is also the mother of Horus, who she had with Osiris. Isis is associated with every aspect of human life and became a powerful goddess represented with a throne on her head in drawings. She is also depicted breastfeeding Horus, which some scholars consider to be the inspiration for pictures of Mary feeding Jesus. Her most famous temple is located in Philae, and she is commonly associated with the Greek goddess Aphrodite. She was one of the last goddesses to be worshiped when the Romans invaded Egypt.

Horus

Horus was the son of Isis and Osiris and was conceived to get revenge on his uncle, Set, for his father's death. He is generally depicted as a falcon or a man with a falcon's head. His most known symbol is the Eye of Horus since one of his eyes represented the sun and the other the moon. Myths say that during his battle with Set, which he won, he lost one eye, the one that represented the moon, which is the reason for the moon's phases.

Set

Set is the god of chaos, violence, deserts, and storms, which he is said to bring to the valley of the Nile. He is the brother and killer of Osiris but is not considered to be evil. According to Egyptian myth, he is a balance to the goodness in all of the other gods. He is generally pictured as a beast with hooves and a forked tail.

Nephthys

Nephthys is the twin sister of Isis and the wife of Set. Although she did not carry a negative connotation, she is considered the funerary goddess and the darkness to Isis' light. She is the Egyptian funerary goddess, mostly believed because she helped her sister set up Set for battle after the murder of Osiris, which she didn't agree with. She is generally represented with a basket on her head and is the mother of Anubis.

Anubis

Anubis is the Egyptian god who cared for the dead and was the god of the underworld before Osiris. He was said to guide the souls through the Hall of the Truth before they were judged by Osiris in the afterlife. He is represented as a jackal or a human with the head of a jackal carrying a staff. Historians believe that the representation of the god as a jackal is because these dogs would surround dead bodies when they were not buried.

Ptah, Sekhmet and Nefertem

This family of father, mother and son was a divine trinity worshiped in Memphis. Ptah appears in the historic drawings during the First Dynastic Period. He is said to be the creator of the universe and the lord of truth, and an early fertility god. He is the patron of the craftsman and the architects since it was believed that he designed the earth's shape. His wife, Sekhmet, is represented as a woman with the head of a lion. She is the goddess of destruction and healing and the patron of the Egyptian military. Some myths say that she is also the daughter of Ra. The son of the couple, Nefertem, is the god of perfume and sweet aromas. He is also considered the god of rebirth and transformation on some occasions.

Hathor

Hathor is an Egyptian goddess represented by a cow or a woman with the head of a cow with horns and sun in the middle. She was believed to protect women during childbirth and was the goddess of music, dancing, inspiration, drunkenness, celebration, and love. Most of the temples built in her honor are located on the west of the Nile River, and the most famous one is located in Dendara. Her characteristics are believed to later have been absorbed by Isis or, in some other stories, she is a later incarnation of Sekhmet. In some stories, she is the daughter of Ra and, in others, the wife of Horus. She was also associated with the Greek goddess Aphrodite.

Bastet

Bastet is a goddess with the form of a cat or a woman with a cat's head. She was associated with the Greek goddess Artemis, divine hunter and goddess of the moon. She is believed to be the daughter of Ra. As the cat was considered a sacred animal in Ancient Egypt, many Egyptians carried a talisman with her in cat form as a sign of good luck and protection.

Heka

One of the oldest gods in Ancient Egypt, Heka was the god of magic and medicine and the guiding force of the universe. He is generally drawn as a man carrying a staff and a knife. He is the patron of doctors due to his healing powers. He is associated by the Greeks with the god Hermes.

Serket

Although Serket is not one of the most famous goddesses, she is known to the public because there was an enormous statue of her made of gold in the tomb of the pharaoh Tutankhamun. She is a funerary and protective goddess who protects children in particular. She was usually invoked for her healing powers.

Thoth and Seshat

Thoth and Seshat were a divine couple associated with writing. Thoth was considered the god of wisdom and writing, having invented the language and the hieroglyphic script, serving as a scribe to the other gods. Due to this, he is the patron of libraries and scribes. He also has magical powers and is the holder of secrets. He was especially worshiped in the Predynastic Period and is considered the last man to rule Egypt and the son of Ra. He is drawn as a baboon or the man with the head of an ibis. Seshat, his wife, or sometimes daughter, is the goddess of writing, notations, measurements, and books. She is mentioned for the first time in the Second Dynasty, and it is said that pharaohs called her when they wanted to properly build their temples. There is no knowledge that Seshat had a temple of her own. She is generally depicted as a woman with leopard skin who has a robe covering her. She is also shown as a woman with a headband holding a stick with a star on top.

Ra, Amun, and Amun-Ra

Before becoming the powerful and most known Egyptian god Amun-Ra, the god was, in fact, two different gods: Amun and Ra. Ra is a god associated with the sun, represented by a human body and the head of a hawk. He used to be the sun-god of Heliopolis and became very popular in the fifth dynasty. Ra is said to drive his sun barge daily across the sky and dive into the afterworld by night, where he faces Apep, the serpent, who threatens him every day. He is one of the most long-lasting gods and is characterized by a sun-disk resting on his head. Amun was also a god of national importance, but he is said to have his origins in Thebes as the sun god. He is represented as a man wearing a crown with two plumes. These two gods merged and became the most powerful god in Egypt—Amun-Ra, the god of sun and air and the King of all the gods.

CHAPTER 6
DEATH AND THE AFTER LIFE

❧❧❧❧❧❧ ❧❧❧❧❧❧

Before you start this chapter, let me tell you that I know talking about death can be uncomfortable and even scary. However, this was a major aspect of the life and beliefs of the Egyptians, so we need to talk about it so you can understand it better. But don't worry. There will be nothing scary about it, just some stories and practices of how they dealt with death and the afterlife. For example, did you know that the pharaohs used to have their tombs filled with offerings to have a comfortable afterlife? See, there is nothing bad about it. It is just people caring for their loved ones who passed away.

However, if you get scared or upset, don't worry. Remember that this is just a book that talks about things that happened a long, long time ago. These ideas were common at the time and part of their culture. They even built temples and magnificent tombs for the afterlife filled with drawings and decorations.

So be brave, hang on and come see some of the beautiful things the Egyptians did for those who died.

Death

Death was so close to Ancient Egyptian culture that many of their symbols are related to death. Mummies? Related to death. Pyramids? Related to death. Tomb drawings and offerings? Related to death. Well, I guess you get the picture of how much the Egyptians related their life to eventual death. Their culture is considered one of the richest when talking about the subject.

They believed in life after death, so, to the people in Ancient Egypt, death was just a temporary passing. They had many rituals they performed when a loved one passed away, including building tombs, making sarcophagi and coffins, embalming and mummifying the bodies and animals, and leaving them with enough possessions to be used in the afterlife. Death was so important to the Egyptians that it was almost considered a celebration when they would honor the life of the person who passed away. They had the knowledge that death would come to everyone at one point or another.

Life in the old ages was short for many reasons. This affected not only the general population but also nobles and kings. Because people often died young in Ancient Egypt, the rituals surrounding the death were popular. The body had to be kept intact if the person's spirit came black to claim it to use in the afterlife, which is why they developed the mummification technique.

The Afterlife

The Egyptians made offerings to the gods and left objects, food, drink, and other objects in the tomb for those who died since they believed that after death, the spirit would depart the body, but only temporarily. In the afterlife, a soul would go to the underworld to be judged by Osiris. However, before reaching the judge and lord of the dead, the soul needed to go through several gates before reaching eternal joy. They would go through the Hall of Truth in the company of Anubis before reaching the final judgment.

When the soul got to Osiris, it would be decided if it would go to heaven, called the Field of Reeds, or stay in the darkness. The most common belief is that the person had the same experience that they used to have while living in the afterlife. Another important thing is that most Egyptians weren't interested in moving on. They believed that everything they needed was in their home, in their land, so they just expected everything to be the same.

These are some of the most common versions of the afterlife, but many kept changing through time. There is also the story about the 42 confessions when a soul would confess their sins in front of the gods, who would judge them and decide if they should go to the Field of Reeds by a magical boat or not. The dead would serve Ra in his daily travels through the sky in another version. This means that not only did they have a very rich culture, but also a very good imagination for storytelling.

Book of the Dead

The Book of the Dead was a book that contained spells that were used when a person died. It was used during most of the period of Ancient Egypt, although it kept changing and improving through time. Even though it is called "the book" of the dead, it had many different copies and no two were the same: Printing came only a long time afterward, so these books were written by hand. The books had illustrations and writing, and because of the difficulty, the high level of personalization, and the elaborate means to make them, only people with a lot of money could afford these writings.

The book was usually buried with the person so that they could use it in case they needed to use the spells. The underworld was a dangerous place, with traps, threats, dangerous animals, and threatening souls. The Book of the Dead also instructed the soul on how to act on these occasions, as if it were a manual on what the person should expect at every stage of the afterlife. This book has become popular recently, with many movies and books making reference to it. You have probably seen it in films such as Harry Potter, the Mummy, or others that deal with magic or Egyptian culture.

Spell 125
If there was one constant in The Book of the Dead, it was spell 125. A copy of this specific spell was found in all of the versions studied by historians. Let's find out what made it so special.

Spell 125 talks about the procedure of weighing the heart, where the gods put the person's heart on a scale to determine if they would go to paradise or not. To pass the test, the person had to know exactly what to say to the gods so that the answer would be positive. The heart was weighed after the individual confessed to the 42 sins and, if it weighed less than the feather of the truth, the person could move on. The spell begins by stating exactly what should be said to Osiris and describes the different situations.

Mummies

Have you ever heard about a creature called a mummy? You have? On Halloween, right? Well, did you know that the Egyptians were responsible for the first mummies ever? And very much like the image we usually have of them, they did, in fact, have their body wrapped. But let's not get ahead of ourselves. Let's start from the beginning, and I will tell you everything there is to know about mummies. Ready?

When a person died in Ancient Egypt, their body went through a process called embalming. This consisted of removing the moisture from the body and leaving it completely dry so that it would not decay quickly. They wanted the body to be preserved so that the soul could return to it in the afterlife and use it if necessary. So, it was important to keep as many good physical traits as possible. This process was so efficient that even today, almost 4000 years later, we can know what the people at that time looked like because their bodies are so well-preserved. This process was so good and efficient that it was used throughout most of Egyptian history and influenced how we put our loved ones to rest today.

Even though it was a good process, it was a really long and unpleasant one, so no details! The mummification took about 70 days to be completed. Can you imagine? Seventy days! That is a little more than two months! The priests were responsible for taking care of the bodies, and they wrapped the body with hundreds of meters of cloth. However, while wrapping the mummy, they would put amulets in between the wraps and write prayers and magical words on the wrappings, all for the good passage of the person who had died.

After the mummy was ready, it was placed inside a tomb, which generally was built long before the person had died, especially if they were a noble or a king or queen. Inside the tomb would be the mummy and a series of offerings for them to use in the afterlife. Sometimes, even their mummified pets were there. Other things that were also in the tomb were food, water, furniture, clothes, scrolls of papyrus, drawings, statues, and pottery. After all of this was prepared, they were ready for the funeral.

Mortuary Temples

Once the pharaohs stopped building pyramids to use as funeral homes for their bodies, they started giving more importance to the mortuary temples. During the pyramid era, they were an attachment to the construction and served as a place to deposit the offerings and house the chapel. These grandiose temples were more common during the new kingdom, where every new ruler or spouse built their own part to be put to rest. Today, the most famous ones are the Temple of Hatshepsut, the Valley of Kings, and the Valley of Queens.

The Temple of Hatshepsut

As we have seen earlier, Hatshepsut was one of Egypt's most famous pharaohs. She determined that her mortuary temple be built as soon as she took power, and she wanted it to be grand. It was supposed to tell the story of her life and her reign and be above any other temple in greatness and beauty. The temple has two ramps, two floors, and many large obelisks. Everything inside the temple was grand and luxurious: pools, sphinxes, statues, art, and much more. It is not only a temple but a sanctuary that includes gardens and memorials as well.

Valley of the Kings

The Valley of Kings is one of Egypt's most visited tourist attractions. The Valley of the Kings is located to the west of the Nile River in the region of Upper Egypt. It was the burial site for almost all the pharaohs of the last dynasties, which added up to more or less 70 kings. The region was chosen because it was in a lonely valley, and the pharaohs believed that their burial site would be protected if fewer people had access to them. Along with the kings, some queens and members of the military are also buried in the complex, as well as the children of some of the rulers. All of the tombs are different in design, as each king built theirs as they saw fit and to their taste. However, they do have some things in common, such as tomb art and sculptures engraved on the walls. It was in this complex that, in 1922, the tomb of the young and famous pharaoh Tutankhamun was found by archaeologists.

Valley of the Queens

The Valley of the Queens, similar to the Valley of the Kings, is a structure also located to the west of the Nile, and it is where the queens were buried after their death. It is located near the Valley of the Kings and even the ruler's children were buried there with their mothers. Although it is composed of 75 tombs, only four are open to the public, including that of Nefertari, the favorite wife of Ramses, the Great. The tomb is colorful, with decorated walls, many corridors, and drawings of the stars on the ceiling.

CHAPTER 7
PYRAMIDS

One of the most iconic treasures known today in Ancient Egypt is the pyramids. Have you ever heard of them? They attract millions of tourists every year who wish to enter them to see and learn a little about what happened during that time. Like I have said before, the first pyramid was built during the Third Dynasty, but it was during the Old Kingdom that most of them were constructed. Once a pharaoh took power, the first thing he would do was to instruct that a new pyramid be built so that it could be ready when he died. Even though most people only know of the three pyramids of Giza, Egypt has around 140 structures of this kind spread across its territory, although mainly to the west of the Nile River.

Although they are the most recognized architecture throughout the country, the pyramid was part of a larger complex that involved gardens, temples, and other constructions. They were initially built only for the pharaohs, but later nobles and members of the higher Egyptian society began building them too. The main objective of the pyramid was to protect and provide for the king's soul in the afterlife and, for this reason, most of them had treasures, food, and other goods stored in them. Historians believe that the pyramids were built in the direction of the sky to help the pharaoh's soul go up to the heavens.

The first known architect of pyramids is Imhotep, a priest during Djoser's reign. Before using pyramids as tombs, the Egyptians used a structure called the mastabas, which were mounds with an angled shape. Imhotep used his creativity to design a building with one mastaba on top of the other. Additionally, tunnels, passages, and rooms were added under the structure to store the offerings to the king or queen, to place his body after death, and even bury other people who were close relatives or servants for the afterlife.

Soon the tombs started having drawings and scripts of the leader's reign and stories and offerings for the gods. These are the earliest registries of Egyptian culture, known as tomb art, which include descriptions of daily life in Egypt, customs, and other rituals carried by them. The inscriptions and art in the Egyptian tombs allowed researchers to better understand the life of these people as well as have a better understanding of their grammar and language.

It is important to say that, while the pyramids remain to be grand structures today, accounts of Egyptologists say that they were even more important when they were built. Today, most of them have gone through a lot of deterioration because they were not properly maintained, which led to the loss of some of their characteristics. Furthermore, robberies and vandalism of the constructions have left the pyramids with little of their original content, such as the remains of the pharaohs, the offerings they had, and the treasures they contained. Finally, it is important to note that even though 138 pyramids are accounted for, a large portion of them was left unfinished, possibly due to the short reign of the kings who ordered them.

Next, you will see, in chronological order of construction, some of the most iconic pyramids which can be found in Egypt. The best part of all is that if you get really curious and decide that you want to see them up close and for real, you can, since most of them are open for visitation.

Step Pyramid

The Step Pyramid was the first structure of its kind built in Egypt. It was built during the Old Kingdom for King Djoser and is composed of six layers. It is 60 meters high and has around five kilometers of tunnels inside. It was named the Step Pyramid because its design resembles steps.

Buried Pyramid

Since this pyramid was not finished, there is little to no information about it. It is believed to have been built under the order of King Djoser's successor and designed by Imhotep as well. However, stories say that the ruler Sekhemkhet Djoserty died before the construction could be completed and, therefore, it was never finished.

Pyramid of Meidum

The pyramid of Meidum, unlike the ones built before it, was the first pyramid to have straight sides instead of a step-like structure. Its original height is believed to be a little over 90 meters and, contrary to the other pyramids, it was built on top of the sand, not stone, which compromised its structure and led to the collapse of a part of it, although another reason could be that it was also left unfinished.

Bent Pyramid

With a height of 105 meters, the bent pyramid was built for the ruler Sneferu in Dashur and has a unique architecture compared to the other pyramids—it appears to be bent! This is because the structure of the building had to be changed during its construction because it began to collapse and crack, scaring the constructors into modifying it before it became completely ruined. This pyramid is today open for visitors to enter and it is possible to see the tunnels and the burial rooms inside.

Red Pyramid

The red pyramid has this name because... Yes! It has this name due to the color of its bricks, which are red. This pyramid was also built by king Sneferu after the construction of the bent pyramid. It is the third-largest structure of the kind in Egypt, only after two of the great pyramids in Giza. This pyramid is considered the first smooth-sided pyramid which was built successfully and is open for visitors. One curiosity about this pyramid, as well as for most of the other pyramids, is that it wasn't originally red, but rather covered with a white layer of limestone so that it would shine. However, tomb raiders and thieves have stolen these parts and now almost none of the structures have them.

The Pyramids of Giza

The complex of the pyramids of Giza is the most known in Egypt since they are the first and second tallest structures of the kind. Like the other pyramids, they have formal names, in order of construction and size, Khufu, Khafre, and Menkaure, names of the kings who had them built. Khufu, the tallest of the pyramids, had an original height of 147 meters; Khafre had an original height of 143 meters, and Menakure had an original height of 65 meters. The pyramids in this complex have many tunnels and burial chambers and are also available for public visitation. However, most of the goods buried with the kings are missing since they have been the object of raids and thefts over the years. The Great Pyramid of Giza is considered one of the Seven Wonders of the world due to its importance.

Also, near the pyramids rests another iconic Egyptian construction, the Sphinx. It is said to have been built to protect the pyramids and the bodies of the kings laid in them. It is 73 meters long and 20 meters high and is the sculpture of a lion with a human head, which supposedly belongs to King Khafre. As you will have noticed, the nose in the face of the Sphinx is missing, and how that happened is unknown. What Egyptologists do know is that the structure has deteriorated over the years and that most of its original paintings and characteristics are gone. Some say that during Napoleon's invasion of Egypt, the nose was shot off with a cannon, but that cannot be verified.

Pyramid of Sahure

This pyramid, although small (it was only 47 meters tall), is important because it represents another change in the way that pyramids were built. In this case, the structure had a tunnel that connected it to all of the other adjourning constructions: mortuary, temple, and valley temple. It was built during the Fifth Dynasty and set the standard for the next pyramids that were built.

Pyramid of Unas

Although the Pyramid of Unas is a relatively small pyramid built by king Unas, the last ruler of the Fifth Dynasty, it is important because it was the first of its kind to have tomb texts on them. It contained spells for the pharaoh's afterlife, and the story of his kingdom, among other information. Although the pyramid is open for tourist visitation, most of its external structure has significantly deteriorated. The inside, however, is mostly intact and allows the visitor insight into what the tombs used to be like.

CHAPTER 8
TECHNOLOGY AND INVENTIONS

❦❦❦❦❦ ❦❦❦❦❦

What would you say if I told you that many of the things we use today were invented by the Ancient Egyptians? I know, it sounds crazy, but did you know that they were the ones who invented items such as the toothbrush and toothpaste and the police? Yes, that police. The Ancient Egyptians were the first ones to have police officers; plus, they even used dogs like we do today! Let's take a look at other inventions made by them that we still use in daily life.

Medical Tools

Can you imagine what it was like if you got sick in Ancient Egypt and had to go to the doctor? Well, you wouldn't need to worry because the doctors in Egypt had some of the most advanced knowledge in the medical field. Some documents describe injuries, treatments, and diagnostics in detail, especially for the upper part of the body. The treatments included bandages and other materials we commonly see today, including some used for surgery.

Toothpaste and Toothbrush

Like I said before, it was in Ancient Egypt that the first form of toothpaste and toothbrush was invented. It may sound a little disgusting, but the recipe for toothpaste was ox hooves, ashes, burnt eggshells, and pumice. Can you imagine the taste? Another recipe, uncovered in a papyrus found in a tomb, probably tasted less yucky. It was made of rock salt, mint, dried iris flower, and pepper grains. Believe it or not, the products also came with advertisements—they claimed that this was the recipe for a powder that would leave your teeth white!

But why would they invent these things? Well, first of all, there were a lot of dental problems in Ancient Egypt; all these pictures that we see of the kings with perfect teeth are probably not true. Second, since Egypt is in the desert, a lot of sand used to get mixed with the food, so they wanted something to get it off their mouths after they ate. This is because if the sand was left in the mouth, it would wear down their teeth to their roots, exposing the pulp and making it easier to get an infection.

Breath Mints

Still, about dentistry, the Ancient Egyptians were also the first ones to use something that is very common today, and you can buy it in any gas station store: breath mints! Because of their poor dental health, their breath was probably also not the best. Therefore, why not invent something that would make it more pleasant to get near a person to hear them speak? So, they did exactly that. Historians believe that these mints were a candy-shaped mixture of frankincense, myrrh, and cinnamon boiled with honey.

Papyrus and Ink

Even though the paper was only invented by the Chinese much later, the Egyptians found a good alternative to write their scrolls and texts: papyrus. Using fibers from the plant that was grown on the banks of the Nile, they discovered that it could be used for writing. However, what were they going to write with? Well, with ink-black ink, specifically. Black ink was a mixture of vegetable gum, soot, and beeswax. As time passed, they discovered that they could substitute the soot for other elements in order to make different colors.

Cosmetics

One thing that the pictures drawn of Ancient Egypt will tell us, is that the Egyptians took care of and worried about their appearance. Maybe because this was so important to them, they invented some things that are very common today: eye makeup, perfume, deodorant, nail polish, and hand mirrors.

The hand mirrors can be seen in several drawings from the time, with men and women alike holding the object. Mirrors were generally sculpted and decorated. The quantity of decoration would tell if the person was a noble or someone from the middle class.

There is something that stands out in every drawing, even those we see today—the black makeup around the eyes. This black eye makeup was created by mixing soot with a mineral called galena, generating a black ointment named kohl, which is still used today. The more noble the person was, the more makeup they wore, especially around the eyes. But the eyeliner was not only used for beauty—but they also believed it could cure diseases in the eyes and protect them from the evil eye.

Haircuts, Wigs, and Shaving

While we are still talking about beauty and how it was important for the Egyptians, let's also talk about how they were the first to wear wigs and have a different shave. Well, first, you need to know that it was very common at the time for both men and women to shave their heads because of lice. Yes, it sounds disgusting, and it is, so they would have no hair at all to avoid this problem. However, a woman with a shaved head was not attractive, so they developed the use of wigs so that it would seem that the woman had hair. But hey, they were not only for the ladies; men also wore them, in the most varied shapes and sizes.

In order to cut their hair and beards, the Ancient Egyptians invented the barber profession, as well as the tools that they would use, such as razors. Since being shaved meant that the person was noble and fashionable while having hair meant that they were poor, everyone wanted to look hairless. But not really hairless, only without their original hair, since they would use sheep wool to make fake beards and wear them around town.

Calendar

You might be surprised to hear that the first calendar resembling what we have today was invented in Ancient Egypt. Invented initially by the Sumerians, the calendar was improved and perfected by the Egyptians. Although we use them today to remember special dates and birthdays, of course, the Egyptians used them to track the floods of the Nile. Much similar to our present-day calendar, theirs was divided into 12 months of 30 days each and five additional festive days in honor of the gods at the end of the year, adding to a total of—you guessed it!—365 days. However, we cannot forget that we have a leap year every four years, so although it was mostly correct, it still lacked some information that we have today until one additional day was added every four years.

Clocks

Since we are talking about time, it is important to say that the first clock was invented in Ancient Egypt. But they were not like the clocks we have today. Rather, they were sun clocks. They used the obelisks they built as an indicator of time according to the shadow that was projected by the construction. They could determine time with a lot of precision, including what was a short day (during winter) and what was a long day (during summer).

Bowling

If you like to go bowling, you must be very thankful to the Egyptians. A game similar to the one we have today was played by them more or less at the time that the Romans invaded the country. Archaeologists have found lanes with a square in the middle and balls of different sizes in their excavations. The game was to try to make the balls reach the square in the middle, while also interrupting the path of the ball of your opponents.

Door Lock

If you are at home right now, look at your door. You see a door, a knob, and a keyhole, right? Well, let me just say that you have got the Egyptians to thank for that: They were the inventors of the door lock which keeps you safe at home at night. However, although they were mostly safe, they were not very practical as they were very big, reaching up to half a meter in length.

Police

Since we are talking about security, let's talk about something that I am almost sure you would not imagine—the police force was created by the Ancient Egyptians. In early Ancient Egyptian times, the local officials kept order in the cities with private police forces but, after a while, it became more centralized. They even used dogs, much like we do today. No one was above the law and punishments of the most varied kind were given to those who committed an infraction.

Tools

The people in Ancient Egypt were very innovative and good tool makers. For example, the first ox plow used in agriculture was invented by them. They also invented canals, reservoirs, and irrigation systems to use the water of the Nile on their farms. Finally, to enable them to build their constructions, the Egyptians developed the lever, in order to facilitate transporting materials.

CHAPTER 9
STORIES AND MYTHS

Like most ancient cultures, the Egyptians had many myths regarding their gods. Some of them were heroes, others were villains. There were myths and stories about wars and about the creation of the earth. Some gods went to war, others stayed with their families. All of these were myths or stories invented by the Egyptian people about the beloved gods and goddesses they worshiped.

However, the Egyptians didn't only have myths about gods and goddesses. They also had tales that told how the pharaoh was deceived or a love story between him and another girl. In this chapter, I will tell you some of the most popular myths from Ancient Egypt and you can choose the one you like the most. Oh, Yes! Keep your eyes open in this chapter for a very special surprise—you just might recognize one of the tales as a popular one told today!

The Myth of Creation

As we have seen in previous chapters, Ra was one of the most powerful gods in Ancient Egypt. Throughout time, people began attributing more and more powers to him. One claim was that Ra was responsible for creating all the gods of the Earth. It was also said that every day, the god would make a journey across the sky in the form of the sun, and, at night, he would go to the underworld and fight with Apep, the serpent. When there was an eclipse or no sun, the Egyptians would say that it was because Ra had lost the fight and was swallowed by Apep.

Another story stated that there was an egg that named all living beings on the Earth and, once that was done, it became a man who was the first Pharaoh of Egypt. This man was said to be Ra and, because of this, the kings claimed that they were the Sons of Ra, since they were from a direct line from the god and, thus, had the right to the throne.

The Myth of Osiris and Isis

Isis and Osiris were two of the five children of Nut, and even though they were brother and sister, they were also married. Because Osiris was Nut and Geb's oldest son, he soon became the king, and boy was he loved. Since everyone adored Osiris, his brother, Set, became jealous and decided that he would kill him. When he did, he spread Osiris' pieces all over Egypt.

Isis, upset because her husband had died, decided to use her powers to bring back her husband to life. She traveled across Egypt picking up Osiris' pieces and resurrected him by using a magic spell. After he was reborn, the couple magically had a child they named Horus. However, even though he was living again, Osiris wasn't allowed to go back to the world of the living and went to the underworld to be their ruler and judge.

Isis and the Seven Scorpions

The tale of Isis and the seven scorpions was a very famous myth in Ancient Egypt. It tells the story of how Isis, after the death of Osiris, tried to hide from Set, but he found her anyway. However, Isis was pregnant, and Thoth thought that she would be in danger if Set found out, so he ran to save her. In order for Set not to find her, she was hidden by seven scorpions who promised to protect Isis and her son.

Isis then used her magic to change her form and adopted one of the poor women. During her travel, she decided to stop at the house of a rich woman and ask for some food and a place to rest. However, this woman was very mean and, when she saw the beggar, shut the door in her face. The scorpions were very angry, but Isis just continued to walk and was sheltered in the house of a poor fisher girl, who gave her food and a place to stay for the night.

The scorpions, however, were not going to forget what the rich woman did to Isis and told Serket, who was the one who sent them as the goddess' bodyguards. She instructed one of the scorpions to sting the rich woman's son. He did and the boy almost died. The mother cried for help, and it was Isis who saw and took pity on her, thus saving the boy and forgiving the woman.

The Myth of Horus and Set

As you know, Horus was the child of Osiris and Isis. He grew up to be a very brave man and decided that he would get revenge on his uncle, Set, for murdering his father. He did this by challenging Set to the throne since he had become the ruler after Osiris' death. Their battle took many years and it involved magic and contests. In the beginning, Set won, because he used tricks and did not play fair.

However, Horus' mother Isis, decided to help her son and set a trap for her brother. When she caught him, she eventually let him go, which made her son and the other gods very angry. Finally, they had the last contest, which was a boat race that Horus won. Set was so very angry that he had lost that he changed his form and became a hippopotamus that destroyed Horus' boat. Of course, because of this, they started fighting again, after all, no one likes to be attacked.

In this last battle, the gods declared that it was a tie, but neither of the men was happy with this result. Therefore, they decided to ask Osiris, who decided in favor of his son, who took his place on the throne.

The Battle of Pelusium

Bastet was the beloved cat-goddess of the Egyptians. However, because their enemies knew of this adoration, they used it to their advantage to win wars. In 525 B.C., in the last battle which the Persians had to conquer Egypt, they used a trick to win.

Knowing about the devotion of the Egyptians to their gods who were represented by animals, especially Bastet, the commander painted images of cats on their shields. He also brought all of the animals that he could find to place on the front line of the battle. No need to say that these animals were dogs, cats, sheep, and ibises, any animal that they knew represented Egyptian gods.

This battle, known as the Battle of Pelusium, was rather curious: The Egyptians lost because they were scared to make their gods and goddesses angry by attacking their images, so they surrendered.

The Myth of Hathor

As you have seen in the chapter about gods and goddesses, Sekhmet was the goddess of love, music, beauty, and more. She was Ra's daughter and represented many good things in the world. However, she also had a bad side to her: She punished people in the name of Ra when they were wicked. One time, Ra was tired of humanity and decided that he was going to destroy them. He asked Sekhmet to do it, but neither he nor the other gods were ready for all the trouble and havoc she would bring.

He tried calling her back but she wouldn't listen to him—she was unstoppable. He then decided to trick her and made large amounts of beer mixed with blood so she would be attracted by the smell. Since she was tired, bored, and thirsty from killing mankind, she decided to drink the beer, but it had magic and she fell into a deep sleep, unable to continue with the destruction. When she woke up, she woke up as Hathor, a benevolent goddess who represented only good things.

The Myth of Anubis

Anubis, who was the guardian of the underworld, was also a protector of tombs. Ancient Egyptians used to tell a story that when a person died, they went to the underworld to be judged by Osiris, and Anubis was there to receive them. He would weigh the person's heart on the Scale of Truth against a feather. If the heart weighed more, the soul would be eaten by a demon: If the heart weighed less, the soul would be allowed to go into the underworld.

The Book of Thoth

A long time ago, there was a prince called Setna, son of Rameses the Great. Setna liked to study a lot and was happy when people left him alone to do so. He knew how to read and write hieroglyphics, and he also knew magic, which he had learned from what he studied. One day, while reading a book, he discovered that a human had read the Book of Thoth and gained incredible magical powers with it, and he decided he would do anything to gain that knowledge.

He left with his two brothers in search of the tomb in which the Book of Thoth was hidden and eventually found it. Guarding the book were two ghosts, who warned Setna not to take the book, as it would bring him trouble. The spirits told him about the challenges faced by Nefrekeptah to find the Book of Thoth—he had recovered the book after a lot of trouble and gained the wisdom of the spells. The Book of Thoth was said to be the most powerful book in all of Egypt. It had all the knowledge of the gods, and the pharaohs were constantly trying to get a hold of it and were never able to. Thoth hid the book in many boxes and placed it on the floor of the Nile, where many serpents guarded it.

However, Nefrekeptah suffered a great loss when he could not save the life of his son and his wife during the journey back home in the Nile, even though he had all the spells from the Book of Thoth. In spite of hearing the warnings, Setna decided that he wanted the book and said he would take it by force, which did not please either the ghosts nor the soul of Nefrekeptah, who came back to life and said that, in order to have it, he must win it in a competition.

They played a game where every time Setna lost, he sank deeper into the ground. He then asked his brother to bring an amulet to save him and, when he was about to sink to the ground, the amulet was placed on his head. He got up fast and snatched the book away from Nefrekeptah. Although the ghosts guarding the book were scared that he lost his power, he claimed that Setna would bring back the book and beg for forgiveness.

Setna read the book and took it everywhere with him. One day, while he was outside a temple, he saw a girl and fell madly in love with her, which even made him forget the Book of Thoth. He was betrayed by her after she made him kill his children and make his wife a beggar, at the promise of marriage and children. When he woke up, he realized that it was only a dream, the result of a spell cast on him. Once the spell was broken, he found himself naked in the street, being made fun of. After a man gave him a cloak, he went back home and found that it was all a dream.

When he realized this meant that he had to give back the book, as the pharaoh had previously advised him to do, he was scared and thought to beg Neferkaptah for his forgiveness. He did exactly that, but the man was not willing to forgive Setna unless he brought the bodies of his child and wife back to his temple to lay with him. If he did not do as asked, the dream would come true. Setna obeyed and immediately set to look out for the bodies, but did not find them.

Soon a man told him that he knew where the bodies were and Setna found them, taking them back to the tomb. After he left, he said a spell that closed the door of the tomb forever, so that no one would find it.

The Girl With the Rose Red Slippers

This myth is an interesting one and it might remind you of a modern story that you most certainly have already heard. Let's see if you recognize it.

There once was a Greek girl named Rhodopis, who was kidnapped by pirates and sold as a slave in Egypt. She had light hair and pale skin, had a kind heart, and knew how to dance very well. Because of this, she was bought by a man who only showed her kindness, giving her beautiful gifts, including a pair of rose-red slippers so that she could dance. She was planning to use the slippers for a festival that the Pharaoh was going to have but all of the other slaves, envious of the treatment that she had from the master, gave her a lot of work so that she couldn't attend.

Tired of working, she took off her slippers for a few minutes to rest, but an eagle passed by, caught one of them, and flew away. Interestingly enough, the eagle took the slipper and dropped it into Pharaoh Amasis' lap, who decided he wanted to meet the owner of the slipper. It just so happens that this eagle is Horus, and Rhodopis seemed to know it, which is why she didn't pay much attention to what happened and continued to work.

The Pharaoh, who also knew who the eagle was, decided when the slipper fell on his lap that he would marry the owner since he believed it was a message from the gods. He traveled through Egypt via the Nile in search of the owner, until he reached the farm where Rhodopis was. The king's men, anxious to please him, just went inside and started trying the shoe on every female slave to see if it fits, which made her scared and so she hid.

When he was leaving, the Pharaoh spotted Rhodopis in her hiding place and told her to try on the slipper. She did, and it fit perfectly. She also removed the other slipper from her belongings, proving that the shoes were hers. It was then declared that she would be his queen and they immediately fell in love and got married.

Does this story remind you of any other? Well, if you said Cinderella, you are correct! This is the Ancient Egyptian version of the very famous fairy tale.

The Prince and the Sphinx

Thutmose was a prince of Egypt, son of Amenhotep, and grand-son of Hatshepsut. He was a very sad prince because, since he was the Pharaoh's favorite, everyone was always plotting against him. His brothers and step-brothers did this so that the king would not favor him anymore and would see him as unfit to become a ruler.

However, Thutmose was very smart and very skilled. In order to escape from these attempts, he would stay away from home as long as he could, even skipping important festivals in honor of the gods. One day, he decided to go hunting near the desert with two servants. They rode until they got to the Great Pyramids of Giza, where Thutmose admired the structures. However, he saw that there was a head and part of a body coming from the sand, and identified it as being from the

Sphinx.

The Sphinx started talking to him and said that he would be a great ruler and the prince, in exchange, said that once he became a Pharaoh, he would request that the parts of the structure that were buried in the sand be exposed again. He went back home and never again did anyone attempt to plot against him.

History said that he did in fact, become a pharaoh—one of the most successful—and that he fulfilled his promise to the Sphinx and built a temple at its feet in its honor.

The Princess of Bekhten

Once there was a pharaoh who was in the country of Nehern collecting taxes when a prince approached him and presented him with his eldest daughter as a gift. Since she was very beautiful, the pharaoh accepted her and named her Ra-neferu. However, years later, during a visit to the pharaoh, the father told the queen that her youngest sister was sick, and asked the pharaoh to send a doctor to see if they could help her.

When she was evaluated by the doctors, they came to the conclusion that she was sick because of an evil spirit. They called priests and other doctors, but the spirit would not leave the girl. The pharaoh did as requested and invoked the god Khonsu, sending a statue of him with some of his power. The god was able to release the evil spirit from the girl and she was cured.

Due to the power that he saw, the prince, the father of the girl, decided to keep the statue. The god stayed there for three years but decided to return to Egypt as a golden hawk. When the prince realized that the god was gone, he felt ashamed of his actions and sent the statue and a large number of offerings back. When everything arrived in Egypt, the pharaoh placed it in the Great Temple, at the foot of the statue of Khonsu.

The Peasant and the Workman

There once was a peasant who lived by selling goods from his country. One day, during his travels, he met a rich man who wished to the gods that he could steal all of the peasant's products and his wish was granted. After tricking the man, the rich man said that he was going to keep all of his products because no one would believe a poor peasant over a lord like him. The peasant cried and asked him not to do that, but it was useless.

The poor peasant then tried to look for justice, but no one would hear them. He wanted his belongings back after they were stolen and he had been beaten. The men of the court could not come to a decision and asked him to bring a witness, which he didn't have. The second time he went looking for justice, the king asked to provide his family with food and water without telling him where it came from.

The man kept coming back—for the third, fourth, fifth, and sixth time. Finally, at the ninth time, the king sent two men to speak to the lord, and the peasant was scared to be beaten again. However, the king had decided that the rich man should be removed from all of his titles and that all of his property be given to the peasant, who started to have a rich life and a good relationship with the family of the pharaoh.

The Tales of Rhampsinit

Rhampsinit was a very famous man in Egyptian stories. He was so popular that he was the main character in not one, but two Egyptian stories: one in which he is fooled by two thieves and the other when he visits Hades, the Lord of the underworld in Greek mythology. Even though he is portrayed as an Egyptian king, there is no record of a pharaoh with this name. Therefore, historians believe that he is a fictitious character, even though some versions of the story claim that the king was Ramses III. Shall we read these stories?

The King and the Thieves

King Rhampsinit was a very rich man who had a lot of gold, silver, and jewelry. Because of the value of his treasures, he wanted to build a safe room where he could store everything and keep it secure. He hired a master builder and his two sons to build this room and, after it was done, all his riches were placed inside. But the builder, who was not a very nice man, built a secret passage into the storage room and, when he was about to pass away, he told his sons about it.

The sons, greedy and want to have some of the riches, started entering the room in secret and stealing part of the king's riches. When the king noticed that part of his precious treasure was missing, he promised to get revenge and set many traps in the room, so that he could catch the thieves. One night, when the thieves were stealing the king's possessions, one of them stepped into the trap and was caught. Since he could not get away and feared that his brother would be caught, he asked to be left there, but that his brother cut off his head so that they would not be recognized.

The king was furious. Not only had they left with more of his treasure, but they were also smart enough not to be recognized. So, he says that there would be a prize to whoever identified the body. The mother of the two men, who found out about everything, begs her other son to get back the body of his brother so that he can have a proper burial. The man then disguises himself as a beggar, gives the guards wine to get them drunk, and steals the body. The king was even angrier, especially because the thief had outsmarted him.

But this story has a happy ending. In a last attempt to catch the men who were stealing from him, the king asks his daughter to help him to find out who the culprits are. She was so beautiful that the thief is enchanted by her but flees as soon as he realizes it is a trick. Finally, the king gave up and promised the hand of his daughter in marriage to the person who could prove that he was the thief. The thief presented himself and the king fulfilled his promise. The man and the princess got married and lived happily ever after.

King Rhampsinit Visits Hades

After King Rhampsinit died, he left the throne to his daughter's husband, the thief. Stories say that when he went to the underworld, he met Hades. Because he wanted to come back to the world of the living, he played dice with a goddess and won, which allowed him to come back. Happy because their king came back to them, the Egyptians celebrated a feast in his honor. A curiosity of this story is that at this time in Ancient Egypt, people used to throw dice to solve problems or make decisions.

The Sacred Lotus

The lotus is a flower that was filled with meaning for the Ancient Egyptians. But before I tell you more, I need to explain that this lotus was, in fact, what we know today as the water lily or the blue water lily, which has a yellow, golden-like center. Because of its importance, it was drawn in tombs in the hands of gods or humans, pottery was made resembling its shape, and many lotus flowers were scattered in the graves of the pharaohs when they passed away. Also, in Ancient Egypt, the lotus symbolized spiritual enlightenment.

In some myths, the flower rose from the water, in the beginning, to give origin to the sun or, in other stories, to the god Amun-Ra. The flower opened every morning for the god and closed at night, but he was lonely and wanted to share the world with other gods and people, so he created everything that exists. The way that the flower opens during the day and closes during the night is closely related to the myth created by the Egyptians.

One characteristic of the lily is that it has a very strong scent, so historians believe that it was probably used as perfume and as decoration at parties and festivals. Stories say that Cleopatra would take a bath every day with lotus flowers for their perfume. Still related to the scent, other myths claimed that the scent of the lily would bring people back from the dead, which is why there are so many pictures of people smelling them in Egyptian art.

Finally, the blue lily was represented in many other places in Ancient Egypt—they were in the jewelry men and women wore, in cups, in engravings, and in pottery artifacts. One of the findings in King Tutankhamun's tomb was a lotus chalice, which is in exhibition today for the public to see.

Monsters and Mythical Creatures of Ancient Egypt

Like so many other past cultures, Ancient Egypt also had its monsters and mythical creatures. They were mostly related to the gods and some kind of challenge that they would have to face. These creatures do not exist in reality, which is why they are called myths. People created them in order to symbolize something or to bring meaning to something that they did not understand. So, there is no reason to fear them, they are just part of a story!

Want to check some of them out? Come on!

Apep

As you have seen before, Apep was a serpent that the god Amun-Ra fought every night when he traveled to the underworld. But Apep was not just a normal serpent, it was a huge one! It was approximately 15 meters long and, because of its size, it caused earthquakes when it moved. But Amun-Ra wasn't the only god that fought the serpent. It also had an encounter with Set, which the Egyptians believed to be the origin of thunderstorms.

Uraeus

Contrary to the negative meaning that Apep has, the snake Uraeus was considered the cobra of the gods and symbolized the pharaohs' majesty. Do you know those tiaras that pharaohs are generally seen wearing in the drawings from Ancient Egypt? Well, if you look closely, you will see that it is a snake. And if you think that the snake represents Uraeus, you are absolutely right! It is the same representation, the only one that allowed a pharaoh to be recognized.

Bennu

Bennu was a self-created firebird related to Ra, very much like the phoenix, and it was a symbol of rebirth. Although the mythical bird became more known in Greek culture, it is believed that they borrowed the story from the Egyptians, since the Greek historian Herodotus claims in his writings that he was told about this specific bird during his travels to the country. It was initially drawn as a small bird but, later in history, was pictured as a huge animal with a long beak, similar to one that was native to the region but is now extinct.

The Griffin

The Griffin is a mythological creature that has the body of a lion and the wings and head of an eagle. It is generally used in Ancient Egyptian mythology to represent war since both animals that compose its body are hunters. It was also the guard of all the gods' treasures and can be seen pulling the chariots of the pharaohs in some of the period's drawings. Since the Griffin can also be found in other cultures, its origin is unknown.

CONCLUSION

Congratulations, you made it! You have reached the end of the book, and now you know a lot more about Ancient Egypt than many people. Here you have learned about the kingdoms, the country's geography, and what their life was like. Do you remember what the name of the important river in Egypt is—the one that is the largest in the world? The Nile! Yes! It was the Nile. The river was very important for the Egyptians and it allowed them to develop as a civilization. Of course, there was also the fact that Egypt is surrounded by desert, water, and mountains, which made it somewhat difficult for anyone to try to bother them while they moved on with their lives. Not that it didn't happen, but it took some time. Meanwhile, they were just there, creating, developing, and, of course, building pyramids!

You have learned a little bit more about the pharaohs, including the stories and traits of some of the most famous ones. Remember how cool it was to find out that King Tut's tomb was found almost untouched and that you can see everything that was inside? Would you have liked to be a king or a queen in Ancient Egypt? What do you think that was like? Do you think you would have enjoyed it? Well, I can say that I would, although I would be scared of having a cheetah as a pet or having to fight hippopotami in the Nile River. I guess you needed to be very smart and very brave to be a leader in Ancient Egypt. For sure you could have done it!

What about the gods and goddesses? You have learned about which ones were worshiped at the time, their stories and myths, and their relationships with each other. I know that it can be confusing with so many gods to keep track of—after all, there are over 2000—but I am sure that you have learned the main points about some of the most important. I think that gods and goddesses were really awesome. They had their magical powers, with which they could almost do as they please. Which god or goddess was your favorite?

There was also a part that talked about death and the afterlife in Ancient Egypt: You hung on like a brave hero and now you know a lot of neat things that they did when a loved one passed away—including building pyramids! Speaking of which, what did you think about the pyramids? Did you like learning more about them? Did you notice how many were built and how different they are from each other? The nice thing is that, if you want to, when you grow older you can go visit them and see them for yourself. That would be really neat!

Were you surprised by how many of the inventions made by

the Egyptians we still use today? Can you remember all of them? I will help you start the list... toothbrush, door lock... can you name the others? I am sure that you can, and that you will now tell all of your friends about the cool things that you learned in this book. Who knows? Someday you might become an Egyptologist who discovers something new about the Egyptians, or you might even learn how to read hieroglyphs. I think it sounds like a great idea!

Finally came the most magical part of the book: the parts with the myths and stories. Did you see my surprise? Yes! I am talking about the first Cinderella story, which came directly from the Egyptians. Which was your favorite story? The one about the Book of Thoth, about the thieves, or about the Princess? What about the myths? Which one was your favorite? I bet you will always remember ancient Egypt every time you see a lily now.

I hope you enjoyed the book and know that it will be here, no matter how many times you want to read it and learn about Ancient Egypt. Goodbye!

GREEK MYTHOLOGY FOR KIDS

EXPLORE TIMELESS TALES & BEDTIME STORIES FROM ANCIENT GREECE. MYTHS, HISTORY, FANTASY & ADVENTURES OF THE GODS, GODDESSES, TITANS, HEROES, MONSTERS & MORE

HISTORY BROUGHT ALIVE

INTRODUCTION

If you have heard about the Olympic Games, you have heard of the Greeks. Want to know the connection? Here it is.

The first Olympic Games ever was held in a place called Olympia in Greece about 3,000-odd years ago. The people who lived there were called Greeks. Greece is still there—a country of great beauty that you can visit—and the people are still called Greeks.

The myths or stories we are about to talk about were all thought up by very clever men who lived in Greece 2,500 years ago. Greece was famous for its intelligent and thoughtful people. These stories are about how the Earth came into being and about gods, goddesses, heroes, and monsters—some very brave heroes and some very nasty monsters.

The Greek gods and goddesses were almost like us humans. They got angry, they were jealous, and they behaved like ordinary people. But they were gods, so they had extraordinary superpowers, somewhat like Superman!

Why do we need to read and understand these stories? They were written thousands of years ago. The reason is that these stories are great tales! They are full of adventure and excitement. They are fun to read, as you will soon discover. And from these stories, you will learn about how people who made up these stories thought about the world around them.

You will be introduced to Poseidon, the god of the Oceans, who lives deep down in the ocean somewhere. The next time you are out on the sea, look down into the water and see if you can spot him! He might actually be there—you never know! That's the beauty of myths. They keep your mind alive with interesting thoughts.

Now, why do you think they imagined a god who ruled the oceans? Well, let's see—years ago the Greeks did not have giant ships going across oceans regularly. They also did not have the scientific equipment to look into the ocean depths. So, the vast oceans were scary, especially when great storms raged across them. The Greeks were convinced that there was a god who caused the storms when angry. They gave this god a name—Poseidon.

So did many other ancient cultures. They too had gods for the oceans, the heavens, and the winds. Even for thunder and lightning! Now ask yourself this: How did all these people think alike? Remember, 2,500 years ago there were no phones, computers, TV—nothing. There were no airplanes either. So, people from one culture could not just pass on their ideas of gods and goddesses to others around the world. Strange, isn't it?

All important cultures had their own myths. There are the Nordic myths, Egyptian myths, Chinese myths, Indian myths, and many more. Myths were very important to people in ancient times. All these myths are also stories about powerful gods, bold heroes, and eventually, ferocious monsters. Only their names are different.

Why were myths necessary? When lightning was seen, it was frightening to say the least. No one knew why it looked like a bolt from the heavens, and the rumbling thunder that came with it made the thing scarier. To explain this, they made up a god of lightning and thunder. When he was angry, this god would cause the lightning and that awful thunder. It gave people a kind of comfort. The gods were doing it. If they prayed to the gods, they would be safe. Today we know what causes thunderstorms, but back then, no one knew.

You may think that ancient cultures needed heroes like Hercules, for example (we shall be meeting him in this book). But think again! You have modern-day heroes: Superman, Spiderman, and Batman, among many others. We need heroes too! And there is another very interesting thing to notice. The words "Herculean Task" are still used and mean a job that is very difficult and needs superhuman abilities to do. So you see, the ancient myths are still around and alive even thousands of years later! Their names are still used!

The terrific thing about myths is that they make your mind soar as you begin to think of the daring acts that the gods performed. You begin to wonder and become curious. Did they really do those things? All great scientists also had this quality of wonder and curiosity. That is what made them discover and invent all the wonderful things that we see and use today.

Did you ever think that it would be nice to have someone like Spiderman around? He could save lives and rescue people from all sorts of dangers. Most people want this in their hearts. But he isn't real, is he? He is a modern myth, just like Hercules of the Greeks! So hero myths are still being created. They haven't gone away. The only difference is in their names. Think about it. The popularity of these imaginary characters means that we still need myths—heroic myths most of all.

The Greek myths are full of action and adventure. The gods too fight wars and call upon monsters to help them in battle.

We will begin with the creation of the Earth and the heavens, as the myths call it. We can also call it the sky. Without the Earth and the sky, the gods have nothing to rule over. They also need people—mankind. There is a myth about how the first humans were created and how they learned to grow food and use fire.

There are many characters in the Greek myths, and we shall be dealing with all the important ones—the gods who were major players in the Greek imagination.

You must understand that different gods became important at different times. Some were deprived of their power and imprisoned and some were just cast out. But how all these things happened forms the basis of these myths and stories.

The story of the creation of the Earth is common to mythologies everywhere in the world. There are differences of course, but every myth talks of gods and goddesses creating the Earth and bringing mankind to live on it. Without mankind, the gods really would have nothing, and you would not have any myths to read. The Greek gods needed mankind to talk about them and write about them. They made mankind and everything else, after all.

However, there is something that you should know: The Greeks actually believed in their gods and prayed to them, offering them food to keep them happy. They thought that their gods were there from the beginning of time and were the ones who created everything. Today, science calls the origin of the universe the "Big Bang." The interesting part is that the Big Bang happened from a void in space—a black hole! It seems that the Greeks had the correct idea about the creation of the cosmos. Of course, they did not know about black holes, they could only guess.

Now we move on to the Greek myths. Who were the Titans? What did they do? Who were the great heroes? In Greek mythology, there are many heroes, and they are very brave and adventurous people. They undertook almost impossible tasks, and they usually succeeded in doing them. Then there are the gods and goddesses—the Divine men and women who ruled the skies, the oceans, the animals, and the lives of the first humans on Earth.

CHAPTER 1
HOW THE WORLD WAS CREATED

In the beginning, a long, long time ago...

There was darkness and a void. Nothing else. The universe had not yet been created. The Greeks gave a name to this darkness: Chaos. This was a time before anything existed.

Then Gaia appeared from the void. She was the mother goddess, the universe in divine form.

However, Gaia felt lonely, as she was alone in the universe. So, she created Uranus—the night sky—and made him so big that he covered everything. You do see the sky wherever you look, right? Then she created the mountains and the seas. But she was still alone, except for Uranus of course.

Gaia fell in love with Uranus and married him. They had 12 children. Six of these were female and their names were: Theia, Themis, Mnemosyne, Phoebe, Tethys, and Rhea. The names of the six male children were: Oceanus, Coeus, Crius, Hyperion, Iapetus, and Cronus.

They were called the Titans. Of the six male children, the youngest one, Cronus, is important, and we shall soon see why. These children were the first race on Earth and they were gods too.

As time went by, Gaia realized that Uranus was a cruel person who treated their children badly. Gaia wanted to be rid of him and asked her sons and daughters to help. She went to 11 of them, but they all refused to help her. They were all scared of Uranus. Then she went to the youngest, Cronus. He agreed to help his mother and destroyed Uranus. But before dying, Uranus cursed Cronus, saying that "one day your son will take power away from you in the same way that you took it from me."

Cronus then took the place of Uranus and became the new ruler. Cronus, however, was not a nice ruler. He remembered the curse that Uranus had put on him and began swallowing all the children his wife Rhea gave birth to. He thought that it was the best way to stop the curse from taking effect. He swallowed five of his children before Rhea decided to stop him from swallowing the next baby, which she knew was a boy.

Rhea went to Gaia and asked for help in saving her sixth child. Gaia told her what to do. When the sixth baby was born, Rhea secretly took him and left him in a cave on the island of Crete. There, the baby was looked after by Nymphs (goddesses of nature) and he grew up big and strong. To fool Cronus, Rhea wrapped a piece of rock in cloth and gave it to him. Cronus, believing it to be his sixth baby, swallowed it!

Rhea named the baby Zeus, and when he was old enough, the Nymphs told him how his father had swallowed his five brothers and sisters. This made Zeus angry and he decided that he would find his father and defeat him in battle.

Zeus then summoned Metis, daughter of Oceanus to his aid. Metis was known for her wisdom. She gave Zeus a potion with instructions to give it to Cronus. Zeus quietly introduced the potion into Cronus's drink. As soon as Cronus drank it he vomited, and out came all the babies he had swallowed, fully grown and alive. Zeus gathered his brothers and sisters— Hera, Poseidon, Hades, Hestia, and Demeter—and declared war on his father Cronus.

The battle continued for close to 10 years with no real result. Neither side could defeat the other. It was at this time that Mother Earth, Gaia, came to Zeus and revealed to him that he should seek the help of the three Cyclops and the three Hecatoncheires—monsters she had also given birth to. She told him that Uranus, their father, seeing how ugly they were, banished them and kept them locked up. Mother Earth advised Zeus to release them. Zeus went to the monsters and realized that they also hated Cronus. He had continued to keep them locked up after seizing power from Uranus, so they agreed to fight for Zeus. These were terrible creatures with superhuman powers! The Cyclops were giants with magical powers that had one eye in the middle of their foreheads. They made weapons that could hurl thunder and lightning at the enemy, and they gave these weapons to Zeus. The Hecatoncheires were also giants with 100 arms and 50 heads and could not be killed easily. The battle was about to become very nasty.

Zeus went to war with Cronus with his new army and the weapons are given to him by the Cyclops. The monsters too went with him, and in no time, he defeated Cronus. Zeus then sent Cronus and the Titans to an underground place called the Underworld, or the Land Of The Dead. There they were guarded by the Hecatoncheires so that they could never escape. Zeus was now the new ruler!

The Titan Children

Some of the Titan children who were not imprisoned by Zeus played very important roles in the affairs of humans.

Cronus, his wife Rhea, and Zeus are well-known in Greek mythology. However, the sons of Iapetus (who was Cronus's brother)—Prometheus, Atlas, and Epimetheus—are also important gods, about whom we shall now read.

The Origin of Mankind

Prometheus and Epimetheus were brothers. When the war was going on between Zeus and the Titans, Prometheus warned the Titans that Zeus had the Cyclops and the Hecatoncheires on his side and that the Titans should change their battle plans. The Titans did not listen, so Prometheus and Epimetheus went over to the side of Zeus. When Zeus won the war, he decided to reward Prometheus and Epimetheus for supporting him. This decision, as you will see, was very important for many reasons.

Zeus called Prometheus and asked him to create mankind. Prometheus took clay and water and fashioned humans. A goddess named Athena breathed life into the clay models and they came alive. These were the first humans.

Epimetheus was given the task of making the animals, birds, and insects. He worked carefully and gave each creature a means of protection. He gave the turtle a hard shell, the bee a sting, and the snake its venom. Prometheus, meanwhile, was busy making humans. He was slow and when he was finally done, he realized that Epimetheus had used up all the protective devices by giving them away to the animals, birds, and insects. There was nothing left to give mankind. Prometheus scratched his head. Mankind needed some form of protection. He thought of fire. The gods had a fire, so if he wanted to give it to the humans, he would need to ask permission from the ruler, Zeus.

Prometheus went to Zeus and asked him, "O great ruler, the humans need fire to protect themselves and to prepare food. With your permission, I will give them fire." But Zeus flatly refused, saying that only the gods had the right to have the fire. This enraged Prometheus. He had never forgiven Zeus for destroying the Titans since he was a Titan himself. Prometheus was determined to give fire to the humans. "I don't need your consent Zeus—I will give the humans fire." He went to the island of Lemnos and stole fire from the forges of Hephaestus (another god). He carried it to mankind and gave it to them. Fire, as we all know, is very important. Without it food cannot be cooked, and candles cannot be lit!

When Prometheus arrived with the fire the people were scared of this glowing light. Prometheus then taught them what to do with it. He showed them how to cook meat, melt iron to make weapons, and how to use fire to scare away wild animals. The people slowly understood the importance of this element called fire and began to worship it.

Prometheus liked the humans more than the gods. But for his theft of fire, Zeus would make him pay a heavy price.

At night, Zeus, on his usual journey through the heavens, saw several lights on Earth and realized that they were small fires. How did they get fire? Then he knew. That fellow Prometheus must have given it to them. The next morning he summoned Hephaestus, the master metal workman. "Prepare chains of such strength that no one can break them. They must be made so that they last for eternity!" barked Zeus.

Hephaestus asked, "and what are these chains to be used for?"

Zeus told him. Hephaestus was aghast. But he went away to make the chains. He did not dare annoy Zeus.

Zeus had Prometheus bound by chains to a rock and had a very large eagle come and feast on his liver. During the day the bird would eat his liver, and during the night it would grow back again. The next day the bird would be back to eat the now grown liver. Zeus wanted Prometheus to feel the pain every day. But Prometheus never surrendered to Zeus. This carried on for about 30,000 years! Until, with the permission of Zeus, Hercules (a popular Greek hero) unchained Prometheus, and killed the dreadful flying creature that was feasting on his liver.

Now you will read about another Greek god, whose name you are probably familiar with—Atlas. Atlas was a Titan, and he had commanded the Titan army. After the defeat of the Titans, Zeus had a special punishment for him. He sent Atlas to the end of Earth and had him hold up the sky for all eternity so that the sky and the Earth shall never meet. They are still separate today. A collection of maps in book form is called an Atlas, in his honor, even today. You see, mythical figures and their impact are still here among us!

Zeus set up his palace on Mount Olympus and went to live there. He decided that the universe was too big for one man to rule, so he needed to have a lottery. The important Olympian gods and goddesses would all draw straws to see who got what to rule over. There were twelve of them. Let's see who they were.

Among the gods there was Zeus, then Poseidon, Hephaestus, Hermes, Ares, and Apollo. Among the goddesses, there was Hera, Athena, Artemis, Hestia, Aphrodite, and finally Demeter. You will get to know who they all were soon.

Zeus was the most powerful, so he got rulership over Ether, which meant that he had lordship over the heavens.

Poseidon was given control over the oceans and Hades was given power over the Underworld. These were the main gods.

The goddesses got positions too. Hesta got to rule over hearth and home, Hera was given marriage and childbirth, and Demeter was made goddess of the harvest. It is important to understand that the rulership of the gods and goddesses was over the affairs of humans, on Earth.

Ares was made a god of war and Hermes was the messenger. Hephaestus was made a god of fire and Apollo became the god of light and music. Artemis became the goddess of hunting and Athena ruled over wisdom. Aphrodite was given power over love.

One day, Dionysus turned up at Mount Olympia. Since he never came to the Council, he had no place to sit. All the thrones were occupied. Hesta, who was Zeus's eldest sister, gave up her place to Dionysus. She wanted to go and look after the fire in the palace—a fire that always burned. Dionysus had power over nature, wine, and fruitfulness, so he was an important god, especially for the humans, who needed their trees to produce fruit.

Now, we come to the stories that tell of wonderful adventures by the gods and goddesses, and of course, the heroes.

CHAPTER 2
THE LABORS OF HERCULES (PART 1)

The first hero you will read about is Hercules. He had to complete the 12 labors given to him. Each one was a very difficult task, but first, you have to know why Hercules was given those difficult and dangerous tasks.

Let us start at the birth of Hercules to understand the reason.

Perseus was the son of Zeus and Danae. Zeus had announced publicly that the first male descendant of Perseus would rule after him. Hera, the wife of Zeus, did not want the son of Perseus to become ruler. So she played a trick and got Eurystheus installed as ruler.

Eurystheus was the grandson of Perseus. Hercules, who was born soon after, never became king. Hera continued to trouble Hercules through Eurystheus, and the most troublesome and difficult jobs were given to Hercules. But he was equal to the tasks.

Hercules showed his strength when he was an infant. Two fearful serpents entered his room. They attacked Hercules, but he was strong. He grabbed one serpent in each hand and wrung their necks. The serpents were sent by Hera to kill Hercules.

When Hercules grew up, he made a mistake and harmed his own family. This too was the doing of Hera, who had sent a disease that made Hercules lose his mind.

Eurystheus, on the advice of the Delphic Oracle, punished Hercules by giving him 12 tasks so that he could be pardoned for his sin. The story of each of these tasks is an adventure by itself. Let us see what Hercules had to do and how he finally succeeded in completing all the tasks successfully.

The Nemean Lion (The First Labor of Hercules)

King Eurystheus, who did not like Hercules much, decided to give Hercules a dangerous task as his first. Hercules arrived at the court and stood expectantly, waiting for Eurystheus to tell him what his first task was.

Eurystheus thought for a moment. "You will go to Nemea and kill the Nemean lion."

"Should I bring the dead lion back here?" Hercules asked.

Eurystheus was annoyed. "What am I going to do with a dead lion? Besides, by the time you bring it here, it will stink. Just bring back its hide. That will do."

Hercules nodded and left the court.

Hercules was aware that so far nobody could kill this lion and that it was terrorizing a place called Nemea. Hercules set out to kill the lion, not knowing if he could really do it.

Arriving at a town called Cleonae, Hercules rested for the night at the house of a poor man called Molorchus. When Molorchus heard that Hercules had come to kill the terrible lion, he was afraid. He wanted to offer a sacrifice. Hercules asked him to wait for 30 days. If he came back victorious, they would perform a sacrifice to honor Zeus.

Hercules then set out to where the lion lived. He knew that this was no ordinary lion, but an extremely strong and fierce animal that no one till now had been able to kill. Hercules began tracking the lion. And suddenly he saw it! He took out his bow and arrows and began shooting at the lion. But although the arrows found their mark, nothing happened to the lion. Hercules now knew that there was only one option left. He picked up his club and approached the lion. The lion disappeared into a cave that Hercules saw had two entrances. He quickly went and blocked one of the entrances. He then entered the cave through the other.

Hercules grabbed the lion and put his strong arms around his neck and held on hard. As you can imagine, there was a terrible battle. The lion was strong and wanted to throw Hercules off. But slowly the lion began to lose strength and finally died. Hercules then took the hide of the lion and went back to Cleonae, to the poor man's house. There he offered a sacrifice to Zeus.

Triumphant Hercules returned to Eurystheus in Mycenae. He had made a cloak out of the skin of the lion and was wearing it when he appeared before Eurystheus. The cloak made him invincible! The king was frightened when he saw Hercules wearing the lion's skin, complete with its head. He did look like a wild and dangerous man.

He decided to send messages to Hercules, instead of calling him to the court.

The Lernean Hydra (The Second Labor of Hercules)

Eurystheus wanted Hercules to fail, so he began to think until he had an idea. He immediately wrote out a message, "kill the Lernean Hydra," and sent it by messenger to Hercules. Eurystheus chuckled to himself. The serpent would certainly kill Hercules. Eurystheus knew how dangerous the Hydra was.

The Lernean Hydra was a terrifying serpent with nine heads! It was huge and lived in the swamps of a place called Lernaea. Another thing about this serpent? One of its heads was immortal! That also meant that as soon as any one of the nine heads was cut off, two heads would grow back again. So you could really not kill it. That was the problem that Hercules faced. It was also said that the breath of the serpent was so vile that it killed whoever stood in front of it.

This time Hercules took his nephew Iolaus with him. Iolaus was an expert charioteer, so Hercules and Iolaus went in search of the serpent on a chariot. They drove to Lernaea and arrived at the swamp where the serpent had its lair. But it was hiding deep in the swamp and Hercules knew that entering the swamp to fight the Hydra was a bad idea. The serpent would be in its element! Hercules decided to draw him out of the swamp to better tackle him.

Hercules fired flaming arrows into the swamp, and the Hydra came out of the murky waters to see who would dare disturb its lair. Hercules, seeing the terrifying creature, knew that he was in for a tough battle. He used his sword to cut off the heads, but as soon as he cut off one of the heads, two heads grew back again! Hercules realized that he was getting nowhere. The Hydra also had a friend—a giant crab—who came out of the swamp and began attacking Hercules. It kept on biting Hercules on his foot.

Better get rid of this nuisance first, thought Hercules, and he killed the crab with one blow of his club. Then he asked Iolaus to light a fire and use a piece of wood fashioned as a burning torch.

Hercules then told Iolaus to burn the headless stump of the neck after he had cut off the head so that the nerve endings would be destroyed. This Iolaus did, and the heads did not grow back again.

Finally, after a grim battle, Hercules cut off the last head, which was immortal. Taking it, he quickly buried it in a hole and placed a huge rock on top. The Hydra could not get at the head and die. Hercules then cut open the serpent and dipped his arrows in the serpent's blood. It was said to be extremely poisonous.

Hercules appeared at the court of Eurystheus and reported the killing of the Lernean Hydra. This enraged Eurystheus even more.

The Hind of Ceryneia (The Third Labor of Hercules)

This time Eurystheus decided to give Hercules a task that he was sure would be impossible for him to perform. Hercules would have to bring back a specific hind that lived in Ceryneia. First of all, let's see what a 'hind' is. It is in fact, just a female deer.

It sounds like an easy job for someone as powerful as Hercules, right? Well, partly right. There is a catch. This particular deer had golden horns and bronze hooves, and it was a pet of Artemis, the goddess of hunting. Killing an animal that was a pet of a goddess was not easy, so Hercules was in a dilemma. He decided to chase the deer. The deer kept getting away but Hercules kept after it. After almost a year passed by, the deer was finally exhausted. It went to a mountain to rest. As she was crossing a stream, Hercules shot her with an arrow. He picked up the carcass and started on his way back to Mycenae to show Eurystheus. But on the way, Artemis and Apollo appeared and Artemis was extremely angry seeing her pet deer dead. Hercules then told Artemis of the tasks he had to perform in order to be pardoned for his sin. Artemis forgave Hercules, and with her powers, brought the deer back to life. But she made Hercules promise to bring the deer back alive once his task was complete. Hercules agreed. Happy at this turn of events, he took the live deer to the court of Eurystheus.

Eurystheus liked the deer and decided to keep it. Hercules then said, "O great king, Artemis, and Apollo made me promise to take the deer back alive. If you keep it, I will have made a false promise and be punished. But Artemis and Apollo will also punish you."

Eurystheus did not want Artemis and Apollo after him. He released the deer.

The Wild Erymanthian Boar (The Fourth Labor of Hercules)

Before we get to the story of how Hercules accomplished his task, let's talk about wild boars. These are fearsome animals— big, strong, and with tusks. They are irritable and attack if disturbed, and bigger animals steer clear of them.

The task set for Hercules this time was to bring the wild Erymanthian boar back alive. Can you imagine bringing a big wild boar back alive? But that was what Hercules had to accomplish.

Eurystheus told his courtiers that this time Hercules would not come back. "The boar is bound to kill him. No one has ever come back alive," he said, rubbing his hands in glee.

Hercules, when he received the message from Eurystheus, went to the court of Eurystheus and asked, "you want the boar brought here? Alive?"

Eurystheus was beside himself with joy. "Yes, alive. I sent you the message. Can't you read?"

Hercules did not say a word and quietly left the court. He understood that Eurystheus wanted him to fail.

Hercules knew that this boar came charging down from the mountain called Erymanthus, and destroyed everything in its path, killing whoever got in its way. Its tusks were dangerous weapons and gored humans and animals alike. Everyone was afraid of the boar.

Hercules did not have trouble finding the animal. He could hear it crashing around and destroying things. Hercules chased the boar round and round the mountain, shouting as loudly as he could so as to scare the animal. Finally, the boar, now tired and scared, hid inside a bush. Hercules thought quickly and thrust his spear into the bush and drove the boar out into an area that had thick snow. Once there, the boar could not run and Hercules threw a net and captured him. He took the animal alive to Eurystheus. Seeing Hercules with the huge boar, alive, scared the living daylights out of Eurystheus. He quickly sent Hercules on his way and released the boar. Who would want to keep a large boar around?

Cleaning the Augean Stables (The Fifth Labor of Hercules)

Eurystheus now hated Hercules even more. Whatever he gave Hercules to do, he did it. So he thought up a real dirty task that would be impossible to do. Or so he thought.

The task was to clean up the stables of King Augeas. This king was very rich and had thousands of heads of cattle. They were all kept in large stables. There were so many cows, bulls, sheep, goats, and horses that no one had cleaned the stables for years. (You can imagine the smell and the muck that had accumulated over the years!) Eurystheus added one important rule—the cleaning up would have to be finished in a day!

Now, my friend, we shall see if you can pull off this one! Eurystheus thought to himself.

Hercules immediately realized that this was going to be a task where he would certainly get dirty, and smelly! But he was determined to do it.

When Hercules arrived at the palace of King Augeas, he saw the stables and all the fine cattle that the king possessed. He wanted some of the cattle from King Augeas, so he devised a plan. He approached the king and said that he would clean the stables in one day if the king promised him a portion of his cattle. The king was so astonished to hear Hercules say that he would clean a large number of stables in a day, that he agreed. Hercules now brought the son of the king to watch. He wanted a witness.

Hercules went to the cattle yard where all the stables were located and broke down a part of the wall on one side, making an opening. He then went to the opposite side and made another similar opening.

Next, he dug large trenches leading from the cattle yard to the two rivers that flowed nearby. Once the trenches reached the river, the water began rushing through them, straight into the yard through one of the wall openings and out the other. The rushing waters carried all the filth and muck with them as they raced through the yard.

Miracle of miracles! All the stables were absolutely clean within no time. Hercules had kept his word. But the king, when he heard that Eurystheus was behind this task, refused to honor his word and give the promised cattle to Hercules. He asked Hercules to leave the kingdom and never return. But Hercules had still completed his task.

The Stymphalian Birds (The Sixth Labor of Hercules)

By this time, Eurystheus was not sure what task to give Hercules. Then he suddenly had an idea. He sent a message to Hercules saying that he must drive away from the enormous flock of vicious birds that gathered at a lake near the town of Stymphalus. This was a very large flock of birds, and they were not ordinary birds, but ferocious ones, as they ate human flesh. Hercules could not decide how to shoo away such a large concentration of birds. But at this point, the goddess Athena came to his rescue. She gave him a clapper, which made a very loud sound and told him to use it to drive the birds away. These iron clappers were made by the master craftsman called Hephaestus, and made a very loud sound. Hercules went up a mountain and from the top, using the clappers. The clappers made such a racket that the startled birds all took to flight. Hercules started firing his arrows at them as they started flying. This time too, with a little help from a goddess, Hercules had succeeded. The myth does not say whether Hercules killed all the birds or only some of them. But he certainly succeeded in driving them all away. The task was complete.

Now let's see what that rogue Eurystheus has in mind, thought Hercules as he made his way back to Mycenae.

CHAPTER 3
THE LABORS OF HERCULES (PART 2)

❧❧❧❧❧❧ ❧❧❧❧❧❧

The Cretan Bull (The Seventh Labor of Hercules)

For the seventh task, Eurystheus wanted Hercules to go and subdue a fierce bull that was terrorizing the kingdom of King Minos and bring it back to him.

King Minos had created this monster by breaking a promise he made to Poseidon. The sea god had given Minos a big bull with the understanding that Minos would sacrifice it in his honor. But Minos liked the bull and sacrificed another bull. Poseidon, when he got to know of this treachery, turned the bull into a fierce animal that began terrorizing Crete, where Minos lived. Minos did not know what to do. He called upon the only man he knew who could do something. He called Hercules, and Hercules was already on his way to Crete to complete his seventh task.

When he got to Crete, he quite easily controlled the beast. He grabbed the bull's horns and wrestled it to the ground using his enormous strength and took the bull back to Eurystheus.

Terrified at the sight of the bull, Eurystheus screamed. "Take it away! Take it outside!"

Hercules took the bull outside and tethered it. He waited for Eurystheus to say what was to be done.

Eurystheus did a strange thing. He let the bull go free and it began its terrorizing activities again. As to why Eurystheus did what he did, we are not sure. Ultimately, another Greek hero, Theseus, killed the Cretan bull. There were lots of heroes in Greek myths, as you will soon see.

The Horses of Diomedes (The Eighth Labor of Hercules)

The myth or story of this task is not very clear. Eurystheus asked Hercules to go and tame the wild man-eating horses of a ruler named Diomedes and bring them back to Mycenae.

Hercules set off on his journey to Bistone where Diomedes lived and where the horses roamed freely. Hercules knew that the Bistones would fight him if he tried to take the horses away, but he was ready for the fight. He attacked the Bistones and defeated and killed them. He then went to the palace and killed Diomedes too.

Hercules tamed the horses and took them back to Eurystheus. But to everyone's surprise, Eurystheus let them go free! Hercules, however, had completed his eighth task, and he was not worried by this strange behavior of the king.

Hippolyte's Belt (The Ninth Labor of Hercules)

The ninth labor of Hercules is very interesting. It involves a tribe of women warriors who were called the Amazons. They lived separately from everyone else and were great fighters. Their queen, Hippolyte, wore special armor in the form of a belt given to her by Ares, the Greek god of war, as she was the bravest warrior.

Eurystheus knew about this special belt and wanted it for his daughter. He cleverly sent Hercules to bring him the belt.

"Don't worry my dear, if anyone can bring back the belt, Hercules can," he told his daughter.

Hercules knew that the Amazons would not easily give up the queen or her belt. He decided to take men with him to help, in case there was a battle of some kind.

Some say the belt that Hippolyte wore was made of gold and it offered her divine protection in times of battle. That's why Eurystheus was interested in it.

Hercules gathered some of his friends, including the brave warrior Theseus, and set sail for the land of the Amazons. When they arrived at the harbor, Hercules was not sure what to do. Then he saw that the queen herself had come to visit him. Hercules greeted the queen. "Why have you come?" was the first question that Hippolyte asked of him. She probably knew why Hercules had come. Hercules, without hesitation, told her that he had come to take her belt and carry it back to Mycenae.

The queen seemed to be ready to hand over the belt to Hercules without a fight. But here, another goddess, Hera, arrived to play tricks. Hera knew that Hippolyte would give Hercules the belt and was determined to stop that from happening.

Hera disguised herself as an Amazon warrior and went around telling all the other warriors that Hercules had come to fight a war and kidnap their queen. Since Hera was a woman like themselves and was dressed as a warrior, they believed her.

The Amazon warriors decided to attack Hercules before he could attack them. They had to protect their queen. Unaware of what was going on, Hercules waited on his ship for Hippolyte to come to give him the belt as she had promised. The only one who grew suspicious was Theseus. "They are going to attack us. I can feel it in my bones," he told Hercules. Hercules was still not sure that the Amazons were preparing to attack them. Hercules, of course, did not believe Theseus. But a little later, he saw the Amazon warriors all dressed up in armor coming towards their ship. They were armed. Hercules realized that they were going to be attacked and drew his sword. So did the other men in the ship.

A massive battle ensued. Hercules was forced to kill Hippolyte, as she was leading the battle. She too had been fooled by Hera into thinking that Hercules wanted to kidnap her and take her away. Hercules removed the belt and sailed away. He later presented the belt to Eurystheus, thus completing the ninth labor.

The Cattle of Geryon (The Tenth Labor of Hercules)

Hercules now waited for the tenth labor. He was sure that Eurystheus would think up something very difficult and dangerous. Sure enough, he received a message from Eurystheus that he was to deliver his cattle from the monster Geryon.

Geryon was no ordinary monster. Chrysaor and Callirhoe were his parents. Chrysaor had appeared from Gorgon Medusa's body (whom we shall read about later). This meant that Geryon was an exceptionally strong and dangerous character. He had three legs and heads—all in one body! That really made him look odd, but that's the way he was. You might be wondering how he got around with six legs, but it seems that he managed quite well.

Hercules realized that to finish this task, he would have to travel to the island of Erythia. Geryon lived on that island and he kept a herd of cattle that were red in color. The cattle were guarded by Orthos, a hound with two heads, and by a herdsman called Eurytion.

The sun, in his admiration, gave Hercules a golden goblet to sail in. It was a large goblet, that much is sure because Hercules was no small man. He set sail for the island where the cattle were.

As soon as he arrived at the island, the two-headed dog attacked Hercules. But it was no match for his strength. One blow from his mighty club killed the two-headed dog. The herdsman, seeing the death of the dog, came to stop Hercules, but was met with the same fate. Hercules was in no mood to play around. He had a job to do. But another herdsman who had seen what had just happened went to Geryon and told him about Hercules. Geryon, being a monster, was enraged and came out to fight Hercules. But he had no chance. Hercules killed him with his arrows.

However, Hercules now faced a bigger problem. How could he drive a whole herd of cattle from Erythia to Mycenae? The island was far away from Mycenae, and to travel with a herd of cattle was beginning to look extremely difficult.

Hercules knew that he had to find a way and started on his journey. In a place called Liguria, the sons of the god Poseidon tried to steal the cattle from him. Hercules killed them. But this, as he saw later, was the least of his problems.

When he was traveling through a place called Rhegium, one of the bulls escaped, jumped into the sea, and swam to a neighboring country (this country is now called Italy). The ruler, Eryx, who was another one of Poseidon's sons, found the bull and put it in his own herd. Hercules, meanwhile, was trying to find the bull and finally tracked it to Eryx's kingdom. He asked Eryx to return the animal, but Eryx refused, saying that he would give the bull back only if Hercules could beat him at arm wrestling. Feats of strength were what Hercules loved. He agreed and not only defeated Eryx but killed him. He took back the bull and put it back in his herd.

After a long and tedious journey, Hercules was close to Mycenae. He thought he had made it, but did not reckon with the evil Hera who wanted to create problems for him. Hera sent a gadfly to disturb and irritate the cattle. The herd scattered in different directions to escape the flying insect.

Hercules spent time running around and brought the herd together again. Finally, he delivered them to Eurystheus.

The Apples of the Hesperides (The Eleventh Labor of Hercules)

After the tiring tenth labor, Hercules was exhausted. But he had to finish another two labors before he would be pardoned. He retired to his house and waited for the next labor, which he knew would be another difficult one. Perhaps something that even he could not accomplish.

After eight months or so, the message arrived. He was to bring back the golden apples, which belonged to the great god Zeus. Hercules understood that Eurystheus wanted him to fail. Something belonging to Zeus, the king of gods, could not be touched, let alone stolen. Hera had given these apples as a wedding gift to Zeus, and Hercules was sure that Hera would not allow anyone to touch the apples.

The apples were in a garden towards the northern edge of the Earth, and were guarded at all times by a dragon called Ladon, who had a hundred heads! There were other guards too. The Nymphs, who were the daughters of the Titan who held up the sky—Atlas.

The problem that Hercules had to solve first was to locate the garden where the apples were. He did not know where the garden was. He started traveling and journeyed through several countries—Libya, Egypt, and Asia—but had no luck.

On his journey through these lands, Hercules came across Antaeus, a son of Poseidon, who challenged him to a fight. Hercules defeated Antaeus, crushing him. Next, another son of Poseidon stopped him, captured him, and took him to be offered as a human sacrifice, but Hercules managed to escape.

Then Hercules came to Mount Caucasus. Here he found Prometheus chained on a rock (on the orders of Zeus—remember?). The giant eagle that came to eat his liver every day was causing Prometheus a lot of pain. Hercules slew the eagle and released Prometheus.

Prometheus was grateful to Hercules and told him the location of the garden where the apples were kept. Prometheus also told Hercules that he would not be able to get the apples himself, but Atlas could get them for him if he could manage to convince him to help. Hercules first went to the garden and saw the tree with the golden apples. He tried to pick them from the branches, but every time he tried to touch an apple, it vanished. He then remembered what Prometheus had said. Abandoning his attempts at getting the apples, he went to see Atlas.

Atlas was tired of holding up the sky and jumped at the chance of shifting the load onto Hercules. He agreed to go get the apples for him. Hercules took over the task of holding up the sky while Atlas went to fetch the apples. But when Atlas came back with the apples, he did not want to hold up the sky and told Hercules to carry on holding it up in his place.

"I'll go and deliver them to Eurystheus for you!" said Atlas.

Hercules now had to think of a way to get out of this trap.

He told Atlas that he did not mind holding up the sky, but could Atlas take over for a minute while he used something to pad his shoulders? Atlas, unsuspecting, took over the load again. Hercules then picked up the apples and walked away, leaving Atlas to continue holding up the sky!

Arriving at Mycenae, Hercules showed the apples to Eurystheus and told him that they belonged to the gods and must be returned to them. Eurystheus knew that it was the truth and told Hercules to return them. Hercules went and handed over the apples to Athena, who in turn took them back to the garden. Hercules certainly must have thought wearily that after all the hard labor he went through to get the apples, they were now back in the garden! But he knew that he was safe from the curse of Zeus.

Cerberus (The Twelfth Labor of Hercules)

Hercules, after the eleventh task, was awfully tired. He had traveled through many lands. There was also his narrow escape from the dreadful task of having to stay for the rest of his life holding up the sky. He thought of what the twelfth and last task would be. Eurystheus was sure to give him something that he would either fail to do or die trying. But he had no other option, so he waited.

By now, Eurystheus was thinking of something that Hercules could not do and then had an idea. He would ask Hercules to kidnap the beast called Cerberus who lived in the Underworld. The Underworld was ruled by Hades and his wife Persephone. Here, depending on what sort of deeds a person did while living, they would either be punished or rewarded. Good souls and bad souls—all went down to the Underworld. Hercules, he thought, would not dare to enter.

Cerberus was a fierce monster who guarded the gates of the Underworld so that no living thing could enter the world of the dead. Cerberus had three wild dog heads, a tail of serpent or dragon, and snakes covered his back. A weird but terrifying monster, as you can guess.

Hercules was wary of entering the Underworld. He knew that no living thing that entered ever came back. It was a one-way trip. He decided to first go to the priest Eumolpus, who was the keeper of secrets. Hercules needed protection before entering the Underworld. He approached Eumolpus and told him what he intended to do and asked for the protection of the Spirits. Eumolpus made Hercules go through several mystery rites before giving him what he wanted. He initiated Hercules into the Eleusinian Mysteries, which would serve to protect him when he reached the Underworld. Armed with divine protection, Hercules was now ready to enter.

Hercules knew that he could not just enter the Underworld through the main gate. That would be dangerous. He decided to enter through a side entrance, a rocky cave. As he entered, he met with many heroes, ghosts, and even monsters. But Hercules was brave and continued on his way into the Underworld. Then, he was confronted by the god Hades himself. Hades asked him what he wanted. Hercules told him about his tasks and that he wanted to take Cerberus with him, alive, to Mycenae. Hades agreed to allow Hercules to take Cerberus with him, but only if he could defeat Cerberus with his bare hands, without using any weapons. Hercules, confident of his strength, agreed and went in search of Cerberus.

Hercules found Cerberus near the gates and, using his strong arms, grasped the monster's three heads and held on tight. Cerberus fought with all his might but could not get out of the grip, although the dragon in his tail continuously bit Hercules. Finally, a weary Cerberus surrendered to Hercules, who took him to Eurystheus.

There is an end to this story. As Cerberus guarded the gates of the Underworld, he had to be returned. Hercules took Cerberus back and released him unharmed, exactly as he had promised the lord of the Underworld.

This task ended the labors of Hercules and he was pardoned for his sin. He was a free man after this. But besides these famous labors, Hercules had many exciting adventures, some of which you will now discover. He was a restless sort of person and he could not stay home and was always looking for something exciting to do.

The Other Adventures of Hercules

As Hercules was wandering around, he heard that Eurytus, the ruler of Oechalia, was offering his beautiful daughter Iole in marriage to anyone who could defeat him and his sons in a contest of archery. Hearing this, Hercules went to Oechalia and defeated the ruler and his sons in the contest. But the king went back on his promise and refused to allow Hercules to marry his daughter. Hercules was annoyed and went away, very angry. But one of the sons of Eurytus, Iphytus, did not agree with his father's actions and went in search of Hercules.

Hercules was resting when Iphytus found him. They sat together and drank and ate and made merry. But then something happened between them, and Hercules, in a fit of rage, killed Iphytus. This was a bad thing to have done, and days later Hercules developed a peculiar disease that he could not cure. He realized that the only way was to go to the Oracle of Delphi and ask for a cure. This Oracle of Delphi was a temple with a priestess who would deliver prophecies. Everyone who went there followed the advice of the oracle.

Hercules went to the temple and asked for a cure. But the oracle refused to tell him anything. Enraged, Hercules started destroying the temple. He took the sacred tripod (known as the Delphic Tripod) from the temple and wanted to carry it away with him. This alarmed the gods. Apollo intervened and began to fight with Hercules. Both were powerful and the fight grew serious. Zeus now saw that it was time he intervened to stop this nonsense. He threw a thunderbolt that separated the two combatants. The tripod was replaced and the priestess then sent forth an oracle. Hercules was to spend one year in slavery. He was given to Queen Omphale (one of the many minor characters in the myths), and there he completed his punishment. The story shows that too much pride and anger are not good and inevitably lead to bad things.

Hercules was also involved in the battle against the Giants. These were ferocious monsters who were as tall as the mountains. These monsters decided to attack Olympus, the place where the gods lived. Zeus knew that he needed the help of Hercules because the Giants were very dangerous enemies. Hercules came and took part in the battle, killing several of the Giants.

Hercules then got involved in another adventure. He told Laomedon, King of Ilium, that he would rescue his daughter, Hesione, from her fate. Hesione was tied to a rock as an offering to the gods to prevent an epidemic. She was to be devoured by a dragon! When the dragon arrived to eat her, Hercules killed it. But again, as had happened many times in his life, the king refused to reward Hercules, going back on his word. Hercules came back with six ships, attacked Laomedon, and killed him and his sons in revenge. He then gave Hesione in marriage to one of his friends.

CHAPTER 4
THE OLYMPIANS

Greek mythology has many gods and goddesses, too numerous to talk about. But in this chapter, we shall talk about the more important ones. The gods and goddesses had big impacts and ruled over important parts of the universe.

Zeus

Zeus was the most important god of the Greeks. He was the son of Cronus and Rhea, though Zeus grew up away from his parents. He was an important god and we shall see that he is perhaps the most important god in all of Greek mythology, as he makes an appearance or is mentioned in almost every myth. He was in fact the king of kings! Although other gods ruled over different parts of the universe, Zeus was master overall. His word was final in all matters. He punished any god who disobeyed him. Remember Prometheus? Greek myth is full of the activities of Zeus. He was the one who would decide the fate of the other gods whenever there was a dispute.

Poseidon

Zeus was the most powerful ruler, but Poseidon, who was his brother, was of no less importance. He was given rulership over the seas and the oceans, and that is quite a lot to rule over.

When Zeus fought the Titans and the Giants, Poseidon fought alongside him.

Poseidon was also known as the god of earthquakes and horses. The trident that he carried had the power to shake the Earth whenever Poseidon threw it down on the ground. Poseidon lived deep in the ocean in a fantastic palace surrounded by sea creatures and monsters.

Whenever he traveled, he fastened his chariot to swift horses with golden manes and bronze hooves. He dressed in golden armor and traveled across the oceans, which parted to let him through. As he swept through the waves, sea monsters came up to pay homage to their ruler. You can imagine the sight of this chariot racing through the seas and sea monsters rising up. An impressive sight indeed! In most Greek paintings, you will see Poseidon with long unruly hair and carrying his famous trident. He was quite a scary-looking character.

Apollo

The exact origin of this important god is not very clear. Apollo was always depicted as a handsome young man, slim and strong. He was said to have ruled over sunlight. As you know, the heat of sunlight is needed to ripen crops and fruit. As a result, Apollo also had rulership over harvests. Accordingly, when people harvested their first grain they made an offering to Apollo, to make the god happy, and ensure that the next harvest was also good. In many cultures, offering the first harvest to the gods is still practiced.

Apollo's mother was Leto. When Apollo was just an infant, he showed that he was not an ordinary god. There was a serpent called Python, who was evil. Apollo decided to kill him. He took with him the arrows fashioned by Hephaestus, the master craftsman, and traveled to Parnassus, where the serpent lived. When the serpent saw him, it attacked. But Apollo hit him with an arrow. The serpent fell to the ground and began moaning in pain. Apollo looked at the serpent with contempt and said "lie there and rot, evil creature."

Apollo was also a shepherd god, looking after the flocks of cattle, sheep, and other domesticated animals. He was important to people who kept cattle and they prayed to him so that their herds were always safe from predators.

Music and song were also said to be Apollo's domain. He was often shown with a lyre in his hands. It was said that the gods often listened to Apollo singing and playing the lyre. Since music and song were always important, he had a very important portfolio. How he got the lyre is in another story that you will read about soon.

He was also known as the Celestial Archer. His arrows never missed their mark.

Apollo, however, was still a very strong god. As you will see, he did not shy away from a fight. In Phocis, there was a man called Phorbas (a mortal), who had extraordinary strength and who waylaid people going to the temple of Delphi and made them fight him. Because he was very strong, he defeated them. He would then torture them and kill them. Apollo decided to put a stop to this bandit. He disguised himself as an athlete and appeared on the road to Delphi. Phorbas challenged Apollo to a fight and Apollo felled him with one mighty blow of his fist. Phorbas had made the mistake of challenging the wrong person!

When Hercules went mad and started destroying the temple of the Delphic Oracle, Apollo fought with him. Hercules, as you know, was known as someone who had superhuman strength, but Apollo did not shy away from fighting him.

He had much respect in the king's council. All the gods honored him when he came in. Even Zeus respected Apollo.

Hermes

Hermes ruled over several things. It is said that he ruled over travelers and ensured safe passage to those who prayed to him. In those days, travel was mostly for business so Hermes automatically became the god of commerce. He is also said to have ruled the wind. His rulership is not very clear in the myths.

One thing is for sure, Hermes was the messenger for Zeus, delivering his messages to mortals and gods alike. And Zeus always kept sending messages to various gods.

Hermes wore winged sandals when he was delivering messages for Zeus. Sometimes he also wore a hat with wings to aid in his travels through the skies.

The son of Zeus and Meia, Hermes was born in a cave. It is

said that on the day of his birth he showed his mischievous nature by stealing cattle that belonged to Apollo. You might think—a newborn baby? Babies can't even get up! But we are talking about gods, remember?

Hermes quietly climbed out of his cradle and snuck out. He then climbed the mountain of Pieria where the sacred herd was kept. He took 50 heads of cattle from the herd and drove them under the cover of darkness to a place called Alpheus. Hermes was so clever that he made them walk backward, so that nobody would know which way they had gone. He put on big sandals so that his footprints would make everyone think the thief was a grown man! He hid the cattle in a cavern, but he wasn't finished yet. He selected two of the fattest heifers and roasted them. He divided up the meat into 12 equal portions and offered the food to the 12 gods. After that, he turned himself into vapor, re-entered his room through a keyhole, and lay down in his cradle again.

Apollo discovered his loss, and by using his divine powers, realized that Hermes was the culprit. In a rage, he went to the cave where Hermes lay and accused him. "Why did you steal my cattle?" Hermes looked up innocently at Apollo and denied having taken the cattle.

Apollo then picked him up and took him to Zeus for judgment. Zeus was amused and could not but praise the ingenuity of Hermes. But he also knew that Apollo was a god and would not tolerate disrespect. He told Hermes to return the cattle to Apollo. Hermes showed them where the cattle were and Apollo got them back.

Zeus and the other Olympians in the court were entranced by

this bubbly child who seemed extremely clever. Hephaestus, who was present at the court, was taken in by the charm that Hermes displayed, sitting on Zeus's lap and fiddling with the god's beard.

All the gods decided that Hermes must become the divine messenger.

Hephaestus decided to give him a gift and made a pair of sandals that had wings. These sandals would allow Hermes to literally zip through the sky to any place that he wanted to go. Grateful for the gift, Hermes gave Hephaestus a great big hug of joy. Hephaestus was not used to being hugged. He was ugly and not many people hugged or touched him. He was so overcome with happiness that he went back to his forge and made a helmet with wings and gave that to Hermes too. This helmet would make Hermes faster through the air. Hephaestus also gave Hermes a silver staff with two snakes entwined on the top.

However, Hermes knew that Apollo was still angry. He had not yet forgotten the taking of his cattle by Hermes. Hermes decided to make amends and made a stringed instrument (later known as a lyre) using the shell of a turtle, and went to meet Apollo. But Apollo was annoyed and showed it until Hermes started playing the lyre. The celestial sound of the instrument delighted Apollo. Hermes knew that Apollo wanted it, but could not ask for it. So he gave it to Apollo as a gift. Apollo now forgot all his anger and he and Hermes became lifelong friends. Apollo entrusted Hermes with the care of the celestial herd.

Apollo became the god of music, as he was always playing the lyre and singing, and Hermes became the protector of flocks and herds. Hermes was part of many adventures and helped many mortals and gods overcome their problems.

Ares

Greek myths say Ares is the god of war and strife. Zeus did not like him and one day in the Council of the gods, Zeus told Ares that he disliked him the most because all he did was enjoy battles, strife, and war. Ares did not mind because he knew that he was the god of war. Somebody had to be.

Ares used to roam around mounted on a chariot that was drawn by swift horses with golden browbands. He himself was clad in bronze armor, with a mighty spear in his hand. He went around battlefields and struck blows on either side. He did not care who was fighting whom or for what reason. He just entered into the battle and fought.

Ares, however, was a very brutal and bloodthirsty god, who was never happier unless he was killing or fighting someone. This made everyone dislike him and even the gods avoided him. But Ares did not always win whatever battle he was fighting. Most often he came away wounded and defeated. Hercules once beat him up and he ran away to Olympus to lick his wounds. Ares got into many difficulties and sticky situations because of his liking for trouble.

Hephaestus

Remember Hephaestus? He was the god from whom Prometheus stole fire and gave it to mankind.

Hephaestus, although a god, was not very good-looking. He was lame in both legs, which meant that they were deformed.

His feet were twisted and he walked at a stumbling pace. The other gods were mean and laughed at his peculiar walk.

Hera, the mother of Hephaestus, was so ashamed of his disfigured body that she threw him into the sea, where he remained under the care of Thetis, another goddess. Later, he was reunited with his mother.

Hephaestus was a master craftsman of metals. He had a forge where he made magical items for the gods. He was extremely inventive, and the gods came to him when they needed something made out of metal. Things like swords, armor, and shields, which the gods always needed, as there was always some war or battle happening somewhere.

Hephaestus may have been ugly, but he was a genius with metals. He made for himself a palace of bronze, which was said to be indestructible. Inside this palace, he had his forge, where he could be seen hammering red hot metal into various objects. He is said to have created many palaces of bronze for the gods. Whenever a god came to see him, he would clean himself up (as he was working with fire and therefore always sweating) and then go and sit on his throne. He would then ask whichever god or goddess had come what they wanted. He knew that he was the best.

Among his famous creations are the golden throne, a scepter and thunderbolts for Zeus, arrows for Apollo and Artemis, a cuirass for Hercules, and armor for Achilles (who was an important figure in the great battle between the Greeks and the Trojans called the Trojan War).

Hephaestus always did whatever Zeus asked him to do. It was

he who created the chains to bind Prometheus to the rock. He did it against his will because he knew that to annoy Zeus was dangerous.

Hephaestus, however, had not forgotten the treatment by his mother. She had not been a good mother to him and had cast him away down a mountainside and into the sea. He decided to take revenge. He built a magnificent throne of gold and sent it as an anonymous gift to his mother Hera.

Hera was fascinated by the throne and sat down on it. Immediately, the arms of the throne closed in and trapped her. She could not get up! Everyone rushed in to free her, but to no avail. Even Zeus failed. A while later, Hephaestus arrived. He pretended he did not know about Hera's problem. He casually asked if Hera was trapped on the throne. Hera, who was terrified and annoyed, said, "can't you see that I am trapped on this infernal throne!"

Hephaestus went towards her and the throne released its grip, freeing Hera. Hephaestus was then treated with respect by Hera. She realized that her son was indeed a special person.

Athena

Athena was known for her valor in the field of battle. Athena liked and protected the brave. She helped Hercules when he was busy finishing the labors given to him by Eurystheus. When Hercules was given the labor of driving away from the Stymphalian birds, he was puzzled. He had no idea how to drive away such a large flock of birds. It was Athena who gave him the clappers. These were special clappers designed by Hephaestus that made such a loud sound that Hercules easily drove the birds away.

Athena had a benevolent side to her character and during times when she was not engaged in battle, she did many useful things. She taught the people of Cyrene to tame horses. She also helped Jason to design and build the ship Argo.

One of her important inventions was her designing and building the first potter's wheel, which was used by the people to make vases and other earthen pots. At the time, this was a great help. These pots and vases were used to store grain, water, and other things. The potter's wheel is still used today.

Athena also taught the women the fine art of weaving and embroidery. If there was no weaving, there would be no clothes today, would there?

There is a particularly interesting and intriguing story about Athena.

In a place called Lydia, there lived a girl called Arachne. This girl was known for her skill in using the needle and spindle. One day she took it into her head to challenge Athena to compete with her. Athena was angry that a mere mortal dared challenge her. She wanted to punish Arachne but instead accepted the challenge. She, Athena, was the goddess who invented the process, after all. She sent word that she was ready for the challenge.

Athena went to meet Arachne disguised as an old woman.

"Withdraw your challenge to Athena. She is a goddess. How dare you challenge her?" she said. Arachne refused to back down.

Athena then took on her divine form, blazing with light, and told Arachne that she accepted the challenge.

Arachne immediately sat on her loom and started weaving. She used colored threads and used, as her design, the loves of the gods. When she finished she offered it to Athena for inspection.

Athena carefully inspected the cloth, but try as she might, she could not find a single flaw. Enraged, she cursed Arachne and turned her into a spider.

"You shall spend the rest of your days weaving using the thread from your own body!" said Athena.

Spiders still use their body fluid to weave their webs. The next time you see a spider, it could be Arachne! What do you think? It's still a myth after all—a story, right? Or is it?

Aphrodite

Aphrodite is the goddess of love and beauty. She was born from the sea and was so beautiful that all the other goddesses were jealous of her. They decided to ask someone, a mortal, to judge who was the most beautiful. The contestants were Hera, Athena, and of course, Aphrodite.

The gods decided that Paris, the son of King Priam of Troy would be the judge. All three goddesses descended on Troy. Paris was tending to his flocks along a hillside when the three goddesses presented themselves. When Paris heard what they wanted him to do, he refused. Paris was clever, he did not want to get involved with goddesses. He knew that if he chose one of them, the others would bear him a grudge, and he could do without grudges from goddesses.

The three goddesses, however, insisted and said that Zeus had made the decision for them to come to him. This time Paris had no choice. The two goddesses, Hera and Athena, promised him land and kingdoms if he chose them.

Only Aphrodite did not offer Paris anything. She had nothing much to offer. But Paris was so struck by her dazzling beauty that he chose her. Aphrodite was the winner.

Hera and Athena were not pleased and later they would avenge this insult by creating the Trojan War in which Paris was killed, and the kingdom of Troy was devastated by the Greeks.

You must have read about the Trojan horse. It was actually a Greek horse. The Greeks hid inside the giant wooden horse and left it outside Troy. The Trojans unknowingly took the horse inside their fortress. The Greeks jumped out of the horse and defeated the Trojans. The Greeks also destroyed the city of Troy. The goddesses had their revenge.

Hestia

The Greek word *Hestia* means 'hearth.' In those days, it meant the place where the fire was kept burning. Nowadays people light a fire when they need it, but remember that in ancient times, a fire was a precious thing. Prometheus risked his life to bring it to the humans. Therefore, a fire was always tended to and looked after, and treated with respect. In those days you didn't just have matches.

When a member of a family went away to set up a new home, he took with him the family fire, so that the continuity of the family was maintained. People also made a place in the community where a public fire was kept burning. Hestia was the goddess of all these fires.

Hestia was also the fire in which men sacrificed things to the gods. Hestia was not a goddess who had many adventures but being the keeper of the household fires, she was still important. In ancient Greece, a fire was a very valuable commodity.

CHAPTER 5
IMPORTANT HEROES (PART 1)

Theseus

Theseus was like Hercules. He was very strong and went about destroying monsters. It is said that when he was still a child, he attacked the body of the Nemean lion, although it was already dead. Hercules had killed it and left the body on a table. Grown, Theseus began getting rid of several bad people who preyed on the innocent.

He heard that Sinis, a son of Poseidon, was torturing anyone who came his way. Sinis would tie the person between two bent pine trees and then release the trees so that the person was torn apart. Theseus decided to punish Sinis and went to see him. Sinis, thinking that Theseus was just another man, tried to hurt him. Theseus, who was also the son of Poseidon, killed him.

One of the great exploits of Theseus was the killing of the

Minotaur, a creature with the body of a man and the head of a bull.

The son of Minos, the ruler of Crete, was killed by the Athenians. Minos exacted revenge by sending his ambassadors to Athens to fetch seven young men and seven maidens. These were to be fed to the Minotaur, which Minos kept prisoner in a labyrinth. This labyrinth was made by the very clever craftsman Daedalus (we shall be talking about him later). The Minotaur was a fierce creature and would kill and devour the 14 young men and women. This was going on for years.

However, Theseus was in Athens when the ambassadors came to collect the 14 unfortunate young men and women. Theseus was angry and decided to go with the youth and kill the creature. When he arrived at Crete, he met Minos.

"And who are you?" asked Minos. Theseus replied that he was the son of Poseidon.

Minos did not believe him. "Well, if you really are the son of Poseidon, then fetch me this," said Minos, and he threw a golden ring into the sea.

Theseus dived into the sea and returned with the ring.

But by this time a daughter of Minos, Ariadne, had fallen in love with Theseus and decided to help him. She knew that the labyrinth was a difficult place to get out of, as it was so cleverly constructed by Dacdalus. It was made this way to keep the Minotaur from getting out.

"Take this ball of string with you, so that you can find your way out of the labyrinth. Tie it to a tree when you go in and let the string unwind as you go. Once you have killed the Minotaur, follow the string back out," Ariadne told Theseus.

Theseus used the string exactly as Ariadne had told him to do, and after killing the Minotaur he followed the string and got out of the labyrinth.

Among his other exploits, he went with Hercules to get the belt from Hippolyte, the queen of the Amazons. He was the one who warned Hercules that the Amazons were preparing to attack.

Theseus was bored one day and thought that he would get rid of the bandits who tortured travelers. That, he felt, would bring him glory. He had already punished Sinis.

So he took off on foot with his sword and a few things in a bag.

The first bandit he met was giant cyclops named Periphetes. He was carrying a huge club.

"What's in the bag?" he asked Theseus.

When Theseus did not reply, the giant began to get angry.

"I am going to smash your head with my bronze club!" he said.

However, Theseus was clever. "That club is not made of bronze, it is made of wood. Anyone can see that."

The cyclops was angry at hearing this and offered Theseus the club to see if it was made of bronze or not. "See if you can hold it."

Theseus pretended that it was heavy and, gripping the club,

hit the giant on its legs. The giant fell to the ground in pain. Theseus then hit him several times and finally killed him. He then went on his way, taking the club with him.

As he moved further on his journey, he came across a menacing bad character called Sciron. Theseus knew what Sciron did. He took people to the top of a cliff. There, he asked them to sit on the edge of the cliff with their backs to the sea and wash their feet. When the victim was doing this, Sciron would kick the man into the sea, where a giant turtle would eat him. As soon as Sciron saw Theseus, he approached him and pointed a sword at him.

"Wash my feet or die!" said Sciron, but Theseus was ready.

"I don't want to. Your feet are dirty and smelly," replied Theseus, standing calmly.

"Either you wash my feet, or I kill you now," said Sciron, pressing the sword point harder into Theseus's body.

Theseus pretended to consider and then said that he needed hot water, oils, and cloth to properly wash Sciron's feet.

The bandit agreed and brought Theseus his hot water, oils, and cloth.

As he began to wash the feet of Sciron, he was pushed right to the edge of the cliff. Theseus suddenly pretended to lose his balance and stumbled against Sciron. He then threw the hot water into the bandit's face, blinding him.

One hefty shove and Sciron was hurtling down on his way into the sea. The turtle was waiting for prey and probably ate Sciron.

The last major adventure of Theseus was to destroy a couple who offered hospitality and then tortured the guest. If the guest was tall, they would reduce the size of the bed. They would then ask the guest to lie down. When the legs of the guest dangled over the edge of the bed, Procrustes would cut them off, saying that the guest was too tall for the bed. The bed had a mechanism to make it longer or shorter. When the guest was short, Procrustes would lengthen the bed and tell the guest that he was too short. They would then use the mechanism of the bed to stretch the guest. Either way, the guests died in agony. Theseus did not know this, but when Procrustes, who was the host, invited Theseus into the hostelry, Theseus became suspicious. He saw that the wife of Procrustes was inside making food, and the two exchanged glances.

Theseus said that he would like to take a bath, and went out to the pond behind the house. However, he did not go to the pond. He circled back to the window and overheard them talking about how they were going to torture him before killing him. Theseus pretended not to know and after dinner, went to lie down. Procrustes went with him. Theseus then threw Procrustes onto the bed. Theseus gave Procrustes a dose of his own medicine. In this way, Theseus ended the terrible deeds of Procrustes and his wife.

Jason of the Argonauts

This myth or story is also sometimes called "Jason and the Golden Fleece." As we shall see, the Golden Fleece does play an important part.

It is one of the oldest myths where a hero goes on a quest. It is a story of adventure and betrayal. But before we begin, you must know why Jason went in search of the Golden Fleece.

The chain of events began when Pelias killed Jason's father, the king of Iolcus, and usurped the throne. Jason's mother, afraid that Pelias might kill the infant Jason too, took him to a centaur called Chiron, who was half-man and half-horse. Chiron carried the infant Jason away and raised him.

Meanwhile, Pelias ruled Iolcus with a tyrannical hand, crushing any form of dissent and protest. He was an oppressive ruler, someone who ruled by the use of brute force. Nobody could remove him as he was so vicious in his vengeance. Pelias was very vigilant because an oracle had prophesied that his throne would be taken from him by a relative wearing one sandal, and his spies were instructed to keep a sharp eye out for such a person.

Meanwhile, Jason had slowly grown up and reached the age of 20. Chiron, who was taking care of Jason, taught him the secrets of herbs and medicines, but realized that Jason was more of an athletic and physical sort of boy.

Chiron then told Jason about his father, and how Pelias had treacherously killed him and taken away the throne. Jason vowed revenge but bided his time. He had learned the benefits of patience from Chiron.

The day came when Jason decided he would travel to Iolcus and demand his rights. He would ask Pelias to give him the throne that was now rightfully his.

He bid Chiron adieu and started on his journey.

Jason walked for days and came to a river—not a deep one, but a river nevertheless. On the bank, he saw an old woman, who was bent over double. He offered to carry her on his back across the river. Hoisting her onto his back, Jason entered the river and began wading through to the opposite side. The old woman on his back kept clawing at him and muttering something.

When he reached the other side, he realized that one of his sandals had come off, and was stuck in some rocks in the river. He tried to wade back in to retrieve the sandal, but the old woman kept clawing at him. By the time he managed to free himself from her hands, the sandal had been washed away. Jason realized that he would have to continue with only one sandal. Meanwhile, he saw that the old lady had vanished without a trace.

The old lady was in fact Hera, a goddess, who wanted to help Jason in his fight against Pelias, whom she hated. Why she hated him is another story, and Hera hated a lot of people anyway. For now, we go with Jason.

When Jason arrived at Iolcus, he wandered around looking at everything. People started staring at this handsome stranger. They were intrigued by the fact that he was only wearing one sandal.

The palace guards ran to Pelias to inform him of the presence of Jason. Of course, they did not know his name as of yet. But the king had to be informed.

Pelias was busy with his own work when the guards arrived.

"Stranger? What kind of stranger?" he asked the guards.

"He is tall with long golden hair. He is wearing the skin of a lion, my Lord!" replied the guard.

Pelias began to think. Who was this golden-haired stranger now?

One of the guards remembered something. "He walks with a limp, my Lord."

"With a limp?" Pelias asked, now more mystified.

The other guard, however, was more observant. "He limps because he is wearing just one sandal."

Pelias now sat up straight. "Wearing just one sandal? Are you sure?"

The guards nodded vigorously.

"Bring him here. I want to meet him," he commanded, beginning to feel uneasy. Was this the one who would take away his throne? The prophecy began to haunt him.

"Wait. I think I will go out and meet him. Where is he now?" asked Pelias.

"He is in the marketplace, my Lord," said one of the guards.

Pelias hurried out to meet this unusual stranger, who wore just one sandal.

Arriving at the marketplace, he found Jason surrounded by admirers. He also saw that the stranger was indeed wearing just one sandal.

Seeing the king, most of the folk made way.

Pelias approached Jason and asked who he was.

Jason believed in the direct approach and said, "I have come to demand what is mine, Uncle."

Pelias was a little taken aback. *Uncle?* Pelias did have a lot of nephews. Then the thought struck him. Here was a relative wearing one sandal! Was this the man the prophecy had spoken about? But Pelias was a devious and cunning man and was determined not to give up his throne so easily.

"So nephew, what is your name?" he asked in a friendly manner.

"I am Jason, son of Aeson, the former king of Iolcus. You killed my father and usurped the throne. I am the rightful heir to the throne and have come to take back what is mine."

Hearing these words, Pelias knew that the past had come back to haunt him. He had to figure out a way to thwart the prophecy from being fulfilled. He thought quickly.

Pelias put his hand around Jason's shoulders and said that he would willingly give up the kingdom to Jason, but there was a problem. The kingdom was cursed.

Jason had not heard of any curse, so he asked Pelias to explain.

Pelias then began to explain the details of the curse to Jason.

Pelias said that he had consulted an oracle when he noticed that there was no peace and prosperity in his kingdom, and the oracle had informed him that the Golden Fleece must be brought back. It must be brought back by the king to Iolcus.

After that, the kingdom would be prosperous. This was a total fib. Pelias had done no such thing.

He then continued with his false tale. He asked Jason whether he had heard of his cousin Phrixus. Jason admitted knowing his cousin Phrixus.

Pelias then told Jason that his cousin had died in a place called Colchis, and had kept the Golden Fleece there. As the new king of Iolcus, Jason must be the one to bring back the Golden Fleece from Colchis. The oracle was firm on that point. The king had to personally go and fetch the Golden Fleece. Only then would the curse be lifted.

Jason considered this and decided to go on this quest for the benefit of the people.

"It shall be done, Uncle! I shall go and bring the Golden Fleece here to Iolcus," said Jason, who was happy that he had a grand quest to go on at last.

Pelias was beside himself with glee. He knew that the task was beset by problems and chances were that Jason would not come back alive. The Golden Fleece was guarded by a fierce dragon that never slept, and just getting there was fraught with danger.

Before we continue, it is important to know how the Golden Fleece came to be in Colchis.

Zeus had given a golden ram to Phrixus (Jason's cousin). Phrixus sat on the ram and flew to Colchis from Greece. Colchis was ruled by a king named Aeetes, who was the son of Helios, the sun god.

Aeetes sacrificed the ram to Zeus and hung the golden fleece in a sacred garden, and put a dragon there to guard it. This was the creature that never slept. Since the ram was a gift from Zeus, the fleece too was a valuable object.

That in short is the story of the Golden Fleece.

Now back to Jason, who was planning his trip to bring back this valuable object.

Jason knew that Colchis was far away and he needed a very good ship to sail in. He approached Argus, an expert shipbuilder. The vessel he built was very strong and had excellent sails and rowing equipment. It was named the Argo in his honor. And yes, you guessed it—the men who sailed in it came to be known as the Argonauts!

Once the ship was ready, Jason announced that he needed heroes to sail to Colchis. Several great warriors came and joined. Hercules, too, joined. He had some time in between his labors and found the idea exciting.

Jason now had a great crew and he set sail. The first port of call was the Isle of Lemnos. Jason did not know that the Isle was populated only by women, who were known as Amazons. They had been sent away from their men and lived by themselves. Jason, however, cleverly managed to leave the Isle without getting into trouble with the women who lived there. (Pelias was sure that when Argonauts reached Lemnos, the women would not allow them to leave. Maybe even kill them. But he was wrong.)

Next, they had to cross the treacherous straits of Bosphorus. The straits were narrow watery passages, and there were rocks on either side of the passage that slammed shut when any vessel tried to pass through, crushing the vessel and killing everyone. Jason was warned of this by an old blind man whom he had helped. The blind man told Jason about a trick he could use to get through the straits without being crushed.

Jason, following the old man's advice, released a dove. The dove flew through the straits and the rocks closed in, but the dove managed to fly through. The old man had told Jason that if the dove could fly through, they too would be able to sail successfully and cross the straits. As soon as the rocks opened, Jason ordered the crew to row as fast as they could. The Argo swept through the straits before the rocks could crush it.

Finally, the Argonauts arrived at Colchis. Jason went to meet King Aeetes, who, although a little surprised to see so many great warriors visiting his kingdom, welcomed them warmly. He thought that they were just passing by. He was wrong.

Jason told the king that he had come to take the Golden Fleece, as it originally belonged to his ancestor Phrixus. The king thought for a moment and told Jason that he was quite willing to give the Golden Fleece to Jason. Secretly, he considered killing Jason and his band of men but realized that other gods and heroes might come back and destroy him in revenge. Besides, the gods might be angry and punish him. The king, exactly like Pelias, now decided to lie. He had a plan that might prevent Jason from leaving with the Fleece.

He called Jason to come close and said, "long ago I prayed to the gods for guidance about the Golden Fleece. The gods told me that the Fleece could be taken only by someone prepared to undertake three tasks and complete them successfully."

Jason believed the king and said that he was ready to perform the three tasks. But the king was not done yet.

"The tasks have to be completed by you and you alone. Your men cannot help you in any way," said Aeetes, trying to ensure that Jason would fail.

Jason nodded his head. He had no other choice. He asked for the details of the three tasks.

The first task was to harness two bulls that had mouths and hooves of bronze and breathed fire and use them to plow a field. These bulls were well-known. They were called The Oxen of Colchis, or the Khalkotauroi. They were fierce creatures and nobody went near them.

"And the second task?" asked Jason.

"I have some dragon teeth that must be planted in the furrows made by the plow. Once you do this, armed men will rise from the ground. You will have to fight and defeat them," said Aeetes with a smile. He was going to make it as difficult as he could.

"The third task is to kill the dragon that guards the Fleece and is coiled around the tree, on which the Fleece hangs," said Aeetes.

Jason wearily agreed but sighed in frustration.

However, the gods Athena and Hera were listening and they decided to help Jason. They asked Aphrodite, the goddess of love, to make Medea, the daughter of King Aeetes, fall in love with Jason. Medea was adept at all sorts of potions and spells. She had been trained by Hecate, another goddess. Once she fell in love with Jason, she would assist him.

At night when Jason was roaming around in the palace, Medea came to him and told him that she was in love with him, and would help him complete the three tasks.

She gave Jason an ointment and told him to smear it all over his body. This would make him invincible.

The next day, the king, queen, and their daughters and son were present to see Jason begin his tasks.

Jason waited for the bulls to be released. The gates were opened and two fierce bulls emerged, breathing fire. Jason waited patiently for the bulls to come to him. He had his sword and shield ready. But in his hands, he had a yoke, which was a wooden piece that fastened animals to plows, and a harness.

The bulls charged him, but Jason did not move. He hit one of the bulls with his shield and stabbed the other one with his sword. The ointment given by Medea saved him from the fire that the bulls were throwing at him.

Slowly, the bulls tired and Jason fastened them to the plow. But as soon as he had plowed the field and planted the dragon's teeth, giant warriors began to emerge from the ground. However, Medea had told him that the best way to defeat these warriors was to throw a large rock into their midst. Jason picked up a large boulder and tossed it. It landed on two of the warriors. Strangely enough, the warriors then began to fight amongst themselves. They killed each other until a single warrior was left standing. Jason walked up to him and cut off his head with one slice of his sword. He had finished his second task. The crowd who had gathered to witness this spectacle were now cheering Jason on, and King Aeetes was scared.

Jason was now ready for the last task: Defeating the dragon and taking the Golden Fleece.

Jason entered the garden where the Golden Fleece was kept and saw the dragon wound around the tree. Medea, who had gone with Jason, put a spell on the dragon and it became paralyzed. Medea then placed a concoction of flowers and herbs into its mouth and it fell asleep. Jason reached out and took the Golden Fleece. Together, Jason and Medea went to the ship that was waiting for them and they set sail for Iolcus.

Jason took over the kingship of Iolcus and ruled for some years happily.

Jason's story is rather long, but is worth reading, as it has several smaller stories in it. Greek myth is sometimes quite complex, with many smaller plots interwoven. But the stories, whether small or big, are all fascinating.

CHAPTER 6
IMPORTANT HEROES (PART 2)

Daedalus and Icarus

Daedalus, if you remember, was a god and a master craftsman. He designed and built many palaces for kings. He had designed a complex labyrinth for King Minos. In this labyrinth, Minos kept the Minotaur imprisoned. Anybody who went in could never get out, so cleverly was it designed.

Daedalus and Minos were great friends, but slowly, Minos began to dislike Daedalus. Nobody is quite sure why their friendship suddenly turned sour, but Minos began to hate Daedalus.

Daedalus had with him his son Icarus, a young boy who he loved very much.

At some point, Minos was so angry with Daedalus that he took him and his son Icarus and placed them in the labyrinth.

Daedalus knew that they would never be able to get out on foot. Daedalus knew that the labyrinth was too complicated, he had, after all, designed and built it himself. Daedalus also knew that the seaports would be watched by Minos's soldiers. There was only one way to escape—by air.

Daedalus began to think. Then he got an idea. He would develop artificial wings for himself and his son and they would fly away to freedom. He set about his task immediately. Using branches from the plants in the labyrinth, he wove them into wings. Now the question was: How to fix the wings onto the body?

Daedalus decided to use wax. He melted the wax and attached the wings to his body. He then did the same for Icarus. They tried to flap the wings first to see if they would work. They did, so Daedalus and Icarus decided to fly out of the labyrinth together.

When they were ready, they both flapped their wings and flew out of the labyrinth and started flying away from Crete. They flew over the sea and everything was working well, until Icarus, with his youthful energy, started flying up and then down. Daedalus realized the danger at once and warned Icarus not to fly too close to the sun, as the heat of the sun's rays would melt the wax and the wings would come off. But Icarus was having too much fun to care. He kept swooping down to the sea and then up again. What Daedalus had feared happened then. Icarus flew too close to the sun and the wax melted. His wings came off and he fell into the sea and drowned. Daedalus managed to get away safely. This story is a little tragic, but it does not end here.

King Minos was enraged when he discovered that Daedalus and his son Icarus had escaped with the help of artificial wings. He decided to find Daedalus and punish him. But where would he find Daedalus? He could be anywhere. Suddenly, an idea came to him. He took a conch shell and set sail. He let it be known that anyone who could thread the shell would be given huge riches as a prize. That meant that the thread had to be inserted at one end and taken out the other.

He sailed from city to city and many people tried to thread the shell without success. Minos knew that only the clever Daedalus would be able to do it. At last, he arrived at the city of Camicus. King Cocalus was interested in the challenge and took the shell from Minos. He took it to Daedalus, who looked at the shell for a minute. Then he got an ant and tied the thread to it. Using honey, he lured the ant through the curvature of the shell until it came out at the other end.

King Cocalus handed the threaded shell to Minos, who immediately knew that Daedalus had done it and that he was there. Minos threatened King Cocalus with a full-blown invasion if he did not hand over Daedalus. The king asked for a moment and went in to consult his daughters. His daughters, when they heard what had happened, drew up a plan.

Cocalus went to Minos and told him that Daedalus would be handed over to him the next day, and meanwhile, he should have a bath and eat a hearty meal. Minos accepted the offer. But when he entered the bathtub, the daughters, trained by Daedalus, introduced very hot water into the pipes. The pipes burst with the pressure and Minos was scalded and killed. The whole thing was passed off as an accident and no one was blamed. Daedalus was safe.

Oedipus and the Sphinx

Oedipus was an abandoned child adopted and brought up by a king and queen. They were not his real parents but raised him with all the benefits of royalty.

Oedipus loved to wander around. He would walk for miles and live frugally. One afternoon, he found himself in the countryside, near the town of Daulis. He found that he was at a crossroads, with three roads going three different ways. He stood undecided when down one road a chariot came speeding at him. The old coachman shouted and cracked his whip at him to get out of the way. Oedipus grabbed his whip and threw him off the coach. When the coach stopped, four armed men got out and came for Oedipus. But Oedipus managed to kill three of them before the fourth fled for his life. He then tore off a branch from an olive tree and started pulling off the leaves, saying the words, "road one, road two, road three," for each leaf he tore off. The final leaf he tore off said road two. Oedipus cheerfully started down road two, not knowing where it would lead.

After a while, Oedipus saw that the road he had chosen led up to a mountain path. He suddenly heard a voice call out to him.

"I would not go that way if I were you!" Oedipus turned to see an old man leaning on a stick.

"Why not?" he asked the man.

"You are heading for Mount Phicium and the Sphinx! Better to go another way," replied the old man, wheezing.

Oedipus realized he was poor and gave him a coin. But he was curious about this creature. He had never heard of anything called a Sphinx.

The old man told him that the Sphinx was sent as punishment to King Laius by the goddess Hera.

"Yes, yes, I have heard of King Laius, but what on earth is a Sphinx?" asked Oedipus.

The old man leaned forward and said, "it is a mortal creature with the head of a woman and the body of a lion. It has wings too, like a bird. It waits for travelers and then asks them riddles. If the traveler fails to reply correctly, it throws them down the mountain to their deaths. So I say, go another way!"

Oedipus was not impressed and said so. He knew that he was good with riddles and went ahead anyway. As he climbed, the pass got narrower and suddenly he was confronted by the Sphinx.

"Halt! You cannot pass," said the creature.

Oedipus saw that the old man's description was spot on. "Why can't I pass?" he asked boldly.

"No one passes without answering my question. If you answer correctly you pass, otherwise..." the Sphinx nodded its head downwards towards the sharp drop of the mountainside.

Oedipus decided to play the game. "What is your question?" he asked.

"What is the thing that walks on four feet in the morning, two feet in the afternoon, and three feet in the evening?" asked the

Sphinx, looking keenly at Oedipus.

Oedipus scowled at the Sphinx and replied, "man. When a child, crawls on all fours, when young, he walks on two feet. In the twilight of his age, he walks with the aid of a stick. That would be three feet." The Sphinx was visibly annoyed.

Oedipus then asked a nasty personal question of the Sphinx, who began to flap her wings and dance around in anger. Seeing his chance, Oedipus pushed the Sphinx off the cliff into the valley, killing it.

When he reached the city of Thebes, he was welcomed and honored by the queen and the people. The Sphinx had been a big headache. Ultimately, Oedipus married the queen, whose name was Jocasta, and he lived for a while in Thebes.

Perseus

Perseus was another hero of the Greek myths. His mother was Danae and his father was Zeus.

Acrisius, the father of Danae, was upset that Danae had a child with Zeus. He decided to put Danae and the child in a wooden box and set them adrift in the sea.

The box drifted along for some time until it was picked off the coast of Seriphos by Dictys, who was a fisherman.

Dictys was a kind soul and looked after Danae and her son, who now had a name—Perseus. As the years passed, Perseus grew into a strong and handsome young man. He was, after all, the son of Zeus!

Danae came to know that Dictys was the brother of the king of

Seriphos, Polydectes, although he lived in humble surroundings and was an ordinary fisherman.

Polydectes slowly fell in love with Danae and wanted Perseus out of the way so he could come and visit Danae. Polydectes struck upon an idea to get rid of Perseus.

Polydectes sent invitations to all the kings and princes, inviting them to come to a feast and celebrate his intention to seek the hand of Hippodamia, a princess. Perseus too was invited.

There was, however, a catch. The suitor who would win Hippodamia's hand would have to defeat her father in a chariot race. Polydectes planned to use this chariot race as an excuse to get rid of Perseus.

At the feast, Polydectes began to talk to Perseus, who he knew was a little vain and proud.

"I want to win this chariot race, but don't have a good horse," he said casually to Perseus.

Perseus said nothing. He knew that he was poor.

"Well, I was hoping you would help me by giving me your horse," said Polydectes, knowing that Perseus did not have one.

"I don't have a horse, but I will do anything to help you win the race," replied Perseus.

This was what Polydectes was waiting for. "Anything?" he asked Perseus.

Perseus nodded.

Polydectes then sprung his trap. "Well," he said. "I would like you to get me the head of Medusa if you can manage that."

Perseus was headstrong and proud, so he immediately agreed to get Polydectes the head of Medusa, unaware of who Medusa was.

When Danae heard what her son was planning to do, she tried her best to dissuade him. She told him that Medusa was a Gorgon who had snakes for hair, tusks for teeth, and talons for nails. She was a terrifying creature with one deadly weapon—her eyes. Anyone who even glanced at her eyes would turn into stone for all eternity.

Perseus, however, was determined to go. He had given his word in front of a lot of people and he was not about to go back on his promise.

Dictys gave him advice that he should not trust anybody and to be careful. He warned Perseus that the mainland was a difficult place.

Perseus set off and arrived on the mainland. What he saw there baffled him. He saw that people were well-dressed, while he was dressed in very ordinary clothes, which made him stick out as an outsider. He decided that he would need assistance if he was to find Medusa, so he went to the Oracle of Delphi.

The words of the oracle puzzled him. The oracle had said that Perseus must travel to the land where people lived on the fruit of the oak tree. Then an old woman told him what it meant.

She told him that he must go to Dodona, where the trees can speak. There, he would find the answer.

Perseus was crestfallen. This was too much. First the Oracle of Delphi, then speaking trees! But he went to Dodona anyway. As he walked through the oak trees, he heard someone speak. Surprised, he stopped. Could the trees *really* speak?

Suddenly, a young man stepped out from behind the trees. Perseus saw that the man was wearing sandals with wings and carried a staff with two live snakes on it.

"I am Perseus..." began Perseus, but he was stopped by the young man, who said that he knew who Perseus was. This baffled Perseus to no end. How did he know who he was?

Then, something even stranger happened. A beautiful woman stepped out from behind the young man. She was holding a shield.

Perseus was rooted to the spot, his head in a whirl.

The woman, who wore a grave expression, said that they were there to help Perseus on his quest.

"We too, are the children of Zeus, like you," said the woman. Perseus never knew that Zeus was his father, so he was taken aback, but kept quiet.

The woman continued to speak and told Perseus that they would give him the weapons he needed to destroy Medusa.

The young man asked Perseus to take off his shoes. Perseus took them off. To his amazement, he found that the winged shoes of the stranger flew and attached themselves to his feet.

"You can go wherever you wish by just thinking about it," said the young man. "And here is a cape and hood. As long as you wear it, you will remain invisible," he continued, handing the article to Perseus.

The woman, who was silent, now introduced herself as Athena, and the young man as Hermes.

Athena gave the shield to Perseus, telling him to keep it highly polished. She next handed Perseus a short-bladed weapon that looked like a scythe, with the instruction to be careful. The blade was extremely sharp. She also gave him a satchel, which mystified Perseus, but he took it graciously.

Perseus, however, had one question. Where would he find Medusa? Which island did she live on?

Hermes and Athena refused to tell him exactly but told him how to find her.

It seemed that there was a trio of old sisters who lived in a cave in Mysia. They had one eye and one tooth between them and used them in turns, to see and to eat. Perseus used his magic sandals and arrived at the mouth of the cave. Using the cloak and the hood to make himself invisible, he entered the cave. He saw the sisters fighting over who should have the eye and the tooth. He grabbed both. The sisters realized that there was someone in the cave, and grew angry. Perseus asked them where to find Medusa. When the sisters refused to answer, he threatened to throw the eye and tooth into the sea. This worked and he got the answer he wanted—Medusa lived on an island off the coast of Libya.

Leaving the cave, he started flying over the Libyan coast, trying to locate the island. It took him a while to spot it. He saw that all three Gorgon sisters were asleep. Only one had serpents for her hair. *That must be Medusa*, thought Perseus.

Perseus also saw several rock formations, which he realized were men and animals and even some children. They were all victims of Medusa's evil eyes. He knew that, at any cost, he must avoid looking into the eyes of Medusa.

Perseus slowly dropped to within a few feet of the sleeping Medusa. He held the shield and the scythe in front of him, ready to do his job. The snakes in Medusa's head began moving and hissing. As soon as Medusa opened her eyes, she saw her own reflection and let out a shriek. Instantly, Perseus cut off her head and put it in the satchel. He then flew away upwards. He had done what he had come to do.

But his adventures were not over yet.

Flying home, he took a wrong turn and saw a beautiful maiden chained to a rock. He landed beside her and asked her why she was imprisoned. She told Perseus that her name was Andromeda and she had been chained to the rock as a sacrificial offering.

Perseus was intrigued and asked her what she had done to deserve such a fate. She told Perseus that it was the fault of her mother, who had said aloud that she was more beautiful than the spirits of the ocean, the nereids, and others.

Perseus said that he kind of agreed with her mother. Andromeda then told him that Poseidon, angry at this announcement by her mother, had her chained and was going to send a dragon called Cetus to eat her. This was the sacrifice he demanded. Since Poseidon controlled the seas, this had to be done, otherwise, Poseidon threatened to stop all ships coming through.

At this point, Andromeda pointed to the sea and said, "here he comes—Cetus. Now I must die!"

Seeing what appeared to be a monster of some kind approaching, Perseus took out his scythe and dived into the sea.

After a few minutes, he surfaced. There was a lot of blood in the ocean. Andromeda knew that he had slain the monster. Perseus flew to where Andromeda was chained and set her free. "Let's get you home," he said with a smile.

Together they flew to the palace in Ethiopia, where Andromeda was greeted with cries of joy by her mother and father. Shortly thereafter, they were married.

After living in Ethiopia for a while, Andromeda wanted to see Perseus's home. Although Perseus told her that it was a humble cottage, she insisted that she wanted to go and live there. Perseus agreed and together they arrived at Seriphos, the place where Perseus used to live and found the cottage in ruins. It had been burned.

There was no trace of his mother, or of Dictys. Perseus then asked around and was told that Polydectes had arrested them and taken them to his court. Enraged, Perseus picked up his satchel containing the head of Medusa and went to the court of Polydectes. He stood behind the throne on which Polydectes was sitting. He saw his mother and Dictys being brought in, bound with ropes. Perseus waited, and then walked forward.

Polydectes was delighted to see him. "Well, well, if it isn't Perseus!"

Perseus asked Polydectes, "why have you imprisoned my mother and Dictys?"

"Your mother was supposed to marry me. Instead, she married this beggar Dictys!" replied Polydectes in anger. "And now they shall die," he added.

Perseus loudly asked his mother, Dictys, and everyone in the court who was on his side not to look at him, and to keep their eyes on Polydectes.

Perseus then said, "you wanted the head of Medusa, here it is."

He produced the head from the satchel and showed it to Polydectes. The curse of Medusa did its work.

What people saw after that was astonishing and frightening. Polydectes and his guards had all turned into stone statues. That was the end of Polydectes.

It is said that Perseus and Andromeda lived happily for many years.

CHAPTER 7
THE ORACLE OF DELPHI AND OTHER STORIES

❧❧❧❧❧ ❧❧❧❧❧❧

The Oracle of Delphi

This oracle was very important to the Greeks. Kings, gods, goddesses, and ordinary mortals all came to the oracle to get answers to their problems. The temple of this oracle was in Delphi. How did it come to be in Delphi, and from where did this oracle stuff come from? Thereby hangs a tale.

Do you remember Apollo? The god with the lyre? Well, apart from being a god of many things, he was also an excellent archer, and his arrows never missed their mark.

In this story, we again come across the goddess Hera, the wife of Zeus, who was an exceedingly jealous woman. When she came to know that Zeus had two children from another lady, she was angry. The two children were Apollo and Artemis. They have hidden away on an island. Hera found out and decided to kill them. Sounds pretty cruel, but that's the way it was.

Let's go back a little. Rhea, who was the wife of Cronus, gave her husband a stone to swallow instead of the newborn child Zeus. Cronus had swallowed it thinking it was his sixth child. Zeus, if you remember, gave a potion to Cronus, which made him vomit his siblings, along with the stone that he had swallowed. This stone was thrown away by Zeus and landed at a place called Pytho. The place where it landed became sacred. Gaia, the mother goddess, then brought forth a large serpent to guard the stone and the place where it fell. This serpent was called Python from the place name Pytho. (Snakes still have the name python. These are enormous snakes that can swallow their prey whole!) The serpent was always present and no one dared to go there, as it was too dangerous.

Hera, in her anger, asked the serpent to go and kill Apollo and Artemis. Zeus, who loved his children, sent word to Apollo about what Hera was up to.

Apollo decided to defend himself and his sister. But he needed a powerful weapon. Python was no ordinary serpent. He sent word to Hephaestus, the man who could make magic weapons. Hephaestus toiled away for several days and made a powerful bow and golden arrows. These he gave to Apollo.

Carrying the special weapons, Apollo went to Pytho and lay in wait for the serpent to show itself. When it did appear, Apollo, with unerring aim, shot an arrow through its eye. As the serpent writhed on the ground, dying, Apollo said, "die and rot here forever."

The serpent did rot there, but it was created by the goddess Gaia so its rotting carcass created a chasm. From this chasm rose vapors that, when inhaled, put a person into a trance. Apollo, meanwhile, had renamed Pytho—he called it Delphi.

As word spread about the vapor and its ability to put people into trances, in which state they could foretell the future, it became a popular place. A temple was constructed and a priestess, called Pythia, was appointed. The priestess would go into a trance and reply to the queries that people asked of her.

The problem was that not all the answers from the priestess were clear. Another priest or a wise man was sometimes needed to decode the meaning. (Perseus, if you remember, faced the same problem until an old woman told him what the prophecy meant.) Sometimes the oracle did not reply and this enraged many people. Hercules, being a strong and impatient sort of character, started destroying the temple when he did not get a response. Apollo had to intervene to stop him from doing that.

However, Apollo had another problem. How would he get people to work in the temple? Cleaning and guarding were some of the things that were urgently needed. The place where he had built the temple was deserted. There was no one around who he could engage for this task. Suddenly, he saw in the distance a ship manned by Cretans. Apollo immediately changed himself into a dolphin and chased the ship. Once he had caught up with it he jumped on board. The Cretans were terrified, especially when they noticed that they had lost control of their vessel and that it was turning around and heading in a different direction. It entered the Sea of Corinth and ran aground on the shores of Crissa. Apollo now changed himself into his divine form and told the sailors not to be afraid.

Apollo then pronounced his will.

"You will never return to your homeland again. You will stay here and guard the temple. Honors and wealth will be yours. Everything that is offered to me, you shall have." said Apollo to the frightened sailors who just nodded in agreement.

"And since you saw me first as a dolphin, you will henceforth address me as 'Delphinian.'"

Apollo had solved his problem. The Cretans did as they were told and the temple had the caretakers it needed.

Over time, the oracle became famous and no god or king ever did anything without a prophecy from the Oracle of Delphi. This oracle has already popped up in several of these stories.

Zeus, Hades, and Persephone

Zeus, as you already know, was the lord of everything in the universe, above ground. But the lord of the Underground, or Underworld, was Hades and his queen Persephone. Hades and Zeus were also brothers.

Demeter was the goddess who ruled over the growth of everything on Earth. Trees, crops, flowers, all of it. She had a beautiful daughter called Persephone who also caused flowers to bloom and the crops to mature. Flowers would bloom with her mere presence.

One day as Persephone was playing around in a garden, the

earth split open and a chariot came charging out of the ground. Before she could do anything, the driver of the chariot, Hades, grabbed her and the chariot disappeared into the crack. Moments later, the crack sealed itself. Persephone had vanished without a trace. As the months passed by, a distraught Demeter was so busy looking for her daughter that she neglected her duties as goddess of the crops and harvest. The Earth began to suffer from famine. Nothing was growing and soon, this news reached Zeus.

Demeter searched everywhere but found no trace of her daughter. Zeus, by this time realizing the danger, got the council together. He was angry that no one had told him about the mysterious disappearance of Persephone.

"And it seems none of you know where she is! What kind of gods are you anyway?" he barked, losing his temper. The gods sat silent.

One day at the council meeting, Helios the sun god suddenly said, "I know what happened to Persephone."

Zeus turned to him. "You know and yet you didn't tell us?"

Helios replied in an offended tone. "Nobody asked me. Everybody thinks I know nothing."

"Well, where is she then?" asked Zeus in anger.

"Hades took her to his palace," said Helios.

Zeus was now really angry. He decided to go to the Underworld and confront Hades immediately.

When he arrived at the Underworld, Zeus went to Hades and

demanded an explanation. He also wanted the return of Persephone without any delay.

"On the Earth, there is a famine and people are dying of hunger! What do you think you were doing, kidnapping Persephone?" said Zeus.

Hades refused. "I love her and she will stay with me."

This enraged Zeus even more. He threatened Hades. "You do not know my power yet. I will ask Hermes to bring no more souls to your Underworld. If required, all mortals shall become immortal. You won't have any souls to deal with. You will become the laughing stock of the gods. What are you going to do then?"

Hades knew when he was beaten. But Hades was the lord of the Underworld, and he still had a trick up his sleeve.

"I will return her to you tomorrow. Let her stay for one more day," pleaded Hades.

Zeus agreed and went back happy.

After Zeus had gone, Hades went to the room of Persephone and told her what had happened and that she must go back to her home.

Hades then produced some pomegranate seeds and asked Persephone to eat some. Persephone picked up six seeds and started eating them. Hades watched with gleaming eyes.

The next day Hermes arrived to take Persephone back to the natural world. Hades called Hermes and told him, "you may take her back, but she has eaten the fruit of the Underworld, so she must return here. She has eaten six seeds, so she must come here to me for six months every year. The other six months she can spend on the surface."

Hermes knew that this was true. He agreed and took Persephone and left.

That began the cycle of regeneration of plants and the seasons. When Persephone was on the surface, everything grew and the Earth was fruitful. But when she went back to Hades, trees shed their leaves and winter stopped the growth of crops. Nature held her breath, waiting for the return of Persephone.

Bellerophon and Pegasus

Nobody knows for sure who Bellerophon's father was. Some myths say it was Poseidon, but Bellerophon was raised by Glaucus, King of Corinth. His mother was Eurynome.

Bellerophon grew up to be, as with all gods, strong and handsome. He had one special characteristic: He loved horses.

Bellerophon never saw gods performing miracles or hurling thunderbolts in Corinth. It was just a very busy city with lots of normal people.

Then one day he heard something that drew his attention. He was 14 years old and had the curiosity of the young. The rumor was that people had seen a white horse that had wings and could fly. Hearing the rumors, Bellerophon tried to find someone who had actually seen this miraculous creature, but he found no one. He dismissed the rumors as fantasy. But this was to change soon.

Bellerophon heard that certain Corinthians were saying that the flying horse was actually present in an area just outside of Corinth. The horse had been seen drinking from a natural water spring at a place called Pirene. Bellerophon decided to go to Pirene and see for himself.

When he got to Pirene, Bellerophon went to the spring and met some people who were standing around. When he asked them about the horse, they replied that it had flown away as soon as it had heard them approaching. It was an extremely shy animal. Bellerophon decided to hide near the spring and wait. Maybe the horse would come back if of course such a thing really existed.

After a while, Bellerophon fell asleep but was awakened by a soft sound. He carefully raised his head and looked at the spring. He saw the horse—a white horse with wings! Bellerophon looked carefully to see if the wings were attached to the horse with wax or something similar. It was not a prank—the horse had real wings.

Bellerophon tried to quietly creep up to the horse and pet him. But horses have an acute sense, and before Bellerophon could get anywhere near, it galloped, spread its wings, and flew away. Bellerophon stared up in amazement. *I have to have that horse*, he told himself as he returned home.

As the days passed, Bellerophon tried all sorts of tricks to get the horse to come to him, but nothing seemed to work. His mother noticed that something was bothering her son and called in the seer Polyidus.

Polyidus then approached Bellerophon and asked him what

the matter was. Bellerophon, after much hesitation, told him. The seer smiled and said that he would tell him how to succeed. Bellerophon was skeptical but listened. He knew that Polyidus had the power of prophecy.

"You must go to the temple of Athena and lie down on the floor and ask for Athena's help. She will definitely help you. There is no other way," said the seer.

Bellerophon was hesitant. He did not believe in gods doing simple favors or working miracles. But Polyidus was a prophet and his words could not be taken lightly.

Bellerophon set out for the temple of Athena. Arriving, he lay down on the floor as directed by Polyidus and waited.

Then he heard a voice. "Bellerophon, you want to ride the white horse? He is shyer than any horse."

Bellerophon nodded his head, not knowing if the gesture was visible to whoever was talking. Then he saw the image of Athena before him and he was amazed. So the gods and goddesses really did exist!

"Only the golden bridle will allow you to ride him. Take it with you," said the goddess before she disappeared.

Bellerophon got up and scratched his head. He did not have a golden bridle. What was the goddess talking about?

Then he saw a bundle on the floor and picked it up. Inside was a golden bridle! *Miracles really did happen*, thought Bellerophon.

Happily, he carried the bridle home, thanked Polyidus for his advice, and prepared to ride Pegasus.

Bellerophon went to the spring where he knew Pegasus came to drink water and waited.

Pegasus arrived as usual and drank from the spring. Bellerophon, golden bridle in hand, approached slowly, making soothing sounds. Pegasus looked nervous but did not run or fly away. Bellerophon put his hand out and patted the horse, and slipped the bridle in place. With a leap, he was astride Pegasus. At his command, the horse slowly started running and, spreading its wings, flew up into the sky.

Bellerophon was ecstatic with joy as he looked down upon Corinth.

After flying around for some time, Bellerophon guided Pegasus to the palace grounds and landed there to everyone's amazement. Many people would come to see this miracle of a flying horse.

Bellerophon and the Chimera

The king of Lycia, Iobates, wanted Bellerophon dead. The reason is somewhat complicated and is not part of this story. This part is about how Bellerophon killed the dreaded Chimera, a fierce monster that was supposed to be immortal.

Bellerophon knew very well that to get the better of a creature like the Chimera, he needed a special kind of lance. So he went to a good ironsmith and had a lance designed specially for himself.

Sitting astride Pegasus, Bellerophon set off to find the Chimera. As he flew around, he noticed that large tracts of the land were on fire. Wildfires happened often, so Bellerophon paid no attention to them. But the swirling smoke from the fires made it difficult to see the ground below. Then he spotted a deer running for its life and being pursued by what looked like a lion, but was not quite a lion. It had a lion's body and head, but there was a goat's head on top too, complete with horns protruding from the back, and the tail was a snake! It was spouting fire from its mouth. Bellerophon had never seen such a creature. He fired several arrows at it, with no result. Then he guided Pegasus lower and when the creature opened its mouth and started spouting fire, he threw the lance straight into the creature's mouth and down its throat.

The creature began growling and screaming and rolling on the ground. Moments later, it was dead. Bellerophon had very cleverly had the lance made of lead. As soon as the lance entered the lion's body, the lead began to melt from the creature's fiery breath, killing it.

Bellerophon cut off the Chimera's head and took it back to show Iobates, who was definitely not happy to see a half-burned lion's head lying in his throne room.

Orpheus and Eurydice

Orpheus is known as the god of good time, fun, and music. His singing was so beautiful that people were hypnotized by it. Orpheus loved his wife Eurydice very much, and when she died of a snake bite and her soul went to the Underworld, he was very sad. He gave up singing and just walked around with an unhappy air around him.

One day Apollo, his father, came to him and asked him how long he would mope around for.

Orpheus did not reply. Apollo asked him again. This time Orpheus said he would be happy if he got his wife, Eurydice, back again. Apollo thought for some time and then said, "in that case, why don't you go and bring her back?"

Orpheus was amazed. "How can I? Nobody who goes to the Underworld ever comes back alive," he said.

"Maybe you can," replied Apollo.

"How?" asked Orpheus, a little surprised.

"Use the power of your music," replied Apollo.

Orpheus sat up. Could that be done?

He decided to try it.

Orpheus took out his lyre, which was lying unused, and restored the instrument.

Then he made a plan. He knew that there were two hurdles to get into the Underworld. The first was Cerberus, the monster who guarded its gates, and the second was the ferryman, Charon, who ran the ferry to the Underworld.

Orpheus started on his journey. When he arrived at the gates, he saw Cerberus ready to pounce on him. He began to play the lyre and sing. Cerberus was hypnotized by the song and slowly fell asleep. Orpheus went past him and arrived at the ferry. There he saw Charon. Before Charon could protest, he began singing. Charon too was charmed and rowed him across to the entrance of the Underworld.

Orpheus, now growing in confidence, entered the

Underworld. There, he began serenading the assorted monsters who guarded the place.

Hearing the commotion, Hades and his wife Persephone appeared.

"What are you, a living mortal, doing here?" asked Hades angrily.

"I came to take my wife back to the world of the living," said Orpheus.

"Don't you know that is impossible!" replied Hades.

Persephone, who was listening, spoke to Hades.

Meanwhile, Orpheus could see his wife in the form of a spirit.

Hades then announced that he would permit Orpheus to sing one song, and if he was happy, he would allow him to take his wife back to the world of the living.

Orpheus sang and Hades and Persephone were entranced by the music.

Hades agreed and let her go. Orpheus and his wife Eurydice started walking towards the gates and back to the world of the living.

Zeus and His Headache

The great Zeus had a headache. Not an ordinary headache, but a very severe and painful one. He roamed around his palace yelling and screaming, with his hands pressed against the sides of his head. No one knew what to do. Some even thought that war had broken out again.

As Zeus howled in agony, Prometheus arrived at the palace. He took one look at Zeus, turned to Hephaestus, and spoke to him quietly.

Hephaestus hurried away.

What was actually going on in Zeus's head was this:

Metis, who lived inside his head, was forging and making metal objects. These needed hammering. The material for these objects came from the minerals that were present in the food Zeus ate every day. It was no wonder that Zeus felt his head was going to split open.

Prometheus knew about Metis being inside Zeus's head.

After a while, Hephaestus returned from his smithy with a large axe. Prometheus then asked Zeus to kneel down and lower his head in prayer. Zeus knelt and lowered his head. Hephaestus then brought up the axe and with one blow, split open Zeus's head. All the gods and goddesses present were stunned. They were also afraid of what Zeus might now do.

But then something strange began to happen.

From inside the split skull, a figure began to emerge. It was a female figure in full armor. She stepped out of the skull and stood in front of the kneeling Zeus. She addressed him as father.

As if by magic, the split skull closed and became whole again. Zeus stood up and recognized his daughter—Athena.

How the Bee Got Its Sting

In the heavens, the marriage of Aphrodite and Hephaestus

was announced. Zeus organized a huge banquet and almost all the gods and goddesses were invited. To add a little spice to the proceedings, Zeus said that there would be a competition. The one who prepared the most original and best wedding dish would be rewarded. He would grant them a favor. Everybody brought what they thought were good dishes and a variety of food turned up. Once the wedding celebrations were over, it was time for the selection of the best dish. Zeus went around tasting the dishes. Finally, he arrived at the table of a small creature with wings named Melissa. She had before her a jar of a kind of gooey substance. Zeus dipped his finger and put some in his mouth. It tasted exquisite. Zeus had no hesitation in declaring it the winner. The creature told Zeus that it was honey.

Melissa then flew close to Zeus's ear and said, "my Lord, it is very difficult to make this honey. I have to go from flower to flower for days to produce a small amount. It is very hard work. But the problem is that animals like bears come and take away my honey. I cannot do anything because I am small. I want you to give me something to defend myself against these robbers. The snake that produces nothing has a deadly bite and poison. Give me a weapon that is powerful enough to kill any who come to rob me of my honey."

Zeus was angry that Melissa should ask for such a boon. But he thought awhile and then he said that he would make the collection of honey easier for Melissa. From now on she would have helpers who would collect the honey. She would be the queen. Zeus also granted her a sting, which all bees now have. Melissa was happy that her wish had been granted.

The honeybee is still called *mélissa* in Greek.

The Legend of the Muses

According to myth, there were nine muses—Clio, Euterpe, Thalia, Melpomene, Terpsichore, Erato, Polyhymnia, Urania, and Calliope.

In the beginning, they were responsible for various things, but ultimately they were said to rule over music and poetry. They served as an inspiration to aspiring artists and poets.

The Muses were the constant companions of Apollo, who was addicted to music, as you already know. They were described as young women with smiling faces, though sometimes grave and thoughtful.

Their offerings were honey, water, and milk.

Nobody knows for sure where the Muses came from, or who were their parents. Some myths say they were the daughters of Uranus and Gaia.

The Muses lived far away from the hustle and bustle of normal life. They preferred the peace and quiet of a mountain called Helicon. The slopes of this mountain were covered with scented plants and flowers, which the Muses loved. They would dance and sing there. The mountain also had several freshwater springs, and anyone who drank its waters would be inspired to write great poetry. At night, the Muses would enclose themselves in clouds and float close to the habitations. The people and gods would hear their beautiful voices singing.

It is said that the Muses were the guardians of the temple of Delphi.

CHAPTER 8
MORE GODS, GODDESSES, AND HEROES

In this chapter, we shall talk about some of the lesser gods, goddesses, and heroes, who, while they were not so well-known as the famous ones, were nevertheless important in their own way. They too played important parts in the lives of the gods and the people.

Themis

Of the lesser gods and goddesses, Themis was important. Themis was the daughter of Uranus and Gaia, the original divinities of the universe. She belonged to the gods called the Titans and despite the defeat of the Titans, was respected and welcomed at the court of the Olympians. She was known to be wise and gave advice to various gods.

When Rhea wanted to hide her sixth child so that Cronus would not swallow it, Themis advised her, took the child from her, and delivered him to the place where he would be safe.

Most of all she is known as the goddess of justice. It was she who had delivered the Oracle of Delphi, which she had inherited from her mother Gaia. She was known as the counselor to everyone and was renowned for her fairness and judgment.

Iris

Gaia is said to also be the mother of Iris. Myth says that she was the goddess of the rainbow, and like Hermes, a messenger of the gods. Zeus especially used her to send his messages when Hermes was not available. When Zeus wanted to send a message to the other gods, he would send Iris. When the message was for the mortals on Earth, Iris would descend onto the Earth and assume a mortal form and deliver the message.

She was known to fly using wings attached to her shoulders and sometimes wore winged sandals, like Hermes. Amazingly, she was just as fast through water as she was through the air! She proved her powers when, at the request of Zeus, she dove into the ocean and went to the Underworld to fill a golden cup with water from the river called Styx. As everyone knows, going to the Underworld is not easy, it is way down, deep in the Earth's bowels. This proves just how powerful she was.

Helios

In the Greek myths, Apollo was the god of sunlight, but he was not the sun god. That title belonged to Helios.

The story goes like this: Every morning Helios would emerge from the east from a swamp. He had a golden chariot that had been made by Hephaestus, the great metal worker. Winged horses were fastened to this chariot, white and dazzling in appearance. The horses breathed fire and were indeed extraordinary. This was because Helios was the dazzling sun god, of course!

Astride this chariot, Helios roamed the heavens, casting light on everything. Try to think of it as a sunrise. By midday when Helios had reached the highest point in the heavens, he started moving downwards, and in the evening it looked like he had plunged into the ocean. Actually, he landed inside a golden cup where his family awaited him. He then sailed the cup eastward until he arrived home. He would emerge again the next morning. It is the rising and the setting of the sun each day of our lives. There is another interesting point to note: Helios knew everything that was going on in the universe. No one knew as much as he did.

Eos

While Helios was the sun god, Eos was the goddess of the dawn—that gentle glow of light that is seen just before the sun rises. Every morning she would rise up in the sky, wearing saffron robes and carrying a torch in her hand. The soft light of dawn was her work. It announced the coming of day and the rising of Helios, the sun god.

Odysseus

This character in Greek mythology is famous for a story that involves the Sirens. Odysseus was setting out on a voyage when a sorceress called Circe warned him of the Sirens. She told Odysseus never to go to the island where these creatures lived. These dangerous creatures sang so well that most men were unable to keep from going over to the island. Should Odysseus go, he would be tortured by the Sirens and ultimately killed and eaten. Odysseus kept that in mind and this saved his life and that of his crew.

When he was approaching the island where the Sirens lived, Odysseus asked that he be bound to the mast of his vessel. He then put wax into the ears of his crew.

When he came close to the rocky islet where the Sirens lived, he saw them. They were weird creatures—half-woman and half-bird.

Then he heard their song. The sorceress had been right. Odysseus, had he not been bound to the mast, would never have been able to resist the song, and would have gone to the islet. Such was the power of the music that the Sirens produced.

The crew members, of course, could not hear anything, and the ship passed the islet safely.

Later, when the Sirens tried the same trick with the vessel Argo, which was carrying Jason and his army, Orpheus, who was present on the vessel, sang a song of such beauty that the Sirens fell silent. It is said that after this the Sirens lost their ability to sing and were turned into rocks!

Pandora

Pandora was not a Greek goddess or anything, but she played an important part in the lives of mortals.

The story begins when Prometheus stole fire from the forge of Hephaestus and gave it to the mortals. Prometheus also taught humans how to use fire.

This made Zeus very, very angry. He loved Prometheus and felt betrayed. The other thing that worried him was the thought that once mortals had the power of fire, they would not need the gods in the future, and would stop making offerings to them. All the good stuff that came from these offerings would disappear! That would not do.

Zeus had Prometheus chained to a rock. This part of the story you already know, but there is another part that needs to be told now.

Prometheus had a brother called Epimetheus. Epimetheus was not as clever as Prometheus.

Zeus, before he had Prometheus chained to the rock, summoned Hephaestus, the god who could work miracles with his hands.

"Fashion a beautiful woman for me out of clay," he commanded Hephaestus.

"Yes, my Lord," replied Hephaestus, wondering what Zeus had in mind.

Hephaestus went back to his workshop and fashioned a clay figure of a woman of exquisite beauty. Aphrodite breathed life into her. All the other gods and goddesses pitched in and gave her jewelry and other ornaments.

Zeus then called to her, "I will give you a vase with a sealed top. You must take this with you to the land of the mortals. But you must never open it!"

Zeus named the beautiful woman Pandora and sent her down to Epimetheus.

Prometheus knew that his brother was not very intelligent and always did things without thinking. Before leaving for distant lands to teach mortals the use of fire, he had warned Epimetheus not to accept any gifts that Zeus might send. Prometheus knew that Zeus was going to try and punish him for stealing fire. He was afraid that Zeus would target Epimetheus, and he was right.

Pandora appeared before Epimetheus, brought to him by Hermes. Epimetheus fell in love with her immediately.

Epimetheus married her and they began living together. Pandora kept the vase without opening it, but she often wondered what was in it.

One day she could not resist her curiosity and went and opened the lid of the vase. Out flew disease, anger, and all of the nasty things that mortals are suffering from even today.

Seeing that ugly things were coming out, she quickly put the lid back on, but it was too late. All the nasties had escaped and they began to spread all over the world.

Zeus had known all along that Pandora would open the lid of the vase.

Pandora was very sad and Epimetheus understood too late why Zeus had sent Pandora to him. He wondered what Prometheus would say when he came back.

Cadmus and the City of Thebes

In Greek mythology, the city of Thebes was very important. But how it was founded is part of an interesting story.

Cadmus (who is the hero of this story) was from a place called Tyre. As it happened, his sister Europa had gone missing. Cadmus's parents sent him to find and bring back his sister. Cadmus took with him a clever and beautiful lady called Harmonia, who he met in a place called Samothrace. He also took with him a gang of men as part of his entourage.

As they wandered around looking for Europa, Cadmus decided that he would need help, so they headed for the Oracle of Delphi. Cadmus, however, was already famous for creating the alphabet. People could now communicate, and everyone sang his praise. He was also known for his athletic prowess.

When they reached the temple at Delphi, Cadmus entered and then asked the question to which he was seeking the answer.

"How do I find my sister?" Cadmus asked the oracle. As usual, the reply was vague.

The oracle said that Cadmus must follow a cow with a crescent moon mark on her back until it lay down with exhaustion. At the spot where the cow lay down, Cadmus must build.

That was all. Cadmus was totally baffled by the prophecy. He could make no head or tail of it. What cow? Build what? He was looking for his sister, that was all. Annoyed, he walked away from the oracle. Even Harmonia was unable to decode this strange message. They continued on their way, still not sure where to look for Europa. The oracle had been of no help at all.

The temple of Delphi was situated in an area called Phocis. The king of Phocis, Pelagon, when he heard that the famous Cadmus was in his area, sent out an invitation for him to come and rest awhile in the royal palace. The tired Cadmus, Harmonia, and his band of men accepted gratefully.

After a meal, Cadmus and Harmonia were strolling in the palace grounds together when the father of Pelagon approached them suddenly. He was a little drunk. He told them that he wanted Cadmus to take part in a local sports event that was slated to start the next day. The king too, as it turned out, wanted Cadmus to participate.

It was just a local event and Cadmus won most of the events easily. The king, who was not very rich, did not know what to give as a special present. A while later, one of the king's henchmen arrived with a cow in tow. The king asked Cadmus to accept the cow as a gift. The courtiers and the public laughed at such a silly prize. But it was Harmonia who suddenly saw the significance of the cow.

"Look Cadmus, the cow!" she said, pointing excitedly at the animal.

"Yes, I see it. It's a cow. So what?" replied Cadmus, somewhat annoyed.

Harmonia still tugged at Cadmus's hand. "Yes, but look at the mark on its back!"

It was then that Cadmus saw the mark of the crescent moon on the back of the cow.

"Whoa!" exclaimed Cadmus, realizing that this was the animal that the oracle had spoken about.

The cow, meanwhile, had started wandering off. Cadmus quickly thanked the king for his superb gift, and together with Harmonia, started after the animal. His entourage of men followed.

Cadmus and Harmonia followed the animal over land and vale. Cadmus by now was getting a little fed up with it all. Where was the cow heading, and why did it not stop and rest?

After a while, the cow suddenly sank down onto the ground, unable to carry on. Harmonia was excited. "Just as the oracle said! You must build here."

Cadmus looked at her and asked sarcastically, "build what?"

Harmonia thought for a while and then said, "let us sacrifice the cow to Athena and see what happens." Immediately, a camp was set up.

Cadmus asked his men to fetch water from a nearby spring and he sacrificed the cow to the goddess. As soon as he had done that, some of his men came running back and said that a giant serpent guarding the spring had killed two of his men.

Cadmus wearily got up and went to see what the serpent was all about. He picked up a large boulder and waited. When the serpent appeared, he threw the boulder at it and crushed its skull, killing it. As soon he did that he heard an unseen voice curse him for killing the serpent. Cadmus ignored the curse and came back to camp.

The goddess Athena appeared in front of them and said that

she was pleased with the sacrifice. She then advised Cadmus that he must follow her instructions exactly, so that he may overcome the curse placed on him for killing the serpent.

Cadmus agreed to do her bidding.

Athena then told Cadmus to make a plow and make furrows in the land using the plow. Once done, he had to extract the teeth of the serpent and plant each tooth in the furrows. Cadmus fashioned a plow and made the furrows, with his men pulling the plow. He then extracted around 500 teeth from the serpent and planted them in the furrows.

Armed men began to grow out of the earth! One for each tooth buried. Cadmus was puzzled.

The men then formed a group and began advancing onwards Cadmus and his men. Cadmus picked a large stone and hurled it at the advancing men. It hit one of them, and they started fighting amongst themselves. After a while, just five of them remained. Cadmus managed to persuade them into surrendering.

He then asked the men if they knew the name of the place where they were standing.

One of the warriors did know. "It is the plain of Thebes."

Cadmus then announced that he would build a great city right there.

Harmonia, standing and watching this whole scene, smiled to herself. The oracle had been dead right, down to the last detail.

This was how the great ancient city of Thebes was built. The myth, however, does not tell us if Cadmus found his sister.

Phrygia and the Gordian Knot

This story is not about a god. It is about an ordinary mortal who became king. How he became king is fascinating to read.

A poor and ambitious peasant named Gordias lived in a place called Macedonia. He used to work the barren fields and live simply. He did not have much money.

One day an eagle flew down and perched on the pole of his oxcart. The eagle looked at him with stern eyes and did not move. Gordias, initially puzzled, took it as a sign that the gods were smiling at him. He thought that he was destined for greater things.

He removed the plow from his cart and decided to go to the oracle of Zeus. The funny thing was that the eagle refused to move even as Gordias drove the cart over rocky paths.

On the way, he met a beautiful girl who he found had prophetic powers. He wanted to take her with him. The first thing this girl said to Gordias was to hurry up and get to the oracle. Gordias agreed to take her with him, only if she agreed to marry him. She nodded her head and said yes.

As this was going on, it so happened that the king of Phrygia suddenly died and left no heirs. The people were worried. Who would now be king? They hurried to the oracle of Zeus to get an answer. The oracle told them that they should crown the first person to enter their gates in a cart. The people were happy and went to their city and waited at the gates to see who would come in a cart.

Meanwhile, Gordias arrived at the gates of Phrygia. The people saw that he was driving a cart and immediately asked him to be king. The eagle had flown away the moment Gordias entered the gates.

Once he was crowned king, Gordias began to rule, and he ruled really well. The oxcart in which he had arrived was treated as a holy relic by the people. They set up a wooden post and tied the yoke of the cart to it using a very complicated knot. The knot was created by Gordias and was so complex that nobody could untangle it. Many warriors and brave men tried but failed. The knot remained secure. It became known as the Gordian Knot. Even today, when a problem is very complicated and difficult to solve, it is referred to as a Gordian Knot!

There is also an interesting ending to this story.

This knot lay unopened for about a thousand years, till a great Macedonian warrior called Alexander came to Phrygia. When he learned about this knot, he went to take a look at it. After looking at it, he drew his sword, and with one slice he cut the knot. He later became famous for his many conquests, and is known as Alexander the Great!

Gordias now takes us to the next story, that of King Midas, who was his son.

Midas

Gordias died after a few years and Midas became king. He was a kind and gentle ruler. But he had one passion—roses. He created a magnificent rose garden and spent most of his time there smelling his lovely roses. He was always respectful, especially to elders.

One day he was walking around his rose garden when he tripped over an old and ugly man who was sleeping. He apologized and invited the man to his palace to eat. The old man agreed. What Midas did not know was that the old man was Silenus, a close companion of the god Dionysus.

Silenus stayed at the palace for 10 days and almost emptied all of Midas's wine and food. Then on the 11th day he said he wanted to leave. Midas was glad. This man had finished a huge amount of his wine and food. Midas was not a rich king, although he wished he had more money to spend on improving his people's lives.

Silenus then asked Midas to escort him to his home. Midas agreed, and along with some of his palace guards, went with Silenus.

After a few days of traveling, they came upon the camp of the god Dionysus. Midas, to his amazement, saw that everyone was drinking and having a merry time.

Silenus introduced Midas to Dionysus, saying that Midas was an extremely good host and that he, Silenus, had drunk all of his wine.

Dionysus looked at Midas and said, "you seem like a kind-hearted soul. Thank you for your hospitality towards my friend Silenus."

Midas just mumbled and nodded his head. He wanted to get

back to the palace and his roses. But Dionysus was not finished yet.

"Ask for whatever you want, and I shall grant your wish!" said Dionysus.

"Anything I wish for?" asked Midas. His mind began to race.

"Anything!" replied Dionysus.

Midas was not sure if Dionysus was joking or not. He did appear a little drunk.

Midas thought hard. He decided that if he had a little more money, he could spend it on important things for his kingdom. He would ask for wealth!

"Whatever I touch will turn into gold. That is my wish!" he said.

Dionysus smiled. "Are you sure that is your wish?"

Midas nodded his head vigorously. "Yes, my Lord, that is my wish."

"Granted. Go back home, and use wine to take a bath. Then go to sleep. The next morning, your wish will come true," said Dionysus.

Midas went home happy. He was still a little skeptical but decided to do what he was told to do.

The next morning Midas awoke as usual and went to the rose garden to touch and smell his lovely roses—and got the shock of his life.

As soon as he touched the rose plant and the roses, they turned into gold! Midas could not believe his eyes. He went around touching other rose plants, with the same result. He was overjoyed. Now he had more wealth than anyone in the world, and he could keep creating more and more gold. He started shouting in joy. His wife, hearing his cries, ran out of the palace and came to see what was going on. She had their infant daughter in her arms. Midas, overjoyed, put his arms around her. Bam! His wife and daughter were now golden statues! Midas was taken aback. What had he done? But this was not the end. Whatever food he touched also turned into gold. Within days, Midas was hungry and extremely unhappy. He did not know what to do, or how to get rid of the wish. Then one night, Dionysus appeared in his dream.

"Foolish man! Always be careful what you wish for! Go to the river Pactolus and dip your hand into its waters. The golden touch will be washed away. Dip everything you turned into gold in the same river, and they will all become normal again," said Dionysus, and the dream ended.

The next morning Midas went to the river and did as directed by Dionysus. His golden touch was no more. He took everything that he had touched to the river, including his wife and child, and dipped them. They all returned to their original form. Midas heaved a sigh of relief! He realized that he had been very foolish.

However, the story of Midas has another twist.

After his episode with the golden hands, Midas lost all love for money and wealth. He became the follower of the god Pan, who was always playing on his flute and enjoying life. Midas liked Pan.

One day when Pan was playing the flute, the god Apollo appeared. All present became silent. Apollo played on his lyre and divine music filled the air. Everyone clapped and said that Apollo was the best musician. But Midas disagreed and said so.

"Pan is a better musician," he said. Apollo could not believe his ears and asked Midas to repeat his statement, which he did.

"You have the ears of a donkey," said Apollo.

Within seconds, a new pair of ears began to grow on Midas's head. They were the ears of a donkey. Everyone saw the ears and started to laugh. Midas ran away, embarrassed. He put on a turban to hide the ears, and went back home.

Midas was aware of his problem and kept wearing the turban so that nobody would know about the ears. But there was one person who had to know, and that was his barber. Midas swore him to silence and threatened to destroy him and his family if he ever let the secret out. The barber was silent for a long time, but he was dying to tell someone. One day, unable to bear the burden of the secret any longer, he went and dug a hole in the ground. Placing his mouth close to the hole he shouted, "the king has the ears of a donkey!" As soon as he said that, he covered the hole with earth so that the secret would not escape. But a seed had fallen into the hole. From the seed grew a sapling, which pierced the earth and came out of the ground. It began whispering in the wind, "the king has the ears of a donkey." Soon, other trees picked up the whisper and the secret finally reached the city. People started laughing and making fun of Midas.

There are two lessons in this story. The first is to be careful of what you wish for, and second is to be careful of what you say.

The Great Flood

Everyone knows about the Great Flood and Noah's Ark. A lot of cultures have a similar story, and there is one in Greek mythology too.

First, a little background. Prometheus married and had a son called Deucalion. Prometheus knew that Zeus was looking for an excuse to destroy all the humans on Earth. Zeus still hated mortals, who were now multiplying and becoming larger in number by the day. Prometheus taught his son everything that would be needed for survival should Zeus do something. That included the craft of carpentry. Together, they built a large wooden box and stocked it with supplies.

Meanwhile, Pandora and Epimetheus too had a daughter, Pyrrha. Deucalion and Pyrrha fell in love and married.

One day, a king called Lycaon, angered Zeus, and Zeus turned him into a wolf. Lycaon's son Nyctimus tried to rule, but his 49 other brothers were destroying everything and setting the land of the mortals on fire. There was mayhem on Earth.

Zeus wanted an excuse, and now he had one. He created huge clouds and they brought down a storm on Earth that drowned every human being. Mankind ceased to exist, except for Deucalion and Pyrrha. They had placed themselves on the wooden box that Deucalion had made, on his father

Prometheus's advice. They floated around until the waters subsided. They found that they were on Mount Parnassus. But the slime and mud were thick on the ground. They had to wait for a few more days for it to dry up.

They realized, however, that they were old and could not help bring children to repopulate the Earth. They decided to go to the Oracle of Delphi.

The oracle, as usual, said something not easily understood. It said that they should cover their heads and throw the bones of their mothers over their shoulders.

Deucalion and Pyrrha thought that since their mothers were probably drowned in the flood, how could they find their bones?

But it was Pyrrha who solved the mystery. She picked up a stone and threw it idly. The stone rolled away and suddenly, Pyrrha understood what the oracle was saying. She turned to Deucalion and said, "stones and rocks, that's what we must use. The Earth Mother is Gaia. She is also our mother. We all came from her!"

Deucalion knew that Pyrrha was right. They covered their heads and started throwing stones over their shoulders in every direction. Wherever the stones and rocks landed, young boys and girls began to appear. The Earth began to be populated with people once again.

It is said that we are all descendants of these boys and girls.

CONCLUSION

By now, you have read most of the interesting mythological stories that the Greeks had created. Some stories have different beginnings and some have different endings. This is because not much is certain about who wrote what. Different writers of ancient Greece have written their own ideas of the myths, but most of the important stories that are here are more or less the best versions.

You should know that Hercules, who is well-known as the mythical strong man, is also called Heracles, but 'Hercules' is what is most popular.

It is not possible to write all the mythological stories in detail, since Greek mythology is huge, with many gods, goddesses, heroes, and mortals all involved in various deeds and conspiracies. There are wars, battles, revenge killings, and other stuff, as you have already read about.

From the story of Hercules, you must have learned about courage and the ability to get the job done, no matter how difficult.

The stories of Perseus and Theseus are very intriguing and exciting. They go through so many problems and pitfalls, but by their courage and cleverness, manage to come out victorious.

Similarly, the story of Icarus and Daedalus teaches us to listen to good advice, especially when it is given by elders. Daedalus, if you remember, warned Icarus not to fly too close to the sun. But Icarus ignored the warning, his wings fell off and he was killed.

The story of Prometheus is very endearing. He knew that he would be punished by Zeus when he stole fire and gave it to the mortals. But he sacrificed his own interest to do so. The punishment that he received was cruel and barbaric, but his action was selfless. He did it for us, mankind.

Greek myth, like all myths, has a number of heroic characters. If you look at history, you will see that heroes are always needed to show the way, and encourage us.

Greek myths are vast, and there are many stories and adventures. They will tell you about exciting places and about how gods and goddesses behaved, sometimes exactly like humans. And it is possible that you may do something heroic someday too—something worth writing a story about.

NORSE MYTHOLOGY FOR KIDS

*LEGENDARY STORIES, QUESTS &
TIMELESS TALES FROM NORSE
FOLKLORE. THE MYTHS, SAGAS &
EPICS OF THE GODS, IMMORTALS,
MAGIC CREATURES, VIKINGS & MORE*

HISTORY BROUGHT ALIVE

INTRODUCTION

(Or, the part of the book no one reads unless they're your parents and they want you to fall asleep quickly.)

If you're the one reading this part, well then HELLO! It's very nice to meet you and tell you what this book is all about. We're sure you're thinking, "What do you mean, 'what the book is about'? Doesn't the title say 'Norse Mythology?'"

You're absolutely right! It is indeed. But we're also going to explore what the words *Norse* and *Mythology* actually mean, and then we'll take a closer look at the myths themselves. Did you know a lot of the Norse myths have also been talked about by other people in different ways? I'm sure you've heard the name Thor, especially with all the superhero movies that came out a few years ago. In this book, we'll tell you all about how Thor was born, how he grew up, and the things he did. Before all that, we'll also take a quick look at what myths are, where they come from, and why they're important. There are many,

many reasons why they're important, but the main reason is because they are wonderful stories which people have loved for hundreds and thousands of years.

Yes, the stories are *that* old. Now, clearly they weren't written in English at first, and when someone decided to translate it into English, they used a very old and very difficult kind of English. But then, some people translated that story from English into their own language and some parts of the story changed! Have you heard the Cinderella story? Well, did you know the Egyptians (Climo & Heller, 1992), the Persians (Climo & Florczak, 2001), the Native Americans (San, 1997) among many others have their own version of the story?

This is what happens when stories evolve. *Evolve* means when you change from what you were to something better. You might have heard in school that monkeys evolved into human beings. In the same way, stories evolved into monkeys — I mean myths!

These myths exist in every corner of the world, even the parts we haven't really explored. There were so many of them that slowly people decided these stories ought to be studied, so that others who want to learn about them will be able to understand them. Like you!

Perhaps once you've grown up, you will decide you want to study the myths properly and will read all those very grown up books such as *The Eddas* or *The Odyssey*. When you begin to study all of this you will discover how the word *myth* comes from the Greek word *Mythos*, which means tales, or story. Then perhaps you will love all the stories you read so much that you will decide to write your own story. And when you do,

I know it will be utterly, and truly, excellent.

History Brought Alive

At History Brought Alive we love learning about things that happened in the past. Even the not-so-nice parts. Which is why, the books we write will invite you to learn about the past in a fun way, and also remind you that the not-so-nice bits are just as important as the nice. We hope you will like what we write and how we write, so that you will read the books first, grow curious and read other books, and maybe one day go on to write books like these yourself! As you read through this book, we especially hope you like our book so much that you make a friend for life.

Citations

When you read through the books, you might find some sentences ending with a name and a date, like so: (Orel, 2003). This means that someone else said the thing you read, long before anyone else. Imagine your friend told you a joke they came up with, but it was so good that you absolutely had to tell someone else. So, you do, but you also tell them that your friend told you the joke first, so that they don't think you came up with it or copied it from somewhere else.

We do this when writing as well. We look at something someone else has written, and we think it is so wonderful, we decide to put it into our stories, but we add the name and date at the end, so people will know we got it from someone else who is very good at writing, too. This is called giving someone *credit*.

It also means that if you want to read that person's stories, you can go to the end of this book, check the list of related books and websites, and use the name and date to see where the person said it. Then, you can get their book to read what they wrote and have an extra book to read!

CHAPTER 1
WHAT ARE THE MYTHS

When you think about the stories you like, which one is your favorite? I'll start. My favorite story is about King Arthur and all his knights, and all the adventures they went on. Perhaps you've read about it. According to the people of Britain, he was the greatest and most noble King who ever lived. And his friend, the wizard named Merlin, was the smartest wizard ever.

How do I know all of this? Well, because I read the story. But, how do I know if it's a true story or not? I don't. However, the people who study history for a living — they're called historians — have studied very old books, some written in 500 A.D and others around 1066 A.D. They realized that although all the other stuff about the wars and things might be true, they still have no proof that a king named Arthur existed (Staff, 2018). So why do people continue to believe these stories are true?

Well, because these stories gave people hope. A lot of the time, people's lives were very difficult, so to cheer each other up, they would tell each other it would be okay. But who would make it okay? How would things like war and sickness ever go away? So, people looked up at the sky when there was a storm and decided the thunder meant there was something or someone up there who was angry. When lightning flashed and someone in the fields got struck by it, they decided that that person must have done something wrong and that's why this happened. On the other hand, when someone fell ill, the person taking care of them must've thought, "Oh, if only someone could make my sister better." Then, a few days later when their sister became well without medicine, they must've thought, "Oh! There was a ray of sunlight in her room that day; maybe there was something magic in it!" And from there they would have talked it over with their friends and those people would have talked about it to others and this way the story would have spread among a whole village.

It was something to pass along to new generations so that they wouldn't forget. Some believed it, and some believed it wasn't true. Those who didn't, preferred to forget it as quickly and as easily as they could. Some people who believed it, decided to write it down and as more and more people decided it must be true because they believed it, it became an official myth or a religion.

Types of Myths

Sometimes the kinds of myths that people told each other were all about how the world was created. But because most of the people in a country such as India had probably never seen a country like Iceland, they would not be able to imagine why people would need stories about a god of ice. But they would both agree when talking about a god or goddess of summer.

Not all of the myths were happy stories. Some were tragic, some were happy-ever-afters, and some were hilarious. But the one thing they had in common, was that the entire world had them.

The Gods

It's difficult to know for certain whether the gods were created from the myths or whether the stories came after the gods. It's a little like the old question, 'Who came first, the chicken or the egg?'. Gods and myths are like the chicken and the egg question, but perhaps you shouldn't call a god "chicken head" to their face.

Did you know they made myths from that question too? The Greeks have a god named Alectryon (Alec-tree-un) who got turned into a rooster for falling asleep while he was supposed to be on guard (*Alectryon (mythology)*, 2021). But in Hindu mythology, a god named Brahma (Bruhm-ah) hatched from a golden egg and then created everything else (Cartwright, 2015).

The gods were said to control everything - from how humans behaved, to when the seasons changed, to how calm the sea was, how hard the wind blew, and even when you sneezed!

They almost always had families, and just like all families, they had good times and bad times. The bad news was, when they fought with each other, it was the humans they decided to mess with. Unfair, right?

If they're going to fight, they should keep it among themselves, don't you think? But because (according to the stories) they created the humans, they thought they had a right to treat us any way they wanted. If they were happy, they would be nice to humans; if they were annoyed, things could go very, very bad. And because they were immortal, their fights weren't the kinds of fights they would forget about — because they would stay alive forever, they would remember what the fight had been about and then they would either involve the humans, hold a grudge, or throw a temper tantrum that would end with a human dying.

The Creation of Humans

After creating the world and everything else in it, the gods became bored. In their boredom, they decided to create humans. I mean, when I'm bored, I just read a book, but gods don't generally do that. I'm not sure if it's because they didn't have libraries or because they didn't think to invent books at that time. Anyway...

When they created humans, they decided to make them just like themselves, but without the immortality and special powers. Which, if I were among the first humans, I would be mad about this and demand to be remade properly with all sorts of powers and everything! Maybe I'd ask for the power to fly. What would you ask for?

The first humans didn't ask for anything of the sort. Some of them even lived in the cold and dark, shivering and afraid until one of the gods felt sorry for them and decided to make them a fire so they would have some light and warmth. I suppose the first humans were just so happy to be made, they did not think of it like that.

After doing this, the gods also gave the humans a bunch of dos and don'ts which they themselves did not follow — this is called hypocrisy (hip-pok-kruh-see). Hypocrisy is basically when someone who gives you rules or advice doesn't do the same. If you've ever heard the phrase, "Do as I say, not as I do," that counts as a form of hypocrisy! But alas, they were gods and they had all the power, so they weren't too bothered by it.

Human Behavior and Emotions

Hidden in the stories we tell ourselves, and all the ones we repeat endlessly and over and over again, are also ideas which ease our pain and sadness. Now we know that our brain is what does this, but did you know that scientists have studied the brain and discovered that stories can make us change what our brains feel (Zak, 2013)? How it works is like this: our brains tell us that emotions are important because they create our motivations. This, in turn, pushes us to take action.

Think of it this way. Imagine you see a little duck on your way to school. When you come back home, you think the duck has gone home. The next day during breakfast, your mum reads a story from the newspaper about how the pond in your city has so much garbage in it that the ducks can't live in it any more. Your brain reminds you of the duck you saw and the story your mum just told makes you think of how sad the duck must feel.

Because of this story, you feel the duck's sadness, so you decide to do something about it. You tell your friends and your family, and all of you gather to slowly clean up the pond. Little by little, news about what you're doing spreads and everyone comes to help. Soon, the pond is clean again, and the ducks come back to the pond.

All of this happened because you understood how sad the duck must be feeling, and because you also took action. This is called empathy. Empathy is when you understand another person's emotions and you try to make it better.

In mythology, when gods have empathy for humans, nice things happen. But more often than not, the gods are in bad moods. So, to try and help improve a god's bad mood so that humans wouldn't suffer, some humans would go on a quest, in the same way you would have for the duck – which would make you a duck hero!

Heroes
Some of the myths we will read about will be about heroes, or legends. Now these heroes were mostly humans, but sometimes they were half-god and half human. Oftentimes the gods would fall in love with humans, and their babies would be half godly and would sometimes even have cool half-

godlike powers, like super strength, or super-beauty (which isn't a word yet, but could be in the future don't you think?).

Anyway, the problem with being super strong or super smart was that the other half of you was human, so that half of you would have human type weaknesses. So, you could be very smart, but you could also be so proud that you would offend somebody and then you would be punished for being arrogant.

Other times, you might be strong enough to win all the wars, but you might forget to keep a promise you made to one of the gods, and they would be so mad that they would let something small like a pin-prick kill you.

There was another reason why people loved stories about heroes and legends - it made them feel as though someone other than the moody gods was on their side. They had a person who was one of them, who would be able to fight for the things they believed were important, and fight the gods if necessary, too!

These stories helped people and the society they lived in work the way it was supposed to. It also allowed kings and queens and leaders to pretend they were just like those heroes, so that more people would follow them. Leaders knew that even though they could fight wars and build huge kingdoms, it was the empathy and love these stories taught which kept those kingdoms strong and healthy.

Where Do Myths Come From?

From wherever people are. There are some people who live on deserted islands and still hunt and live all on their own. They don't want to talk to people like us, and scientists believe that if we tried to contact them, they could die of something as harmless as measles (Survival International, 2018)!

Imagine the kind of stories they would have told their children and grandchildren about us: about people who sailed on the sea in large ships, or people who flew in the air on a giant metal bird that had blades for arms! You and I know it is a helicopter, but they wouldn't know that. That's how myths begin and spread, and as they spread; sometimes we discover what we have in common.

Do you remember me telling you about King Arthur at the beginning of this chapter? The legend of King Arthur is a famous one in Great Britain, and the most famous part of it is how he was the only one who was able to pull a magic sword out of the stone to become king (White & Shadbolt, 1998). But did you know that there is a Norse hero named Sigmund who also pulled a magic sword out of a tree, placed there by the god Odin (*Branstock*, n.d.)? We will read more about this particular story later on, but isn't it incredible to realize we have so many stories that echo each other?

Depending on where we live, our stories about what we believe in can be very different, but sometimes the ideas behind the stories are the same. The stories we tell ourselves and our friends can sometimes be so strong, that they can shape how we and others who come after us see the world.

CHAPTER 2
WHO WERE THE NORSE

You see, the word 'Norse' is a mix of languages from old Scandinavia (Scan-dee-nave-ya). Between the years 800 and 1066, Scandinavia was made up of a bunch of countries which today are known as Denmark, Sweden, Iceland, and Norway (Encyclopedia Britannica, 2018). All the people who lived there were called the Norsemen, the Norse, or — and you might have heard this word before – the Vikings.

The Vikings were a fierce but fun-loving lot. Have you heard grown-ups use the phrase, "work hard and party hard"? That's what the Vikings did. They would work from early in the morning to early evening. Some of them would take their ships out to the sea and go fishing, or go looking for new, nicer places to explore and claim, while others would stay behind to grow food, weave cloth, hunt, and sew clothes.

The last part sounds very dull, doesn't it? But did you know the Norse loved colorful clothes and lots of jewelry?

If you showed up in old Scandinavia wearing a pair of blue silk trousers, a red t-shirt, green and blue beads, and orange converse shoes, they would think you were someone very rich and very fashionable (Skov Andersen, 2015)!

Which is why, when the Vikings who had gone out exploring other lands would finally return, they would make it a point to bring all sorts of pretty things for everyone. And then they would gather together in a large space around either a bonfire or an indoor fireplace and they would drink something called mead, eat lots and lots of really nice food, and tell stories.

Some of you might think all of this sitting around and talking was boring, but their stories were anything but boring. They would tell story after story of gods and goddesses who lived in places where it was always either spring or summer, like endless summer holidays, and others who lived in an icy, dark place, like the inside of a freezer.

You see, Scandinavia was, and still is, a place of long, cold winters, and long, dark nights (Stavrou & Tchetchik, 2017). In other parts of the land, during summer, the sun doesn't set at all for months (*Northern Norway – where the sun never sets*, n.d.)!

Imagine how weird that would be - your parents tell you to come home before it gets dark, but since it doesn't grow dark you don't know when to head home! But here's what could have happened.

The Vikings, who were pretty smart, could have waited and watched when the birds began to return to their nests. Or perhaps as they worked, they waited to see when the goats would lie down after what they thought afternoon was. That way they knew it was time to head home and get dinner ready.

They didn't know any other way of life, so it's not surprising that they believed their gods and goddesses lived in lands like theirs, and sometimes with problems like theirs.

So, these were the stories they told each other, and their children and their grandchildren and their great-grand-children and their great-great-grand-children and...well, you get the idea. This was how the myths began and stayed relevant throughout history.

The Norse Myths

Do you and your friends tell each other stories? Or perhaps your mum tells you stories about what she did when she was your age, and your grandma corrects her. This is how history and myths began. If someone could prove something had happened long ago, then it was written down and it became history. If there was no proof, then people would still write them down but they would call those stories, myths.

And their myths about their gods and goddesses are wonderful! In fact, they even wrote them down in many different ways. Two of the most famous ways are two different kinds of books: a book called the Poetic Edda and the other, called the Prose Edda (Wikipedia Contributors, 2019). The Poetic Edda is one very, very, very long poem about all the gods and the things they did.

Not everyone wanted to read one very long poem, so a man named Snorri Sturluson decided he would try and write them like stories. But, because he lived in the year 1200, the language he used to write the stories was old-fashioned and difficult for anyone over the age of very old.

Some of the stories you're going to read in this book have been taken from the Prose Edda, some from other Norse poems or stories. These were written by people who are not so old, so we can all understand them.

You'll read about dwarfs who live deep underground and make things for the gods, frost giants and their general frostiness, someone who was first a human then a deer, an eight-legged horse (like an octopus horse, but one that can fly!), what the world is really made of (no, it isn't what you think), a god who decides to do something really crazy in exchange for knowledge (ouch!), and so much more.

How It All Began

Perhaps you've read about other myths and they explain how the world was created. And if you've read other myths, then you know every story borrows a little from each other and then they tell their version — a little like copycats, but not. But with the norse myths, do me a favour and forget every other story you've heard, because this is unlike any other beginning.

Before anything, and I mean *anything*, including sea and sky and earth and light and noise and even food, there was only fire and ice. That's it. The entire world was made up of fire and ice and nothing nice. In one direction, (no, I don't mean the music band.) was the fire, burning endlessly. If you're going to ask me what was burning, well, I just answered that earlier. Fire. Fire was burning. What was burning in the fire? That is a very good question and one I do not know the answer to. Probably fire. Perhaps you will be the one to find out.

Anyway, the place which was burning was called Muspell. I know your next question. If nothing and nobody existed, then who named this place? The best I can tell you is that they probably named the place *after* everyone came into being. They must've sat down and said, "Well, we can't keep calling it That-Place-of-Endless-Fire, so let's come up with a name." Though between you and me, That-Place-of-Endless-Fire sounds like a super cool name to me, because Muspell isn't pronounced the way it is spelt, oh no. The way the people of Iceland pronounce it is 'Moosh-peth'. Sigh.

On with the story.

In the other direction (which really should've been the name of another band, don't you think?) was ice. What did the ice rest on? MORE ice! It was just ice all the way up, all the way down, and all the way inside and all the way outside. Just ice. And this land of ice was called Niflheim. Which sounds like a sniffle that was startled in the middle, and is pronounced the same way, too. Say it with me: 'Niffle-hime'. Do you see what I mean? And if you think these place names are weird, buckle your godly seatbelts my friends, because we are about to get a *whole* lot weirder.

In between the-place-of-endless-fire or Muspell and Sniffle...sorry, *Niflheim*, lay a huge empty space. A little like the space between your study desk and your bed. You're never sure quite what you want to fill that space with. A beanbag. Maybe a nice rug. A cat-bed. A pillow fort. Clothes that you meant to put away but got knocked off the bed so you've just left them there. The empty space between Muspell and Niflheim was a bit like that. And it was called Ginnungagap. I told you we would get a whole lot weirder with the names, didn't I? I'm sure you're very smart and can say it, but it took me a while to understand that the G-sounds like what it would be if you were saying 'Golly'. Or 'God'. So, it would be pronounced 'Ginh-un-guh-ghap'. It could be a fun game to dare your friends to say it fast about ten times, don't you think? But on with the story. Where were we? Oh yes, Ginnungagap was the empty space between Niflheim and Muspell, except Niflheim also had rivers of ice, but because they were all frozen over, I suppose we could call them river pavements of ice.

Now, if, like me, you are wondering how ice can make rivers before it melts, wonder no more. See, deep, deep, deep below Niflheim was a well. It was so deep, that the word deep had to be invented to describe how deep down it was. This well was called 'Fer-eh-gel-mer' but is written as Hvergelmir. All the rivers came from this well, but by the time they reached Niflheim, they froze into pavements.

It apparently wasn't enough for these pavements to be just made of ice, because they were also full of poison! They were poisoned ice river pavements that wound around Niflheim and reached Ginnungagap. However, on the other side was Muspell, the-place-of-endless-fire, remember? And I'm sure you know what happens when fire and ice meet. The ice melts and if enough ice melts, the fire goes out. That isn't what happened here.

The poison ice river pavement met the heat of Muspell and began to melt. As it melted and the water dripped, the drips magically formed two living beings that were larger than you can imagine, and I'm sure your imagination is incredible. A cow named Audumla (Ay-doo-mlah) and the first-ever frost giant who called himself Ymir (Yee-mir). I suppose Ymir named the cow after naming himself because he didn't want to be called Drip. But that might have been a better thing than what came next.

Ymir, His Sweaty Kids, and A Cowlick
The first thing Ymir did after he came into being, was take a nap. We can all understand that, because naps are nice. But Ymir took a nap near Ginnungagap and because it was so hot he was sweaty (and probably a little stinky, too), which was not so nice. However, Ymir's sweat was magic sweat and his magic sweat turned into his children. I know, EW!

His oldest children were twins, a male giant and a female

giant, and they came from the sweat under his left arm. His third child came from the sweat on his legs, and this giant had six heads.

Let's ignore the giant with the six heads, he's not important. Anyway, eventually, Ymir's children went on to have many of their own kids, who in turn had more kids, and so on and so forth until there were dozens of frost giants everywhere. They would usually want to hang out with Grandpa Ymir and Audumla the cow, but Audumla did not particularly enjoy this. She'd often wander off on her own in search of much-needed solitude.

One day, after wandering off, Audumla was licking a block of ice and salt. As she kept licking it, she tasted something stringy. So she looked at it and realized there was hair on the ice. She shrugged in a way that only cows can shrug and went on about her day. The next day as she was licking the same salty ice block, she realized that the hair was attached to a man's head. While she was curious, she let it be for that day probably because her mouth was tired and cold. On the third day, she went back and licked at the block until the man's full body emerged.

I'm sure by now you've guessed Audumla's spit was magic spit. Gross, but effective. It's magic in the same way when there's a bit of dirt on your face and you try to clean it with your palm, it doesn't always go away, but when your mum tries to clean it with a bit of spit on her hanky, your cheek is perfectly clean! Or if you still think it's too gross, think of it as Audumla giving the salty ice block a spit shake.

Audumla's ice-block-spit-shaking son was named Buri (bhoorhi) and he was kind, tall, and good-looking. Ymir's kids were anything but. They were probably good-looking, but most of them were cruel, unkind, and just plain mean and this made them look ugly.

After Buri had been around for a while, he met a rather nice frost giant and married her, and had a son. They named him Bor, but not because they thought he was a bore; they just liked the name. Bor was also lucky enough to marry a nice frost giant named Bestla (Best-lah).

Bestla and Bor had three sons, and they had names you might recognize. Their names were Odin (Oh-din), Vili (Vill-uh), and Ve (Vay). They became the first Aesir (Ice-ir) gods.

The Gods of the Aesir Age

The Aesir Age. Get it? Because it's pronounced like Ice, and we've all read about the Ice Age in school? It's not funny if I have to explain it.

Moving on. The Aesir age started when Odin, Vili, and Ve decided to go exploring. Except they didn't have anywhere to go except into the nothingness of Ginnungagap. After they had explored some of the nothing, they went further and found more nothing. This was a problem. This is also why when you ask someone if something is wrong, and they answer "nothing", they're probably right. Ginnungagap was a big space of nothing, and nothing was a problem.

Odin, Vili, and Ve wanted to do something about it, so they went to ask Ymir if they could use their new godly powers to make stuff. Ymir said no. When they asked why, he told them because he liked saying no. Then he went back to lazing

229

around and doing absolutely zero things. The three brothers thought this was unfair. If Ymir wasn't going to do anything, the least he could do was let them do something. They tried to tell him this, but Ymir shouted at them and told them to go away before he hit them. This wasn't anything new, because Ymir and most of his frost giant kids were horrible, violent, and wicked. They picked fights and were mean to people just because they thought it was fun. Do you know people like them? They are the sort of people who are unkind to others because they think it is fun, or because they think it makes them look stronger. You and I know better. It doesn't.

Odin, Vili, and Ve also knew better, but their solution was a little extreme. They decided to attack him, and after a long fight during which no one was sure who would win, Odin managed to stab him. But because he was larger than anything in the universe, he had a lot of blood in him. In fact, he had so much blood, that when Odin stabbed him, all of it began to flow out and become a flood that drowned all of the frost giants that were wicked like him.

But one of them named Bergelmir (Bear-gil-mer) and his wife hid from the flood in a hollow tree trunk. Then they had the bright idea to turn it into a boat and sail away. "Sail away where?", you ask? To Jotunheim (Yo-tun-hime), of course. "But where's Jotunheim?", you ask me again. It's going to be formed in a bit. "How can they sail away to a place that doesn't exist yet!?", you ask. My, you certainly have a lot of questions, don't you? Well, as they're sailing away, Odin, Vili, and Ve get busy working on everything. And before you ask me any other questions, just wait for a minute. Some of them will be answered in the next chapter.

After Bergelmir and his wife sailed away, they promised they would never forgive any of the gods for killing Ymir. When they had children and grandchildren and great-grandchildren, all of them also never forgave or forgot, and they became enemies with the gods forever.

The World is Like a Body

Now, you would think Odin, Vili, and Ve would at least hold a funeral for Ymir, but no. They knew Ymir's body was full of magic, so they shoved his body into Ginnungagap. And then they set to work. They created the world from what's left of him. Yes, you heard me correctly. While the lesson here is 'don't kill people and definitely don't do what Odin and his brothers did', at least they used every part of Ymir instead of wasting anything!

His flesh became the earth and his bones turned into mountains. This is probably why they're so bumpy. His teeth turned into rocks, which isn't really as surprising as it should be since some rocks are made of calcium — the same stuff teeth are made of. But perhaps a god's teeth were made of something else? Rocks, probably.

Anyway, what's left? Plenty, actually. Hold on to your seats for a minute. If you're not sitting down, hold on to the wall for a minute because do you know what part of him was made into the rivers? His blood. I suppose we should all be grateful that Ymir had very odd-colored blood.

They made his hair into trees, and this is the really crazy part. They played volleyball with his skull for a bit before kicking it up so high that it got stuck there and became the sky! But I guess they forgot to take his brains out of the skull, because the next thing you know, his brains floated out of his skull, and instead of following the rules of gravity and falling to the ground, instead they turned into clouds!

So the next time someone tells you that the clouds are made of water vapor and air, you can tell them the truth. Clouds are made up of *brains*. Which also explains all the squiggly lines of the clouds! Have you ever seen a cloud that is a straight line? No. That just proves it.

I have to admire the three brothers for not wasting even a little bit of what they thought would be useful in creating the world. This could be why the Norse are so eco-friendly about the things they use.

The Sun, The Moon, The Stars, And The End
After the three brothers had finished creating the world, they decided the skull - I'm sorry, I meant the *sky* - up there looked empty. To sort this out, they wandered over to the edge of Muspell and sat staring at the fire.

As the fire burnt endlessly, it suddenly shot sparks into the air, and all three brothers had the same idea at the same time. They decided to catch some of the sparks and throw it into the sky to make stars, and they did just that.

They looked at the skull-sky and thought it needed something more. They decided to go into Muspell and see what else they could find to use over there, instead of using whatever was left of Ymir.

So, they went into Muspell and were wandering around, when suddenly they heard a great booming voice. "WHO ARE YOU AND WHAT DO YOU WANT?" the voice said. The brothers were confused because they thought they were the only ones around and Muspell was supposed to be empty, so instead of answering the question, they yelled back "TELL US WHO YOU ARE FIRST, THEN WE'LL THINK ABOUT ANSWERING YOU!" Now, first of all, this is a rude way to answer a question, especially when you are exploring a place you are not supposed to be in. But because they are gods, I suppose the rules don't apply to them, or they hadn't been invented yet.

The voice was a little annoyed when it replied, "YOU CAME TO *MY* HOUSE, SO YOU TELL ME FIRST!" Now, even though they had been rude at first, Odin and his brothers had been brought up by Bor and Bestla to be polite. They realized they weren't behaving very well, so they remembered what their parents had taught them and answered politely, "We are sorry Mr. Voice. Our names are Odin, Ville, and Ve and we are the Aseir. We've just finished creating the world and were looking for something else we could create."

"Hmm. Like what?" asked Mr. Voice.

"Well, we aren't quite sure. You wouldn't happen to have something shiny, would you?" answered the brothers.

"I might," said Mr. Voice. "Let me show you around."

The brothers heard loud footsteps coming toward them. The footsteps were so loud, that the ground shook with every thump.

Soon, Mr. Voice stood before them and they looked up. And they looked up. And they looked up some more. Finally, when they had looked so far up, there was not much 'up' left to look at, and they saw his face. His face was made of *fire*.

They gulped and took a deep breath. Then because they were gods and gods were not supposed to show fear, and also because their parents had taught them to be polite, they just smiled and said hello.

Mr. Voice looked at them and said, "I suppose I should introduce myself. My name is Surt."

Odin almost asked him where the rest of his name was, but thankfully Ville stomped on his foot, and Ve shook his head at him. Ville spoke, "It's nice to meet you, Mr. Surt. Would you show us what you think we could use? Please," he added quickly because some words are magic words even if they aren't god magic.

"Of course!" Surt replied and led them to a pool of what looked like hot, melted gold. Ve dipped his hands in it. It *was* hot, melted gold!

The brothers were ecstatic, which is a word for very very happy. They thanked Surt over and over again and began to pack some of the gold away.

Surt was curious. "What are you going to make with that?" he asked them.

"We thought we would try and create a sun chariot and a moon chariot," they replied.

"Oh," said Surt. He thought for a moment. "That's all very well, but who will draw the chariot? I don't think you can make the chariot self-driving, after all, Artificial Intelligence hasn't been created yet."

"We've thought of that," said Ville. "We're going to create horses and then we're going to invite someone we know to drive it across the sky in an endless race."

"Interesting," said Surt. "But, there's just one problem." "You do realize the fire and gold of Muspell are so hot, that the chariot will end up burning whatever is on the ground, right?"

The brothers looked at each other. They looked at Surt. Surt looked back at them. Then they looked at each other some more.

In the middle of all of this looking, Ve had an idea. "What if we cool the moon chariot down enough so that the fire is almost out and the gold is so light it looks like silver?" Ville and Odin liked that idea. In fact, they liked it so much that Odin had an idea of his own. "What if," he exclaimed, "we put a shield under the sun chariot so that the sun only warms the world instead of burning it up?" (*NORSE GODS: SÓL – Ýdalir*, n.d.)

Everyone was delighted with both these ideas. Everyone, that is, except Surt. "Hey, you three, we've still got a problem," he said somewhat unhappily. "Now that you're going to create things, you do know I'm going to have to destroy all that you've created right along with all of you, don't you?"

"Right now?" the brothers asked.

"Oh no! Not for thousands and thousands of years!" Surt reassured them. The brothers looked at each other and shrugged. "That's alright then," they said. "Ragnarok (Rahg-nuh-rok) has to happen sometime. Everything has to begin for everything to end and for everything to begin again."

(Ragnarok | Encyclopedia.com, 2019)

"Oh phew! No hard feelings then?" Surt asked, relieved.

"No, no, none at all," they replied.

They all said a cheery goodbye to Surt and went back to Ymir-Land to start making the sun and moon chariots. After they'd finished making them, they went to find Sol (Soul) and Mani (Maah-ni).

Sol and Mani were Mundilfari's (Min-thil-fa-rey) children. Mundilfari was the god of time. Where were Mundilfari and his kids while Ymir was being born? At a guess, I would say they were existing outside of time. How can you exist outside of time, you ask? Well, have you ever sat watching the clock on your classroom wall, on the last day of school just before summer vacation begins?

The clock ticks and the clock tocks and it feels as though you're living in the space between the tick and the tock.

That's probably where Mundilfari and his kids were living, too. In the space between Ginnungagap and Ymir, which was the creation version of the tick and the tock.

Odin, Ville, and Ve went up to Sol and Mani and asked them if they'd like a job. By this time Sol and Mani were sick of just sitting around all day with nothing to do, so the minute they were asked, they said yes. The brothers told them they would need to make a full circle around the world every twenty-four hours. Without hesitation, Sol climbed into the sun chariot, Mani climbed into the moon chariot, and away they went. And that is how the hours were divided into night and day.

Another interesting little tidbit is this. Did you know certain days of the week are named after Sol and Mani? Because Sol is also called Sunna in Old German, the best day of the week, Sunday, is named after her, while the first day of the week, Monday, is named after Mani.

CHAPTER 3
THE NINE WORLDS

According to some people, Bor and Bestla planted a tree long before the brothers were born. Now, as you've probably guessed, this was no ordinary tree. This was Yggdrasil (Ig-drah-sil), the hugest, largest, most giganta-enorma-saurus magic tree that ever existed or will exist. It was so huge, that instead of Ginnungagap, Yggdrasil became the center of the universe.

The World Tree Is Also Named Yggdrasil

After it became the center of the universe, it continued to grow so much that both Niflheim and Muspell became part of the tree!

But did it stop there? No. Oh no, it didn't. It grew and grew and grew, the same way your younger sibling who was once shorter than you, grows taller than you. But Yggdrasil was super-magic because you know how most trees grow fruit or have nests in their branches? Yggdrasil instead had the whole, entire worlds resting on them! Nine worlds, to be exact. This is also why sometimes it is called The World Tree.

All of these nine worlds were connected to each other because of Yggdrasil. Which are these worlds? Well, you already know both Nifleheim and Muspell; the others are Asgard (Ahsguard), Midgard (Mid-guard), Jotunheim (Yo-tun-hime), Vanaheim (Vah-na-hime), Alfheim (Alf-hime), Svartalfheim (Svuck-tarv-hime), and Helheim (Hale-hime).

You might be wondering how a tree is strong enough to hold all of that plus all those humans, animals, grass, and trees —

do you think the trees in those worlds would be baby Yggdrasil trees? Sorry, I got distracted. I think the answer could be that because Yggdrasil grew so big, it became the universe. And as you know and have probably learned in your science classes, the universe can hold many, many different kinds of worlds, all at the same time. Perhaps when you grow up, you will discover a different answer.

Some of you might be wondering whether Ymir's skull, which made up the sky, was on the outside of the tree or on the inside. Again, I think it was both.

"That's impossible!" you cry. I know it sounds like that, but hear me out. Think of it like bubble wrap. You know, the kind that you unwrap from something and start popping the bubbles? That. Imagine you've got a piece of bubble wrap and a mug. Now you know that the bubble wrap is smooth on the outside, but has bubbles on the inside. When you wrap the outside of your mug, the mug can feel the bubbles. But when you fold the wrap over *inside* the mug, it feels the smooth side of the bubble wrap. That is how I think it works. Do you have any ideas on how it might work?

Anyway, let us get back to Yggdrasil. Between the branches of the tree were many animals. Do you know how some of the trees you have seen on walks or while camping will have birds, squirrels, and snakes? The World Tree is not so different in that way. There are many animals who live in it, but the four main ones you should know about are the no-name giant Eagle and his friend Vedrfolnir (Vey-thruh-vol-ner) the hawk, Ratatoskr (Rat-tuh-tos-ker) the mean squirrel, and Nidhogg (New-thong) the evil snake-dragon.

Among the others who live in the tree are four deer which represent the four winds, and a goat and a stag. They dash around on the tree's branches like they're in a race and eat all its leaves. The goat, whose name is Heidrun (Hi-dhoon), provides the warriors of Valhalla with an endless supply of something called mead. The stag is named Eikthyrnir (Eykh-thir-nir), and he spends his entire day eating the new, young leaves of The World Tree.

But let's talk about the first four — the eagle, the hawk, the squirrel, and the snake-dragon. These four are not friends, except for no-name Eagle and Vedrfolnir who lives on top of no-name Eagle's head. That might sound uncomfortable, but because the Eagle is pretty gigantic and Vedrfolnir is *mostly* normal-sized, Vedrfolnir has plenty of space to relax in.

He also flies all around and brings back news about what's happening where. You know that one time you stuck your finger in your nose when you thought no one was looking? Vedrfolnir probably saw you and told the eagle. But don't worry, I'm sure eagles do the same in their own eagle way, too.

Next is Ratatoskr, the mean, gossipy little trouble maker. Why am I saying nasty things about him? Because he truly is a tattle-tale. The trouble he creates is his main job. Every time he hears no-name Eagle insult Nidhogg, he runs down The World Tree to where Nidhogg lives and tells him all that Eagle said. Perhaps the eagle may have said something like, "I think Nidhogg has a fat head."

Ratatoskr would immediately run down the tree, and march over to where Nidhogg would be nibbling at the roots of the tree because he wanted to destroy it and be all, "Bro, did you hear? Eagle called you a great big stinking fathead who likes to laze around doing nothing!"

At which point, Nidhogg growls, snarls, and sputters, "Well...well, you can tell that birdbrain, he looks like a *feather duster*!" So, off Ratatoskr would go. He would climb up the tree till he reached the top and tell Eagle what Nidhogg had said, but he would add to it and lie about what was actually said, making them even more mad at each other. And then all three of them would do it over and over again.

The thing is, Eagle is supposed to be very wise, but I don't think it's smart to pick a fight with someone. Especially based on the lies of someone else. Moral of the story: Don't trust Ratatoskr. He is a lying liar who lies.

Five Plus Four Worlds Sitting In A Tree
That makes exactly n-i-n-e!

Okay, I may be bad at poetry, but I do know some things about the nine worlds that are a part of The World Tree. Let's take a look at all of them one-by-one, starting with the ones who get a nice view of everything at the top, and the ones who get a different sort of view at the bottom:

Asgard: The Place the Aesir Call Home
Asgard is the home of all the Aesir gods and goddesses. Which is why, it is no surprise it's got the best view of everything, all high up in the sky among all the brain clouds. Every god and goddess has their own mansion made of gold and silver, and Odin is the ruler of Asgard and the supreme leader of the Aesir.

Odin's mansion has a huge inner mansion, or hall, called

Valhalla (Vahl-ha-lah). This is where half the good people who died in battle go. The other half goes to another nice place called Fólkvangr (Fork-vahn-gur) which is ruled by the goddess Freya. You must be wondering why only the people who died in battle go to these nice places. You see, battles can be any kind of battle. They could be someone saving another person from getting crushed by a car, it could be someone who is sad, lonely, and upset deciding not to give up and keep on living and kill themselves, or it could be someone standing up and being a decent person when no one else is.

A battle is simply a fight you have inside yourself when some part of you wants to do something mean, and will hurt both you and someone else, while the other part of you wants to do the decent thing and be firm but kind. If you die in the middle of doing something good and honest for someone else, the gods of Valhalla or Folkvangr will welcome you with open arms.

Every night, Valhalla has a party to celebrate all the new people who arrive and they swap stories with the others who have been there. The new people are brought to Valhalla by the Valkyries (Val-kuh-rees). Valkyries ride flying horses and decide who gets to go to Valhalla and who doesn't. Everyone loves hanging out in Valhalla because it is pretty incredible. The roof is made up of gold shields, while the pillars on which they rest are actual spears!

Folkvangr is Freya's place for warriors. Unlike Valhalla, Folkvangr is a large meadow where the sun shines, but the weather is always the perfect temperature and instead of the type of party in Valhalla, the people who go there tend to have very fun picnics.

As you can see, Asgard is a wonderful place. One out of three of Yggdrasil's massive roots reaches into The Well of Urd (Oord), also known as the river of fate, which lies deep underground in Asgard and is guarded and watered by three ladies known as The Norn (rhymes with *corn*).

Odin and his wife Queen Frigg (Free-guh), rule it and fill it with wonderful things made either by them or by others - such as the wall around Asgard. What's so wonderful about a wall? The fact that it was built through trickery! Which is not a *good* thing, but when you're a god, people tend to say most of the things you've done are amazing. We'll read about that in a couple of chapters.

Vanaheim: Home of the Vanir

For the Vanir, the land of Vanaheim was home. Who were the Vanir? They were an ancient group of gods – gods as old as the Aesir. They were the ones who cared most about things like health, growing things, and wealth. They were and are masters of witchcraft and magic, and every single person knew that the Vanir had the ability to correctly tell the future. Though they could and did fight, they were not known as gods and goddesses of battle like the Aesir. They preferred to do a little gardening, or maybe learn new ways of improving things, and they liked making, buying, or selling pretty and expensive stuff. The most famous of all the Vanir were Njord (Nigh-ord) and his two children, Freyr (Fray), and Freyja (Fray-yah), who came to Asgard as a sign of peace.

The story goes that a Vanir named Gullveig (Gool-Vag-uh) was among some of the best witches who practiced a form of magic called seidr (say-dur). Seidr is magic that allows you to see and sometimes shape the future. Gullveig wandered from place to place showing people her seidr skills, and occasionally teaching them, too.

When she reached Asgard, they invited her to stay and show off her seidr skills. Except, the more she used them, the more the Aesir gods began to want only that. They wanted it so much, in fact, that they grew selfish and began to forget the things which made them loved and respected by the people in the first place - things such as loyalty, honor, and doing the right thing. They no longer valued what they were good at or the qualities that made them who they were and were instead focused on what they didn't have.

Except, instead of accepting the fact that it was their fault, instead they decided to blame Gullveig for their actions. In fact, they blamed her so much, they decided the only way for them to stop behaving so badly was for them to kill her. No Gullveig, they thought, no more problem.

So, they gathered a lot of wood and they burnt her. But, she stepped out of the fire as though she was stepping out onto a beach. They got some more wood, and burnt her again, but she yawned and stepped out of the dying fire as though she was bored when actually she was very angry. But she would give them one more chance to stop behaving in this manner.

However, the Aesir were furious — which is another word for super angry – that their plan had not worked. So, this time, they got more and more and more wood to make sure the fire would be hot and would burn properly. And this time when they shoved Gullveig into it, she burnt down to ash.

The Aesir were very happy and were sure that now their

problems were over. Except, they weren't. They were only beginning.

They heard a whooshing noise behind them, and when they turned to look, the ashes swirled up into a pillar, and the pillar of ash transformed into Gullveig. By now, she was so angry, that she could barely talk.

Have you ever been that angry? So angry that all the words you want to say seem to burn up in your blood before they even reach your mouth? Gullveig was that angry.

Instead of saying anything, she turned around and stormed away all the way back to Vanaheim and told everyone there exactly what had happened. Njord, who was the leader of the Vanir, was even more angry than Gullveig and told everyone in Vanaheim to get ready for war against the Aesir.

The Aesir knew they had messed up, but instead of accepting what they did was wrong and saying they were sorry, they thought the best way to deal with this was to go to war against the Vanir.

So, they fought against each other. The Aeisr used battle strategies to fight, while the Vanir used some battle strategy and some magic. People on both sides died, but eventually, it looked as though the Vanir might win.

At this point, Odin sat down with the other Aesir and said, "Look guys, I know we thought we were doing the right thing, but clearly not. We were wrong and we should tell them so, or this war will go on forever." Some of the other Aesir weren't sure if they wanted to stop, but Odin simply said, "Well, too bad. I'm the King and what I say goes, so you can deal with it."

Of course, if he'd just said this right at the beginning, there might not have been so many problems, but then we would also not have had a story.

Anyway, both the Vanir and the Aesir called a truce. And as a sign they wouldn't fight with each other anymore, they sent people from their land to live with the others. The Aesir sent Hoenir (High-neer) and Mimir (Mee-meer), two of Odin's relatives and friends, to live with the Vanir. The Vanir sent Njord, Frey, and Freya to live with the Aesir.

After this, while there were small fights, there was no war between both these places – even when the Vanir cut off Mimir's head. But that's a story for another day. Since no one really knows the exact location of the land of Vanaheim, or even what it looks like, that is also probably why no one went to challenge them to war again!

Alfheim: Where the Pretty Elves Live

Alfheim (Alf-hime) means home of the Elves. It is roughly close to where Asgard is on The World Tree. Alfheim is where all the elves live and these elves are the most beautiful creatures you've ever seen. This is why they are called light elves, because they are so beautiful to look at, and it feels as though you are looking directly at a light bulb. You know how if you look directly at a light bulb, you can't look at it too long, so you close your eyes, but it feels as though you can still feel the light and see the shape of the bulb in your mind? That's what it felt like to look at the elves of Alfheim.

The leader of the elves was the Vanir god Frey and he ruled the land of Alfheim. Frey was as powerful as Odin and Thor and was also the god of summer and fertility, which is a word for growing things. Even though Frey could fight as fiercely as Thor, he didn't like to fight unless he had no other choice. He was a kind and a happy god who preferred to look after nature and help others learn how to do the same. The elves were also gods, but they weren't as powerful as any of the others like the Aesir and the Vanir. They used what little power they had to take care of nature and made sure all growing things were fruitful.

They weren't always nice to humans, but would also try to help them because Frey didn't want them to be mean. They knew how to make humans fall sick, and they knew how to heal them. The elves and Frey also loved poetry and the arts and music, so they would wait to see which human seemed to have talent. Then, they would help that human think of words for their poem or story, or see the colors they needed for their art in their mind's eye. So, if you ever wanted to act, dance, or paint something, you would ask Frey for help. Then, he would make sure the elves of Alfheim who were good at the stuff you wanted help with, would give you the inspiration you needed to make your art.

Today, a large number of people think Alfheim was just another word for fairyland, while some people think that is where all of our stories about fairies and elves come from (*Álfheimr*, 2021). What do you think? Do you think Alfheim and Fairyland are the same places? Perhaps, you will be the one to find out!

Niflheim: Ice Here, Ice There, Ice Ice Everywhere

We've already read about Niflheim, so I'm sure you remember what it is all about. Think of it like the old rhyme "Old Mac'Donald":

On Yggdrasil's branch was a land, Niflheim was its name!

With an ice block here, and a river there,

Here an ice, there an ice, everywhere an ice, ice.

On Yggdrasil's branch was a land, Niflheim was its name!

You also know about the snake-dragon called Nidhug who lives there and nibbles away at one of Yggdrasil's roots. Though why he wants to eat an uncooked root is between him and his taste-buds. The same way some people like eating kiwi on pizza...yuck.

Moving on.

We also read about the river or well named Hvergelmir. This river is the river from which all living things come and the place where all living things will go back. One of Yggdrasil's three roots is also watered by this spring, which probably explains why it is always so green.

CHAPTER 4
MORE ABOUT THE WORLDS OF THE
WORLD TREE

We've already read about some of the worlds,

especially about the ice world. Now let's read about the other worlds, starting with the one that is the opposite of ice.

Muspel: It's on FIRE

Do you remember reading about Muspel? The place where Odin, Ville, and Ve went for a little trip, ended up meeting the fire giant Surt and let's see, what else? Oh yes, the land was on FIRE!

By now, Muspel had minor fire demons and other fire giants. I mean, Surt probably got bored waiting to destroy the world at Ragnarok and created some of the demons out of lava or something, and maybe he found a nice fire giant to marry and they had fire giant children. I don't know for sure, but I'm guessing that's what happened.

Just to recap, which means to repeat the main points of an explanation (*recap*, n.d.), Muspel is a fiery hot place and everywhere you look, there are lava rivers, mile-high flames which shoot sparks, and it looks mysterious because of all the smoke and also because all the walls are covered with soot. It is ruled by Surtr, who is waiting for Ragnarok to arrive, so he can go out and destroy Asgard and everything else.

I have to say, though, I'm sure the heat of Muspel makes for a great barbecue place — as long as we aren't the ones getting barbecued.

Midgard: The Human Home
Midgard is also called Middle Earth because it sits right in the middle of The World Tree. It is below Asgard, and because the gods like to visit us often, Midgard and Asgard are connected by a bridge. But like everything else with the gods, the bridge

is no ordinary bridge. It is called the Bifrost (Bif-roast). It is also called the Rainbow Bridge, because it is made of, you guessed it, a rainbow!

The bridge starts in Asgard, goes over the ocean which surrounds Midgard and ends up in locations wherever the gods decide. The ocean surrounding Midgard has a serpent living in it. The serpent is so big, it can curl its body all the way around the world without having to stretch! Not something you should think about the next time you're at the beach and some seaweed clings to your legs. If you think that is scary for you, think of how scary it must have been for Ask and Embla, who were the first humans. "But can the giant serpent get out? And where did Ask and Embla come from?" You cry. To answer the first part of that question, no. The giant serpent won't leave the ocean until the end of the world arrives. If you're at the beach and you see a snake head as large as a jumbo jet coming out of the water, you'll know it's the end of the world. As for the second question? Patience, my gentle reader. We are soon coming to those stories. Read on, read on.

Jotunheim: A Gigantic Home

Jotunheim is the home of the giants. Not just any giants, but the frost giants. You remember - the ones who are the grandchildren of Ymir. They're the ones who promised themselves that they would remain the enemies of the Aesir gods forever and ever until Ragnarok, when they will all be busy fighting each other.

Not all frost giants hated the gods. Some of them were even invited to live in Asgard and were also called gods, like Loki (Low-key), the god of mischief. Some of the giants married gods and had children with them. Frey married Gerd (Geard), Njord married Skadi (Skah-di), and so on. The gods didn't much like visiting Jotunheim, but then they were used to beautiful lands where the grass was always green, the sun was shining, and everything looked like a photograph. Jotunheim was not like that. What is Jotunheim like, then?

Well, Jotunheim is made up of mostly rocks, ice, snow, and thick forests where the trees grow so close to each other, you have to hold your breath, suck your stomach in, squeeze through them sideways, and hope you don't get stuck. It also has the ocean on one side and is separated from Asgard by the river Ifingr (Ee-ving-er) on the other. This river doesn't ever freeze over, flows very fast, and is deep enough to drown a giant, so the giants can't cross over to Asgard. The third water source is the spring of wisdom, better known as Mimir's Well, and it sits deep under Jotunheim watering the third root of The World Tree.

Since the ground in Jotunheim is rocky, pebbly, and hard, thanks to the cold, no one can plant anything or have any kind of a farm, despite the water from the river. So, the giants go fishing and hunting twice or three times in a single day, because they're giants and they have to eat as much as I imagine giants need to eat. Which is probably a hundred times more than you and me.

Svartalfheim: The Home Under the Ground
Svartalfheim (Svuck-tarv-hime), is the underground home of the dwarves. Dwarves cannot live above ground because if they come in contact with sunlight, they turn to stone. For this reason, they live inside hollowed-out rocks, deep inside caves, or create underground tunnels which connect to underground homes.

The dwarves can create things no one else can — not even the gods! They are such skilled crafters that they can make any sort of weapon or treasure, and have, in fact, made many of the weapons and jewelry which the gods of Asgard have in their keeping. They created jewelry such as the magical ring Draupnir (Drope-near), and hair for the goddess Sif (rhymes with *tiff*) — yes, *hair*. They also made weapons such as Odin's spear Gungnir (Goong-near) and Thor's famous hammer Mjolnir (Myol-near).

But, where did the dwarves come from? Well, that's a story I can't wait to tell you. And I won't. Wait, I mean; sorry. Here goes.

Do you remember when Odin, Ville, and Ve shoved Ymir's body into Ginnungagap? And after they'd finished building the world from parts of him, they left his remains to rot. As his flesh was rotting, worms started to crawl out of it and guess who those worms turned into? That's right. *Dwarves!*

Anyway, once the gods saw this happening, they decided to help the worms — sorry — *dwarves* along, and gave them intelligence and skills and shapeshifting abilities and other useful stuff. Then, they asked for volunteers for a special task which could possibly turn those volunteers to stone. The task was to hold up Ymir's skull which formed the sky. So, four dwarves named Nordri (Nor-duh-ri), Sudri (Shud-rih), Austri (Esh-tri), and Vestri (Wes-tri) went off to hold up the sky. And *that* my friends, is where we get the directions North, South, East, and West from.

The other dwarves probably didn't want to be picked for any other such tasks, so they thanked the gods politely, and went off underground where the gods wouldn't be able to find them in a hurry.

Helheim: Where the dead go on living

The name sounds scary, doesn't it? Don't worry. Helheim is not a bad place, nor is it *not* a place where all the dead people go to be punished. The bad dead people are punished and cursed by the gods in different ways, but all those who died of old age, illness, or anything other than battle or drowning, go to Helheim.

Helheim is ruled by the goddess Hel, and while she is scary to look at, she is also very wise, just, and kind. In this place, once the dead people arrive, they simply go on and live the lives they did while they were alive (*Hel (The Underworld) - Norse Mythology for Smart People*, 2012). In Helheim, you can continue to do things like swimming, meeting your friends — if they're also there — for a meal, working, or taking a nice long nap. It wasn't a constantly happy, exciting place like Folksvangr or Valhalla, but it wasn't a sad, unhappy place either. It was just more like life after death in a place you didn't expect.

Other Facts About The World Tree

As you can see, those are the nine realms, and how they are connected and placed in The World Tree!

The Norns

In addition to this, while you know Yggdrasil is cared for by the Norns, did you also know that if they don't water it from the Well of Urd, the universe will begin to fade away? However, watering the tree is only one half of their job.

The other half of their job is to weave a tapestry. A tapestry is a cloth which has a scene or a picture woven into it with lots and lots of different threads. Each thread the Norns use are said to belong to a living being — including the gods. When the Norns have finished using your thread in the tapestry, they cut the thread and that is when you die.

The Numbers Game

The numbers three and nine, are an important part of Norse culture and mythology (Skjalden, 2020).

The number three is a holy number for the Norse, because of the three brothers who created the world. It is also important because the three Norns take care of every person's fate, and also because when the war with the Vanir ended, three of the most important and powerful Vanir became part of Asgard.

Add those together and you get the number nine. Nine was said to be the number of Magic. You know there are nine lands, but there are also other things that make that particular number important. When Odin wanted to learn something called rune magic, he hung from The World Tree for nine whole days! When Heimdall was born, he had nine mothers. Yes, nine mothers! And afterwards everyone knew his birth was a very special event because of all that he would do in his human life and his godly life.

CHAPTER 5
HUMANS, GODS, AND MONSTERS

Well, so far we've read about the creation of the world and we've read the names of gods we don't know yet. Don't worry — that's what we're going to read about now.

Creation of Humans

After Odin, Vile, and Ve had finished creating most of the world, they were taking a walk through Midgard, and were admiring all they'd done. Gods are like this. They like to admire what they've made, just like us. Unlike us, if people don't say nice things about what they've made, they tend to lose their temper and fight or curse everyone. But since there wasn't anyone around to say nice or nasty things, they complimented each other and were happy.

They admired the sparkling rivers, the mighty mountains, the green, green fields, and the blue skull-sky. They stopped, took a look around, patted each other on the back, and then twisted around and patted themselves on the back. Pat, pat, pat. "Good job, brother!" said one happily.

"Don't you mean, 'God job?'" snickered the other.

"Goodly godly job!" chuckled the third.

It was a good thing no one was around to tell them their jokes were terrible.

Vile took a look around again. He began to smile, but frowned instead. "What's wrong, Vile?" asked Odin. "I'm not sure, but something doesn't feel right." Answered Vile. "Hmm. You're right" said Ve. "Feels like something is missing, but what could it be?"

Odin looked around too. Then Vile looked around in another direction. Ve looked around in a third direction. Then they all switched places and looked again.

"I've got it!" said Odin excitedly.

"Tell us, quick!" said the other two in unison.

"Walls," said Odin. He was proud of himself for figuring it out.

"Walls?" asked Ve. He wasn't sure Odin had found the solution.

"Walls?" asked Vile. He wasn't sure what was going on.

"Walls," Odin nodded determinedly. "See, we've made a beautiful world here. But do you know who's going to want to live here?"

Vile understood immediately. "Giants," he said in an understanding tone.

"Giants?" asked Ve in confusion. He still didn't get it.

"Frost giants, to be precise," replied Odin. "They will want to find a way to move here instead of staying in Jotunheim. Except, if they move here, they will ruin *everything*."

"Oh. Oh no!" Ve was horrified. "They'll break all the trees!"

"They'll muddy up the rivers!" cried Vile. "They'll tear up the grass and make the ground all icy and horrid!"

"Yes," Odin said grimly. "That is why we need walls!"

"You're right!" said Ve.

"That's all very well, but what could be strong enough to keep out the giants?" asked Vile.

"Eyebrows!" exclaimed Ve.

"*Eyebrows?*" Odin said in disbelief, raising his own..

"Can all of us please stop repeating everything the other says?" huffed Ve in irritation. "We sound like a video stuck on pause."

"What's a video?" asked Odin.

"What's a pause?" asked Vile.

"It hasn't been invented yet, and that's not what is important," said Ve, shaking his head.

"Okay. Let's go back to the eyebrow wall idea," Odin suggested.

"Look, if we turned Ymir's skull into the sky and it was big enough to cover the whole world, then it stands to reason his eyebrows will be useful," reasoned Ve.

"Good point, Ve! Let's go get this done," Vile said. Then he turned to Odin and whispered, "so what *is* a pause?"

"It's like a stop, but only for a minute." Odin whispered back. "Wouldn't that just be a stop?" asked Vile in confusion. "No, when you stop, you have to start from the beginning. When you pause, you can pick up from where you left off," said Odin. "Now hurry, or Ve will yell at us again." And he hurried away.

The brothers went to Ginunngagap, plucked out Ymir's eyebrows, planted them like trees all around Midgard, and they turned into a wall no one could break through, including the frost giants.

The brothers were very pleased with themselves and they went to Asgard to check on how they wanted their palaces and halls built, and also to take a break. After a while, they went to look at Midgard again, decided they had done a good job again, and patted themselves on their backs *again*.

It still didn't feel quite right to Vile, but he didn't say anything. He was trying to pause his thoughts and start them again.

It didn't feel right to Ve, but he didn't say anything. He was wondering if the walls would grow bushy like regular eyebrows do.

It didn't feel right to Odin, but he didn't say anything. He still wanted to know what a video was.

As they were walking along the beach, all three of them tripped on a tree trunk.

"Why would anyone put that there?" Odin said crossly.

"Who would put that there?" said Ve grumpily. "It's not as though there's anyone around except us."

"That's it!" Vile was excited. "That's what Midgard is missing, you guys! Let's make *people*."

The other two were thrilled. "Vile, you're a genius!"

They decided to make the first ever humans out of the driftwood they had tripped over. This could also be why when people use the phrase, "knock on wood" to avoid bad luck, they knock on their own skulls, because according to the Norse, we are like Pinocchio.

So, the brothers made the first humans. Odin gave them the breath of life, while Vile and Ve made their brains work. Then the brothers blessed the humans with creativity, speech, sight, movement and so on, before hurriedly making them some very pretty clothes.

The man was named Ask (Aye-sk), and the woman was named Embla (Ehm-bla). Then the brothers gave Ask and Embla the whole of Midgard, so they could make it their home. That's how they became the parents of the entire human race.

Science will tell you we evolved from monkeys, and that could be as true as anything else. It depends on what you want to believe. If you like monkeys, you can decide that's where you came from.

If you like trees, you can decide that's where you came from. And the next time you look at a tree, you can thank the three brothers that they decided to make humans, instead of furniture.

Where Bad Poets Come From
Odin and his brothers left Midgard to the care of Ask and Embla and went back to Asgard. As they were walking across the Bifrost, the sparkly rainbow bridge, Vile and Ve were talking about the things they were thinking of doing back at Asgard. They also wanted to spend time with their children and with the gods and goddesses who were beginning to make Asgard their home.

Odin, however, was planning an adventure. He loved to know things. The more things he knew, the more he could become better at them. The better he was at whatever he knew, the happier he was. And a happy Odin, was a not-so-dangerous Odin, which was a good thing.

On this adventure, he had decided to try and get The Mead of Poetry from the giants. What is The Mead of Poetry? The

Mead of Poetry is a drink made from the blood of Kvasir (Kwey-see-urh), who was murdered by two horrid dwarves for being the wisest and most intelligent of all the gods. After they murdered him, they mixed his blood with honey and kept it in three barrels to sell as an energy drink for your brain. Or super-smart-brain-juice. And if you think that's gross, just you wait my friends, because we are about to get more gross than you could ever imagine.

After the dwarves had murdered him and made Kvasir honey juice, they hid it away because they didn't want the Aesir gods to know what had happened. But the two dwarves were the kind of people who would quarrel with others and then murder them. This is what they ended up doing when a giant and his wife came visiting. First, they sat down to supper. Then they picked a fight for no reason. Then they pretended to be sorry. Then, they murdered the giants by tricking them.

Except this time, they couldn't get away with it because the giant's son came looking for his parents, realized what had happened, and was going to kill the dwarves himself. But they made a deal with him – they said they would give him all of the mead of poetry if he would let them live. Now, Suttung (Soo-toong) the giant knew how valuable god blood was, so he agreed. He took all three barrels back to his home inside a mountain in Jotunheim. He then hid it deep inside a hole in the mountain and told his daughter Gunnlod (Gwin-lorth) to guard it day and night.

However, there was a problem, as there usually is in these cases. That problem was Suttung's mouth. He would not keep quiet about the treasure he had, so practically everyone knew what had happened.

When news reached Asgard, all the gods including Odin also knew what had happened. They were upset that Kvasir had been murdered and they were upset that a frost giant had taken his magic blood juice to Jotunheim. But what could they do?

Odin knew this was his moment. Not only would he have an adventure, but he would also get to teach the giants a lesson, and he would be able to drink some of the mead and learn many things.

He disguised himself as a giant named Bolverk (Bowl-verkh), and off he went. He walked for a long time, and after he got to Jotunheim he walked some more. Everything was rocky and gray to look at, so he walked faster to get away from such a boring view. Soon, he came to a place near the mountains that made him think he had found the right place. The place was green and was being cared for by nine greedy human men.

They were cutting the grass with their scythes. Scythes are long knives which curve in a half circle. Since tractors and lawnmowers would not be invented for a long, long time, people used to use scythes to cut the grass or wheat stalks, or prune small tree branches. But the scythes these nine men were using were not what they were supposed to be.

What were they supposed to be, you ask? Sharp. They were supposed to be sharp. Have you ever tried cutting a tomato or a stalk of celery with a blunt knife? You have to press down harder on the tomato, and saw the knife back and forth before you can manage to even cut through it. Also, once you've cut through it, the more force you've used means the squishier the vegetable is.

This is what had happened to the scythes, and the nine greedy men were tired, sweaty, and irritated.

Odin knew these men were mean and greedy and wouldn't help him if he asked, so instead he asked them if they wanted help. They looked at him suspiciously, and asked what kind of help he could offer.

He took a whetstone out of his pocket and said he would sharpen their knives for them if they liked. A whetstone is a rock – which was part of a giant's forehead – that is often used to sharpen knives. The men looked at each other. They weren't sure if this old giant would be able to help or not, but they were interested in seeing how the whetstone worked. If it worked, they would ask him for the stone. If he refused to give it to them, they would simply kill him and take the stone for themselves. You and I are better behaved, clearly. If someone says no, we know they have a good reason for saying no. And if a god says no, they have a *very* good reason for saying no!

Finally, one of them said okay and gave Odin his scythe. Odin sat down and carefully sharpened the scythe before giving it back to him. The man took his scythes and started swinging them at the grass. The scythe went through the tough grass like a hot knife through butter. All the men were impressed and they immediately wanted Odin to sharpen their knives, too.

They asked him if they could have the whetstone, and Odin knew what would happen if he said no. Instead, he said, "sure; the one who catches it, can have it all to themselves." As he said that, he threw the stone high up into the air and moved out of the way.

The men were so eager to be the first ones to get the stone that they tried to shove each other aside to catch it. They forgot they were all still holding their scythes, so when they shoved each other aside, they stabbed each other to death.

Odin picked up his whetstone, put it back in his bag and walked down the road until a few days later he got to Baugi's home. Baugi (Bi-yee) was Suttung's brother, and Odin knew he would know where Suttung kept the mead.

Odin introduced himself as Bolverk and asked if he could spend the night in a barn. Baugi said, "Alright, but you'll have to take care of yourself and your luggage." Odin as Bolverk said, "That's not a problem. But you look upset. Is something wrong?"

"Oh, you bet something's wrong," said Baugi. "Someone murdered my nine slaves and now I've got no one to help me cut the hay."

"I could do it for you, for a price," offered Odin.

"You? You look quite scrawny for a giant," Baugi laughed.

"Yes, but looks aren't everything," said Odin. "I can do a lot of work in very little time."

"Okay, and what do you want for doing all the work?" Baugi asked.

"Just one sip of the mead of poetry your brother has." Replied Odin

"Sure", said Baugi. "If you finish cutting all the hay and stacking it neatly, I'll try and convince my brother to let both of us have a sip of the mead." *But,* he secretly thought to himself, *there's no way he can finish all of that work on his own. And even if he does, there's no way my brother or my niece will let him anywhere near the mead.*

All through summer, Odin stayed with Baugi, and worked and worked and worked as hard as nine men. When summer was over and winter started, he went to Baugi and said, "Well, I've kept my end of the deal. All the hay is cut and stacked neatly and now that summer is over, nothing is growing anymore. Let's go talk to Suttung."

Baugi was impressed by Odin, but was scared of his brother. However, he had to keep his promise, and so off they went to go talk to Suttung.

Once they arrived, he introduced Odin to his brother. "Hey Suttung, this is my friend Bolverk. He helped me all summer cutting the hay and asked for a sip of Kvasir's mead as payment."

"WHAT!?" roared Suttung. "How dare you!"

"B..b..but," Baugi stuttered.

"NEVER!" cried Suttung. "Not a single drop will I ever give ANYBODY! Now, get out!" and he stormed out of the room.

"Well," said Odin, once he and Baugi were alone, "I hope you aren't going to agree with him? Tell you what, why don't we try to steal some of it for ourselves?"

Baugi hated looking like a fool in front of other people, so he agreed.

"But we'll have to make a careful plan, Bolverk," Baugi told him. "You do know where it is hidden, right? Deep in the heart of the mountain, and it is guarded by my niece!"

"No problem," replied Odin. And from his bag, he pulled out a drill called Rati. "See this drill? It can drill through any rock as easily as if you were pushing your finger through pudding!" Saying that, he handed the drill to Baugi.

But Baugi was feeling lazy. So, he drilled through the stone for a minute or two and stopped. "There!" he shouted. "I've finished drilling through."

Odin knew he hadn't, but he pretended to believe him. He put his mouth over the opening and blew into it. Bits of stone and lots of dust flew into his mouth. He spat it out, and looked at Baugi and waited patiently.

"Fine." Baugi rolled his eyes, put the drill to the stone, and drilled some more. He felt the rock give way, so he turned to Odin and said, "I've done it! This time I really have got through!"

Once again, Odin blew into the hole and this time, the dust and bits flew out the other side. Baugi frowned at the size of the hole and said, "Wait a minute, how do we get through this? It's much too small!"

"Not for me!" said Odin. He quickly shapeshifted into a snake and slithered through the hole. By the time Baugi realized he had been tricked, Odin was halfway through to the other side. When he slithered out of the hole, he found Gunnlod, Suttung's daughter, lounging on a stool. He quickly turned back into Odin the god and as soon as Gunnlod saw his godly form, she got a huge crush on him. Odin was supposed to be quite handsome after all, and Gunnlod had had no one to talk to because her father had made sure she did nothing except guard the mead.

They spent three days and three nights getting to know each other, laughing over what they thought were good jokes, but weren't that good at all. At the end of the third day Odin told Gunnlod that he had to get back home before his friends and family came looking for him. She wanted Odin to remember her, so she asked him what he wanted. Odin said, "Do you think it would be okay for me to have three sips of the mead of poetry?"

Gunnlod didn't care about the mead; she cared about her friend and lover, Odin. *Besides*, she thought. *He just wants three sips.* "Sure," she replied and showed him where the three barrels were.

Odin picked up the first barrel and drank all of it down in one gulp.

Oh, thought Gunnlod.

Odin then picked up the second barrel and drank all of that down in one gulp.

Oh dear, she thought again.

Odin picked up the third and last barrel and drank all of that in one big gulp.

Oh no, thought Gunnlod, *If he keeps drinking that quickly, he'll get a stomach ache.* So, she told Odin that.

Odin grinned at her, "Don't worry about it babe, I'll be fine. Gotta go now before your dad catches me."

Gunnlod smiled and wished him luck. Odin transformed into an eagle and flew out of the mountain.

In the meantime, Suttung realized what had happened. How? Baugi probably told him. As soon as he saw the eagle, he knew it was Odin. So, he shape-shifted into an eagle as well and raced off after Odin. But Odin the Eagle was faster, and he flew out of Jotunheim, over Midgard, and was back home in Asgard before Suttung could catch up with him.

Once he was back in Asgard, he got three barrels and vomited the mead of poetry into them. And that's what the mead of poetry is. Kvasir's blood, Odin's vomit, and a little dash of honey.

EWWWWW! Right?

Anyway, Once he was back in Asgard, Odin took a proper drink of the mead and now he knew poetry, he had wisdom, and he knew many, many smart things. The gods were sad at having lost their friend Kvasir, but they were happy they had managed to get his blood back from the giants.

Odin, unlike Suttung and the dwarves, was generous. He shared the mead with the gods who wanted a drink of it, and occasionally he would share some with the nicest humans who wanted to become poets and writers and so on, and that's how some of the books we love best came into existence.

However, I told you we would get more gross than you could imagine, didn't I?

Some people believe that as Odin flew away from Jotunheim while Suttung was chasing him, he pooped some of the mead out as he was flying over Midgard. It didn't look like poop, so some people picked it up and ATE IT.

EW! EW! EW! EW! EW!

Any person who ate Kvasir-juice-Odin-Eagle-poop went on to write bad poetry or terrible stories that not many people like (Skjalden, 2018). Now that you've read this story, what do you think I've had? A sip of Kvasir-juice? Or Odin-eagle poo? I hope it's not the latter!

CHAPTER 6
GODLY ADVENTURES

All of the gods, whether Vanir or Aesir, would grow bored just sitting at home. Instead of reading a book, or going out to play basketball, they would go off on adventures which usually ended with either them getting hurt, or giants getting killed. I suppose that was their version of playing basketball.

Odin is Stuck to The Tree

After his adventure in Jotunheim, Odin wandered around learning more and more things. He even went to visit the Norns. When he visited them, he discovered they knew a form of magic he didn't. It was called rune magic. He wanted to learn it, but the Norns told him he couldn't learn it unless he wanted it so much he was willing to give up something very dear to him.

Odin didn't like not knowing things. He asked them what he should give up, and they said that he had to figure that out all on his own. Don't you hate it when people tell you that? Well, Odin did too. So, he sat for a while trying to think of all the things he could give up, but he couldn't think of one single thing that was important enough to sacrifice.

The other gods tried to distract him by telling stories and throwing fun parties where everyone was laughing and talking. Odin, however, was quiet.

He really, *really* didn't like not knowing things - he wanted to know it all. He wanted to know how to do Rune Magic. He wanted to understand the cycle of Ragnarok. He wanted to know what a video was. As soon as he got back to his house in Asgard, he sent his crows Huginn (Hoo-nin) and Muninn (Moo-nin) out, so they could search for an explanation and then give him an answer.

Odin was strange that way. He wanted knowledge the way you want a nice, big slice of chocolate cake with ice cream after eating a dinner you don't like. In fact, he wanted knowledge *even more* than that.

As he waited for Huginn and Muninn to get back, he decided to make a list of the things he could give up. Could he give up the mead of poetry? No, it wasn't only his, so he couldn't give that up. Could he give his magic away? No, then he wouldn't be able to help others. On and on he thought, but nothing occurred to him. When Huginn and Muninn got home, they didn't have any answers for him either.

He decided to make himself a nice hot drink of Kvasir juice and take a nap. A nap is always nice, and sometimes it helps you understand what you have to do, he thought. So, he took a nap.

As he was sleeping, the answer suddenly came to his mind and bolted upright in bed. Oh no. Oh no, no, no. Now he wished he could have slept a while longer without knowing the answer, because the answer hurt. Just like he was going to hurt.

He didn't want to tell anyone. He walked sadly from one end of Asgard to the other end of Asgard. He smiled sadly whenever people told funny jokes. He even ate his food sadly and one night the food was so good every single god except Odin was happy.

Finally, the others couldn't take it anymore. They poked at him, they talked to him, and they asked him and asked him and asked him till they were all asked out. Odin sighed sadly, and told them what was troubling him.

Once they heard what he had to say, they were horrified. "No.

Don't do it!" said one. "It's not worth it."

"No. You can not do it," said another, "It will hurt and hurt and hurt."

"No. You shouldn't do it," said yet another god. "It won't mean anything."

Odin replied sadly but grandly, "It will mean everything, because knowledge is always worth having. Even when it hurts."

Now the gods were sad too. Odin knew that the only sacrifice that would be acceptable would be his own death. It was why very, very, *very* few gods and goddesses knew Rune magic. But Odin being Odin, he had a plan.

First he told all the gods and goddesses not to help him. Then he told No-Name Eagle, Ratatoskr the lying squirrel, the goats, the stag, and the deer not to help him or feed him.

Then he took a deep breath and climbed Yggdrasil till he reached a high branch from where he could look down and see the Well of Urd. He took a rope and hung himself, and then took a spear and speared himself with it on to The World Tree like a human or godly fly pinned by a dart.

Don't try this at home, kids! In fact, DON'T DARE TRY THIS AT ALL. If you want to hang something, hang a photograph on a wall.

Where were we? Ah yes. Odin was being a pinned fly.

He hung on Yggdrasil for nine whole days and for nine whole nights, and afterward he was still alive, looking down into the

Well of Urd. The Well of Urd looked back at him. The water in the well was so clear and still, it looked like a mirror or a screen. The well considered whether to reveal the secret of Rune magic to Odin and decided to wait the full nine days to see if he was serious.

If you ask me, the fact that he stuck himself with a spear as though he were a kebab, would prove he's pretty serious. But what do I know? I'm not an all-knowing well of fate.

So for nine days and nine nights Odin looked at the well, The Well looked at Odin, and all the gods and the animals living in the tree looked at them looking at each other. As the days went by, the well first showed him nine magical songs and waited to see if he would leave. But Odin was stubborn. He wanted to learn the runes, so he stayed on the tree.

Next, the well showed him nine words of stupendous power. The well was sure Odin would leave now. Clearly, the well didn't know everything, because Odin stayed there stuck to the tree. Oh erm...you know what I mean. He didn't go anywhere.

The Well of Urd was impressed. So, on the end of the ninth day, when Odin was almost mostly dead — 'mostly dead' is not *completely* dead, as we all know — the well decided to accept his sacrifice and show Odin the runes.

You must be wondering what runes are. Runes are the Viking or Norse alphabet and are still used today. But for the Norse gods and the Norse people, the alphabets were more than something you could use to write a word or sentence, the way I am doing right now. Each alphabet was magic and when it was placed together to form the right words, the symbols could create very powerful magic — the same way the Norns could.

When the well showed him the secret of rune magic, the spear loosened and Odin fell off the tree. Thankfully, he didn't have very far to fall and everyone else was waiting and watching, making sure he wouldn't hurt himself more than he already had.

After he recovered (gods tend to recover very quickly if they're only *mostly* dead), Odin was more knowledgeable and more powerful than any of the Aesir gods. However, Odin quickly put the rest of his plan in practice. He wasn't usually a selfish god, and he believed if people wanted to learn, then they should be able to do just that. So, after he learnt rune magic, he went and taught others who wanted to learn how to read and write the runes as well.

Finally, he thought, everything was how it was supposed to be. Now he could get on with doing god-like things such as fighting battles, playing tricks, and serving justice, all of which were just human things but remember, on a godly level.

Mimir Loses His Head

Do you remember the story of the war between the Aesir gods and the Vanir gods? Or how Njord and his two children Frey and Freya came to live in Asgard as a truce?

Well, Odin was supposed to send people to the Vanir as well, so he chose Hoenir the handsome and Mimir the wise to live in Vanaheim with all the other Vanir.

Since Njord had gone to Asgard, the Vanir had to choose a new leader, but they didn't know whom to choose.

The Vanir didn't always make smart decisions, and since Hoenir was so handsome to look at, they thought he must be just as smart too, so they elected him to be their new leader.

This is why you don't pick people based on what they look like, because as you can guess, this story does not end well. But not for the person you would expect.

After he became the leader, Hoenir made one smart decision. He made Mimir his adviser, and that was the only smart decision he ever made. So, when the Vanir came to him to ask him for his advice, or to sort out a fight, he would turn to Mimir. Mimir would step in and answer questions, help them sort out their troubles, and generally be a very clever person.

The Vanir were happy to have such wonderful people and they thanked the Aesir for sending them to Vanaheim. For a long time, that was how things worked. Mimir would be happy to use his wisdom, and Hoenir would be happy to look at himself in the mirror or have people admire him.

Then one day, when Hoenir was admiring his new cape and brushing his beautiful hair, some of the important Vanir came rushing into the room. There was an emergency and they desperately needed Hoenir to tell them what they should do.

Hoenir began to panic; he knew there was no way he would be able to give them intelligent advice. He tried to stall the Vanir while he searched for Mimir. But he couldn't find Mimir anywhere, because Mimir was taking a break away from everything. Without Mimir telling him what to do or say, Hoenir could barely open his mouth.

The Vanir couldn't understand why he wasn't saying anything the way he usually did. They asked him again and again, until he finally began to talk. Once he began to say something, the Vanir grew more and more horrified and started to wish he would stop talking.

Do you know people like that? When they start talking, they talk and talk and talk but they have nothing intelligent to say? And then because they don't stop talking, you become angry? That is exactly how the Vanir were feeling. They began to feel as though the Aesir had cheated them by giving them Hoenir and Mimir in exchange for Njord, Frey, and Freya. They were so angry, they thought perhaps Mimir wasn't as smart as he was either. And since Mimir wasn't as pretty to look at as Hoenir was, they thought it was better to get rid of Mimir instead of Hoenir. So, when Mimir got back from his picnic and before he had a chance to open his mouth to even say hello, they cut off his head, packed it up neatly in a box, and sent it as a surprise package to Odin.

Odin was relaxing at home with everyone else when the package arrived. Njord also came to look at what the Vanir had sent. Perhaps they had sent something nice for him, too, to remind him of home. You and I know they had not!

Odin opened the package and everyone standing around it gasped in horror. Odin was upset, Njord was angry, and everyone else was shocked. Njord wanted to go punish his people for doing something so terrible, but before anyone could tell Odin anything, Odin began to work some magic. After all, he didn't stick himself to The World Tree with his spear for nothing. One of the magical songs that The Well of Urd had taught him, was how to give the gift of speech and thought back to someone who had died.

Odin picked up Mimir's head and started singing to it. The song echoed around the hall and everyone stopped to listen. Even Njord calmed down long enough to listen and smile. Once Odin had finished his song, he reached into his pocket and took out some special lotion and rubbed into and over it, so that it wouldn't grow moldy and gross.

Then Mimir opened his eyes, looked around at everyone and smiled. His head now looked like one of those head statues you see in a museum, except it was alive and talking. But he no longer wanted to answer any questions from anyone else except Odin, because Odin had brought him back. Who knew what someone else would cut off if they became angry with him?

The other gods wanted to know what to do about the Vanir. Should they not be punished for doing something so horrible, especially to someone who did not deserve it even a little bit? "Well, yes," said Odin. "And I've thought of the perfect punishment."

"What is it?" said Nord. "Shall I make the waves of the sea rise up and swallow them?"

"What is it?" said Thor. "Shall I go and beat them all up?"

"What is it?" asked Skadi. "Shall I go turn everything into ice?"

"No," Odin said. "We shall let Hoenir continue to stay there and rule them. He talks too much and says so many stupid things, so that will be punishment enough."

CHAPTER 7
MORE GODLY ADVENTURES

The Gods do seem pretty quarrelsome, don't they? It seems as though every story we read is one in which the gods are picking fights with each other, or simply *waiting* to pick a fight with each other.

The gods knew this was a problem. They knew not everything could be solved by picking a fight, or with magic. But how would they sort out this problem? Well, one day the answer came to them. Literally. And it arrived in the form of a person.

The Other God Of Poetry

Do you remember Gunnlod? The giantess who guarded the mead of poetry and then gave it to Odin to drink? Well, she and Odin had a son whom Odin didn't know about. Gunnlod named him Bragi (Bra-yee) because even though he knew how to fight, he liked to bring peace instead by having fun conversations. He wanted to talk about things, help people, write stories and poems, solve problems, and help people think for themselves so they could do the right thing.

Unfortunately, in a place like Jotunheim, all the giants thought he was a wuss. Why, they wondered, would anyone sit around and come up with stories, when they could fight? Gunnlod knew the giants wouldn't appreciate her son's talents and they might even try to kill him. So, she called him, and told him she was sending him to his father, Odin, and to be a good boy when he got there.

Bragi was excited to get to know his father, so he hugged Gunnlod and set off for Asgard. When he arrived there, the gods were in the middle of a deep discussion on how to stop themselves and humans and everyone else from picking useless fights that would lead to war.

Bragi walked up to Odin and explained who he was and asked if he could help in any kind of way. Odin was happy to meet his son, and pestered him for news about Gunnlod. When Bragi had convinced Odin that Gunnlod was happy and fine on her own, he once again offered to help the gods solve their problem.

"But it could be really dangerous, son," protested Odin. "Your mum may not want you to do this."

"Some people talk too much while others talk too little, and even *that* causes them to fight," sighed Frigg. "Are you sure you want to do this?"

"I like talking to people and helping them with their problems," Bragi answered. "Sometimes, if they don't want to listen to advice, they will agree to listen to stories – and I'm pretty good at making advice sound like fun stories, writing your hero moments so that others will remember, and just stories in general."

"Hm. I don't know," Odin said worriedly.

"Come on, dad. Mum won't worry because she knows I can fight, but she also knows I like to try every possible peaceful solution first, before I kick someone's butt!"

"Okay, you've convinced me." Odin continued. "Tonight, we will hold a party to welcome you properly and then you can start to do what you do best. How does that sound?"

"Awesome!" replied Bragi excitedly.

That night everyone gathered for a party that had everything - streamers, fireworks, and delicious food that was so good it made you cry happy tears, along with games and music.

In the middle of the party, Frey wandered up to Bragi, slung an arm around him and took him around the room introducing him to everyone. When they stopped in front of Idunn (Ee-thoon), the goddess of youth, she blushed while Bragi, who was never at a loss for words, stammered out a "H...h...hi."

Oho! thought Frey. *They like each other. How cute! I should try and help them.*

Just then, the musicians stopped playing to take a little break. Frey had an idea.

"Hey, Bragi. I heard you know how to sing? Why don't you sing something for us, huh? I'm sure we'd all like to listen – especially Idunn. She loves music."

"Oh no, I couldn't," said Bragi

"Please. I'd love to hear you sing," said Idunn shyly. Frey hid a grin. His plan was working!

"Okay, but you have to promise not to laugh if I get it wrong," he said, smiling at Idunn. Then he began to sing.

As he sang the entire party fell silent. The fireworks stopped fireworking, the streamers stopped streaming, and even Yggdrasill didn't move a leaf. Bragi's voice was beautiful. Imagine the most beautiful music you've ever heard in your life, and it *still* would not compare to how wonderful Bragi's voice was.

When he finished singing, Bragi looked around. Everyone was either smiling, or happy-crying, or smiling and happy-crying, while Idunn looked at him as though she wanted to give him all the apples of youth from her garden. This time, Bragi blushed.

Then Frey quickly told them to go take a walk together before everyone else decided to come and talk to Bragi.

"Freeeyyyy!" whined Thjalfi (Th-yal-way), Thor's human servant, "Why did you send him away? I wanted to talk to him."

"I wanted to talk to him as well," Frigg protested.

"None of you are looking at the larger picture," said Frey, rolling his eyes. "Bragi likes Idunn, Idunn likes Bragi, and if they fall in love and get married, Bragi will be one of us forever."

"Oohhh, I like that!" said Freya.

"You sure do some quick thinking, Frey," said Odin. "I do too. Quick thinking, I mean. I thought we should make him the official singer of the royal court and the god of poetry and knowledge."

"Ooh! Yes!" the gods said in unison.

"While no one can replace Kvasir – may I rest his soul – Bragi seems just as kind and smart and therefore is more than qualified. We should start planning the whole thing!" said Odin. Then he began to make a list.

And it happened exactly the way they had hoped. Bragi and Idunn fell in love and got married. Odin made Bragi the god of poetry and knowledge and gave him the right to travel through all the worlds without needing a godly passport. As a wedding gift, Idunn, who also knew rune magic, carved runes onto Bragi's tongue to make his speech skills even more excellent than they already were.

I mean, I would have settled for some cake, but to each their own.

How Loki Built a Wall and Odin Got a Spider Horse

Do you remember reading about the war between the Aesir and the Vanir? How could you forget. It seems as though everything started there, instead of when Odin, Vile, and Ve created the world, doesn't it?

This story is also set a little while after the Aesir and Vanir war. After the war, and after Hoenir and Mimir had gone to Vanaheim while Njord, Frey, and Freya had settled in Asgard, everyone was a little worried. Why was everyone worried? Because even though the war was over, they were anxious that someone might try to invade or attack them again.

Odin walked around Asgard while the other gods trailed after him. Everyone looked around and they knew they needed something, but what? What would help?

Thor looked around and saw wide, lush green grasslands, and just beyond that he could see the other worlds, too. But if he could see the other worlds, that meant they could see them as well! Maybe they needed to put up curtains, thought Thor.

Sif looked all around and saw wheat fields which would soon be ready for cutting. She was the goddess of autumn and of the harvest, so she noticed stuff like that. She could see the wheat fields of Midgard, and the no-wheat, no-field land of Jotunheim. But if she could see all of those lands, then it was possible they could see all that was in Asgard, too. Perhaps, they needed to grow giant fields of wheat around the edges of Asgard.

"I know what we need," said Odin decisively. "What we need is what Vile, Ve, and I made in Midgard."

"Humans?" asked Freya.

"No. Walls."

"How will no walls help?" asked Tyr (Teer).

"Ugh, I meant, no, we don't need humans. I meant we need walls," huffed Odin irritably.

"Ohhh, that makes more sense," said Tyr. "But didn't you already use all of Ymir's eyebrows to make the walls around Midgard?"

"Yes. And my magic isn't strong enough to build a wall which will keep out the frost giants, and who knows what else."

"Then what are we going to do?" asked Heimdall (Hime-dal).

"We'll have to hire someone. Let's go back to the house and make a list of all the people we know who can do this." said Odin. So they all traipsed back to Odin's mansion. As they were making their list, which really was just a blank piece of paper because they couldn't think of even one person, a stranger wandered into Asgard.

"Who are you and what do you want?" asked Frigg.

"I am the best builder in this whole universe. In fact, I'm so much the best, you can call me the Master Builder."

"Why should we believe you are as good as you say you are?"

"Because I can build you a wall," smirked the stranger. Odin and all the gods sat up straight when they heard that.

"Anyone can build a wall," sniffed Odin dismissively.

"Not like my wall, they can't," the stranger boasted.

"Oh? Tell us what makes your wall so special, then," Odin said, trying to play it cool.

"My wall will be made of stones so large and thick that the wall itself will be so tall and thick that no one – even the frost giants – will be able to break it down. And I'll do it in a year and a half, not a day more," boasted the stranger. "Of course, I make no promises that it can stand against anyone when Ragnarok arrives," he added hastily.

"Of course, of course. Ragnarok is a different matter altogether," agreed Odin. "And if you manage to build this wall, what do you want as payment? Gold? More gold? A medal made of gold?"

"I don't want gold at all, thanks," said the stranger.

"What do you want, then?" asked Loki. He was immediately suspicious, because he knew how people played tricks. He was the god of mischief and tricks, after all.

"Three things. One, I want the sun. Two, I want the moon. And three, and most importantly, I want Freya to be my wife."

"Anything else? Would you like us to give you the throne of Asgard, and the mead of poetry too?" Odin drawled sarcastically.

"Nope, just the three things I mentioned," the stranger said.

Freya stamped her foot. "I AM NOT A *THING!* HOW DARE YOU!" she yelled.

"Okay, I think we need to discuss this privately. Can you wait outside please?" asked Loki.

" Sure," the stranger replied, leaving to wait outside the hall.

"What do you mean, discuss?" asked Frey. "There's nothing to discuss! We'll find another way to build the wall, but we are not giving my sister to whoever that person says he is."

"He said he was the master builder. Weren't you listening?" asked Loki.

"I don't care who he says he is," yelled Freya. "I am not marrying him!"

"And *I* am not giving up Sol and Mani to whatever he says he is," said Baldr (Bal-door), the god of light.

"No, of course you aren't marrying him, Freya, and no we're not giving up the Sun and the Moon either, Baldr," Loki said soothingly.

"What I meant was, how about we let him think he's going to get all that he asked for, but we trick him so he ends up building the wall for free and we keep Freya and Sol and Mani?"

"Sounds like a recipe for disaster, but I like that plan," Odin nodded.

"Well, I don't!" said Freya crossly. "It's not your freedom that is being discussed here! You marry him if you feel that strongly about it."

Baldr wasn't very pleased either, but he tried to be fair. "Okay, explain your plan and then we'll see."

"Simple. We make it harder. Instead of a year and a half, we give him only six months, no help from anyone, and when he can't finish it, he doesn't get anything or anyone."

All the gods considered Loki's plan. Given how impossible it was to build a wall in that short a time, it did sound like a good plan to everyone except Sol, Mani, Baldr, Freya, and Frey. They called the stranger back into the hall, and told him since he was such a fantastic builder and everything, they were sure he could do it in less than half the time.

He frowned and hesitated.

Loki came forward with a smile and put his hand on the stranger's shoulder. Look, MB...can I call you MB? You know, short form for Master Builder?"

The stranger shrugged.

Loki went on sweetly, "Look, MB, we're offering you a pretty good deal. You work for six months, and you get the Sun and her chariot of pure Muspel-ien Gold, the Moon and his chariot of Muspel-ien silver, and Freya herself, the goddess of love and beauty and all that awesome stuff! You'll be the envy of every single person in the universe. All we're asking is for you to complete the work in six months. If you don't, you get nothing, but if you do, you get everything you wanted! Do we have a deal?"

MB thought about Loki's words and said, "Hm. Okay, but I have conditions of my own."

"Alright, let's hear them."

"I want my horse Svadifari (Sva-thil-fa-ree) to help me." MB folded his arms across his wide chest and stared at all the gods.

"Your horse?" asked Loki.

"Yes," nodded MB.

"You want your horse to help you build a wall?" asked Odin disbelievingly.

"Yes, I do." MB nodded harder.

Loki shook his head with barely hidden amusement and asked, "Okay, what else?"

"That's it," MB said.

"That's it?" the gods asked together.

"Yeah," he replied, wondering why they needed to have everything repeated.

"Sure! We can agree to that. All the best!" said Loki, as Odin and MB shook hands.

What a fool MB is, thought Loki. *He isn't just going to be fun to trick; he is going to be easy to trick too!*

MB started work immediately. As soon as he did, the sky grew stormy and it grew cold and every single person who didn't have to be outside, was sitting inside their house by the fireside drinking some nice hot cocoa.

The storm was, of course, the work of the gods, who were planning to keep the weather horrid and uncomfortable so MB wouldn't be able to finish his work on time. But MB surprised them.

He marched off to the mountains, and piled twenty boulders on to his cart. Each boulder was the size of three grownups standing on top of each other and was just as wide too. The gods were standing in a tower and watching him pile boulder after boulder onto the cart and they laughed and went downstairs. No horse was going to be able to pull that cart on his own. The gods were safe. Or so they thought.

As soon as MB had finished piling the boulders onto the cart, Svadilfari pulled the cart as though there were nothing but feathers in it. The next day, there was already a circle of stone halfway round Asgard. The gods were shocked, and so this time they kept a close watch.

As they monitored his progress, MB finished the first line of stones around Agard. It wasn't a wall; instead it looked as though MB had made a circle bench all around Asgard. Once MB had finished with the first line, he didn't stop for a sandwich or a soda, or a . . . well, whatever the gods ate back in the day, and went off to the mountain once more. This time the gods were waiting to see how he was able to do this, and they saw how his horse pulled the cart with the boulders in it. Their worry began to grow again.

MB was working day and night. Or rather, MB and his horse were working day and night. They worked through bad weather and good weather and just weather, but they didn't stop – even for half a minute.

As MB built the wall, he stacked the stones together the way you used to play with building blocks. He kept working and the wall got closer and closer to completion while Freya grew closer and closer to sending Loki out to be used as building material for the wall as well.

Finally, the sixth month arrived and every day of that last month, the wall grew a little stronger and higher and the panic inside the room of the gods also grew stronger and higher. What could they do? By this time Freya was planning how to make Loki suffer, Baldr was planning to kick Loki like a football, and Loki was planning on running away and hiding.

Apart from that, not one of them had an actual plan.

"Loki, what have you done?" thundered Odin.

"Me?" squeaked Loki.

"You've ruined everything!" roared Heimdall.

"Me?" yelped Loki.

"Find a way to fix this, or I'll throw my hammer at you!" growled Thor, as he gripped his hammer tightly.

"Of course, I'll fix this, it's all part of my plan! Why does no one trust me?" asked Loki sadly.

"LOKI!" yelled all the gods in unison.

"Alright, I'm going! But you'd all better have a party ready for me when I get back from saving all of you," he called over his shoulder as he sauntered out of the door.

As soon as he was outside and no one could see, he leaned against a wall and wiped the sweat from his forehead with a soft "Phew!" Then, he walked near to where MB was working and hid himself so he could spy on him and come up with a plan.

"Why did I think he would be easy to trick? Now I have to figure something out and I have no idea what, so I can make sure the others aren't mad at me. Argh. Think brain, think!" He thought hard and long, but quickly since he didn't have much time.

Loki wasn't a nice god, but he wasn't a mean god at first. In the beginning and during the middle, he really didn't want anything bad to happen to the others. He just found it funny when they got in trouble usually because of him, but he liked getting them out of trouble, too. It was only towards the end that he let his jealousy grow so much, that his anger turned into hate, and he turned into the meanest, most horrid god ever.

This story happened around the beginning, so while everyone would get irritated with him, they still sort of liked him and he still liked them. Which was why he was trying to come up with a plan to get Freya and the others out of this mess. As he watched MB and Svadilfari the horse work, he got an idea. He thought it was such a good idea he almost did a little dance, but stopped himself just in time. He knew he would have to wait for the darkness of night, to make sure his idea had the best chance of succeeding. He then walked off deep into the forest.

That night as MB headed to the mountain to get more boulders, Svadilfari trotted next to him not even a bit out of breath from the day's work. Suddenly Svadilfari heard a noise and his ears twitched; the noise came again and since he was curious, he turned his head to look. There at the edge of the forest was a black mare – a female horse.

Svadilfari's breath caught in his throat. This mare was the loveliest mare he had ever seen. She looked as though she were made out of starlight and a piece of night sky. He wanted to get to know her.

Just as he thought that, the mare turned away and ran into the forest. Svadilfari was already halfway in love with the mare, so instead of staying and helping MB with the boulders, he chased after the mare into the forest.

MB ran after him, shouting at him and telling him to stop, but Svadilfari didn't listen. The only thing he was listening to was the sound of the mare's hooves as she ran fast. So he ran faster. He ran so fast that MB couldn't keep up.

MB was in despair; his horse had disappeared and so had his chance of completing the wall in time. There was only a little bit left, but that bit still required more boulders than he could carry. He tried, but he couldn't do it. His horse hadn't come back, and he wasn't able to finish the wall.

At the end of the sixth month, he went to meet Odin and all the other gods. "I've completed most of the wall," He told them.

"The agreement was for all of the wall, or nothing," Odin reminded him.

"Yes, I know. I am willing to give up the Sun and the Moon as payment, but I want Freya."

"And we wanted the wall completed on time, but we don't always get what we want, do we?" smirked Freya.

MB looked at all the gods and grew angry. "I know you've tricked me somehow, so you'd better give me part of my payment."

Frey looked around and said in a fake innocent tone, "Trick you? How would we do that? Do any of us look like we know how to play tricks?"

MB grew so angry that first he grew purple in the face, and then he grew and grew and grew until his real self was revealed. He was a frost giant in disguise! He tried to grab Freya, but before Freya could kick him and set her cats on him, Thor grabbed his hammer and struck him over the head with it.

He hit him so hard that MB's skull shattered and turned into pebbles all over the world and the gods all cheered and began to plan a party. Odin stopped them. "We have to plan a party for Thor for killing MB of course, but where is Loki? I'm sure he tricked the giant, but how?"

Everyone looked around and felt a little bad. Only a very little, since some of them were still irritated with him.

"How about we plan the party now, and then have the party once he gets back?" suggested Baldr.

"Good idea. Till then let's not worry about him too much," said Freya.

Everyone agreed and went back home to do what they usually do.

A couple of months later, Loki walked into the throne room calling out cheerily to everyone. But he had someone with him. A young horse with a shiny silvery coat, and eight legs! It had four legs in front and four legs at the back, and it walked as though it was going to start running at any minute. *Was it a horse, a spider, or an octopus?* wondered some of the gods.

Odin was just as surprised, but he was also pleased to see Loki. "Where have you been all this time? We were beginning to worry that you were either in trouble or that you were being trouble," he teased.

"Har Har, you think you're so funny," sniffed Loki. Then he grinned and said, "But enough of that; let me introduce you to my son, Sleipnir (Sleyp-neer), the eight-legged horse who can fly, walk and run on water, and run faster than any horse ever."

"WHAT?" yelled everyone in surprise.

"I was the black mare. How else do you think I distracted MB's horse, Svaldilfari? With sugar cubes?" asked Loki scornfully.

"You tricky trickster!" said Freya admiringly.

"You sneaky little shapeshifter," laughed Thor.

Loki laughed. He liked being admired for his brains and his cunning. He gave Sleipnir to Odin as a gift, and then all of them got on with the serious business of partying the night away.

CHAPTER 8
THE OTHER TWO STRONGEST GODS

W̲e all know how smart and cunning Odin is, but many people believe Thor and Frey were and are Odin's equal. It is a little unfortunate that Thor is now shown as a bit of a dumb god who only like fighting and drinking, while some of the people who have read about Frey like to dismiss him as a god who was a fool.

The truth is Thor was smart and clever when he needed to be, and Frey was quick-witted and a strong warrior when he needed to be. And they were both very loyal to the people they loved, as we will see in these stories.

Why Thor Gets Headaches

Thor's problems start, as they usually do, when he ends up fighting someone because of someone else. This is what happened when Odin decided to go off on a little adventure on his own, to Jotunheim (*Thor's Duel with Hrungnir - Norse Sagas - Norse Mythology*, 2017).

Now, if you and I dislike someone, we don't visit their house, because we don't want to end up picking a quarrel with them. When Odin is in one of his moods, on the other hand, he likes nothing better than picking quarrels.

So there Odin was, riding Sleipnir and talking to him the way we do to our dogs and cats, except Sleipnir understood Odin and Odin understood Sleipnir. As he was riding through the mountains and looking at all the rocks and ice, he came to the edge of a deep crater. It looked like a bottomless pit, but since there was a bridge, Odin didn't really care much about the pit. He and Sleipnir moved to the bridge to cross it.

See, if I had a magic, eight-legged horse that could walk on water, or fly through the sky, I would've just flown over the bridge. But that is me. And if Odin had done that, we would not have had a story. Also, perhaps Sleipnir was tired, or grumpy, and he just did not want to fly. Either way, they decide to walk over the bridge instead of flying over the pit.

In front of the bridge was a large boulder - much, much larger than the ones MB used to build the wall around Asgard, which is one of the reasons Odin didn't really trust boulders. In this case, he was right not to trust it, because as he stood in front of it, the boulder moved. It moved and stretched and stood tall, and Odin sat on his horse and sighed and thought resignedly, *Here we go again.*

The rock giant grumbled, "Who are you and what are you doing here?"

For a minute Odin was surprised and a little insulted. How many people did this giant know who had an eight-legged horse, or had a shining spear, or looked so handsome even with only one eye? How did he not know who he was? Did he live under a rock? Or maybe he didn't know anything because he *was* a rock. Hm.

"My name is Odin, and I am the ruler of all the gods," Odin informed him. Now step aside, whoever you are, because I'd like to cross that bridge."

"My name is not 'Whoever'; my name is Hrungnir (Thoong-nir), and I am the rock god," answered the giant.

"No such thing as a rock god. You're making that up," said Odin dismissively.

"Am not!" answered Hrungnir. "I'll prove it to you; my heart and my head are made of stone."

"That doesn't prove anything about you being a god except for the fact that you've got rocks in your head," said Odin.

"Oi! Don't you talk to me like that, or the only way you'll cross this bridge is in a coffin!" said Hrungnir.

Odin looked up at him for a minute. "Alright, tell you what? We'll have a race across the bridge. Me on Sleipnir and you on your horse, and if you win you can cut my head off."

"Hahahahahaha! My horse Gullfaxi (Gool-fa-she) is a hundred times faster than your weird horse, so sure! I'll race you and win and then use your head as a bowling ball!" sneered Hrungnir.

This time Sleipnir was insulted. How dare that stinky rock call him slow! He would show him.

Hrungnir climbed onto his horse and as soon as the race started, Sleipnir was off like a bullet. Gullfaxi wasn't far behind, but Sleipnir had eight legs. He could have run twice that distance without growing tired. Hrungnir was angry; he thought he would win without a problem, but no.

But by the time he reached the end point of the race, which Odin had cleverly chosen to be Asgard, Odin had already showered and dressed and was sitting on his throne.

Since Odin had won the race, he was feeling generous. So, he invited Hrungnir into the hall the way they usually would as a guest. Then Odin invited him to stay for dinner as well.

At dinner, Hrungnir ate a wonderful dinner of chicken in rock sauce, roast ox with pebbles, and stone salad. And then Odin offered him some mead. Unfortunately, the cup the mead was poured into was Thor's cup. Nobody noticed since Thor was away visiting friends and fighting trolls. Even more unfortunately, Hrungnir would not stop drinking mead. And the more he drank, the more drunk he became.

The more drunk he became, the more he talked. But his talking wasn't the "fun conversation" sort of talking, oh no. Hrungnir's idea of small talk was to threaten people. He turned to Odin and told him, "You watch. I'm going to turn Asgard into a pile of rocks. Before I do that, I'm going to kill all of the gods, starting with you." And he pointed at Odin. Or rather, he meant to point at Odin, but he was so drunk, he ended up pointing at an empty chair instead.

Odin spoke soothingly. "Sure, Hrungnir. Sounds like a great idea, but for now why don't you put the cup down and go to bed? Let's talk about this when you're not drunk."

"Drunk? WHO ARE YOU CALLING DRUNK, YOU ONE-EYED BEETLE!?" yelled Hrungnir. "I am absolutely, completely, and totally not drunk!"

"No, he may not be drunk, but he certainly is a jerk," Freya muttered to Sif.

"Yup. And if he doesn't stop talking, Thor will return and thump him," replied Sif.

Hrungnir saw them muttering to each other and got a drunken idea which he simply had to announce. "After I've killed all of you, I'll leave Sif and Freya alive and take them with me to Jotunheim as my wives!"

"Uh Oh," Odin said.

"Oh no," Frey also said.

"WHY DO PEOPLE I DON'T KNOW KEEP WANTING TO MARRY ME?" yelled Freya. "All I want is to practice my magic and take care of my cats."

"And why do people forget who *I'm* married to?" asked Sif, annoyed.

She had a point. The goddesses of Asgard and Vanheim were as dangerous and sometimes even more so than the gods. They, like Frey and Bragi and the others, didn't fight because they didn't want to, not because they couldn't.

Anyway, while all of this yelling was going on, Hrungnir lumbered out of his chair and said, "I'm going to take them with me now, and no one can stop me, so there!"

As he moved towards them to grab them, the entire dining room heard thunder roaring outside just before the hall was flooded by a flash of lighting. When the light dimmed, Thor was standing in front of Hrungnir and hefting his hammer.

"You! Not only do you drink out of my cup when I'm not here, but you threaten to KILL MY DAD AND EVERYONE ELSE, AND THEN KIDNAP MY WIFE AND SISTER-IN-LAW? YOU'RE DEAD!"

When he saw Thor, Hrungnir got un-drunk in a hurry. "No, no, that's not what I meant at all!" he tried to lie.

"Really? What exactly did you mean, then?" snarled Thor.

Hrungnir thought since he had nothing to lose, so he might as well challenge Thor. "I meant, I'll do all of what I said, after I kill you in a proper fight. Or are you telling me you're going to be brave and fight an unarmed man who is a guest in your house?"

Thor was mad, but he realized he couldn't hurt the giant while he was a guest in his home. It would break the rules of being a good host, and for the Norse, this was an unbreakable law — except of course there were lots of people who broke it and were then punished for it.

But Thor could not break this law. He was a god and he was supposed to be a fair god most of the time.

So, he said, "Fine. I won't kill you here. Instead I will meet you in a proper fight, and we can choose where, because I won't fight you in Jotunheim, and you won't fight me in Asgard."

Hrungnir wanted to fight in Jotunheim, because that way he could cheat, but now he did not have that option. So, he said, "Okay, what about the rock field near Jotunheim?"

Thor agreed, they decided they would each pick a helper, and then decided to have their fight the next day.

Hrungnir got on his horse and raced back to Jotunheim. He got all the frost giants together and told them what had happened. Some of the giants were scared. They had met Thor before and they knew he was strong enough to fight and kill a group of giants if he was truly angry.

Some of the other giants were planning to use this fight to make the frost giants famous. After all, Hrungnir had a head and heart of stone, so he would be very difficult to kill. If he managed to kill Thor, they would be famous! But Hrungnir would need help.

Since the gods had said each of them was allowed a helper, the giants decided to make a helper for Hrungnir. They made him out of clay, but since they could not find the heart of a giant to bring him to life, they decided to use the heart of a small mare instead. They named this clay-giant "Mist-Calf".

They made him so tall his head was in the clouds, the clouds which were once Ymir's brains. They made him so wide, that his chest was almost the size of a football field. The giants were satisfied. Surely, Thor would take one look at this giant they had made, and be terrified. When the next day arrived, both of them went to the rock field to wait for Thor.

Thor had gotten ready for the battle and he had picked Thjalfi, his human servant, as his helper. Thjalfi was the fastest human runner in all the worlds, no one except Sleipnir could beat him.

He raced ahead of Thor and got to the field well before Thor reached it. He saw Hrungnir and Mist-Calf waiting, and Hrungnir was holding his whetstone and his stone shield. Mist-Calf did not have a weapon, because everyone thought his size would be enough to give him an advantage, but they forgot about the heart they had used while making him.

Thjalfi took one look at Hrungnir and started laughing, "Hah! This fight will be over before you know it! You're holding your shield out in front of you, but every single person who's fought Thor knows he'll attack you from under the ground. Of course, you can't ask anyone he's fought because they're all dead — just like you will be soon!"

Hrungnir said, "Oh yeah? We'll see about that." And promptly put his shield down and stood on top of it instead. "Let's see him try to attack me now", he smirked. Thjalfi pretended to be upset at having told him this, but inside his head he was laughing. Their plan was going well.

Barely a second later, all of them heard the sound of loud thunder and Thor flew down from the sky in a bolt of lightning. Hrungnir knew Thjalfi had tricked him so he promised himself he would deal with the human later, and he turned to face the god of thunder. As he faced Thor, Thor threw his hammer at Hrungnir's head with all his strength and at the same time Hrungnir threw his whetstone straight at Thor.

Thor's hammer flew through the air with so much force that it hit the whetstone and shattered it, flew straight through that, and hit Hrungnir in the head, shattering his head too. People say that all the whetstones in the world today are pieces of Hrungnir's original weapon.

Anyway, when Mist-Calf saw this, he was so scared he peed his pants. Thjalfi attacked Mist-Calf, cut off his legs, and when he fell over, quickly killed him. Thjalfi looked around for Thor, and all the gods who were pretty sure Thor would defeat the giant also looked around for the god of thunder.

And then Thjalfi saw him. He was pinned under Hrungnir's leg and he felt a little wooly headed. He tried to get up from under the giant, but the rock giant was much too heavy for Thor to push off. First, Thjalfi tried to help, but as nice a gesture as that was, he was only human. Then Odin tried. Then Njord tried, and one by one all the gods tried, but they couldn't lift the giant off Thor.

Then, Thor's three-year-old son, Magni, who hadn't seen all that had happened, noticed his dad couldn't move. So, he went right up to Thor and lifted the giant's leg up so Thor could crawl out from under it. At three years of age, *I* was drawing on the walls with crayons, but you should talk to your parents. Perhaps you were as strong as Magni and were able to lift very heavy things!

Thor and the other gods were so impressed, they praised him and Thor hugged Magni and told him that when he grew up, he would probably be stronger than Thor himself! Then, as a thank you present, he took Hrungnir's horse Gullfaxi and gave it to Magni to ride.

Odin was feeling a little selfish, so he said, "What will three year old Magni do with such a fancy horse? You should give it to me instead."

Thor looked at Odin in annoyance and asked, "Did you manage to lift the giant's leg off me? Don't answer that. Let's talk about why I was fighting that giant in the first place. Because I don't remember racing a rock giant and then inviting him to have dinner with us and then letting him insult and threaten everyone in the hall. Do you want me to remind you who did that?"

"I don't know what you're talking about," said Odin sulkily.

"Sure you don't," said Thor. "For now, let's go home. I have a headache."

This was curious, because Thor almost never got a headache. He was the one giving trolls and giants a headache. So Frigg looked at his temple closely and gasped. In the fight with

Hrungnir, one of the pieces of the whetstone weapon had struck Thor's forehead and was now so deep in his head that it was stuck and no one, even the sorceress Groa, was able to get it out.

This is why, if you lose your temper and throw a whetstone across the room, it moves the stone in Thor's head and gives him really terrible headaches, which makes him so mad that he creates storms of thunder and lightning. Is it stormy where you are right now? Are you sure you didn't throw a whetstone across the room?

How Frey Got a Stag's Head

Frey was bored. Have you noticed how trouble often starts because gods are bored? It was no different this time. Since Frey was bored, he wandered all around Vanaheim. Then he went to visit the gods in Asgard, but his dad Njord and his stepmom Skadi were away.

Freya was busy practicing her sword fighting skills with Sif in an open carriage drawn by her cats, Thor was away smashing some giant's head in, and Odin and Frigg were off on a date. Everyone was busy and Frey was lonely. His wife Gerd was off busy wrapping up her duties as the goddess of winter, so that he could get ready to bring summer to the worlds, especially Midgard.

So, he went back home, sat on his throne and tried to complete a few kingly and godly duties, but he grew bored of that as well. As he was reading, he dozed off for a while. Soon, his nap turned into deep sleep and while he was sleeping, he had one long terrible nightmare.

He dreamt that because he had gone to sleep for longer than he intended to, summer was late. Because summer was late, on Midgard, even though winter was over, nothing had begun to grow, or thaw. The skies were still gray, and because the weather was so strange, food was in short supply.

He dreamt that soon there was very little food and the humans were beginning to fight with each other. "Why doesn't Frey bring the summer?" one cried. "Perhaps we have displeased him!" cried another.

In their hunger and confusion, some evil people decided to convince a village that the only way to gain Frey's approval was to sacrifice nine people to him and to give him gold equal to that sacrifice, too. These evil people planned to then come back and steal the gold.

At this point his dreams became sharper and clearer, the way they do when you feel as though you're going to come awake at any moment.

As the villagers returned to their village to try and collect enough gold and choose who would be the nine sacrifices, they saw the priest's little son Saklauss (Sok-ley-si) sitting in the dirt by the temple playing with an idol of Frey. Saklauss thought it was a doll or an action figure, so he was playing with it and dragging it through the mud and having a grand time imagining adventures for the doll.

The villagers were outraged! "No wonder Frey had abandoned us," they yelled, "look at how this little boy insults him!" As they began to hit little Saklauss, he cried out loudly. He managed to escape into the forest, but he got lost. And in the dark and dangerous forest, wild animals killed him.

As soon as Frey heard the boy cry out, he woke up and went frantically to look at Midgard. He was horrified, because his nightmare had been a vision. Saklauss had been killed all because Frey had taken a nap.

However, Frey was going to set this right as soon as possible. He got on his magic boar Gullinbursti (Good-lin-push-teh), and sped to Helheim where Saklauss's soul would go. He and Gullinbursti raced through the worlds faster and faster until they were both just a blur of light and soon reached the dark world of Helheim. He looked at the long queue of people waiting outside the gate to get inside — there were millions of people. How would he ever find Saklauss?

Just then, he heard the sound of a child crying. It could have been any child, but Frey did not like seeing children cry, so he went to find them - and there he was. It was Saklauss after all. Frey got off his boar, went to Saklauss, and pulled him into a hug. The light and warmth from Frey calmed the boy and he hugged Frey back. As he opened his eyes, he felt something burrow under his arm. Gullinbursti had snuggled his nose under Saklauss's little arm and was comforting him, too.

Just then, Frey heard a tap-tap-tapping noise behind him and he turned. Saklauss gasped, and Frey just sighed. It was the goddess Hel tapping her foot.

"What do you think you're doing, Frey?" demanded Hel icily. She wasn't mad, she was just cold.

"I can explain," said Frey.

"Oh? Well, go on then." She raised her only eyebrow on the side of her face that had a face. Hel was half-skeleton plus half normal, which equaled a whole goddess. One side of her face and body was just bones, while the other side looked like a beautiful woman. Despite what she looked like, she was a kind, but stern, goddess.

"I took a nap, but the nap turned into a deep sleep of magic, and so I couldn't bring summer and because of that Saklauss got killed. Please let him go, Hel."

Hel looked at Frey as though he was crazy, before saying, "What? No, I got the second part," she interrupted him before he could start talking, holding up her hand. "Explain how this was your fault, and explain in detail." So, Frey explained in detail.

After he had finished, Hel looked at Saklauss in sympathy and then regretfully at Frey. "I'm sorry, Frey. I'd like to help, but he doesn't have a body to go back to. And while it is unfair that he died before he was supposed to, he won't be treated badly in my home, you know."

"I know, but I have a plan for that. Listen, I promise to buy his soul from you with gold, and then give him a new body. I'm just worried Odin might yell at you," Frey said.

"Odin can't tell me what to do," sniffed Hel. "Ignore him. And if you can find a body, this might work. And having all that gold warming my hall will make the people happy, too. You have a deal."

They shook hands with Frey promising to send the gold to Hel as soon as possible. Then he and Saklauss climbed on top of

Gullinbursti and went to Saklauss's village in Midgard. There Frey asked him, "So, what kind of body would you like?"

Saklauss thought for a minute and answered, "I don't want to go back to the village because they were all mean to me. And even though the forest was where I got killed, I still love how beautiful it is. Can you give me a body that will let me live there without having to be afraid?"

Frey smiled at the smart boy and answered, "Yes, I'll turn you into a stag with such huge antlers that all the animals in the forest will be afraid of you and will leave you alone. Is that what you want?"

"Yes please, and thank you!" said the excited little boy. Frey sang a magic song known only to the Vanir gods, and where Saklauss had been standing, there now stood a bigger than big stag with massive, grand antlers on his head.

Satisfied that he had done all he could, Frey went home where Gerd was waiting for him and told her everything. She was happy the little boy was safe, but was a little worried too. "You made sure none of the other animals would be able to hurt him, but what about the humans and giants?"

"Hadn't thought of that, babe. What do you think I should do?" asked Frey. He loved it when Gerd got involved like this. He just loved Gerd, and didn't regret giving his sword away to win her love for an instant, even though he now had no weapon. She was always kind, caring, sensible, and had lots of wisdom to give.

"I think you should check up on him once in a while. Maybe have some kind of warning system for him just in case he gets in trouble."

"Good idea. But I think he should be okay," Frey said, crossing his fingers.

Unfortunately, Gerd was right. For a good number of years Saklauss the stag lived in peace, and neither human nor animal bothered him. But one day while Frey was out in the woods throwing truffles for Gullinbursti to eat, and making Gerd laugh, he heard Saklauss the stag cry out in his head.

Quickly he told Gerd, and called Gullinbursti to him so they could go see what was wrong. But he hesitated for a minute. "Gerd, Odin is supposed to come to Vanaheim today. He wants to grow grapes inside Valhalla and he wants to learn Vanir magic to do it."

"Don't worry about him. Odin's grapes can wait, and if they can't I'll cover for you. But you need to go. Now," She urged.

"You're the best, babe." He kissed her quickly and set off for Midgard.

When he reached the forest, he and the boar searched the woods swiftly. There in a small clearing was Saklauss the stag, alive but hurt badly. He had an arrow in his side, and was bleeding profusely. Worst of all, it seemed as though someone had hit him on the head as well, because his beautiful antlers were twisted and bleeding as well.

This time, instead of feeling guilty, Frey was angry. "Who did this to you Saklauss?"

The stag grunted softly at Frey.

"Beli (Bel-yah)? Who is Beli? And why would he do this?" asked Frey.

The stag grunted a few more times, telling Frey everything, and Frey grew angrier and angrier. "So, you're telling me Beli is a frost giant and he's hunting animals in Midgard because he finished hunting in his part of the forest in Jotunheim? How did he even get past the eyebrow wall?" The stag made a sound between a huff and a bleat.

"Ah. He tricked the humans into giving him a ride. Foolish humans," he said, irritated. Just then, both he and the stag heard footsteps stomping along to where they were. Frey told Saklauss, "I will heal you so you can run away, but since I don't have a weapon, this fight might take a while, so stay away from this part of the forest, alright?"

Saklauss looked at Frey with affection, grunted at him again and gently bowed his head before The Lord of Summer.

Frey gasped. "Are you sure?" he asked.

The stag bobbed its head.

"I would be honored, Saklauss. And once I'm done, I'll give you a new set." promised Frey. He placed his hand on the stag's head, whispered magic words, and lifted the antlers off Saklauss' head as easily as though he was removing a baseball hat. He finished healing the stag's wounds and told him to run and hide as the footsteps grew closer and closer.

Just as the stag had run away, Beli the frost giant shoved his way through the clearing. He didn't notice Frey at first since he was busy looking for the stag with the enormous antlers.

"Hey, where did the stag go? Here, staggy staggy!" He called.

Frey hated frost giants just as much as Thor did, but he didn't usually fight them. However, this time he was so mad, he wasn't going to let the giant get away scott-free.

"Hey!" yelled Frey. "Hey you. I'm talking to you, stinky!"

The giant looked up, then he looked around, and then finally he looked down. "Who are you calling 'stinky', you tiny torchlight?" he shouted. "Who are you anyway, and what did you do with my stag?"

"I set the stag free! My name is Frey, and you aren't just stinky. You're a stinky, rotten, poo-faced coward!"

"WHAT DID YOU CALL ME?" Beli roared.

"Oh, I'm sorry. I didn't realize you were deaf. I'll say it louder. YOU'RE A POO-FACED COWARD WHO WON'T PICK ON SOMEONE YOUR OWN SIZE!"

"You're hardly my size, puny. And besides, I've heard all about Frey the dumb god who gave away his sword for love," sneered Beli. "What are you going to fight me with? A love song? A cushion? A stick?"

"How about I fight you with this?" Frey said, and in one swift motion he pulled the antlers from behind him, and held it up high in one hand. As he held it up, the antlers began to glow with the ancient magic of the Vanir gods, and the heat and power of summer.

Frey leapt up and struck Beli under his jaw with the antlers. Beli staggered and swung wildly at Frey with his club, but Frey dodged the blow, ducked under his arm, and hit him again. Beli shook the blood and sweat out of his eyes and snarled at Frey, "You're dead, buddy. And once I kill you, I'm going to go find that stag and smash its head in, too."

This was a mistake. You can tell it was a mistake. I can tell it was a mistake. All the animals of the forest, and everyone else were able to tell this was a mistake. Except for Beli. Who decided the best way to deal with an angry god was to make him even more angry?

As Beli swung his club, Frey saw Saklauss's blood on the club from before. He was so angry that the heat of summer turned into a raging fire. He leapt straight at Beli, and swung his antlers at his head so hard that his head went flying off his shoulders in the opposite direction.

Then Frey calmed down and summer became normal again. Everything was green, blooming, and lovely.

"Saklauss!" called Frey, and Saklauss trotted out of the thicket he had been hiding in. "Thank you for the gift of your antlers. They are a wonderful weapon, and I know I shall use them at Ragnarok to fight Surt."

The stag bleated at Frey, and Frey reassured him, "Oh no. Not for a long while. But let's not talk about that. Instead, here's what I can do. I can take you to a forest far away from humans or giants and you can stay there, or I can hide this forest so that humans and giants won't discover it for a thousand years. What would you like me to do?"

Saklauss grunted.

"Okay, option number two it is," Frey said. Then he stood back and sang a song of secrets and hiding. The forest blinked in and out of focus as though it was television switching itself on and off. "There you go," said Frey. "Live in safety and in happiness, little buddy. I'll visit when I can."

Then he climbed on to Gullinbursti, and set off towards Vanaheim to tell Gerd all about his adventure and show off his new weapon.

CHAPTER 9
NINE MOTHERS FOR HEIMDALL

I'm sure you know plenty of people who have two moms, or two dads, and that makes sense. But have you ever heard of someone who had *nine* moms? You and I know that moms are loving but scary people at the best of times, now imagine having nine! If you can't, well, let's read and imagine it together.

Half Rig, Half Heimdall

We've heard about so many of the gods already. Did you know that while Njord is the god of sea and the winds, there is another god who is the god of the sea and the waves? This god's name is Aegir (Ey-yir). He and his wife Ran (Rah-nh) live under the sea in a huge hidden castle.

Now, they don't really have mermaids in the castle. Instead, they have ghosts. Do you remember how we read about Hel being a place for normal dead people? In the same way, Aegir and Ran's underwater kingdom was home to all the souls of people who had drowned in the sea.

Aegir and Ran also had nine daughters. They were as beautiful as the ocean on a sunny beach day, and as dangerous as a tsunami. A tsunami is what you call a tidal wave so big and wide it looks as though it is touching the sky and can destroy entire islands in one go.

That is how dangerous Aegir and Ran's daughters were when they were angry. For the most part, they liked to talk with their ghost friends, explore the sea, and sometimes go exploring the land. Their names were Kolga (Kool-gah), Duva (Doo-vah), Blodughadda (Blow-do-gat-ha), Bara (Bow-rah), Bylgja (Bilg-yah), Hronn (Hrun), Hevring (Hevh-ring), Unnur (Oon-nur), and Himinglava (He-ming-lavuh), and they were super protective of each other.

Once, during a trip to Vanaheim, Odin met one of the sisters and they fell in love and had a baby. But Odin had to go back to Asgard, and she couldn't go with him. So, they parted sadly and promised to be there if ever one of them needed the other.

Now, no one knows which sister had the baby, because they knew their dad and mum would be angry because they didn't like Odin very much and would have blamed him. So, all nine sisters hid in the deepest, darkest part of the ocean — it was even deeper and darker than the Marianas Trench. There they stayed and promised each other that they would never tell which one of them had the baby, and the baby would instead be known as the child with nine mothers.

When Aegir and Ran eventually found out, because one: it is impossible to hide a baby, and two: it is impossible to hide stuff from your mum and dad, they were mad. But no matter how much they yelled and threatened to ground them forever and ever, not one single sister tattled. My sibling tattles on me if I take half an extra helping of dessert. Is your sibling like mine, or are they more like the nine sisters?

On with the story.

The sisters wanted to keep the baby, but they knew he would have a better chance of surviving with Odin. So, they put him on a little boat and called Odin to come pick him up from the boat. Odin came immediately, and was so happy with the way the baby grabbed his finger, that he promised to take the baby to Asgard immediately.

When Frigg saw Odin coming home with the baby, she went straight up to him and smacked him on his head. Odin, I mean; not the baby.

"Ow!" said Odin, "What was that for?"

"You're carrying the baby all wrong!" she snapped at him. "Just because he's a demi-god, doesn't mean you can dangle him like a noodle. Give me the baby," she said, snatching him out of Odin's arms. "Isn't that right, darling? You're not a noodle, are you, precious?" she cooed at the baby. The baby cooed back at her. Frigg was so delighted and loved the child so much, that she named him Heimdall and then glared at Odin, daring him to disagree with her name choice.

"I think it's a wonderful name, Frigg, but uh, it's a very godly name, isn't it?" he said cautiously.

"In case you hadn't noticed, he *is* a god, Odin." Frigg rolled her eyes.

"Only half," muttered Odin.

"What was that?" asked Frigg sharply.

"I said I forgot my staff," said Odin loudly.

"Hmph," Frigg said and went inside. After a couple of days, Odin came to the nursery where Njord, Skadi, and Frigg were sitting and playing with Heimdall. Skadi was making flurries of snow above his crib, while Njord made the winds blow the snow around.

Odin waggled his head at Frigg who understood he wanted to talk to her privately, so she followed him out into the hallway. "Yes dear, what's on your mind?" she asked.

"I did a bit of seidr magic, the way you taught me, about Heimdall," he confessed nervously. Frigg just smiled serenely and said, "I wondered when you would try to see his future. I did it the day he arrived!" she snickered. But then she grew serious. "I know sending him to Midgard is the right thing to do, but Odin, it'll be so long till we see him again!"

"I know, but he has a human life and destiny that he has to fulfil, Frigg. Besides, we're gods! Time isn't a big deal for us, remember?" he reminded her.

"I know, but I'll miss him," she said sadly.

Odin had looked in Heimdall's future and seen that he must live as a human before he could become a god. The humans needed a hero anyway, so Heimdall would first become a hero and complete his duties on earth, and then become a god.

Odin took him to Midgard and left him near a fisherman's house. The fisherman found the child crying, so he took him inside and cared for him. He named the baby Rig (Ree-hg), and Heimdall grew up on Midgard as Rig. Unlike his fisherman-dad, Rig was a little wary of the water, because he always felt as though the sea was watching him. He didn't know he was right, since all of his nine mothers would watch him from afar just to see how he was.

Rig grew up fast, and as a fisherman's son, he grew up to be patient, strong, brave, humble, and true. He also grew up to be very handsome, and many women wanted to marry him. Once he was old enough, he went away to fight in wars, and fight dragons and all kinds of monsters — even the human kind of monsters.

Soon, because of all the battles and adventures, the Norse people admired and loved Rig so much, they made him King.

Everyone always had plenty to eat, fights were settled calmly and fairly, and everyone was happy. Odin, Frigg, and his nine mothers who were always watching from afar, were very proud of him.

But even though he was a demi-god — something he didn't know yet — the human half of him grew old, and died. Everyone was standing around and crying and sobbing, when a whopping great flock of birds flew down and fluttered around his body. Then, the birds put him on their back and flew him all the way up to Asgard.

There, Odin sang his rune song over him, and Rig woke up. He looked around and saw Odin and Frigg standing there waiting to welcome him. He got slowly out of the bed the birds had placed him in and noticed that the way his bones used to creak and hurt when he was old had all disappeared. He looked at himself and was astounded — which means he was shocked in a good way — to see he was young and strong again!

Odin and Frigg explained all that had happened and told him that the human half of him had to die, before he could live properly as one of the Aesir gods. They told him his godly name was Heimdall, and that he would be the guardian god of Asgard.

Then they told him about his nine mothers, and he decided to go visit them on the shores of Vanaheim before taking up his godly duties. And that is how Heimdall is the god with nine mothers (Arithharger, 2013).

CHAPTER 10
THE END, OR IS IT?

Well, here we are. We're at the end. Or are we? We're almost at the end, but there's still a little more. So, let's go. Together.

The End is The Beginning is The End

The end doesn't always have to be a sad thing. Have you seen a lotus flower? It grows once a year in swampy places. The roots reach deep down into the mud, while the leaves float on top and then, slowly the flower unfurls. One petal at a time. Despite the dirty surroundings, the flower stays clean and beautiful. Once it has finished blooming, it closes its petals, folds up on itself and sinks into the water. It seems sad that such a beautiful thing could have such a fleeting life.

But underneath, there is magic. The seed hidden inside the lotus sinks into the mud, and there, it waits to grow again. That is what endings and beginnings are like, like an echo which ends where it starts – at the opening of a cave. Or like a story which finds another story like itself and ends and begins at the same time.

Do you remember how we read about King Arthur? When Arthur died, the legends say he was taken away to rest in the land of Avalon, until Great Britain needs him again.

This is similar to what happens in the story of Sigmund. King Volsung (Fol-zong), Sigmund's (Seeg-mond) father, built a beautiful palace built with a large tree growing in the center of the throne room. The tree, which was named Barnstock, stretched through the roof and out into the open.

One evening when King Volsung had given a party to celebrate King Siggeir (Si-gah) and his daughter Princess Signy's (Sig-nee) engagement, an old one-eyed stranger came into the hall wearing a hood. He stood in front of the tree, drew a sword and plunged it down right to the hilt into the trunk, saying, "Whomever can pull the sword from the tree, shall keep it and always find victory." And the old man, who was Odin in disguise, disappeared.

All the people present there tried to pull the sword from the tree, including King Volsung and King Siggeir, all without success. Then Sigmund came forward, put his hand on the hilt, and pulled the sword from the trunk as easily as though he were drawing it out of butter.

Everyone congratulated Sigmund, but Siggeir was full of envy, and offered to buy the sword in exchange for gold.

Sigmund refused, saying, "The will of the gods sent this sword to my hands and I will not give it away."

With the sword, Sigmund became a great warrior and a mighty king, until he was betrayed. When he was betrayed, he mistakenly did something which caused Odin's favor to be taken away from him, and he died. But, some legends say he and his wife sleep in a cave, while others say it is his son who sleeps, only to wake again when he will be needed in battle with his trusty sword Gram by his side.

Perhaps some parts of these myths were true. Perhaps there was a king who was that amazing. Perhaps there was a sword so sharp it could cut through a solid block of iron (Sigmund, n.d.).

Perhaps, you will read The Volsunga Saga and realize it meant something else entirely!

CONCLUSION

(Or the part everyone reads in the hope there is one last story left).

We've read all about endings and beginnings, so you know that even though we've reached the end of the book, the stories you will read or imagine are just beginning.

So, let me leave you with one last story which will take you right back to the start. The story of Ragnarok — which isn't as sad as it sounds.

It will begin with wars in every single country on earth. Heimdall will blow the horn and all the gods and warriors will then ride into battle against the frost giants, monsters, and Loki, who is now completely evil.

Odin will be killed by Fenris (Fen-rhis), the wolf who will break free of his chains, but his son Vidar (Vee-dar) will kill Fenris. Thor will fight the giant snake, and it will be his greatest battle. He will kill the snake, but the snake poison will allow him to take only nine steps, before he falls down dead. Heimdall will fight Loki, and they will kill each other.

Frey will fight Surt, the fire giant of Muspel. If he had his sword, he would have survived, but he would still manage to wound Surt a little, before he himself is killed. Then Surt will use the fires of Muspel to burn everything and everyone, and he will die as well.

But then, once the fires have burned down, water will wash over the world, and a new world will rise up out of it, with sparkling rivers, evergreen forests, a blue sea, a bright sun in a clear sky, and fields upon fields of flowers. And two people, a man and a woman, will walk through those fields. They are the two people The World Tree hid in its trunk and kept safe.

And on another branch, Asgard and Vanaheim will rise out of the smoke and fire, more beautiful than ever before. Thor's sons Magni (Mak-nih) and Modi (Moody), Vidar and Vali (Va-lih), the sons of Odin, Hel, Baldr, and other gods and goddesses stroll through the worlds, talking, laughing and making everything seem bright (Wikipedia Contributors, 2020).

"But I thought you said it wouldn't be as sad as it sounds!" you cry. My dear confused friends, I promise you an ending is not a sad thing at all. It makes way for something new - a new plan, a new song, a new painting, a new job, a new life... and even, a new story.

Write your own stories. Write your own version of the myths. Maybe you read a myth and something deep inside you said this was not how it happened, and you decide to take parts of that story and make something new of it the way I did with Frey's story of the antlers (How Frey Gained the Antlers of Saklauss | Thomas Hewitt's Poetry, n.d.)!

Start somewhere. But if you can't decide where to start, start at the end. I know that sounds strange, but a poet named T.S Eliot (1971, p. 21) once wrote a poem called, "Little Gilding". The poem says *What we call the beginning is often the end / And to make an end is to make a beginning. / The end is where we start from.*

We may have come to the end of this book, but you now have the chance to read (or create!) something new. No ending is truly final or forever. So, enjoy the end, and celebrate the promise of a new story.

Good luck!

MYTHOLOGY FOR KIDS

EXPLORE THE GREATEST STORIES EVER TOLD BY THE EGYPTIANS, GREEKS, ROMANS, VIKINGS, AND CELTS

HISTORY BROUGHT ALIVE

INTRODUCTION

Most people just skip the introduction, so if you're reading this, well, that's all right. There won't be any stories or myths in this bit, but maybe we'll get to know each other a little bit better. I'm not saying that you should skip it, but no one will tell you off if you do.

Still here? Good! Let me tell you a little bit about this book. Just like this is the introduction to the book, this book is an introduction to mythology. No one could ever write just one book about all the myths. There are way too many! But that's good because it means you will never run out of stories.

Hopefully, after you've read this book you'll put it down (or maybe read it again!) and think—I WANT TO READ MORE! I know I would because myths are the greatest stories that anyone has ever written. Imagine, for thousands of years people have been telling each other stories. If it's a boring story, they just forget it (a lot of boring stories have been forgotten over the years). But if it's a good story, they tell it again and again and again. And everyone they tell it to tells someone else who tells someone else. Eventually, someone might even decide it's such an AMAZING story that they should write it down. Those are the myths we have today!

Of course, that means there are a lot of myths and a lot of books about them. At the end of this book, we will give you a list of some really good ones so you can keep reading and discovering more myths (we're not going to tell you what they are just yet, though—we want you to read our book first!).

Who knows, maybe one day you will want to read the really serious, long stuff like *The Iliad* or Ovid's *Metamorphoses*. Maybe you'll even decide to be one of those crazily intelligent people who learn Ancient Greek and Latin and how to read the Egyptian hieroglyphs (I'll tell you more about those later). Then you'll be able to read loads of really, really old books in strange languages and discover myths we had forgotten about. Or maybe you'll discover that there was a mistake in one of the myths and it actually said the exact opposite of what we thought (it has happened!).

For now, though, this book is just an introduction. It's like a tasting menu. Have you ever been to a really expensive restaurant? Me neither, but I've seen them on TV and a tasting menu is where instead of giving you just one big plate of spaghetti they give you lots and lots and lots of little plates of really weird food. I think they just want to show off how good at cooking they are. I would prefer a big plate of spaghetti.

But sometimes you just can't choose between the spaghetti or the pizza so it's nice to have a little bit of both. Maybe a slice of pizza and a bite of spaghetti. But then, which kind of pizza do you want? Maybe pepperoni or Margherita? Or something with pineapple on it? Or are you one of those crazy people who like chicken on their pizza?

Well, with this book you get to have a slice of everything—a slice of Ancient Egyptian, Ancient Greek, Roman, Norse, and Celtic. Maybe you'll get to the end and think, "You know what? I actually *like* chicken on pizza!"

Enjoy your meal.

I mean your book! Enjoy the BOOK!

But don't eat it. It will make you sick.

History Brought Alive

At History Brought Alive we have a passion for everything from the past. The books we write are full of fun facts and even more fun stories that will make you think about the past and our ancestors in new and exciting ways. While we hope you will go on to read many more books about the subjects in ours—that is why we are writing them in the first place!—our books are ones you will return to throughout your life for information and entertainment.

Citations

Sometimes you might see a name and a date at the end of a sentence like this (Achilles, 2021). This means that someone else said the thing you have just read. It is important to give people *credit* for their work. Giving someone credit means saying, "I thought what you said was so good that I want to copy it, but I don't want people to think I said it first, so I will tell them that you did!"

This also means that if you want to know more about what that person said, you can go to the end of this book where there is a list of books and websites. This will tell you where the person said it. Then you can get their book or go to their website and read what they actually said!

CHAPTER 1
WHAT ARE MYTHS?

Have you ever thought about where you come from? You are not the only one. People have been wondering about where they come from and why they exist ever since they were able to think. No one knows how long ago that was exactly, but it was definitely many, many thousands of years ago. It probably wasn't the first thing they thought. The first thing they thought was probably, "I'm hungry," or "Oh my God! There's a saber-toothed tiger—run!"

The thing is, they wouldn't have been able to think "Oh my God" because they had not thought about gods yet. That would only have happened once they had escaped from the saber-toothed tiger and were safely in their cave. They would have sat around the fire and now that they had time to relax, they could wonder about less serious things like where they came from, or where that round silver thing in the sky came from, or where that round yellow thing in the sky during the day came from.

A lot of the time, as we will see, they decided that everything came from the round yellow thing in the sky. I am of course talking about the sun, but you knew that. They decided that the sun was so big and hot and powerful that it must have created everything, including the Earth and including them. In other places, they decided that everything was created by the thing they were sitting on, the Earth. They decided it was their mother.

But that wasn't enough. Once they had decided where everything came from, they had to explain where all the things came from. Nowadays we use science to explain these things, but for a lot of human history we weren't very good at science—everything takes practice, after all. So instead of science, people used stories to explain the things they saw around them. They had to explain why there were storms and why thunder was loud and why it was raining and where the animals came from and why life was so difficult. It was a lot more difficult back then than it is for you and me.

So they invented stories. Clearly, if there was a storm then someone was angry, weren't they? That was obvious. Storms are loud and noisy, just like angry people. A lot of the time, they decided the angry person must be a god. The god was angry because of something the humans had done. So the humans prayed and told the god that they wouldn't do it again. But that meant that someone had to decide why the god was angry in the first place and what exactly it was the people should not do again. In some places, they decided that the god must be angry because someone had killed their own brother and that killing was wrong. They promised never to kill again.

In other places, they decided the god was angry because not enough people had been killed so they decided to go to war and kill a lot more. Sometimes they decided they had to make sacrifices to make the god happy. A sacrifice is where you give up something important to show how much you love or fear your god. It might seem like a horrible and not very intelligent solution to stopping a storm to you, but people used to think it worked!

But that wasn't everybody. In a lot of places, they thought one god was boring and obviously, the god of that tree over there can't be the same as the one in that river or in the sky. For those people, it made more sense that the storm was two gods arguing and that the thunder and the lightning were the gods hitting each other.

You will have guessed by now that these myths used to be religions! People thought this was how the world worked. But religions don't just explain the world around us—they also give us rules to live by. Myths often use stories to show these rules, telling us stories where someone didn't follow them and the terrible consequences that happened. A lot of these rules were things like, "Do what your parents tell you or you'll be eaten," or "Obey the gods or they will make you go and live somewhere very hot for a very long time." This second one is a bit like being sent to your room for being naughty, but a lot worse. It also caused a lot of problems because people often couldn't agree on what the gods actually wanted or how to obey them.

Myths are stories, and people have always told each other stories. A lot of the time they were stories about things like brothers and sisters fighting. Maybe that sounds familiar to you—if you're anything like me and my brother, you fight together all the time! Other stories they told were about love, jealousy, sadness, and happiness. Anything a human could think or feel was turned into a story. I love stories, you love stories, I guess, or you wouldn't be reading this right now! Myths are stories from a time when people had no television or films or internet or even books. All people had back then was the smelly old man who came and told some stories by the fire if you gave him some food and a bed for the night! Maybe that doesn't sound as good as watching a film with popcorn and a drink, but just imagine how good the stories had to be for people to put up with that smelly old man! Of course, I might be a smelly old man but you will never know.

Types of Myths

We've already talked about the myths about the creation of the world but there are many others. Here are just a few more subjects that myths tell stories about.

The Gods

There would be no myths without the gods. These often represent parts of nature like the sea or rivers or forests. They sometimes represent other things like beauty or death or war. Whatever they represent, the gods are like a big family that is always arguing about silly little things. Unfortunately for humans, what is silly and little for them is very big and serious for us. Gods also have the added bonus of being immortal. This means that they can never really die. They can be mean or nice, beautiful or scary, peaceful or violent. Many of the gods are all of these things at different times! This does not make them a very happy family, but it definitely makes the myths about them very entertaining.

The Creation of Humans

Following the creation of the world and the birth of the gods, there is a period in which the gods have fun falling in and out of love with each other, arguing and fighting, and generally causing trouble. After a little while, though, one of them will often get bored and decide they need something new to entertain them. So they create humans. They make these humans similar to themselves, which seems silly afterward because they always end up scared that the humans are better than them and will one day take over the world (maybe they were right!). To stop this from happening they give the new humans some rules. They tell the humans that if they follow these rules everything will be great and they will always be happy. You and I know what rules are though—annoying! Even the gods thought rules were annoying, so why they thought people wouldn't is a great mystery.

I am sure you have broken some rules. Well, so did the early humans. They often broke the only rule they were told not to break exactly because they were told not to! It is like an itch you just have to scratch or a big red button that says "Do Not Push!" The itch will be scratched. The button will be pushed. The gods become angry and they punish the humans. These myths are an explanation for everything bad in the world. Of course, we all know that it was really the gods' fault. They knew we would break the rules.

Human Behavior and Emotions

Just as there is a myth to explain all the bad things in the world, there is often a myth for everything a person does. These often also explain where our words come from. Did you know that another word for selfish is *narcissistic*? We have this word because a very handsome man called Narcissus was cursed, so when saw his reflection in a pond he fell in love with himself! He thought he was so handsome that he couldn't stop staring at himself and stayed there, admiring his own reflection for so long that he turned into a flower.

An emotion that is explained by a myth is *fury*. This is another word for anger and comes from the name of the three sister gods called the Furies. People prayed to the sisters when they were angry and wanted an enemy punished.

Heroes

Another type of myth tells the story of a hero. Sometimes these are human heroes, sometimes they are demi-gods. Demi is an old word for half, so a demi-god, as you have probably guessed, is a half-god. This means their mother or father was a god but their other parent was mortal. A demi-god is stronger than a normal person, but they always have a weakness. Sometimes, the weakness is in their personality— maybe they get angry too easily. Other times the weakness is physical. Achilles was a demi-god. When he was little his mother dipped him in a magic river to make him invincible. If you are invincible it means that nobody can hurt you. Too bad for Achilles, his mother forgot to dip the part she was holding him by—his ankle! He went on to become a great warrior until he was shot with an arrow in his ankle and died. Now we use the phrase "Achilles heel" to name someone's weakness. Chocolate is my Achilles heel—give me some chocolate and I will do anything for you! We also call part of the back of our foot our Achilles tendon.

Where Do Myths Come From?

Everywhere! Every country has myths. Sometimes even different parts of the same country have their own myths and during different times people told different myths. An interesting fact is that sometimes countries on opposite sides of the world have very similar myths even though it is unlikely they ever spoke to each other. In this book, we will read myths from Egypt, Greece, Italy, Scandinavia, and Ireland but there are also great myths from China, Japan, India, Saudi Arabia, Nigeria, and every other country in the world! Myths are something that all people have in common because we all wonder about the same things. Sometimes we come up with different ideas—someone who lives by the sea will tell different stories than someone who lives next to a volcano—but it is surprising how often we come up with the same ideas. Myths are stories, and stories bring people together.

CHAPTER 2
ANCIENT EGYPT

꧁ ꧂

Who Were the Ancient Egyptians?

Ancient Egypt started so long ago that people aren't even sure when it started! But we can be sure that their myths are from more than 5,000 years ago. I don't know how old you are, but that's 148 times older than me! The point is, even if we don't know exactly how old Ancient Egypt was, we know it was definitely *very old*.

You probably know a little about Ancient Egypt already. Maybe you have seen the pyramids and their writing—the hieroglyphs. Hieroglyphs use little pictures instead of letters and are very beautiful and fun to read and write but also very difficult to translate! A lot of the myths we have from Ancient Egypt come from people reading the hieroglyphs they found inside the pyramids. The pyramids were where kings and queens were buried. I am sure you have heard of mummies as well, but do you know why the Ancient Egyptians wrapped themselves up in bandages like that? They did it for the same reason we put food in the fridge instead of leaving it out in the sun—so that it doesn't go bad! This was important to the Ancient Egyptians because they believed they would wake up again in the Afterlife, and they needed their body and all their things when they did. That's why the pyramids were full of treasure and artifacts; these objects tell us how the Egyptians lived when they were alive. Maybe they wrote the myths on the walls because they knew they would need something to read when they woke up as well—they were worried the Afterlife would be boring!

The Myths of Ancient Egypt

Creation

The Ancient Egyptian myth of creation starts with a sea of nothing which they called Nun. From this rose a pyramid, and from this pyramid the god, Atum, created himself. You might be thinking, "Well, that doesn't make much sense, how did he create himself?" This is a good question. Explaining the beginning is a problem all myths have. Even our modern science has a little difficulty with it.

Your teachers have probably told you that the beginning of everything was the Big Bang, but the greatest scientists in the world are still arguing about what happened before the Big Bang. Maybe when you are older you will become a scientist and find out the answer, but then someone will ask you, "What happened before the thing that happened before the Big Bang?" Then, you will have to keep looking.

So you can see, this isn't just a problem the Ancient Egyptians had. Once Atum had created himself, things started to make a little more sense (but not much). Atum had a lot of names, but he is probably best known as Ra. Ra was the sun god. The fact that the Egyptians thought he came first is understandable because it is such a hot country and mostly desert.

Sitting on his pyramid with nothing to do and no one to talk to, Ra got bored and lonely. You and I know how boring things can be if there is nothing on television or our parents have told us not to use the computer, and even then we could read a book or go outside and play or visit our friends. Ra had none of this. He just had to sit there staring at the nothing all around his pyramid, probably wondering why he had wasted any time creating himself.

But Ra was a god, and gods can do whatever they want. Ra decided he would make some other gods so that he would have company. His way of doing it was a bit strange though—he spat and he sneezed. When he spat he created Tefnut, the god of moisture. When he sneezed he created Shu, the god of the air.

Now, I don't know about you, but to me, that sounds a lot like *atishoo*! Think about it, you have a tickle in your nose and your head goes back and you go, "Tef-tef-tef- TEFNUTSHU!" and out of your nose and mouth come moisture and air. The only difference between when you and Ra sneeze is that he is a god, so when he sneezes the moisture and air that came out were gods like him. Crazy, right? But try not to think about the fact that everything in existence comes from Ra's boogers!

That was just the beginning. Tefnut and Shu then had two children: Geb and Nut. Geb was the Egyptian god of the earth, Nut was the Egyptian god of the sky. Geb and Nut had some kids as well. They were called Osiris, Horus the Elder, Isis, and Nephthys.

From these nine gods came everything else in the world, not to mention a lot of trouble!

Ra's Real Name

Something you are going to find out from reading this book is that gods are not the easiest people to get along with. The Ancient Egyptian gods were no exception. They were constantly fighting with each other for power, tricking each other, making and breaking agreements, and generally being difficult. Maybe this is because Ancient Egyptians thought of their gods as being like pharaohs. Pharaoh is another word for king. In fact, many Egyptian pharaohs became gods themselves. At least, they said they did. It's up to you whether you believe them or not. The pharaohs were always fighting for power, so it seemed only natural to the Egyptians that the gods were too.

One day, Isis decided that she wasn't powerful enough. She thought the best way to get power was to get control over Ra, her great grandad. He was the most powerful at the time, even though he was very old. If she had power over him, then she would have power over everything. The best way to get power over a person was to discover their real name. Now, when it comes to you and me it isn't too difficult to discover our real names. It's the one we use every day! Ra was different though. We already know he was also called Atum, but he had a lot of other names as well. This was because he was the creator of everything and had different names when he was doing different things. In some ways this makes sense. Think of one of your teachers for example. You might call them Mr. Jones or Ms. Jones. But their friends might call them Tom or Alice. Their husband or wife might call them love or sweetheart or darling (ew! I know!). Maybe they have kids, so their kids probably call them dad or mom. In the future, those kids might also have kids and they will call your teacher—Mr. or Ms. Jones to you—grandad or granny. Which of those is their real name? It's hard to say, isn't it?

Isis had to discover Ra's real name. He wasn't stupid though—he knew the power that names had, and he wouldn't tell it to anyone. Isis had to find a way to trick him. She was clever, though, and she had a plan. She knew that if she got a bit of his body—some hair or skin or a toenail, for example—she could make a spell that would injure Ra very badly. As Ra was now very old, he drooled all over the place. We already know how powerful some of Ra's drool could be—he used it to create Tefnut and Shu! All Isis had to do was follow behind him and scoop his drool up off the floor. It was icky, but it was worth it. Once she had enough of his drool, she mixed it with some dirt to make clay and from the clay, she made a giant snake. She nailed the snake to the ground (so it was already very angry!) on a path she knew Ra went down.

Poor Ra, old and weak, didn't know what was coming when he set off on his daily trip around Egypt to check that everyone was okay. He was the creator, after all, so he still had a lot of responsibility. Maybe because he was old, but his eyes and ears were getting so bad that he didn't see or hear the snake. Or maybe he had been that way so many times he wasn't being careful. Either way, the snake bit him and injected him with all its venom. Remember, this wasn't a normal snake. It had been made from Ra's own spit, so it was very strong and had powerful venom.

It was the most painful thing Ra had ever felt, and he had been around forever and had felt everything! He was in *agony*. He called to all the gods and everyone who knew magic and begged someone to make the pain go away. All of them tried, but no one could find the cure.

Then Isis came and said, "Oh, what's wrong, Grandad?" Like she didn't know. Ra explained that he had been bitten by a deadly snake and that he was in a lot of pain. Now Isis knew her plan was working and she said, "Well, the only way I can cure this type of snakebite is with the real name of the person who has been bitten."

Ra began to list all the names of the things he had created and done because these were also his names and he thought he could trick Isis into using one of these. But Isis shook her head, "No, it has to be your *real* name, otherwise there's nothing I can do."

By this time Ra had probably figured out what had happened, but it was too late. He tried to ignore the pain and refused to say his real name but he couldn't take it. "Fine!" he said, finally, "My real name is written on my heart. Here." And he gave his heart to Isis.

His great-granddaughter did as she had promised and performed the magic to cure the snakebite. It worked and he was cured, but now Isis had Ra's heart *and* his real name. This meant that she also had his power. So while Ra was no longer in agony, he was also no longer a god.

I would love to tell you what Ra's real name was. Maybe if we knew it *we* would have all the power of a Ra. But Isis wasn't about to share that secret with anyone. She was now the most powerful god in Egypt and she wanted it to stay that way.

CHAPTER 3
ANCIENT GREECE

❧❧❧❧❧ ❧❧❧❧❧

Who Were the Ancient Greeks?

The Ancient Greeks lived on the other side of the Mediterranean from the Ancient Egyptians. In fact, a very famous Greek soldier called Alexander the Great invaded Egypt more than 2,300 years ago and became a pharaoh (National Geographic Society, 2019). The Ancient Greeks are very famous for their philosophy and learning. Alexander the Great's teacher was one of the most famous philosophers ever: Aristotle. And, of course, they are famous for their myths. We know Alexander the Great knew the myths because he copied some of the things he had heard or read about in them (Encyclopedia Britannica, n.d.). He did this because he wanted people to think of him as one of the heroes from the myths. That way they would respect him more, and maybe be afraid of him.

This is another reason myths were important in the past. They were often used by rulers to connect themselves to heroes and gods from mythology. If they could make themselves seem like a hero in a myth it told people something about them. A ruler who was a soldier like Alexander wanted people to think of him as strong and powerful. Maybe he also wanted people to think of him as a demi-god.

The Myths of Ancient Greece

There are some similarities between the Ancient Greek and Ancient Egyptian myths. They both say that the world was created from nothing, but the Greeks called nothing *chaos*. This is a word we still use today to mean something is badly organized. To the Ancient Greeks, it meant emptiness. Another similarity is that the Ancient Greek gods were always fighting for power, just like the Ancient Egyptian ones. They had two different names for their gods, though: gods and Titans. Titans were actually gods as well.

In Ancient Greece, Zeus was the king of the gods. He had taken his throne on Mount Olympus from his father Cronus, one of the Titans. Zeus imprisoned Cronus and the rest of the Titans, apart from Prometheus and Epimetheus. He left these two free if they agreed to help him create men and all the animals and plants and things of the Earth that men would need to live.

Some of you reading this might be thinking, "What about women?" The fact is, Zeus decided he didn't want any women to be made because his wife, Hera, would be jealous (Fry, 2017). Hera's jealousy was completely understandable—Zeus was a terrible, terrible husband and could never be trusted.

The Creation of Humans

Why Zeus thought the world needed human is a difficult question to answer. He had a lot of brothers and sisters, just as many wives and lovers, and even more children! It seems that wasn't enough for Zeus, though, who felt like something was missing. Some people think he was just bored (Fry, 2017).

Either way, he ordered Epimetheus to get to work and for Prometheus to keep an eye on him. They had to make all the animals and give them the tools they needed to survive—claws and wings for birds, teeth for tigers and lions, scales, and the ability to breathe underwater to fish. Unfortunately, Epimetheus wasn't watching what he was doing and by the time he came to the men, there was nothing left to give them! So he had to ask his brother, Prometheus, for help (Bullfinch, 1885).

Prometheus made the men out of clay, but they had no way to survive. Prometheus felt bad for the men and decided there was one thing that would help them—fire. There was one problem, though. Zeus was scared of the men becoming too powerful! He'd asked for them to be made in the first place, yet now he was scared of them! And he knew that the one thing that would help them become more powerful was fire, so he told Prometheus that they could never have it.

Prometheus Steals Fire

But Prometheus wasn't one to follow the rules. He had also become very fond of his creation and didn't like to see them suffering as they were. He decided that he would steal the fire from the gods. The best place to get it, of course, was the sun. Obviously, only an idiot would try and chase down the sun while it was flying across the sky. It would be too hot and moving too fast. But during the night, it was a different matter. By then the sun had cooled down, like a fire that was about to go out.

So Prometheus crept into the cave where the sun was hidden, waiting for the next day, and stole a piece of it. He took it down to the men and showed them how to use it. Finally, they were able to make all the tools they needed to survive and to cook and warm their homes.

Pandora's Box

Of course, when Zeus found out that Prometheus had disobeyed him he was furious. Perhaps you remember the word "fury"? Well, furious is the word for describing a person who is feeling very angry.

Furious, yes, but not out of control. A lot of gods might have started throwing thunderbolts and letting off volcanoes and flooding the world (he would do that later). Instead, he decided to set a kind of trap for the men. So he made the first woman. Her name was Pandora. He asked all the gods to give her something. Aphrodite gave her beauty, and Athena taught her how to sew which, to be honest, does not seem much of a gift. Some people said that other gods made her jealous and cruel and a liar, but that is just because those people were angry with Pandora for what she did. Her only real weakness was curiosity, which is not a weakness at all unless a god has tricked you. And Zeus definitely did trick her because before she went he gave her a gift: A box which he told her never to open.

I'm sure you know what it feels like to be carrying around something you can't open. Just think of what it's like the night before your birthday, or on Christmas Eve, when you know there are presents in the house! You know you will be able to open them the next day, and still, it's difficult not to go and look, to peel back just a tiny bit of the wrapping paper and see what's inside. Imagine if you were given a present and told you could *never* open it! Do you think you could do it? I know I couldn't.

Pandora couldn't either. She managed for a while but her curiosity won in the end. She opened the lid of the box just a tiny bit, just for a peek, and out flew all the bad things in the world, things like illness and murder and hatred and disease and lies. As soon as she realized what was happening, Pandora shut the box again, trapping inside one last thing—hope.

People argue about whether this means we still have hope, kept safe in the box for all time, or if it is the opposite. If only she'd left the box open for another second, there would be hope in the world as well. You will have to decide which sounds correct yourself. I'm afraid I can't help you there.

The Flood

A giant flood happens in almost every mythology and religion in the world. There is one in Babylonian mythology, Arabic mythology, and Ancient Egyptian mythology, as well as in Christianity and Judaism. These floods often happen because the god or gods of the place were said to be unhappy with the humans' behavior. Zeus was the only one who was angry at the human behavior he had *caused*. Imagine, all the trouble that humans were experiencing in the world, all the lying and the cheating and the stealing and the war was because of the box he had given to Pandora! And we all know that he knew she would open it. He created her and he knows, just like you and

I know, that you can't ask someone not to open their present!

It doesn't seem fair, then, that he was angry about the bad things the humans were doing. We should be thankful that he didn't go with his original plan—to burn everything. That might have been worse. But the only reason he didn't do that was that he was scared the fire might reach Mount Olympus, where he and the other gods lived.

So he called on Poseidon, his brother and the god of the sea, to help him send a flood. Zeus himself made earthquakes and storms and between them, they washed away all of humanity. All apart from two—Pyrrha and her husband Deucalion. Zeus remembered that of all the people these two were the only ones who had worshipped him as much as he liked to be worshipped (which was a lot), so he sent away the storms and told Poseidon to relax and bring the oceans and rivers back down.

Zeus was happy again, although I'm not sure he deserved it. Poor Pyrrha and Deucalion had to start all over again. Humanity had to start all over again.

The Trojan War

Washing humanity off the face of the Earth wasn't a permanent solution. That's probably because the humans weren't really the ones causing the trouble. Yes, you guessed right, it was the gods. Zeus was what we call a hypocrite. This means someone who tells people they believe one thing but then does the exact opposite. Zeus being annoyed at humans for arguing and causing trouble was very hypocritical. The greatest war in Ancient Greek mythology, the Trojan War, was actually the gods' fault as much as it was the humans'. The

Trojan War is probably the most famous of all the Greek myths. There is a whole book about it called *The Iliad* by someone called Homer.

The Golden Apple

The Trojan War started because someone wasn't invited to a wedding. That might sound like a silly reason to start a war, but a lot of wars start for silly reasons. In this case, it was Eris, the goddess of discord, who wasn't invited. Discord means not getting along or fighting or causing trouble. Perhaps that is why she wasn't invited to the wedding. No one wants arguments and trouble at their wedding. It made her very angry, though. Or maybe she started out very sad and lonely, but you and I know that our emotions can change when we think about them too long. Sometimes sad people act in very angry ways.

Have you ever not been invited to a wedding? Okay, maybe a wedding is a bad example. They're boring and it's better not to be invited! But have you ever not been invited to something like a birthday party? Everyone else is going but for some reason, the birthday girl or boy hasn't invited you. If that has happened to you, you know how bad a feeling it is to be left out. If that hasn't happened to you, you are very lucky.

It is not nice to be left out, and Eris was as sad about it as you or I would be. Being the goddess of discord, her solution to being left out was to cause trouble. She found a golden apple and wrote "For the most beautiful" on it. She then crept up to where the wedding was happening. Everyone was drinking and laughing and having fun (imagine how Eris must have felt hearing and seeing all of those people enjoying themselves without her!). She rolled the apple into the middle of the

365

dancefloor and as if by magic, there was discord. Who was the apple for? It said the most beautiful, but at least three of the wedding guests thought that meant them!

In an attempt to stop the arguing, the three most beautiful guests—Aphrodite, Hera, and Athena—went to Zeus. They wanted him to decide who was the most beautiful. Now, Zeus wasn't the most tactful god in history—if you are tactful that means you are good at talking to people without being rude or making people angry—but this time he knew he had to be careful. Hera was his wife, and Aphrodite and Athena were his daughters. He knew that if he chose one, the others would hate him. Of course, if he had been a good parent or husband, he might have done what parents have done throughout history and told them that they should share!

Instead, Zeus decided to avoid the question and said that the three goddesses should ask someone else. He even chose the person: A very handsome prince called Paris. Paris was from a city called Troy, which is where we get the name the Trojan War from. You might have guessed, then, that things are not going to go well for Paris.

Why Zeus thought Paris was a good choice to make this decision is a mystery. Knowing Zeus, he probably thought Paris was the worst person to decide the winner. But Zeus seemed to enjoy discord as much as Eris did.

Aphrodite, Hera, and Athena went to Paris and demanded that he tell them who was the most beautiful. You have to feel sorry for Paris in this situation. The gods are very scary. It doesn't matter if they are beautiful or not, they can still do terrible things to people, sometimes just for fun! So imagine you have to choose between three! It would be something like your parents coming and standing in front of you and asking who you think is best! You don't want to have to make that decision.

Poor Paris had no choice. I say poor Paris, but he probably managed to make the worst decision possible for the worst possible reasons. He accepted one of their bribes. Aphrodite promised him the most beautiful woman in the world, Helen, would be his wife if he chose her. Paris, the idiot, accepted her bribe. Aphrodite was declared the winner of the golden apple. Paris had Helen.

Helen

Now, there are several problems with this situation. The first is that we never really hear what Helen thought about this. No one asked her if she wanted to be with Paris. The second problem is that Helen was already married to a very powerful man, Menelaus. She had chosen Menelaus out of many men and was happy with him. To make matters even worse, all Menelaus' friends and supporters had promised to protect her.

Then, Paris turned up at Menelaus' house and was welcomed as a friend. Hospitality, being nice to people in your house, was very important to the Greeks. It was also important for the guest not to be rude to their host. There are not many things ruder than stealing someone's husband or wife. That is what Paris did. Some people say that he persuaded her to run away with him, but that seems a little strange. Why would she leave her husband to run away with someone she barely knew?

Whether he kidnapped her or she chose to run away with him, in the morning Paris and Helen were gone and Menelaus was very, very angry. Furious even. Nowadays, if someone is kidnapped, we would probably call the police. But in Ancient Greece, there were no police. So Menelaus got all the people who had promised to protect Helen together and said they were going to war. They agreed, maybe because they felt bad because they had let her be kidnapped in the first place!

The Trojan Horse

The Trojan War lasted ten years. There was a lot of fighting, and a lot of people on the Greek and the Trojan sides died. But Troy was a big city with big walls and the Greeks never managed to break them. As long as the Trojans were safe behind those walls and the Greeks were outside, the war would never end.

A Greek king called Odysseus, one of Menelaus' friends realized the war could go on forever this way. But Odysseus was famous for being very intelligent, and so he came up with a solution. You might wonder, if he was so smart, why didn't he come up with this solution ten years earlier? I don't know. He could have saved a lot of lives. But it was a very unusual solution, and over the ten years, the Greeks tried all the normal ways of attacking a city. They tried climbing over the walls during the night—that didn't work. They tried knocking the walls down with big boulders—that didn't work. They even tried just hanging around until the Trojans ran out of food and water. You guessed it, that didn't work either.

This maybe explains why Odysseus thought the best solution was to build a giant wooden horse. Even some of the other Greeks probably thought this was a bit weird. But they knew

Odysseus was smart, so they did what he said and they built the horse.

One morning the Trojans woke up and went up to the walls, ready for another day of fighting. But when they looked out they saw that all the Greeks had taken their ships and left during the night! All that was left behind was a giant wooden horse. The Trojans were happier than they'd been in a long time. They had won the war! The Greeks had gotten tired and went home. Not only that, but they'd felt so bad about the whole thing that they had built this lovely wooden horse to say sorry. So the Trojans opened the gate and went out and pulled the wooden horse inside and had the biggest party they'd ever had. They probably drank too much alcohol, which is what adults do at parties. And as any adult will tell you, when you drink too much alcohol you will regret it the next day. They have probably never regretted it as much as the Trojans, though. They drank and they partied and they drank some more until eventually, they all fell into a deep sleep.

Maybe if they hadn't drunk so much they would have woken up when the second part of Odysseus' plan started. Because the Greeks didn't build the horse as a present. They built it as a trick. Inside the horse, hiding the whole time, was Odysseus and some other Greek soldiers. When they heard the party coming to an end and the snores of all the drunk Trojans, they opened a hidden trapdoor and climbed out of the horse. They then ran to all the gates and opened them. Outside, the Greek army was waiting. They had not run away, they had just been hiding out of sight. And while the Trojans were partying they came quietly back, ready for Odysseus to open the gates.

Troy was destroyed. Paris was dead. Menelaus was back with

Helen. She had always loved him. She had even helped the Greeks during the war, so her husband knew she had been kidnapped and was happy to have her back. And we have Odysseus to thank for the phrase "a trojan horse", which we use when something disguised as something good turns out to be something very bad.

We also have Odysseus to thank for the word odyssey. If something is an odyssey it means it was a very long and difficult journey full of danger and excitement. We have this word because, while Menelaus and Helen were already back home playing happy family, it took Odysseus another ten difficult years to make it home!

That is nothing, though, if you think about the poor Trojans who no longer had a home to go to. But this was not the end of their story, as we will see.

CHAPTER 4
ANCIENT ROME

Ancient Rome and Ancient Greece had a lot of things in common. A lot of their culture is very similar and most of their gods were the same but with different names. This is because, even after they conquered Greece, the Romans still felt that Greek culture was better and they sent their children to study with the Greek philosophers.

But that didn't mean they thought the Greeks themselves were better. Obviously, the people who conquered the Greeks were better than the Greeks. Yes, they had culture, but if they were really better than the Romans, then they wouldn't have lost all the battles. That was how the Romans saw it.

In order to show this, the Romans used myths in a way that was a bit like how Alexander the Great used them. They told stories to show how they were superior to the Greeks. To do this, they actually used some of the Greek myths.

One thing they said was that when Zeus defeated his father Cronus, he didn't actually manage to imprison him. Instead, Cronus, who the Romans called Saturn, escaped and went to live with Janus. Janus was the god of Rome. He had two faces, one looking forwards and the other looking backward. The one looking forward represented the future, and the one looking backward represented the past (although, how you know which way is forwards or backward when you have two faces, I don't know). From his name, we get the word January.

The Romans worshipped all the other Greek gods as well but, as mentioned, they gave them different names. The gods weren't the only part of Greek mythology the Romans stole, though.

The Origins of Rome

We've already seen how myths were used to explain the beginning of the world and the beginning of people and the beginning of a war. The Romans also used myth to explain the beginning of their city. Maybe because Greece had such a powerful culture, the Romans wanted to be clear that they were different. Maybe you have a brother or sister who is very close to you in age. Do people say that you look the same, or that you could be twins? If that has happened to you, you will know how annoying it is! Or maybe you have an older sibling who you copy a lot. You think they are cool and you want to be like them (even if this annoys them!). Someday, you will decide you want to have your own identity and you will decide to dress very differently from them and listen to different music. But still, you will always know your older sibling taught you a lot of things.

The Romans were like the Greeks' younger siblings in that way. They had copied them for many years, but now that they were older and more powerful, they wanted the world to know that they were different. To do this, they took the story of the Trojan War and made a kind of sequel.

Some of the Trojans survived when their city was destroyed. One of them was called Aeneas. He was a cousin of Paris. When the Greeks came in and destroyed his city, he ran away to Italy and started a family. Some of his descendants—his great, great, great-grandchildren—would be the founders of Rome. Their names were Romulus and Remus.

Rhea Silva and Mars

Romulus and Remus' family got along about as well as the Greek gods, which is to say not well at all. Their mother was called Rhea Silvia.

Rhea's father was a king called Numitor. He had a brother called Amulius. One day Amulius imprisoned Numitor and made himself king. But he was still scared of Numitor's children, especially the boys. He was afraid that they would come back when they were older and kill him for what he had done to their father. So he decided to kill them first. He didn't kill Rhea because she was a girl. This was pretty sexist of Amulius, but I'm sure Rhea didn't complain about that at the time. Instead, he made her become a nun. He did this because nuns were not allowed to marry, so she would never have children.

We've already seen what happens when someone tells a person they can't do something in myths. Rhea didn't marry anyone, to be fair to her, but one day she met a man walking in the woods. He had a woodpecker and a wolf with him, which is a hint that he wasn't a normal man. In fact, he wasn't a man at all. He was Mars, the Roman god of war.

Rhea and Mars fell in love and Rhea became pregnant. When Amulius heard about this, he used it as an excuse to throw Rhea in prison for breaking the rules. Then, when she gave birth to two boys, he ordered that they should be taken to the river and drowned.

The Wolf and the Shepherd
There is a saying that Amulius had obviously never heard: If you want something done right, do it yourself. The people he sent to drown the twin boys didn't do the job he had sent them to do. Instead, they just threw the boys and the basket they were in into the river. Eventually, the basket bumped against the bank and the babies fell out.

It was cold and they were wet and hungry so the babies did what babies do and they cried. A she-wolf heard them crying and came to them. Maybe it was the same wolf that had been with the boys' father, Mars, or maybe it was another one. Either way, the wolf looked after the boys, cleaning them and giving them milk to drink until a shepherd, Faustulus, found them.

Faustulus took the boys home and brought them up as his own children. He was pretty sure they were the children of Rhea. Everyone had heard what Amulius had done by then. Faustulus knew that they were safer with him. The two boys grew up not knowing who they were. They had a good life, even if they weren't rich. Shepherds are normally peaceful people who do not attack their brothers and kill their nephews so, in many ways, it was better than being a king.

Romulus and Remus

Romulus and Remus *were* kings, though. More than that, they were demi-gods. So while the life of a shepherd might have been nice, they got bored of it quickly. Instead of looking after the sheep, they ran around the countryside and played together, and went hunting. Other boys thought the twins were very cool, and they followed them around in a gang. Soon enough, the twins thought hunting and running and playing were boring too and, together with their followers, they started robbing people. They were good boys, though, so they decided only to rob bad people. They decided to rob a gang of robbers!

Unfortunately for Romulus and Remus, these robbers were friends with King Amulius. This isn't surprising really. We already know Amulius was a bad guy, so it makes sense that he was friends with other bad guys. But it made the whole situation a lot more dangerous for Romulus and Remus.

The robbers soon found out where the twins lived. Romulus was able to escape, but the robbers caught Remus and took him to Amulius' prison. When Romulus ran home and told the shepherd what had happened, the old man was worried. If Amulius realized who Remus was, he would kill him! So he told Romulus that he and his brother were really princes.

Escape from Prison

Do you remember Numitor? He was Romulus and Remus' grandfather. For some reason, Amulius wasn't particularly scared of him. He had been scared of all the other boys in Numitor's family, so why wasn't he scared of Numitor?

Numitor was the only one who could actually hurt him. The others were just babies! Perhaps Numitor was a coward. That is the only thing that explains why Amulius even let him out of prison and let him stay in the castle!

Romulus sent a message to his grandfather. The message said that Numitor had two grandsons and that one of them was in the castle's prison. Numitor was so surprised that he didn't believe the message at first. Maybe he thought it was his brother trying to trick him. To see if it was true, he went and looked at Remus in the prisons. Remus looked so much like Rhea that Numitor knew he was his grandson. He agreed to help them.

Numitor tricked Amulius into thinking that an army was coming to attack. Amulius sent his soldiers to fight the army. Once again, he made the mistake of not going himself. As soon as the army was gone, Romulus attacked the castle. He had all the shepherds and his and Remus' followers to help him. With no one to defend the castle, Amulius was helpless, and Romulus killed him. Maybe if Amulius hadn't been lazy and had gone with his army he could have come back and taken over the castle again. Fortunately for Romulus and Remus, he was lazy.

Numitor was made king again, although you have to wonder why. He had not shown many kingly qualities. But he was made king, and Romulus and Remus agreed to help him.

The Foundation of Rome
Romulus and Remus soon became bored again. Perhaps, just like the king part of them meant they weren't happy being shepherds, the shepherd part of them meant they weren't

happy being kings! Either way, they decided they wanted to make their own city instead of helping their grandfather with his. If only they had been happy with what they had. That would have saved them a lot of trouble.

They went back to the hills where they had been shepherds and looked for a good place to put a city. By this time the twins had a lot of followers. They agreed to go with them to find the city. Some of them were the ones who had followed them when they were children. Others were probably people who thought, like us, that Nimutor wasn't a very good king and didn't want to hang around when the twins had gone!

So the two brothers wandered the hills with their followers, looking for the best place to build a city. Remus chose one hill and said it would be the best place. Romulus chose another. Some of the followers agreed with Remus. Some of them agreed with Romulus. The ones who agreed with Remus said *he* would be the founder. The ones who agreed with Romulus said that it would be *him*. In the end, they couldn't agree on who was right, so each of them started building their own city.

Now, I don't know if you have any siblings, but if you do you know that sometimes things can become very competitive. If you see your sibling doing something, you want to do it bigger and better. Sometimes you might start trying to annoy your sibling, saying that your thing is better than theirs. This is how a lot of arguments start.

The argument between Romulus and Remus started like that, but it got out of control. One day Remus came over to see how Romulus's city was coming along. Romulus had started building his wall. He said it was going to be a great wall and that no one would be able to get through it. Remus laughed. The wall was still very low. He said it was a useless wall. "Look," said Remus, still laughing, "I can just jump over it!" And he did. He jumped one way and then the other, laughing all the time about how small Romulus's wall was.

"Stop it," said Romulus. "Shut up! It's obviously not finished. When it's finished you won't be able to jump over it!"

But Remus wouldn't shut up, and he wouldn't stop jumping over the wall and laughing. We all know what it's like when someone is annoying. We try to control ourselves, we try to ignore them, but sometimes it just gets too much. Unfortunately for Remus, Romulus had a sword and when he got annoyed, he killed him.

He probably didn't mean to kill his brother. He probably just got angry. Sometimes when we are angry we don't think about what we are doing and bad things can happen. That is why our parents tell us that when we are angry we should count to ten. If Romulus had counted to ten, he probably wouldn't have killed his brother. But he didn't count to ten, so he had to live with that for the rest of his life.

He did build his city, though, and he called it Rome. Which makes you wonder how bad he actually felt about it. If he had felt bad, surely he would have named the city after his dead brother and called it Reme. Maybe he decided that just didn't sound as good.

CHAPTER 5
THE INFLUENCE OF GREECE AND ROME

✤✤✤✤✤✤ ✤✤✤✤✤✤

Of course, there are many cities in the world, but there are not many as famous as Rome. This is because Rome once had an empire that ruled most of the world. The Roman Empire changed so much that we can still see its effects today, nearly 2,000 years later. The most obvious effect is in the languages we speak and the words we use. While languages like French and Spanish have a lot more in common with Latin, the language they spoke in Rome, English has a lot of words from Latin as well.

This is because Latin was the language of business and trade. In some ways, Latin was then what English is now. Even countries that have their own languages are influenced by English. This makes some people very annoyed, which is understandable, but it is the way things are. In the same way, many languages in the past were influenced by Latin. Some were almost totally replaced, others just took a few words. Of course, all these places knew how much influence the Greeks had on Rome as well, especially when it came to philosophy and science.

What this means is that a lot of names from the Roman and Greek myths are present in our lives today. You can see this if you look at the names of the planets: Mercury, Venus, Earth, Mars, Jupiter, Saturn, Uranus, Neptune, and Pluto (some people say that Pluto is not a planet, but whatever it is, its name comes from Rome, so I am including it here!). These names—apart from Earth and Uranus—are all the names of the Roman gods. Uranus is the name of a Greek god, but all the others are the same as the Greek gods but with different names. Venus, for example, is the Roman name for Aphrodite—the goddess of love who promised Helen to Paris. Jupiter is Zeus and Saturn is Cronus. Uranus, on the other hand, is the Greek name for the Roman god Caelus.

I will give you a warning here—some very *pedantic* people might say that the Greek and Roman gods are not always *exactly* the same. A pedantic person is someone who takes little things VERY seriously. Yes, maybe they are right about those little things, but this is a book about stories, and stories are supposed to be fun.

Maybe, when you are older, you will enjoy being pedantic. Then you can read long books about how Jupiter was only the same as Zeus in the year 341 BCE on the second Friday of June at 11:35 a.m. if you are lying down with your arm in the air. I, for example, get very angry if someone boils my egg for seven minutes instead of six minutes and thirty seconds. This is why I do not have many friends.

Mercury

Mercury is the Roman name for the Greek god Hermes. He is most famous for being the messenger god and is shown with wings on his shoes. He was fast, clever, and mischievous, which means that he enjoyed being naughty. Jupiter was his father and his mother was Maia.

Maia was not a god but a nymph. Nymphs were similar to gods but they are more associated with nature and represented things like trees or rivers. They could also represent ideas like love or, in Maia's case, growth.

Mercury was born at dawn. By lunchtime, he had invented a new musical instrument called a lyre. A lyre is a little bit like a harp. Normally they are made out of wood, but for some reason, Mercury decided to make his one out of a turtle shell. And it wasn't a turtle shell he'd found lying around, ready to be made into a lyre, either. When Mercury found it, it still had a turtle in it. I won't go into the details about what happened to the turtle, but let's just say that Mercury's first day on Earth was the poor turtle's last.

All that inventing made Mercury a little peckish and, for a young god like him the only thing that would feed his hunger was meat. Mercury wasn't happy with just going down to the local butcher, either (although, perhaps that wouldn't have been the best idea as he was still a baby and a talking, walking baby is enough to scare the bravest soldier, let alone an innocent butcher).

Instead, Mercury decided that the only thing to do was to steal some of his half-brother Apollo's best cows. So off he ran, just as the sun was going down, and herded some of the cows away from the others. He was just about to leave with the cows when he saw an old man watching him. This annoyed Mercury. He had almost gotten away with the perfect crime and now this man was a witness. He went over to the man and said, "What's your name?"

"Battus," said the old man.

"I'll give you one of these cows if you keep quiet about what you've seen," said Mercury.

Battus laughed and pointed, "See that stone over there? That stone will tell before I will."

Mercury smiled, handed over the cow to Battus, and ran away with the rest. But he stopped around the corner. He didn't trust the old man. Making sure the cows couldn't escape, he put on a hat, changed his clothes, and ran in a big circle to return to Battus from the same direction he'd come from before. He put on a strange accent and said, "Hey old man. Someone's stolen my cows. You haven't seen anything, have you? If you tell me, I'll give you a cow and a bull!"

Now, if you or I met two talking babies in one day, we would probably guess they were the same one, right? After all, how many talking babies can there be in the world?

Battus, on the other hand, thought one talking, a cow-herding baby was nothing strange so he wasn't surprised when he met another. He did not suspect a trick. He wasn't a very honest man either so when the second baby offered him a cow and a bull, Battus pointed and said, "The other baby and all your cows went that way!"

At which point Mercury threw off his hat and his coat and said, "Ah-ha! It's me. You thought you could lie to me, did you, Battus?" And he turned Battus into a stone. Which you will either think served Battus right or was a bit mean, depending on your point of view.

Mercury was happy turning people into stones, anyway. He ran back to the stolen cows and carried them on his way, driving the cows ahead of him. He even made them walk backward for a while to confuse anyone who followed him.

After a while, he separated two unfortunate cows from the herd, drove them into a cave, wrestled them to the ground, and killed, cooked, and ate them. The rest he let go, presumably terrified of the baby that had just eaten two of their friends.

Now, I don't know about you but I sometimes have difficulty getting together the energy to cook, let alone catch and butcher *and* cook my own meal. But Mercury was a god, and a very fast and strong one as well, so it isn't really fair to compare ourselves to him.

Once he had eaten enough, Mercury crept back into his mother's house and into his bed and went to sleep like nothing had happened, pretending that he was a baby like any other.

Apollo, of course, noticed that some of his cows were missing and set about tracking them down. He followed their hoofprints, looking around for someone who might have seen something but there was no one. He stopped next to a stone and sat down to rest on the way. Leaning down, he looked closer at the hoofprints and saw there were some tiny footprints in the middle of them. This made him a little suspicious. Battus thought *talking* babies were normal, but Apollo was pretty sure there weren't many *walking* babies in the world. He got up and followed the hoofprints again.

After a little bit, he stopped and scratched his head. The hoofprints showed another herd of cows coming from the opposite direction! For a second he looked around, wondering which direction to go. Then he saw the tiny footprints of the baby. They were still going in the same direction. Suddenly, he realized the cows were walking backward! Angry that someone had tried to trick him, he started following the tracks again.

Eventually, he found the cave with the still-hot fire and the clean bones, and found the little footprints everywhere around and guessed from the prints that this tiny baby had first fought and then eaten the cows. Now he was sure. Maybe, *maybe*, there were a couple of babies in the world who could walk, but there definitely wasn't more than one that could walk, steal cows and kill, cook, and eat them! He came to what seemed the most obvious conclusion to him—it was his new half-brother Mercury who had done this.

He went to Maia's house and went into Mercury's bedroom where he found the little god sucking his thumb and pretending to be asleep. The baby's cuteness had no effect on Apollo. He gave it a poke and said, "Hey, little brother. You better tell me what you did with my cows or I'll chuck you in prison with the Titans and even your mom and dad won't be able to get you out again."

Mercury opened his eyes and yawned and stretched and said,

"Think about what you're saying, big brother. I'm a baby, how am I going to go and steal some cows and kill and eat them? That's just ridiculous. I can't even walk!"

There are a couple of problems with this answer. The main one is that if Mercury wanted to convince Apollo that he was a normal and helpless baby, he probably shouldn't have said anything at all. He should have screamed and cried and maybe drooled a bit. Those are three things that babies are good at.

Obviously, Apollo was not fooled. He laughed and said, "Oh, really? I bet you stole lots of stuff today. I bet there are shepherds and cow-herds wondering where their sheep and cows are from here to Timbuktu." Well, maybe he didn't say Timbuktu, exactly. But he would have said somewhere very far away, which is what 'Timbuktu" really means in English, even though it is a real city in Mali, Africa. What people who actually live in Timbuktu say for somewhere very far away, I do not know. New Jersey, maybe? Or Manchester? Sorry, I got distracted. Where were we? Oh, yes.

But even though he knew Mercury had done it, Apollo also knew it didn't look very good for a fully grown god to attack a baby. So he decided to go to Jupiter instead, and he told him what had happened and demanded that the baby be punished. Mercury—again, not being a very convincing baby—said, "Dad, I'm telling the truth. This guy came to my house and started accusing me of stealing his stupid cows even though you can both clearly see that I am a baby. He doesn't even have any witnesses. I swear I didn't do it."

Jupiter laughed. He didn't believe Mercury, perhaps for the obvious reason that the baby was talking long before it should have. He said, "Very clever, son. I'm very impressed. But you better tell us where those cows are."

"Okay! Fine," said Mercury, "I stole them. I'm sorry, but I was hungry. I ate two of them, but the rest just ran off. I don't know where they are."

Jupiter was impressed. Parents are often impressed by the things their children do. Sometimes they shouldn't be. But I think you will admit that what Mercury did was quite impressive. On the other hand, it is probably not a good thing for a parent to be impressed by their children's lies, but Jupiter was not a great parent. Or husband. Or son. Or friend. He wasn't a very good husband either, but that is another story.

Jupiter laughed again, "Good boy. Now go with your brother and find those cows which you stole." And he sent his two sons away.

Apollo was still very angry. His father's attitude had not helped. He made clear to Mercury that if they did not find those cows there would be trouble. He was also a little worried now. If Mercury had managed to do all this on his first day on Earth, what would he be able to do in a few years? He was just thinking about tying him up forever (the gods often look for extreme solutions) when Mercury started playing the lyre that he had made.

It was the most beautiful thing that Apollo had ever heard. He listened, amazed until the song was finished. Then he said, "Little brother, I don't care about the cows. If you give me that lyre, we can forget about the whole thing."

Mercury looked at his older brother and smiled, "You can have it. And I'll teach you to play it beautifully as well. I'm sorry I stole your cows. I didn't mean to make you angry."

And from that day onward Apollo and Mercury were best friends. This is probably the only time in history two gods ended an argument peacefully.

Venus

Venus is the Roman name for the Greek goddess Aphrodite. Maybe you remember her from the story of the Golden Apple. Maybe you blame her for the whole Trojan War thing. After all, if she hadn't offered Helen to Paris, a lot of problems could have been avoided. On the other hand, without her, there'd be no Rome and no Roman Empire, which might seem like a bad thing if you're Roman, but maybe not so bad if you're the rest of Europe. There are two sides to everything, after all, just like there are two sides to Janus's face.

We are going back further in time for this story about Venus, back to before the Trojan War, back to before the Golden Apple. But you might have noticed two things about Venus's personality from the story of the Golden Apple: She didn't like to hear the word no, and she wasn't afraid to cheat. Some people think cheating is very bad, but the gods don't seem to have minded it. In fact, a lot of the time they seemed to think it was funny or even clever. They thought that if you cheated and got away with it, that just meant you were smart. Which is something that a lot of people in prison thought as well. Until they ended up in prison that is. Unfortunately for the humans of mythological times, you couldn't really imprison a god, so they normally got away with it.

So you have to feel bad for the Trojan prince called Anchises. He was an honest young man. He just wanted to live a normal life, looking after his herd of cows. Most princes don't even want to look after themselves, let alone hundreds of animals, but that's the kind of man Anchises was. He used to take the cows out in the morning, make sure they had all the best grass to eat, and then bring them home again in the evening. That was what he was doing the day when Venus first saw him.

She thought he was very, *very* handsome and decided that she wanted to marry him. When she came over and said hello, Anchises thought she was very, *very* beautiful as well. So beautiful that he suspected she was a goddess.

Now, a lot of people in the myths fall in love with the gods and have no problem with it. They never seem to realize, though, that falling in love with a god rarely ends well. Take a man called Tithonus. Tithonus fell in love with the goddess Aurora and she fell in love with him. They wanted to be together forever, but Tithonus was just a man so they knew he would die one day. Aurora went to Jupiter (the Roman name for Zeus, remember) and asked him to make Tithonus immortal. The problem was that she forgot to say immortal *and forever young*! Jupiter being Jupiter didn't point out the mistake on her part. You can, I guess, add "bad father-in-law" to the list of things he was bad at. As a result, Tithonus lived forever but he also got older and older and older—older than anyone had ever been before. Like Ra in Egypt he ended up drooling, but he also got so weak that he couldn't move or speak. Presumably, he's still alive, and older than ever. We can agree, I think, that this was not a very nice thing for Jupiter to do. But then, we have a lot of evidence now to say that Jupiter was not a nice god.

Maybe Anchises had heard this story. Or maybe he had heard one of the many other ones where things didn't go well for a human who fell in love with a god. Or maybe he just didn't want Jupiter as a father-in-law, which seems very wise. Either way, he was pretty sure that Venus was a goddess and tried his best to stay away from her.

But we know what Venus was like, don't we? She said, "Goddess? What goddess? There aren't any goddesses around her. I'm just a princess from that town over there, here to marry you because you're the most beautiful man I've ever seen. Don't you think I'm beautiful too?"

Anchises couldn't really say anything but yes to that question. Venus was known for her beauty, after all. She could probably have won that Golden Apple without cheating if she'd been patient.

So Anchises agreed to marry Venus. He loved her, so how could he say no? Later he would say that she had lied to him, which was true, but you have to wonder, don't you if he wasn't really lying to himself. You think you can't lie to yourself, do you? Well, you can if you want something badly enough. It's like putting your fingers in your ears and going, "LALALALALALALA," so that you can't hear the voice in your head telling you the truth. This is probably what Anchises did when it came to Venus. He knew she was a goddess but he pretended he didn't so that he could ignore the voice in his head telling him that bad things happened to people who fell in love with gods.

Venus waited until their baby, Aeneus (perhaps you remember him), was born to tell Anchises the truth.

"How could you lie to me?" he said, acting all surprised and shocked.

To which Venus probably said, "Come on! Don't pretend you didn't know. Oh, and by the way—don't EVER tell anyone Aeneus is my baby, okay. Bad things will happen if you do that." And then she left! Just like that. Gods don't often hang around once they have gotten what they want from someone.

Of course, we already know what happens when you tell someone not to do something in a myth. Yep, that's right, they do the thing they were told not to do. They might do it instantly, or maybe in a month, or maybe years later, but they will definitely do it.

In Anchises's case, it might have been understandable if the person he told about Venus was Aeneus himself. After all, a little boy is going to be curious about who their mother is. But no, Anchises just got drunk and told some people in a bar. He was just showing off. Unfortunately for him, as soon as he revealed the truth, Jupiter knew. I don't know how he overheard the conversation, but he is a god so I'm sure he has powers we don't know about. However he heard it, he was furious and threw a lightning bolt that blinded Anchises. You might feel bad for Anchises, but you have to say that Venus did warn him.

Mars

Mars is the Roman name for Ares, the god of war. The Greeks didn't actually like him that much. The Romans on the other hand thought the war was the best thing there was, and that they were the best at it. That's why they said that Mars was the father of Romulus and Remus, the founders of Rome. They wanted the world to know that war was in their blood.

Mars wasn't always a great god though. One time he even got himself kidnapped by two giants and had to be saved by Mercury and Diana (the Roman name for Artemis, the goddess of the moon).

The two giants were called Otus and Ephialtes. They grew very quickly and by the time they were nine years old they were already as tall as a very tall tree. They decided they were going to fight the gods and beat them so they stacked two mountains on top of each other to reach the gods on top of Mount Olympus.

Their attack wasn't successful, but they came away with one prize: Mars, who they squeezed into a big jar and kept trapped in their house. Quite how the god of war managed to get kidnapped and stuffed into a jar by two nine-year-olds is a good question. It makes you wonder why the Romans wanted him to be their god.

However it happened, he was stuck in that jar for 13 months and would have stayed there for longer if the giant's mother, Iphimedia, hadn't heard him calling for help. She realized who it was in there and told Mercury. Why she thought she should tell on her two boys, we will never know. Maybe she just thought it was bad to keep someone in a jar.

Mercury and Diana came up with a plan to help Mars escape and went down to the giants' house. Diana went to the front door and knocked and asked to be let in. She was very beautiful and the two boys instantly fell in love with her. She chatted with them and laughed and distracted them while Mercury snuck in and grabbed the jar and ran away.

When they realized what had happened, Otis and Ephialtes were very angry with Diana. She turned into a doe, which is a female deer, and jumped between them. Both the boys tried to kill her with a spear but they missed and killed each other instead.

Mercury was waiting for her outside. He hadn't let Mars out yet because he was having too much fun laughing at him. But Diana told him to smash the jar and let their brother out. He did, and the three of them went back to Mount Olympus together.

Jupiter, Saturn, and Uranus

You already know that Jupiter is the Roman name for Zeus and Saturn is the Roman name for Cronus. Uranus, remember, is actually the *Greek* name for Caelus. We are going to talk about these three together because their story is the story of fathers and sons.

We also talked about how Jupiter fought his father Saturn, beat him, and imprisoned him. But we haven't talked about why they had a fight in the first place. It is true that this is partly because Jupiter was very ambitious and wanted to be king of the gods, but another reason is that Saturn was an even worse father than Jupiter! I know, I didn't think it was possible either. Saturn wasn't a great son either. If Jupiter might have had an excuse for fighting his father, Saturn didn't have a great one for fighting Uranus.

Uranus, the sky god, was the oldest of all the gods. He was the husband of Gaia, which was what the Greeks called the Earth. Apparently, she didn't like her husband very much, because she asked her children, the Titans, for help getting rid of him. Most of the Titans were too scared—or maybe they even loved their father, you never know—but Saturn was more than happy to help. He wanted to be king of the gods and the only way he could do that was to defeat his father.

He didn't kill him, though. He just injured him so badly that the old god was too weak to fight anymore. Uranus knew he had lost, but he had a warning for his son.

"Your own children will do the same to you as you have done to me," he said.

This worried Saturn. If he could do it, then of course his children would be able to as well.

His solution is probably the worst example of fatherhood in the history of fathers. Our parents would probably think, "Well, when I'm old, of course, my children will take over from me." Or maybe they would decide they just needed to bring us up correctly, to teach us to share and to be nice, and not to fight or argue.

But we already know that Saturn didn't think like that. Just look at what he did to his own dad! Anyone who is capable of something like that is normally afraid that everyone else is just like them.

So Saturn decided he had to eat all his children as soon as they were born! He was so big that he didn't need to chew, just popped them in his mouth and swallowed, and because they were gods, they didn't die.

The children's mother, Rhea, wasn't too happy about this so when it came to the last one to be eaten, Jupiter, she came up with a plan. She hid the little baby away and wrapped a rock in his baby clothes instead. Saturn came as soon as he heard his wife had had another baby. He grabbed it from its bed and gobbled it up. We can assume that he didn't have a very good sense of taste because he didn't notice anything different between this one and the ones he had swallowed before. Rhea, meanwhile, took the little baby and hid him with some nymphs who kept him in a cave.

So Jupiter grew up in secret. This was easier said than done, especially when he was a baby because, as we already know, one thing babies are really good at is making a lot of noise. The nymphs came up with a plan to stop Saturn from hearing the baby screaming. They hired a load of soldiers to dance and sing every time the baby cried. They could probably have got the same result by banging some pots and pans together, but that might have driven the nymphs crazy. Not that having people singing and dancing was much better because, while babies are very good at making noise, they are also very, *very* bad at sleeping. Imagine the poor soldiers having to wake up at all hours of the day and night to drown out the noise. I wouldn't do that job if you paid me, but I'm not a very good singer or dancer, so I don't think anyone *would* pay me. On the other hand, why soldiers would be your first choice I don't know either.

Eventually, Jupiter grew up. He got hold of a drug—a drug is a type of medicine that is not always good for you—which he gave to Saturn. Presumably, Saturn was happy to drink it because he thought all the people who could hurt him, his children, were safely digesting in his stomach along with the last hotdog he ate. Unfortunately for him, this was not the case. The drug Jupiter gave him made him throw up. First came the hotdog, then the stone, then the children.

These kids were a little bit angry that he had eaten them. You would be too if your dad ate you, I'm sure. So they agreed to help Jupiter fight against Saturn and the other Titans. As we already know, that was a fight they won and the Titans were imprisoned.

Is there a lesson to be learned from this? Definitely. The lesson is to be nice to your parents and your kids because if you aren't, they won't be nice to you!

Neptune

Neptune is the Roman name for Poseidon. Neptune was the god of the sea and earthquakes. He had a fearsome reputation. This means that people were very scared of him because they believed he sent sea monsters to attack their boats and even cities on the coast.

After defeating the Titans, he, Jupiter, and Pluto had put the sky, the sea, and the Underworld in a hat to see who got to be a god of which. Jupiter won the sky, Pluto got the Underworld and Neptune got the sea.

He was happy with the sea, but he wanted more. He wanted to be the king of the gods and he was jealous of his younger brother. After all, who wants their little brother to be in charge of them?

For a long time he let things be, but one day Jupiter's wife Juno (the Roman name for Hera) came to him with a proposal. She was annoyed with Jupiter. He was not a good husband and was always running away with other women and goddesses. Apart from that, a lot of the gods were not happy with how Jupiter was behaving like a king. They said he was a tyrant, which means he was a cruel and unfair ruler. Juno suggested that if Neptune helped her trap Jupiter and tie him to his throne and stole the thunderbolt he got most of his power from, then Neptune could be king of the gods.

Neptune liked the sound of this. He was sick of his little brother being king. He was not the only one. He, Juno, and some other gods worked to trap Jupiter and they were successful.

They weren't successful for long, though. Thetis, the mother of the Greek hero Achilles, didn't like the idea of Neptune being the king of the gods. Perhaps this was because she was herself a sea nymph and didn't like how Neptune ruled the sea. She sent a great sea monster up to Olympus to break the chains holding Jupiter down.

Jupiter had been getting angrier and angrier while he sat there chained to his throne. Now he was free he was furious and he punished the rebel gods.

He tied Juno up in the sky for a long time to think about what she had done. Neptune's punishment was more simple. He sent him to be a slave of the king of Troy for a year. This was before the Trojan War and it is because of Neptune that the war lasted so long. The king of Troy made him build the walls around the city. He built them so well that they were the strongest walls in the world. That is why the Greeks were not able to break them down and had to use the trick of the Trojan horse instead.

Pluto

Pluto, known as Hades to the Greeks, was the god of the dead. We already saw how Pluto got the Underworld, which is where people go when they die and is generally quite gloomy and dark. Hell, in other words. Pluto pretended he liked things gloomy and dark. He said he liked sad music and wore dark clothes and tried to act like being the god of the worst place in the Universe was just what he had always wanted.

But even the gloomiest person needs a bit of sunshine on their face and likes to go swimming in the warm sea. And we all like someone to sing us a happy birthday and bring us a cake on our birthday. In short, even the god of the dead needs someone to love. He found it difficult, though. Most of the people he met were dead which meant they were either very old, annoyed, or very depressed about being in the Underworld. It was only natural, though definitely unfair, that they blamed Pluto for the situation they found themselves in. Added to that was the fact that looking after the Underworld was a full-time job, which meant that Pluto didn't get out much.

So when he did find the time to go into the world above he kept an eye out, searching for a beautiful woman or goddess who might like to come and live with him in the Underworld.

Up until then, the world was a very different place from the one we know now. It was summer all the time, the flowers were out, the trees had leaves on them, and animals were running around in the fields. People just had no idea how depressing winter could be because they'd never seen one. There was a simple reason for this. Ceres (the Roman version of Demeter), who was the goddess of things like flowers and fruit and grain, had a daughter who made her very happy. Because she was very happy, she wanted everyone else to be happy, so she made the crops and fruit, and flowers grow all the time.

This daughter of Ceres was called Proserpina. In Ancient Greece, her name was Persephone.

Beauty might be a subjective thing, but most people agreed that Proserpina was very beautiful. Pluto certainly thought so when he saw her. In fact, he fell in love instantly. Love, you may be aware, has a habit of making people (and gods) do very stupid things. When Pluto fell in love with Proserpina he did something very stupid and, in fact, very, *very* bad. He did something you should never, *ever* do—he kidnapped her!

There are several reasons you should not kidnap someone. The first is just that it is bad. The second is that it is illegal and you will go to prison for a very long time. And the third is that if you kidnap someone, they are probably not going to like you, let alone love you. Especially if you take them straight to the Underworld. Maybe if you kidnapped them and took them to the Bahamas they would be happier, but they still will not like you.

Another reason you should not kidnap someone is that their parents are going to be very sad. They are going to wonder where their child is and be afraid that something bad, worse even than kidnapping, has happened to them. When her daughter didn't come home that evening, Ceres went out to look for her. She looked everywhere and asked everyone, but she couldn't find out where she had gone. The next day she went up to Sol, who was the god of the sun and asked him to look for Proserpina while he crossed the sky. He could see the whole Earth from up there, so he would be able to find her easily.

Of course, the one place Sol couldn't see was the Underworld. The sun never went there, which is one of the reasons it was so gloomy. So it was that at the end of the day, when he had looked everywhere, Sol went to Ceres and said, "Sorry, I couldn't see her anywhere."

Ceres was scared for her daughter. Sometimes when people are scared, they become very angry as well. This is because they feel like they are powerless, and don't want people to know they are actually sad. They think being sad is being weak, which is not true, but people often believe things that are not true.

So Ceres was very sad and very angry. And when the gods feel something, there are consequences (normally bad ones) for the rest of us. This is because, even if they feel powerless, gods arc actually very powerful. It might not have been much of a problem if Ceres was the god of something nobody likes anyway, like slugs, but she was the god of flowers and plants and crops, which basically means *food*! And when she couldn't find her daughter she said, "Until someone brings her back to me all the plants and flowers and crops will *die*!"

And they did. And all the people were very hungry because there was a famine, which is what it is called when nothing grows and there is no food.

"But it wasn't *the people's* fault," you say. I know, I agree. It seems very mean of Ceres to blame people. They didn't have anything to do with the kidnapping of her daughter. But you might have noticed by this point in the book that the gods don't really care whose fault something is. Perhaps that's why they aren't our gods anymore.

Eventually, Jupiter noticed what was going on. Personally, I think this is another black mark against Jupiter. He doesn't seem to ever pay much attention to what is happening in the world. If he wanted to be President, I wouldn't vote for him.

Unfortunately for the people in mythological times, Jupiter was the *king* of the gods, which means he didn't need people to vote for him and he could do whatever he wanted. He did at least realize that it wasn't a good thing for everybody to be hungry. They might not be able to vote for him, but they could stop worshipping him and making sacrifices for him. Why, after all, would you worship someone who lets you go hungry?

Because he was very narcissistic (remember the selfish Narcissus we spoke about at the start of the book?) and always wanted to be the center of attention, Jupiter didn't want people to stop worshipping him. Being worshipped is the best way to be the center of attention and it made him feel great.

The point is that while he didn't really care that the people were hungry, he *did* worry that they might stop worshipping him. So he looked around for Proserpina. Being the king of the gods he could see everywhere and he soon found her with Pluto in the Underworld.

Pluto was Jupiter's brother, though, so he didn't really want to annoy him by telling him to give Proserpina back. He needed Pluto to look after the Underworld. As we know, it was gloomy and depressing down there and Jupiter didn't want to have to deal with gloomy and depressing things.

Instead, he decided to delegate the job to Mercury. Delegating is when a powerful person tells someone else to do something. They do this for different reasons. Sometimes it is because they think that person has a special skill which makes them better for the job. Sometimes it is because they are busy with other, more important things. Sometimes it is because they know it is a difficult job and if it goes wrong they want to be able to point at the *other person* and say, "They did it!"

Jupiter probably delegated because he was lazy.

But whatever the reason, Mercury went down into the Underworld and spoke to Pluto. "Look, Uncle," he said. "I agree that Proserpina is very nice, but you shouldn't have kidnapped her. Ceres is furious and is causing all sorts of problems. Jupiter, well, he sent me to ask you to please, please send her back."

Now, Pluto might have been the god of the Underworld, but Jupiter was king of the gods. Pluto was just a little bit scared of his younger brother. Maybe he also thought that he owed Jupiter for saving him from Saturn's stomach!

With a sigh, Pluto agreed to give her back. He went down to Proserpina's room. He hadn't been mean to her, apart from the kidnapping. He'd actually treated her very well (not that that makes kidnapping okay!) and she didn't hate him. But she was overjoyed when he said she could go home. She got all her things together, and put on her shoes, smiling and excited to see her mother and flowers and sunshine again.

"It's a long way back, though," said Pluto, "Here, have something to eat before you go." He held out his hand. In it were six red pomegranate seeds.

Now, pomegranate seeds are very tasty, but they are also very small. Why Proserpina didn't ask for a burger or some chips, I don't know. Maybe she thought it would be rude. Either way, she smiled and said, "Thank you." And then she ate the seeds.

Perhaps you have realized by now that the gods don't do many things out of kindness. Perhaps you realized that the pomegranate seeds were a trick. You might not know why, yet, but you're smart. You know that you shouldn't accept anything from strangers, or gods, least of all a god who has kidnapped you. You were probably screaming at Proserpina to say, "Actually, I just ate, thanks. I'm stuffed! I couldn't eat anything else, even something as tiny as a pomegranate seed."

But Proserpina wasn't as smart as you. Or maybe it was just that she was very innocent and too polite for her own good. Either way, she ate the seeds and ran out of the Underworld, laughing.

Ceres was overjoyed to see her daughter again. Instantly, the flowers bloomed and the crops grew and the trees were full of fruit and nobody was hungry anymore.

But, even though she was happy, Ceres was also worried. Mothers are often worried. They are worried because they love their children and don't want bad things to happen to them.

So she asked Proserpina to tell her everything that had happened in the Underworld.

When you discover that there was no reason to be worried, you are relieved. Listening to Proserpina talk, Ceres started out relieved. Pluto really had been nice to her daughter. But then, right at the end of her story, Proserpina told her about the pomegranate seeds, and Ceres was horrified!

Why was she horrified? Because she knew that if you ate anything in the Underworld you had to stay there! She could have killed Pluto!

When Jupiter heard what had happened he held up his hands and said, "Sorry, there's nothing I can do! She ate the pomegranate seeds, so she has to go back to the Underworld."

"But she only ate six!" said Ceres.

"All right," said Jupiter. "So she has to go back to the Underworld for six months every year."

Ceres didn't like this. She loved her daughter and she wanted her around all the time. But there was nothing she could do. Every year, for six months, Proserpina went to live with Pluto in the Underworld. And for those six months, no plants grew, the flowers died, and there was no fruit on the trees.

So whenever you are feeling cold and wish the sun would come out and wonder why there are no colorful flowers or oranges and apples on the trees, blame Pluto. It is his fault we have fall and winter. Those are the six months when Proserpina is with him.

It wasn't all bad, though. Proserpina, as we know, was a very nice and kind goddess. She was probably the only goddess who could ever actually like Pluto. And while we're up here suffering through the winter, Proserpina is in the Underworld, making Pluto and all the dead people very happy. She became the queen of the Underworld, and she is a good queen.

It all worked out well in the end for Pluto, then. But that does *not* make it okay to kidnap anyone.

CHAPTER 6
THE NORSE MYTHS

The Norsemen came from northern Europe. They are probably best known as the Vikings, who I'm sure you have heard of. They came from Denmark, Sweden, and Norway but they traveled all over the world. They invaded Great Britain, which includes England, Scotland, and Wales. This is where the English language comes from... They invaded Ireland, and Iceland and even made it as far as America nearly 500 years before Columbus did (Encyclopedia Britannica, 2018).

Just as famous as the Viking name is the fact that they were very warlike. This is a word that means they enjoyed fighting. In a lot of history classes, you will hear how they went places and killed people and destroyed their homes. This is true. They did do all those things. The people of Great Britain, who were called the Anglo-Saxons, often complained about being attacked by the Vikings, which is funny because around 400 years earlier they had done the same to the people who lived in Great Britain before them. In fact, the Anglo-Saxons and Vikings were practically related, a bit like the Greeks and the Romans! They even had a lot of the same gods and myths.

We know their myths were very similar because they used similar names for their gods. For example, the Norse god Odin is the same as the Anglo-Saxon god Woden! Tyr, the Norse god, is the same as Tiwes, the Anglo-Saxon god. And Thor— you've probably heard of him—is the Norse version of the Anglo-Saxon Thunor.

Have you noticed anything else about those names? What if I give you a hint?

The days of the week.

Okay, it isn't obvious at first, but if you screw your eyes up a bit and say the Anglo-Saxon names very quickly with the word 'day' after them you get our days of the week. Tuesday is 'Tiwes'-day', Wednesday is 'Woden's-day', Thursday is 'Thunor's-day', and Friday is 'Frigga's-day'!

So while you might think of Tuesday as burger day or sports day, or the day your favorite TV show is on, the Norse and Anglo-Saxon's thought of it as the day of the god Tyr or Tiwes and had lots of stories to go with it!

"Why are you telling me all this?" you're shouting, "I don't care! I'm just here for the stories."

Which is fair enough. Let's get on with the myths!

The Norse Gods

Odin

Odin was the oldest and most powerful of the gods. He was their leader, just like Zeus had been the leader of the Greek gods. There was one small difference, though: Odin took his responsibility a lot more seriously than Zeus ever did.

He worried that something bad would happen to the world—his world—one day, and he decided he had to do something to save it. He needed wisdom. He was already smart, he knew that, but he needed to be wise. With wisdom, he could protect the world from anything.

And he knew exactly where to get wisdom: at the Mimir's well. It was said that if you drank from the well you would become the wisest person in the world. Odin knew, though, that nothing was free in this world, especially not wisdom. He wondered what Mimir would want in return for a drink from the well.

Still, he decided he would do it, whatever the price. So he dressed up as an old man with a stick and went out into the world of humans and giants. When a human saw him, he looked like a human, and when a giant saw him, he looked like a giant. Nobody knew he was actually Odin, the god.

One day he met a giant and asked him who he was. The giant said, "I am Vafthrudner, who are you?"

"My name is Vegtam the Wanderer," Odin lied. Then he said, "I have heard of you, Vafthrudner. People say you are very wise."

"I'm not just very wise, I am the wisest giant that ever was."

"In that case," said Odin—*Vetgam*! I meant Vetgam, of course.

"In that case," said Vetgam, "I have a question for you."

The giant rolled his eyes. Everyone was always asking him questions. He kind of regretted his little boast about being the wisest. He said, "Okay, okay. I'll answer your question, but only if you play a game with me. We each ask each other three questions and if either of us gets one wrong, then the other one gets to chop off his head!"

Perhaps he had said it as a joke. Most people would not play a game like that with the wisest giant that ever was. It is like you or me betting an Olympic runner that we can beat them in a race—a bad idea (unless you are an Olympic runner, in which case I am very impressed. Well done).

Vafthrudner was very surprised, then, when the old giant with a walking stick agreed.

The giant looked closer at him, frowning. "Really?" He shrugged. "All right. It's your head. My first question is this: What river separates Asgard from Jötunheim?"

"Ifling," said Vegtam.

"Okay, okay," said the giant, smiling now. "Not bad. What about this: Name the horses that Dagr and Nótt ride."

Dagr was the god of the daytime and Nótt the god of the night. Each of them had a horse that they rode across the sky. Now, Vafthrudner had chosen this question because he knew that no normal man or giant could possibly answer it. Only a god or a very wise giant would know the answer. So he was very surprised when this Vegtam he had never heard of said, "Skinfaxe and Hrimfaxe."

"That's right," said Vafthrudner, probably running a finger around his collar and starting to sweat. "Yes. Wow. You're good. I'll admit that. Okay." He stopped now, thinking hard. If he couldn't catch this Vegtam out with the next question, it would put his *own* neck at risk! "Your last question then. Here it is: On which field will the last battle ever be fought?"

"Vigard," said Vegtam.

The giant laughed a little nervously, "That's right. Yes. Vigard. I'm impressed." But then he stood a little straighter. He was still the wisest giant in existence. What could this old guy ask him that he wouldn't know the answer to?

"What," said Vegtam, "are the last words Odin will whisper to his son, Baldur?"

When he heard that question the giant probably swore. He might even have shouted, or maybe he cried. He knew he couldn't answer. No one but Odin could answer that question. And as soon as he thought that he realized how stupid he had been. He pointed. "You're Odin! Only Odin could know the answer to that and only Odin would have asked that question!"

Odin smiled and said, "Maybe you're right. Maybe. But if you want to keep your head you have to tell me something: What will Mimir ask for a drink from his well of wisdom?"

The giant grumbled a little when he heard this question. He

would have answered that without putting his neck in danger if he had known it was Odin asking. Gods were very annoying, he thought. They couldn't do anything the normal way. They always had to show off and make you feel small. He didn't say any of that though. After all, he now owed Odin his head, so it was best not to argue. Instead, he sighed and said, "He will ask for your right eye."

"My right eye?" said Odin. "Nothing but my right eye?"

"Yep. A lot of people and giants have gone and asked for a drink from Mimir's well. I even went myself once. But no one's ever given up their right eye. No one thinks it's worth it. I definitely didn't. Can I go now?"

Odin nodded and the giant left. He wanted to run away in case Odin changed his mind. He was too proud of that, but he did walk very, very quickly.

Odin on the other hand walked on very, very slowly. He liked his right eye. He looked at things with it. He even thought it might be better than his left eye. He tried covering one and then the other and looking at things. First, he would look at something far away, like a mountain. Then he would look at something very close, like his hand. Yes, he was sure of it. His right eye *was* better.

He sighed and walked on. He knew he should go to the well of Mimir, but he didn't want to. Instead, he just walked in circles, trying to find another solution. He couldn't. He knew there was a great fight coming, a fight between good and evil, and the only way he could save the world was to drink from that well. Then he would be so wise he would know what to do.

Finally, he forced himself to walk to the well. It had to be done. It was better to do it quickly, like pulling off a Band-Aid. The slower you do it, the more it hurts.

Mimir was standing by the well when Odin arrived. He tried not to yawn, but guarding the well was quite a boring job.

"How can *eye* help?" he said, laughing to himself. Nobody else even knew it was a joke when he said it, but he still laughed every time.

"You know what I want," said Odin. He didn't think the situation was very funny.

"All right," said Mimir, annoyed. "You know the price?"

"No," said Odin, suddenly hoping that the giant had been lying. He took out his money bag and shook it. "I've only got a few pieces of gold on me."

"It's your right eye," said Mimir, pointing at his own. "Your right eye. Nothing more, nothing less."

Odin sighed. He nodded. Then he took a deep breath and just did it.

It was not like pulling off a Band-Aid. It was a lot more painful and the pain lasted for a long time. It also took him quite a long time to get used to having only one eye. He bumped into quite a lot of things and ended up with bruises all over his right side. He did learn to live with it, though, and the pain did go away.

And it was worth it. He drank from the well and instantly he knew everything. He even saw the future. It wasn't pretty.

Humanity would go through many difficult and terrible times. But he also saw how to bring an end to those times and how to save humanity.

Mimir didn't even want the eye. He threw it in the well. It's still there, floating around, staring up at anyone who looks down. It probably makes people think twice about drinking the water. Firstly, you have to give up your eye, and secondly, that water obviously isn't very clean.

Thor

The guy with the hammer! Yes, that's right. I'm sure you have heard of him. But there are plenty of stories about him I'm sure you haven't heard. He was the god of lightning and storms and, of course, thunder.

He might be most famous because of his hammer, but Thor wasn't always very careful with it. He should have been extra careful seeing as the hammer was the first line of defense for the gods' home, Asgard!

One evening he and Loki went to the giant Thrym's house for a feast. You might have heard of Loki. He was the Norse god of mischief and caused a lot of trouble. The worst trouble he was to cause was yet to come. For the moment he and Thor were best friends so they went to Thrym's feast together.

The Norse gods, just like the Vikings, liked to drink alcohol. They didn't have beer, though. They had something similar called mead. The effects of drinking mead were the same as drinking beer. Loki and Thor drank too much of it that night. So much, in fact, that they were halfway home before either of them noticed Thor's hammer was missing. Perhaps you can take this as a warning against drinking alcohol. As I'm sure you can guess, you have to be pretty stupid to forget something as big as a hammer, especially Thor's hammer. But that's what alcohol does to you, it makes you stupid. Being stupid can sometimes be fun, but generally, it is best to avoid it.

Thor was frantic with worry. He had promised never to let the hammer out of his sight and now he couldn't even remember where he had lost it. Loki, on the other hand, had obviously had a mom who had told him to retrace his steps whenever he lost something. This was good advice. Advice from moms is normally good advice.

Thor, by this point, was no use. Another thing that alcohol can do is make you very sad about very silly things and Thor was now sitting against a tree, crying. He was probably a bit scared of what Odin was going to say when he found out his son had lost the hammer.

So Loki ran to the palace where all the gods lived and up the stairs to speak to Freyja. She had a special coat made of falcon feathers. Anyone who wore the coat could fly. Loki asked to borrow it from her so he could fly back to the giant Thrym's house and look for the hammer.

Freyja knew how important the hammer was. She probably also knew how furious Odin would be if he ever found out it was gone, so she didn't hesitate to hand it over.

Loki flew back to Thrym's house but he found him outside in the garden, putting the leashes on his dogs so they could go for a walk. I don't know if you are a cat person or a dog person.

Maybe you are a lizard or a snake person. Or maybe you prefer spiders. Whatever kind of animal you like, you know that sometimes people speak to their pets. It is silly. Obviously, they can't understand us. But we do it anyway. Thrym was no different. Loki, dressed as a falcon and sitting in a tree, heard him talking to his dogs.

"I'll be able to get you some nicer collars soon, boys," he told them. "Don't you worry. Now that I've got Thor's hammer, things are going to get a lot better for us!"

"Ha!" said Loki, jumping out of the tree. "You might have the hammer, Thrym, but we know you have the hammer and we'll find out where you've hidden it no problem!"

Thrym was a little surprised, it's true, but then he laughed. "Search all you like, Loki. You'll never find it. I've buried it eight miles under the earth."

Loki pursed his lips and put his hands on his hips. "So there's no point looking for it then, is there?"

"Nope," said Thrym, grinning.

"What do you want for it, then? Gold? How about this falcon feather coat? Have you ever flown? It's amazing."

"I don't want any of those," said Thrym. "I'll never give the hammer back."

"Come on, Thrym, my old friend." Loki put an arm around the giant's shoulders. "There must be something."

"Well," said Thrym, blushing and twisting the dogs' leash between his fingers. "Freyja is very beautiful, you know."

Loki smiled and winked. "She is, isn't she?"

"I guess, if you get her to be my wife, I might think about giving the hammer back."

As soon as he heard this Loki said, "Don't worry—you'll soon be married!"

And jumping into the air, he flew away, straight to the palace.

By the time he got back, everyone had heard what had happened. It is easy to notice an enormous hammer, especially when Thor is supposed to have it with him *at all times.*

"What did he say, Loki?" they asked him, as soon as he had taken his coat off.

Loki cleared his throat. Freyja was there with the rest of them, waiting to hear what Thrym had said. Loki avoided her eyes. "Well, he said... He said he would give it back if Freyja married him. So I promised him she would." He was speaking very quickly when he finished and made sure to be far away from Freyja.

He was right to be nervous. Freyja was disgusted and angry. "What! How dare you offer me as a wife like some kind of..." She was so angry she didn't know what to say for a moment, but then she spoke again, "Never! I will never marry that stupid little giant!"

Then Heimdall, the gatekeeper of the gods had an idea. "Why don't we just dress someone else up as the bride. If we put Freyja's necklace on them, Thrym will think it's her and won't notice until it's too late, after we've got the hammer back."

"Hey," said Loki, nodding. "That's actually a good idea. Who?"

Now, what I am about to tell you might seem a bit strange. I mean, Thrym wasn't blind, and there were plenty of other goddesses who could have pretended to be Freyja. If the plan was just to get the hammer back and then run away, why couldn't Freyja just pretend to get married and then run away with the hammer?

But as you might have noticed, the gods do not go for the obvious solution. They go for the craziest one they can think of, which in this case meant dressing Thor up as Freyja. Loki, who was a pretty skinny guy, would have made a lot more sense. But even with a veil, it is hard to imagine anyone could have confused Thor for Freyja.

Maybe the gods just wanted to punish Thor for losing the hammer. He certainly wasn't happy to be dressed up like that. Loki, who promised to go with him as his maid-servant, was a lot more comfortable about it and was actually quite enjoying himself.

So the two of them went off to the wedding, the other gods laughing about how beautiful the bride looked, Thor trying not to trip in his high-heels.

A tear appeared in Thrym's eye when he saw his bride. The ceremony was beautiful and all the giants were full of joy at the happy occasion. After the ceremony, there was the feast.

Thor had learned nothing from the whole experience up to this point. He ate and he drank, he ate and he drank. He ate (apparently) one whole cow, eight salmon, and all the little snacks. To wash that down, he drank three tonnes of mead!

"Have you ever seen a woman eat and drink so much!" said Thrym, very impressed. He was so impressed that he tried to sneak a kiss but jumped back when he saw his new bride's eyes. "Wow! I've... I've never met a woman with such," he cleared his throat, trying to think of a polite word, but he couldn't, "*scary* eyes!"

Loki, still dressed as a maid-servant, jumped in and said, "Oh, that's just because she's very, very tired, you see. She hasn't slept for eight nights because she's been so excited about marrying you!"

Thrym frowned, trying to catch glimpses under the veil, but Thor just giggled and pretended to be shy. Thrym smiled. "Okay. That's understandable. Oh, by the way—and what about the *dowry*?"

A dowry was a gift that the bride's family gave to the groom when they got married. As Freyja was one of the gods, Thrym was expecting a lot of gold. If we are honest, he was just as excited about this as he was about marrying the goddess of his dreams.

Loki held up a finger. "No dowry until we get that wedding gift you spoke about with Loki."

"The hammer?" said Thrym. "A deal's a deal, I guess." He waved one of his servants over and said, "Go and get the hammer."

While they waited they drank and ate some more. Once again, we can probably blame the alcohol for Thrym not noticing that his new wife had very muscly arms, a very deep voice, and a beard.

Loki was sweating under his dress. It was a very hot dress, it is true, but mostly he was sweating because he was scared the giant would realize he had been tricked before the hammer arrived. Thor, on the other hand, was not the type of god to worry. He just kept drinking and eating.

"Here it is." The servant returned, holding out the hammer.

Loki almost laughed with relief.

Thor jumped up, grabbed the hammer, threw back his veil and, with a great big smile on his face, began smashing up everything in Thrym's house, starting with Thrym himself.

Loki rolled his eyes and went outside to wait.

Tyr

Tyr was the bravest of the Norse gods. You might be thinking, "What an idiot! No, he wasn't, that was Thor. I've seen the movies."

You're right, Thor was very brave. But he wasn't as brave as Tyr. When they heard about Tyr, the Romans thought he must be the same as their god Mars. And Mars was their favorite god, so this meant they were very impressed.

That's not the main reason we know he was the bravest, though. We know he was the bravest god because of how he tricked the great wolf, Fenrir, who was Loki's son.

Loki had three children with the witch, Angerboda.

One of their children was a giant snake called Jörmungand. Thor had no difficulty dealing with the snake. He grabbed it by the tail, swung it around his head a few times, and threw it into the sea. It wasn't a perfect solution! The snake liked it at the bottom of the sea and grew until it reached around the Earth. It was, however, at the bottom of the sea, so the gods felt like they didn't have to worry about it anymore.

Loki and Angerboda's second child was a girl called Hela. The gods were terrified of her because half of her was a normal woman and the other half was dead! If she looked at you from the right side, she had healthy skin and a beautiful blue eye. If she looked at you from the left, there was just bone and teeth and a black, empty eye socket.

We should not judge anyone by how they look. It is very rude and is also not a very reliable way to decide if someone is good or bad. I myself have broken a few mirrors in my time, but I promise I am a very nice person and quite a good cook. If you decided you didn't like me because of how I looked we would never be friends and you would never get to eat my famous spaghetti.

The Norse gods were powerful and intelligent and beautiful, but I don't think they were very nice. They didn't want Hela anywhere near them, so Odin took Hela and threw her into the caves under the Earth.

Hela didn't seem to mind this too much. She made her own world down there and made herself queen of it. This is where our word *hell* comes from. The Norse gods said that it was a nasty place down in her world, but the Norse gods only liked people who enjoyed fighting and killing, so maybe Hela's world was actually quite nice! As we mentioned before, beauty is a question of opinion.

"You were supposed to be telling us about Tyr and Fenrir!" you say? I am getting there. I just wanted to tell you about his brother and sister first because the other gods weren't afraid of them—at least, not so afraid that they wouldn't even touch them.

They *were* too afraid to touch the wolf Fenrir. Fenrir was very powerful and loved destroying things. That sounds bad, I know, but I think you'll agree that sometimes breaking stuff can be fun.

The only one who wasn't scared of Fenrir was Tyr. He still couldn't control him, exactly, but he could calm him down so that he wouldn't break too much stuff. He did this by feeding him some nice, raw meat every day. He stuck it on the end of his sword and held it out for Fenrir to eat.

Perhaps you have a dog, or a cat, or a spider. If you feed them, they start to like and trust you. It was the same with Fenrir and Tyr.

That didn't stop the wolf from destroying things, though. Eventually, the gods decided something had to be done. They decided to tie the wolf up so he couldn't break any more stuff. They had a slight problem, though. They were all too scared to go near Fenrir.

They had a plan, though. They knew Fenrir was proud of his strength, so they challenged him. They made the thickest, strongest chain they could and then they went to Fenrir and said, "Wow. Fenrir. Wow, you really are *strong*. But how strong are you exactly? I bet you couldn't break these chains if we tied you up."

Fenrir laughed and said, "Of course I can!"

And he lay down and let them tie him up. Standing, dusting their hands, the gods smiled. But then Fenrir broke the chains and they stopped smiling. Fenrir really was strong. They were right to be scared of him.

So they tried again. They made a new chain, thicker and stronger, and they tried again. "Hey, Fenrir," they said. "Okay, you broke that last one, it's true. But what about this chain?"

Fenrir snorted. These gods were idiots, he thought. "Look, I'm *Fenrir*, okay? There is no chain that I can't break."

"You're just scared. I told you he couldn't break it," the gods said to each other.

"Of course I can break it!" snapped Fenrir. And he lay on the ground again and let them chain him up.

The gods stood up, dusting their hands. They weren't smiling this time, they were just hoping—hoping Fenrir couldn't break the chain.

But he could and he did, easily.

The gods threw up their hands. This plan clearly wasn't working. They needed something stronger than a chain. And they knew who to go to—the dwarves.

The dwarves listened to the gods' order, nodding as they did. "Yes," they said. "We can make something that will keep Fenrir tied up, no problem. We will make it out of six things."

"Which six things?" said the gods, worried about the price.

"The roots of stones, the breath of a fish, the beards of women, the noise made by the footfalls of cats, the sinews of bears, the spittle of a bird," (Colum, 1920).

"The roots of stones? Beards of women? But fish can't breathe," said one god.

"And I've never heard the footfalls of a cat!" said another.

"Sounds expensive," said a third.

"Do you want Fenrir tied up or not?" said the dwarves.

"Fine," said the gods. "Whatever the price. It'll be worth it."

So the dwarves set about collecting the six things. Where they got them, we don't know. Sometimes it's important to keep things secret. If the dwarves revealed where they got the materials, then the gods could have made the chain themselves!

What they made wasn't exactly a chain, though. In fact, it was more like a piece of string. At first, the gods thought they had been tricked. Then, the dwarves said, "Just try it out. You will see that it is the strongest material in the world."

There was another problem. When the gods took the string to Fenrir he looked at it and said, "Why do you need me to prove I can break that? I've just broken two massive chains! Obviously, I can break that piece of string."

The gods said, "Well... No... I mean. Yes, it's a piece of string, but it's really strong. Like a spider's cobweb. It looks thin and weak, but if you get a load of it together it's pretty strong, you know?"

Fenrir narrowed his eyes. He sensed a trick. "I bet there's something magic about that string. No, I'm not letting you put that on me. I'm not stupid. I'm strong, yes, but I can't break a magical piece of string."

"There's nothing magical about this piece of string. We promise, Fenrir."

Fenrir said, "Well, I don't trust you. I'm not going to do it."

Tyr came forward. He said, "You trust me, don't you Fenrir?" Fenrir still wasn't sure, but Tyr kept talking, "How about this: I will put my hand in your mouth while they tie you up, and then if there's anything magical about the string, you can bite my hand off!"

Fenrir agreed. Tyr came forward and put his hand between the wolf's fangs. "Not your left hand," Fenrir mumbled, slobbering all over the hand. "Your right hand." He knew Tyr was right-handed and that the right hand was worth a lot more to him.

Tyr switched his hands and stood still and calm while the other gods tied the string around Fenrir.

When it was all around him, Fenrir tried to break the string. He tried and he tried but he couldn't do it. That was how he knew he had been tricked. He would have been able to break any normal string. So, furious, he bit Tyr's hand clean off.

Now, when you see a picture of Tyr, you will see that he only has one hand. He sacrificed his other hand so that Fenrir couldn't destroy the world anymore.

CHAPTER 7
THE CELTS

When most people hear the word *Celtic* they think *Irish*. If you said that to a Scottish or Welsh person, they would probably be quite annoyed, as they are also Celtic cultures. If you had said, "Celtic just means Irish," a thousand years ago, *a lot* of people would have been annoyed because back then the Celts were spread all across Europe (Proinsias, n.d.).

They gradually got squeezed into the corners of Europe, first by the Romans, then by the Germanic people like the Anglo-Saxons, and of course the Vikings. Now they are only found in a couple of very western parts of the continent. You can often tell where the people have a Celtic background because they have two languages: The main language of the country and a Celtic language.

These places are very proud of their Celtic roots. This is often because these countries were invaded by other places over the centuries but always kept their own sense of identity. And perhaps this is one reason why people think of Ireland when they think of the Celts; just as Alexander the Great and the Romans used their myths to connect themselves to gods and heroes, so the Irish used theirs.

The Irish did this a lot more recently though. In the 20th Century they did this with the main aim of separating themselves from the British Empire. During this period, writers, teachers and politicians used the old language, sports, culture and myths of Ireland to recreate the Irish identity and to make sure it was very different from that of the British Empire. As a result, the Irish myths have been told many more times, by many more people and are the most famous. These are the myths we are going to look at in the next part of this book.

Their myths are full of giants and warrior queens and gods and goddesses and sacred bulls and magical salmon and all sorts of crazy things. But for any country that wants to free itself from the control of another, the things it needs most of all are heroes. Luckily for the Irish, their myths had plenty of those.

Celtic Heroes

Cú Chulainn

One of the most famous Irish heroes is Cú Chulainn (which is more or less pronounced "coo-hull-un"). His exploits, or adventures, started when he was very young and carried on right until he died which, coincidentally, was also when he was very young.

No one is quite sure who exactly Cú Chulainn was, which is to say that no one was sure *what* he was. Some people say he was the son of Dechtire and the Celtic god Lugh of the Long Arm. Other people say he was actually Lugh in human form.

Whether he was a god or a demi-god, all the myths agree that Cú Chulainn was very strong, very handsome, and very smart. He was blessed with seven fingers on each hand and seven toes on each foot. He even had seven pupils! This was supposed to make him better than normal people like you and me, although you could probably argue that having seven of any of those things would be more of a problem than a help. Having seven fingers would just get in the way. And where are you going to find shoes that fit seven toes?

For Cú Chulainn, though, having all these extras was a big help in performing some of greatest deeds. He is most famous for defeating the army of Queen Maebh single-handedly when he was just seventeen. You might think that one person, even one god, couldn't defeat a whole army. But, apart from being strong, handsome, smart and having all those extra fingers, toes and pupils, he was also a berserker.

Berserker is a viking word for a warrior who goes so crazy when they fight that it is impossible to stop them. The stories say that Cú Chulainn's eyes would bulge and his muscles would expand and his veins would stick out like ropes when this happened to him. You didn't want to be anywhere near Cú Chulainn when he went berserk because he would pretty much kill anything in sight, and those seven pupils meant that he could see a lot of things!

But Cú Chulainn was famous long before he fought Queen

Maebh's army and there are many stories about his boyhood and even how he was born.

The Birth of Cú Chulainn

The confusion about whether he was a god or a demi-god probably comes from the circumstances around his birth, which were far from normal. His uncle, Conchubar, was king of Ulster in the north of Ireland and was having a feast to celebrate his sister Dechtire's marriage to a man named Sualtim. As you might have noticed, this is not the name of Cú Chulainn's father, and that is because the wedding did not go ahead as planned. In fact, it went very, very wrong.

Dechtire was celebrating with everyone else, dancing and chatting and having fun. All the excitement left her very thirsty and so she went to get a drink. Being all excited, and perhaps already a little drunk (the Celts enjoyed a drink just as much as the Norsemen), she didn't notice the mayfly that had landed in it. She swallowed the fly.

If this were anything other than a myth, she would have made a face, drunk some more and carried on having fun. But you know that isn't what is going to happen here. Instead, she became very tired and had to go and lie down. Being a queen, she couldn't go and lie down all by herself, so 50 of her friends went with her.

While she was sleeping, Lugh appeared in her dreams. He said, "That wasn't just any old mayfly you swallowed, Dechtire. That was me. And now you, and all your friends, have to come with me."

And he turned them all into the most beautiful birds. We don't know which kind, exactly, but myths tend to have people turn into swans, so if you want to picture it, picture 51 swans taking off across the sky.

Conchubar and Sualtim had no idea what had happened. They went and looked in Dechtire's room and she wasn't there. Nor were any of her friends. It was the greatest mystery of the age and it took a whole year before it was solved.

Aside from missing 50 of their number, life for Conchubar and his kingdom returned to normal until one day a flock of beautiful birds appeared from the sky and started to destroy and eat all the crops and plants.

As beautiful as the birds were, the sight of all their hard work and food being destroyed angered Conchubar and his men. They ran outside shooing the birds away. After the birds had flown off, the men decided getting rid of them wasn't enough. They jumped in their chariots and chased after the flock, admiring them all the time but still determined to make sure they never came back.

By nightfall, they still hadn't caught up with the birds, so they decided to find somewhere to sleep. Luckily, there was a castle nearby that they went to see if they could sleep there.

A man answered the door. He was young, strong, handsome and wearing armor. There was a woman standing next to him. Conchubar and his friends asked if they could stay the night. The young man laughed. "Don't you recognize this woman?"

The men looked at her for a moment. They shrugged. They didn't recognize her.

"Aren't you missing 51 women?" said the young man.

"Yes, we are," said one of Conchubar's men.

"So look again!"

Suddenly one of Conchubar's men, who had been standing at the back shouted, "That's my girlfriend!"

The young man laughed again. "It is!"

"So you have my sister too?" said Conchubar.

"She is here, but she can't see you now."

"Why not?"

"She is giving birth. But come in, have some food, have a rest."

If you or I suddenly discovered 51 of our loved ones after a year, we would probably call the police. Conchubar and his friends didn't seem to find the whole situation too strange, though, because they went in, ate, drank and slept, no questions asked.

Conchubar was the first to wake up in the morning. He went looking for the young man whose castle it was, but couldn't find him anywhere. No one ever saw him again. Instead, Conchubar heard a baby crying and followed the cries to find Dechtire with a baby.

And that is how Cú Chulainn came into the world. This explains why some people think he is just a demi-god and other people suspect he might be an actual god. After all, what happened to the young man of the castle?

Either way, Cú Chulainn went home with his mother and grew up with her and his step-father Sualtim. He wasn't called Cú Chulainn yet, though. When he was young he was known as Setanta. How he got his name is another story, which we will get to now.

How Cú Chulainn Got His Name

The Romans never made it to Ireland, but they came across the Celts in Britain and heard about the god Lugh from there. They decided that he must be the same as their god Mercury. This makes sense when you hear about Cú Chulainn's personality. Whether you think he is Lugh or is just his son, he is bound to have many of his characteristics. It is both a curse and a blessing that we all have things in common with our family.

And, if you remember what Mercury was like, you will remember that he was precocious. Precocious means that you are doing things people do not normally do until they are older (such as running around, stealing cows and turning old men into stone). Cú Chulainn was precocious too. He was very strong and smart and could defeat boys much older than him at sport and fighting when he was still very young. He would often travel around on his own, visiting people and having adventures.

When he was around seven, he went to stay with uncle, Conchubar. He hoped to be a great warrior one day and he thought it was more likely to happen living there. There were also other boys there who he could play games with. They were much older than him, but still he beat them easily, often playing with him on one team and everyone else on the other. He was one of those annoying people who was good at everything they did.

His favorite sport was hurling. Hurling is an Irish sport where each player has a stick called a hurley and two teams of hurlers try to score goals with a ball like a baseball. One day, while he was playing (and winning) his uncle called out that he was going to see a friend of his called Culain. Cú Chulainn was enjoying his game too much to leave just then and shouted back that he would come later, following his uncle's chariot tracks to find the way.

"All right," said his uncle. "But don't come too late. Culain has a guard dog, a hound the size of a shed with teeth as long as your arm. It has killed many intruders and the whole country is afraid of it. Culain puts him out as soon as the sun goes down."

Cú Chulainn shouted "Okay!" It wasn't long at all before his mind was already back in the game. Conchubar left him there and went to see his friend.

Even if he was precocious, Cú Chulainn was still a young boy, and young boys do not often pay attention to what adults tell them. He had not paid attention to his uncle's warning and continued playing until late in the day.

Eventually he set off, playing a game he liked to play to make a journey more fun. He would hit the hurling ball as far and high as he could then throw his stick after it and run after them, catching both before they hit the ground. That made the time pass faster for him. The sun began to go down as he went, and it was starting to get dark by the time he arrived at Culain's castle. Everyone was inside. The guard dog was prowling around the garden, ready to attack anyone it saw.

Unfortunately for the dog, the next person it saw was the little boy, Cú Chulainn. It ran at him, spit flying from its fangs, ready to eat him. Cú Chulainn wasn't afraid. He was almost never afraid. He took his hurley and hit a ball at the dog. He hit it so hard that the dog died! Which seems a little unfair, since it was only doing its job. Yes, people were terrified of it, but that's exactly what you want from your guard dog.

Inside the castle they heard a howl. Conchubar turned to Culain in horror, "I forgot my nephew was coming after me! He's been killed!"

When Cú Chulainn marched through the door without a scratch on him, the horror turned to anger. You might think that Cú Chulainn's uncle would be happy that his nephew hadn't been eaten, but actually he was more annoyed that his friend's dog was dead. He knew Culain would never find another one like it. He told the little boy off.

Cú Chulainn felt bad and promised to train a puppy to be a new guard dog for him. He also promised that, until the puppy was grown and ready, he would guard Culain's house and cows and property himself.

Culain accepted the offer and said, "From now on, you will be called Cú Chulainn—the *Hound of Culain*."

"I don't know, I'd rather keep my old name—Setanta," Cú Chulainn said.

Culain shook his head. "Don't be silly. One day the whole world is going to know the name Cú Chulainn!"

Cú Chulainn thought about it before saying, "Well, if it'll make me famous, I'll keep it."

Which is why we are talking about Cú Chulainn instead of Setanta right now!

Fionn MacCumhaill

Fionn MacCumhaill (or Finn McCool) was another very famous Celtic mythological hero of Ireland. He was the leader of a group of soldiers called the Fianna, who had many great exploits. In some stories, he is described as a giant (as was Cú Chulainn at times). He was said to be descended from druids and was very wise.

How he became so wise is a story in and of itself. When he was a boy, Fionn went to learn poetry from the poet Finnéces. The poet lived by the River Boyne. He had been living there for seven years, trying to catch the great salmon of wisdom that lived in a deep part of the river called Fec's Pool. Once he caught the salmon, he would eat it and then he would know everything there was to know in the world.

So Fionn lived with Finnéces and did all the dirty work for him, things like making fires and cooking and cleaning the tent. Anything the poet told him to do, he did it. Then, one day, after many years and even more hours of boredom fishing for the salmon (Odin just had to give up his eye, which was painful, yes, but also quick), Finnéces finally caught it.

He gave the salmon to Fionn to cook, with a warning not to eat it. It was a big salmon, plenty for both of them, but whoever ate the first bite would take all the knowledge. Of course, Finnéces didn't tell Fionn that.

Now, you might be thinking that you know what happens when people are told not to do something in a myth. 99 times out of 100 they do it. But Fionn was an obedient boy, which means that he did what he was told. Unfortunately for Finnéces, but fortunately for Fionn, he burned his thumb on the salmon while he was cooking it. The burn hurt so much that Fionn instantly stuck his thumb in his mouth to cool it down. The problem was that the thing that had burned him was a drop of grease and in that drop of grease was all the wisdom in the world. Fionn, sucking his thumb, suddenly knew everything there was to know about the past, present, and future. From that moment on, whenever he had a question, he just had to suck his thumb to find out the answer.

You have to feel sorry for Finnéces, though. Fionn brought him the salmon and the poet grabbed it and took a big bite, expecting to become the wisest man in history. But nothing happened. Then he looked up and saw the strange new look in Fionn's eyes and realized that all the wisdom was in the boy. Poor Finnéces. He threw the plate of salmon away and walked off in a huff.

Fionn left the poet and went on to have many great adventures. He built the Giant's Causeway, which you can still visit if you are ever in Northern Ireland, and became a great king. There was only one person he was afraid of, someone we have already met: Cú Chulainn.

Now, it often happens in mythology that a character changes. In later stories, they might be a giant, like Fionn or Cú Chulainn, when they had been a warrior or demi-god in others. This is because people always like to exaggerate. This is a bit like lying, but not quite. Maybe you have a friend at school whose stories you do not believe. They are always telling you about some amazing thing their mom or dad did but it seems impossible. It might be a lie, in which case none of it is true, or it might be an exaggeration, in which case some of it might be true. For example, their mom or dad probably did really catch a very big fish, it just wasn't nearly as big as a car.

Another thing that happens in myths is that a character who is a hero in one story will become the villain or bad guy in another. How does this happen? Maybe it is like the broken telephone game. Have you ever played that game? You whisper something like, "I like chocolate," to one person, and they whisper what they heard to the person next to them and *they* whisper what *they* heard to the person next to them until it gets to the last person who thinks you said, "My bike has a lock on it."

Well, a similar thing can happen with stories over the years, and if there is enough time and enough people tell them, they can change completely. Perhaps that is how in the story we are about to read, Cú Chulainn got a magic finger to match Fionn MacCumhaill's, only Cú Chulainn's gave him strength rather than wisdom. And perhaps that is also how Cú Chulainn, who was a hero before, became a villain to Fionn MacCumhaill.

However it happened, Fionn was terrified of him. One day Fionn was sucking his thumb and it told him that Cú Chulainn was coming to kill him. Fionn ran home to his wife Oonagh and said, "What am I going to do? What am I going to do? He's coming to kill me!"

Oonagh, who was smarter than Fionn, despite all the wisdom

he had in his thumb, said, "Don't worry, love, I've got a plan."

She told Fionn to go and get into the baby's bed, leftover from when their son had been little. She dressed her husband in baby clothes and pulled the blankets up to his chin.

Now, we've come across this a couple of times in the myths in this book. Something that seems so crazy there is no way it could work. We weren't fooled by Thor dressing up as Freyja, but Thrym was, and we weren't fooled by Mercury the talking baby either. You might be thinking now, how could Fionn, a GIANT, pretend to be a baby?

I don't know. It is very strange. But it worked, as we will see. You will just have to suspend your disbelief, which is a very complicated way of saying to forget that this is silly.

Cú Chulainn arrived and knocked on the door. "Is this Fionn MacCumhaill's house?" he shouted.

Oonagh came out and said, "Oh, hello. Yes it is, but he isn't in at the moment. You could wait here with me and the baby until he gets back."

"That would be nice, thanks," said Cú Chulainn. He went over to take a look at the baby. "He's a big one, isn't he?"

"Yes, he is. Big and strong." Oonagh smiled, and asked, "Care for a cup of tea?"

"Yes, please."

"Ah," she said, sounding annoyed. "It's so dark in here. I've been asking Fionn to turn the house around so the sun comes in through that window for ages now, but he never does it. I'll do it tomorrow, he says. What good is tomorrow?"

"I could do it for you if you like," offered Cú Chulainn.

"Would you?" said Oonagh.

Cú Chulainn cracked the knuckle of his right middle finger three times. Then he went outside, picked up the house with Fionn and Oonagh still in it, and turned it around so that the sunlight came in through the window.

Fionn was even more scared now. "Get rid of him, Oonagh," he whispered.

"Didn't you see, Fionn? He cracked his finger three times, that is where he gets his strength and power from, just like you get your wisdom from your thumb!"

Then Cú Chulainn came back in and sat down so they had to be quiet.

Oonagh said, "I'm just going to make some muffins, if you'd like one."

"Sounds delicious," said Cú Chulainn.

Now, Oonagh wasn't just going to make any old muffins. She made two batches, carefully keeping what she was doing hidden from her guest. In one batch of muffins, she put some rocks in the middle so that they were very hard. The others she made like normal. They were chocolate muffins. Those were Fionn's favorite.

When they were ready, she gave Cú Chulainn one of the ones with rocks in and a normal one to Fionn.

Cú Chulainn shouted in pain when he bit into his muffin. "I've lost a tooth! What do you put in these?"

"What are you talking about? They're just normal muffins. Look, the baby's eating them fine." She pointed to Fionn who was munching happily on his muffin, chocolate rubbed all over his face so that he looked more like a baby.

Cú Chulainn was very impressed. "He must have very strong teeth," he said. He went over to the baby's bed and stuck a finger—the finger from which all his strength came—into Fionn's mouth to check his teeth.

Fionn bit his finger off. Cú Chulainn instantly lost all his power and Fionn jumped out of the bed and said, "It's me! And now you are powerless and I can defeat you, Cú Chulainn!"

Which he did. He killed him, actually. Which seems a bit mean. Cú Chulainn was powerless now, so Fionn didn't have to kill him.

Maybe Cú Chulainn wasn't the villain in this story, then? Maybe it was Fionn. Do you see how confusing these things can be?

Oisín

Ireland is famous for its writers and poets and it always has been. A lot of the Irish poets are seen as heroes too. One of the most famous heroes of all was the poet Oisín. Oisín was the son of Fionn MacCumhaill, but in the myths he had just as many, if not more, adventures and was respected as much as his father.

Oisín is best known for his journey to Tír ná nÓg and his love for Niamh. This is the story we will tell here.

Tír ná nÓg means the Land of Youth in English. When you were there you aged so slowly that it was like living forever. The king of Tír ná nÓg, Niamh's father, was a paranoid man. He constantly worried about things when there was not really anything to worry about. One of his biggest worries was that someone would steal his crown.

The phrase "steal his crown" does not mean take the gold crown off his head and run away with it. It actually means to take his place as king. He asked his druid if he should be worried about this.

The druid said, "You don't have to worry about anyone stealing your crown. Oh, unless your son-in-law takes it from you. Sorry, I almost forgot to mention that part."

The king laughed. He didn't have a son-in-law so he felt a lot better about the whole thing. But then he saw his daughter, Niamh, and he started to worry. She was smart, she was beautiful, and she was a princess. Her beauty worried him most of all. He didn't have a very high opinion of young men. He thought that beauty was the main thing they wanted in a wife. This was probably because that was the main thing *he* had wanted from his wife.

So he had some words with his druid. The druid suggested that they turn Niamh into a pig. Then she wouldn't even be human and no man would ever marry her. The king thought about this but then decided it was too cruel.

"No," he said. "That's too much. Just give her a pig's head."

The druid nodded and said, "Your wish is my command—"

No. Wait. Sorry, that's from Aladdin.

The druid nodded and said, "A pig's head. Not a problem."

And the next day, Niamh woke up with a snort. Which is something a lot of us do after a long night snoring, but the difference here was that Niamh couldn't stop. She looked in the mirror and found that the druid had done what her father had asked. She still had her old body, it was true, but in the place of her head was that of a pig.

When the druid saw how sad the poor girl was, he felt very sorry for her. One day, when the king was busy somewhere else, he called Niamh to him and whispered, "Look, you don't have to be this way forever, you know?"

Niamh snorted with excitement, then covered her nose and said, "Really?"

"Really. All you have to do is marry one of Fionn MacCumhaill's sons. Do that and the pig's head will be gone and you'll be back to normal."

"One of Fionn MacCumhaill's sons? Where can I find one of them?" Niamh asked.

"They're from Ireland."

The words were barely out of his mouth before Niamh was gone. How exactly she got to Ireland, we don't know. If everyone knew the way to Tír ná nÓg, the place would be crowded with people who want to live forever.

When she arrived in Ireland, Niamh walked all over the island asking people if they knew Fionn MacCumhaill or any of his sons. Some people said that no, sorry, they didn't. Others said they had seen Fionn going in the opposite direction, or that they hadn't seen him for a while. A lot of people screamed and ran away when Niamh put her hood down and revealed her pig's head. This isn't necessarily because they thought she was ugly; they just thought it was terrifying that anybody had a pig's head instead of their own. They probably would have been just as scared of a pig with a person's head.

Oisín, meanwhile, was out hunting. He was such a good hunter that he ended up with a small mountain of dead pheasants, boar, and deer. There were so many that his servants threw up their hands and said it was too much to carry. They left him there with his dogs, wondering what to do. It would be a terrible thing to leave so much food when so many people were going hungry.

Niamh saw him standing there, thinking. She went up to him and asked, "Excuse me. You don't happen to know Fionn MacCumhaill, do you?"

Oisín looked up to see who had spoken. He couldn't help but jump with fright when he saw the pig's head, but he was polite, so he tried to pretend he had meant to jump by doing some jumping jacks.

When he had finished, he said, "Sorry, I was just doing some warm-ups before I try to carry all this stuff home." He pointed to the dead animals.

"There's certainly a lot to carry," said Niamh. "So, do you

know Fionn MacCumhaill?"

"I do, actually. He's my dad."

"Really?" said Niamh. She took a closer look at Oisín. He was handsome and strong, she thought. Not that any of that mattered. She would have married almost anyone to get rid of the pig's head. "Tell you what, I'll help you carry all this if you take me to Fionn."

"That would be great!" Osin happily agreed. "I was worried it would all go to waste."

So they bundled up the game and set off walking through the forest.

As they walked, they chatted and got to know each other. Oisín laughed a lot and found himself thinking that Niamh was quite cute when she laughed too, even though she snorted. She knew some great poems as well, which Oisín liked as he was a poet. He found himself enjoying her company so much that he took her the long way home.

It was starting to get dark when he said, "You aren't any normal woman, are you Niamh?"

"Was it the pig's head that gave it away?" said Niamh, laughing.

"No. I mean, yes—that is unusual. But you're different in other ways too. I like you."

"I like you too, Oisín," said Niamh, and it was true. "You're right, I am different. My father's the king of Tír ná nÓg. He put this stupid head on me and the only way I can get rid of it is if one of the sons of Fionn MacCumhaill agrees to marry me."

Oisín was smart enough to recognize a marriage proposal when he heard one, even if it was a little strange. He turned to her, grinning. "Right here and now. Let's get married!"

The game was forgotten. They ran to find a druid and were married before nightfall. Niamh got her normal head back and they were both very happy. But that wasn't the end of it. Niamh looked at her new husband and told him, "I can't stay here long, Oisín. I have to go back to Tír ná nÓg or I will grow old and die. Will you come with me?"

Oisín didn't hesitate. "Anywhere you go, I go."

He didn't even say goodbye to his family. As far as Fionn MacCumhaill knew, his son had disappeared off the face of the Earth. Which was true in a way because Tír ná nÓg is not part of this world.

And then the poor king's worries came true. His son-in-law did indeed become the king, though he didn't steal the crown, he won it in a race.

One of the stranger things about Tír ná nÓg was that it was ruled by whoever was the fastest person there. To decide this, there was a race every seven years. Until then, Niamh's father had never been beaten.

It was different this time, though. The other runners had barely left the start line when Oisín was already at the finish, which was the throne itself.

Oisín was happy as the king of Tír ná nÓg for many years. He and Niamh never grew old. They had two kids, and they were very happy.

But eventually, Oisín became homesick. He missed Ireland and his family and he wanted to go home.

Niamh didn't want him to go. She said that if he went he wouldn't come back to her ever again. He would grow old and blind and, finally, he would die.

"I'll be fine," Oisin promised.

Niamh shook her head, but she knew he would go whether she wanted him to or not. So she gave him a great white horse and said, "Don't ever step off the horse. Don't even touch the ground of Ireland. If you do, you will grow old and die."

Maybe you are rolling your eyes right now. Are you? I bet you are. You know what happens in myths when someone is told not to do something, don't you? That's right, they go and do it.

Well, maybe Oisín will surprise you. Maybe he will be smart and stay on the horse and go back to Tír ná nÓg and continue living happily with Niamh and their two kids.

The Ireland he returned to was nothing like the one he had left. You know how they say one human year is the same as seven years for a dog? Well, one year in Tír ná nÓg was like a hundred in Ireland. So what had seemed like ten years to Oisín in Tír ná nÓg was a thousand in the real world.

The Ireland he had left had been full of forests and small towns with wooden buildings and maybe a couple of stone castles. The Ireland he came back to was full of churches.

Fionn MacCumhaill and even Oisín himself had become myths. They had lived so long ago that people had forgotten that they were even real. One young girl even told the story of how Fionn's son had been stolen away by a fairy from another world.

He traveled to where his father's castle had been, but there was nothing left. At least, that was what he thought. He had just been turning to leave when he saw a stone sticking out of the ground. It was the stone bowl they had washed their hands in when they came in from the fields.

The sight of something he remembered in this strange land, the only thing that remained from his home, filled him with a powerful need to touch it. Forgetting what Niamh said, he got off his horse and bent down to feel the stone.

Between the time his foot touched the ground and when he touched the stone with his finger, a thousand years came over Oisín and he found himself lying on the ground, weak, blind, deaf. Powerless and dying.

Of course he touched the ground. You knew he was going to.

CONCLUSION

W e have reached the end of the book. We hope you enjoyed all the myths. If you look in the acknowledgments and references you will find many more to read.

Maybe one day all the things happening now will become myths, just the way Oisín and his father did. Maybe things we learn about in history books will get exaggerated and changed until the stories say that George Washington sucked his thumb for wisdom, or that Hitler was thrown into the center of the Earth by gods called America, Britain, and Russia and that he rules over Hell.

Maybe there really was a king called Ra who lost his throne to a queen called Isis, but it was so long ago that we will never be able to find the proof. Maybe a boy really did kill a guard dog. Maybe a man called Oisín really left Ireland a long time ago, traveled the whole world, and then came back as an old man.

Maybe all these stories have a kernel of truth, which means

that there is a tiny, tiny bit of truth hidden in the middle of all the make-believe.

That said, there doesn't seem to be much truth in Fionn MacCumhaill dressing up as a baby. It makes for a good story, though, which is all we need from myths. They are the greatest stories ever told and the greatest stories to read and enjoy.

Thank you for reading.

Acknowledgments

We mentioned at the start of the book that it is very important to give people credit for their work. This is not just about being honest, it is also so that we can recommend some other great books about myths that you will love.

A lot of the stories in this book come to you directly from the original translations of the very old books where they were discovered. Some of the myths about Egypt, for example, were translated *directly* from the walls of the pyramids!

Because these books are so old, a lot of them are available for free. The best website for all things mythological is Sacred-Texts, which you can find at this link: https://www.sacred-texts.com/index.htm.

The problem with some old books is that they are very difficult to read. The Pyramid Texts, for example, are copied down exactly as they were on the walls of the pyramids. Maybe you have noticed that the paint falls off the walls in your house after a few years. Well, imagine what it would look like after a few thousand years! As a result, the Pyramid Texts are missing a lot of stuff that people have had to fill in, using things they have read on other pyramids, or they have heard from other people.

One excellent writer who was very good at taking these difficult-to-read texts and making them fun is Padraic Colum. His book, *Orpheus: Myths of the World,* is an interesting and fun book that tells stories from all over the world, including Japan and Latin America, and New Zealand—places we didn't get to visit in this book. A lot of his books are also available on the Sacred-Texts website.

Another great writer who has many books about myths and other amazing stories like King Arthur and Robin Hood is Roger Lancelyn Green. If you enjoyed this book, you should definitely read his.

This book owes a lot to many other writers and books. If you want to see a full list of other books you might like, or to know where some of the stories and facts in this book came from, look at the references at the end.

We hope you enjoy all your future journeys through mythology! You have a lifetime of them to come.

REFERENCES

EGYPTIAN MYTHOLOGY FOR KIDS: DISCOVER FASCINATING HISTORY, FACTS, GODS, GODDESSES, BEDTIME STORIES, PHARAOHS, PYRAMIDS, MUMMIES & MORE FROM ANCIENT EGYPT

Adhikari, S. (2019, April 9). *Top 10 Fascinating Facts about the Egyptian Pyramids.* Ancient History Lists. https://www.ancienthistorylists.com/egypt-history/top-10-facts-egyptian-pyramids/

Allen, R. C. (1997). Agriculture and the Origins of the State in Ancient Egypt. *Explorations in Economic History, 34*(2), 135–154. https://doi.org/10.1006/exeh.1997.0673

Britannica. (2020). *Ancient Egypt - The Early Dynastic period* (c. 2925–c. 2575 bce). https://www.britannica.com/place/ancient-Egypt/The-Early-Dynastic-period-c-2925-c-2575-bce

Britannica. (2020). *Ancient Egypt - The Predynastic and Early Dynastic periods* https://www.britannica.com/place/ancient-Egypt/The-Predynastic-and-Early-Dynastic-periods

Ancient Egypt Online. (n.d.). *The Princess of Bekheten | Ancient Egypt Online.* https://ancientegyptonline.co.uk/princessbekheten/

Art in Context. (2021, July 14). *Egyptian Art - An Exploration of Ancient Egyptian Art and Its Influences.* https://artincontext.org/egyptian-art/

Arun. (2018, September 12). *10 Interesting Facts About Religion In Ancient Egypt | Learnodo Newtonic.* Learnodo-Newtonic.com. https://learnodo-newtonic.com/ancient-egypt-religion-facts

Atkins, H. (2018, June 20). *10 Famous Ancient Egyptian Pharaohs.* History Hit; History Hit. https://www.historyhit.com/famous-ancient-egyptian-pharaohs/

The Australian Museum. (2018, November 21). *Art in ancient Egypt.* https://australian.museum/learn/cultures/internatio nal-collection/ancient-egyptian/art-in-ancient-egypt/

Bevan, R. (n.d.). *The greatest pharaohs of Ancient Egypt.* Sky HISTORY TV Channel. Retrieved April 9, 2022, from https://www.history.co.uk/shows/legends-of-the-pharaohs/articles/the-greatest-pharaohs-of-ancient-egypt

The British Museum. (2017, August 2). *Everything you ever wanted to know about the Rosetta Stone.* The British Museum Blog; The British Museum. https://blog.britishmuseum.org/everything-you-ever-wanted-to-know-about-the-rosetta-stone/

Canadian Museum of History. (2019). *Egyptian civilization - Government.* Historymuseum.ca. https://www.historymuseum.ca/cmc/exhibitions/civi l/egypt/egcgov1e.html

Carnegie Museum of Natural History. (2020, September 14). *Egypt and the Nile.* https://carnegiemnh.org/egypt-and-the-nile/#:~:text=Ancient%20Egypt%20was%20located %20in

Chalmers, M. (2021, April 4). *Life after Death in Ancient Egypt | History Today.* Www.historytoday.com. https://www.historytoday.com/archive/history-matters/life-after-death-ancient-egypt

Digital Giza. (n.d.). *Daily Life in Ancient Egypt.* Giza.fas.harvard.edu; Harvard. Retrieved April 10, 2022, from http://giza.fas.harvard.edu/lessons/ancient-egyptian-writing

Dorman, P. F. (2019). Valley of the Kings | archaeological site, Egypt | Britannica. In *Encyclopædia Britannica*. https://www.britannica.com/place/Valley-of-the-Kings

Dorman, P. F., & Baines, J. R. (2017). ancient Egyptian religion | History, Rituals, & Gods. In *Encyclopædia Britannica*. https://www.britannica.com/topic/ancient-Egyptian-religion

Ducksters. (2019). *Ancient Egyptian History for Kids: Geography and the Nile River*. Ducksters.com. https://www.ducksters.com/history/ancient_egypt/geography_nile_river.php

Ducksters. (2019). *Ancient Egyptian History for Kids: Mummies*. https://www.ducksters.com/history/ancient_egyptian_mummies.php

Egyptian Myths. (2014). *Ancient Egypt: the Mythology - The Book of Thoth*. http://www.egyptianmyths.net/mythbookthoth.htm

Egyptian Myths. (n.d.). *Ancient Egypt: the Mythology - The Peasant and the Workman*. Www.egyptianmyths.net. Retrieved April 11, 2022, from http://www.egyptianmyths.net/mythsekhti.htm

Egyptian Myths. (n.d.). *Ancient Egypt: the Mythology - The Prince and the Sphinx*. Retrieved April 11, 2022, from http://www.egyptianmyths.net/mythsphinx.htm

Egyptian Myths. (n.d.). *Ancient Egypt: the Mythology - The Treasure Thief*. (2014). Egyptianmyths.net. http://www.egyptianmyths.net/mythtthief.htm

The Editors of Encyclopedia Britannica. (2019). *Book of the Dead | ancient Egyptian text.* https://www.britannica.com/topic/Book-of-the-Dead-ancient-Egyptian-text

The Editors of Encyclopaedia Britannica. (2019). *Egyptian architecture.* In Encyclopædia Britannica. https://www.britannica.com/art/Egyptian-architecture

The Editors of Encyclopaedia Britannica. (2018). *11 Egyptian Gods and Goddesses.* https://www.britannica.com/list/11-egyptian-gods-and-goddesses

The Editors of Encyclopedia Britannica. (2010). *Lower Egypt | geographical division, Egypt.* https://www.britannica.com/place/Lower-Egypt

The Editors of Encyclopedia Britannica. (2020). *Mortuary temple | Egyptian temple* https://www.britannica.com/topic/mortuary-temple

The Editors of Encyclopedia Britannica. (2020). *Mummy embalming.* https://www.britannica.com/topic/mummy

The Editors of Encyclopedia Britannica. (2016). *Pharaoh | Egyptian king.* https://www.britannica.com/topic/pharaoh

The Editors of Encyclopedia Britannica. (2019). *Pyramids of Giza | History & Facts.* https://www.britannica.com/topic/Pyramids-of-Giza

Eunice, M. (2019, January 14). *26 Strange Facts About The Pyramids Of Egypt Very Few Know.* TheTravel. https://www.thetravel.com/26-strange-facts-about-the-pyramids-of-egypt-very-few-know/

Flinders Petrie, W. M. (n.d.). *The Peasant and the Workman | TOTA*. Www.tota.world. Retrieved April 11, 2022, from https://www.tota.world/article/213/

Garnet, T., & Dorman, P. F. (2019). Egyptian art and architecture | History & Facts. In *Encyclopædia Britannica*. https://www.britannica.com/art/Egyptian-art

Handwerk, B. (2010, October 21). *Egypt's Valley of the Kings Provides a Window to the Past*. History. https://www.nationalgeographic.com/history/article/valley-of-the-kings

Handwerk, B. (2017, January 21). *Pyramids of Giza | National Geographic*. History. https://www.nationalgeographic.com/history/article/giza-pyramids

Hays, J. (n.d.). *WORSHIP AND RITUALS IN ANCIENT EGYPT | Facts and Details*. Factsanddetails.com. Retrieved April 9, 2022, from https://factsanddetails.com/world/cat56/sub403/entry-6114.html

Heritage Daily. (2021, January 19). *The Ancient Egyptian Pyramids*. https://www.heritagedaily.com/2021/01/the-ancient-egyptian-pyramids/134365

History for Kids. (2019). *Animals of Ancient Egypt - Facts for Kids*. https://www.historyforkids.net/egyptian-animals.html

History on the Net. (2018, April 25). *Egyptian Social Classes and Society - History*. https://www.historyonthenet.com/the-egyptians-society

History.com Editors. (2018, August 21). *Egyptian Pyramids*. HISTORY; A&E Television Networks.

https://www.history.com/topics/ancient-history/the-egyptian-pyramids

History.com Editors. (2020, February 21). *Ancient Egypt*. HISTORY; A&E Television Networks. https://www.history.com/topics/ancient-history/ancient-egypt

Hoch, J. (2019). Egyptian language | History, Writing, & Hieroglyphics. In *Encyclopædia Britannica*. https://www.britannica.com/topic/Egyptian-language

HowStuffWorks. (2021, December 16). *10 Amazing Ancient Egyptian Inventions*. https://science.howstuffworks.com/innovation/inventions/5-amazing-ancient-egyptian-inventions.htm

Hughes, T. (2019, October 30). *13 Important Gods and Goddesses of Ancient Egypt*. History Hit. https://www.historyhit.com/important-gods-and-goddesses-of-ancient-egypt/

Jarus, O. (2012, September 10). *Step Pyramid of Djoser: Egypt's First Pyramid*. Live Science; Live Science. https://www.livescience.com/23050-step-pyramid-djoser.html

Kasawne, S. (n.d.). *Myth Project: The Treasure Thief*. Sites.google.com. Retrieved April 11, 2022, from https://sites.google.com/site/mythprojecthetreasuret hief/

Kashyap Vyas. (2018, February 25). *Egyptian pyramids have been fascinating us since long. Despite a lot of research, there are still many secrets*. Interestingengineering.com; Interesting Engineering. https://interestingengineering.com/explore-33-interesting-facts-about-the-ancient-egyptian-pyramids

Kiger, P. J. (2021, July 26). *8 Facts About Ancient Egypt's Hieroglyphic Writing.* HISTORY. https://www.history.com/news/hieroglyphics-facts-ancient-egypt

Kinnaer, J. (2013). *Bent Pyramid at Dashur | The Ancient Egypt Site.* Ancient-Egypt.org. http://www.ancient-egypt.org/history/old-kingdom/4th-dynasty/snofru/pyramids/bent-pyramid-at-dashur.html

Mark, J. (2009, September 2). *Pharaoh.* World History Encyclopedia. https://www.worldhistory.org/pharaoh/

Mark, J. (2016a, January 18). *Predynastic Period in Egypt.* World History Encyclopedia. https://www.worldhistory.org/Predynastic_Period_in_Egypt/

Mark, J. (2016b, January 20). *Ancient Egyptian Religion.* World History Encyclopedia. https://www.worldhistory.org/Egyptian_Religion/

Mark, J. (2016c, January 22). *Early Dynastic Period In Egypt.* World History Encyclopedia. https://www.worldhistory.org/Early_Dynastic_Period_In_Egypt/

Mark, J. (2016d, March 18). *Pets in Ancient Egypt.* World History Encyclopedia. https://www.worldhistory.org/article/875/pets-in-ancient-egypt/#:~:text=The%20ancient%20Egyptians%20kept%20animals

Mark, J. (2016e, March 28). *Egyptian Afterlife - The Field of Reeds.* World History Encyclopedia. https://www.worldhistory.org/article/877/egyptian-afterlife---the-field-of-reeds/

Mark, J. (2016f, April 14). *Egyptian Gods - The Complete List.* World History Encyclopedia. https://www.worldhistory.org/article/885/egyptian-gods---the-complete-list/

Mark, J. (2016g, September 26). *Old Kingdom of Egypt.* World History Encyclopedia. https://www.worldhistory.org/Old_Kingdom_of_Egypt/

Mark, J. (2016h, October 13). *Ancient Egyptian Government.* World History Encyclopedia. https://www.worldhistory.org/Egyptian_Government/#:~:text=The%20government%20of%20ancient%20Egypt

Mark, J. (2017a, January 10). *Ancient Egyptian Agriculture.* World History Encyclopedia. https://www.worldhistory.org/article/997/ancient-egyptian-agriculture/

Mark, J. (2017b, June 15). *Trade in Ancient Egypt.* World History Encyclopedia. https://www.worldhistory.org/article/1079/trade-in-ancient-egypt/

Menes | Pharaoh, Accomplishments, Definition, History, & Facts | Britannica. (n.d.). Www.britannica.com. Retrieved April 9, 2022, from https://www.britannica.com/biography/Menes#:~:text=Menes%2C%20also%20spelled%20Mena%2C%20Meni

Millmore, M. (2007, December 31). *Ancient Egyptian Gods and Goddesses.* Discovering Ancient Egypt. https://discoveringegypt.com/ancient-egyptian-gods-and-goddesses/

Millmore, M. (2008, January 1). *Ancient Egyptian Inventions.* Discovering Ancient Egypt.

https://discoveringegypt.com/ancient-egyptian-inventions/

Ministry of Tourism and Antiquities. (n.d.). *The Red Pyramid.* Egymonuments.gov.eg. Retrieved April 9, 2022, from https://egymonuments.gov.eg/monuments/the-red-pyramid/

Ministry of Tourism and Antiquities. (n.d.). *Valley of the Kings.* Retrieved April 11, 2022, from https://egymonuments.gov.eg/archaeological-sites/valley-of-the-kings/

National Geographic. (2021, July 16). *How the Rosetta Stone unlocked the secrets of ancient civilizations.* https://www.nationalgeographic.com/history/article/how-the-rosetta-stone-unlocked-the-secrets-of-ancient-civilizations

Nix, E. (2018, August 23). *What is the Rosetta Stone?* HISTORY. https://www.history.com/news/what-is-the-rosetta-stone

Reading Museum. (2020, May 11). *Sacred animals of Ancient Egypt.* Reading Museum. https://www.readingmuseum.org.uk/blog/sacred-animals-ancient-egypt

Reuters. (2019, July 14). *"Bent" pyramid: Egypt opens ancient oddity for tourism.* The Guardian; The Guardian. https://www.theguardian.com/world/2019/jul/14/bent-pyramid-egypt-opens-ancient-oddity-for-tourism

Smithsonian. (2012). *Egyptian Mummies.* Smithsonian Institution. https://www.si.edu/spotlight/ancient-egypt/mummies

Smithsonian. (2019). *The Egyptian Pyramid*. Smithsonian Institution. https://www.si.edu/spotlight/ancient-egypt/pyramid

Society, N. G. (2019, March 1). *Pharaohs*. National Geographic Society. https://www.nationalgeographic.org/encyclopedia/pharaohs/#:~:text=As%20ancient%20Egyptian%20rulers%2C%20pharaohs

Storynory. (2021, May 16). *The Doomed Prince*. https://www.storynory.com/the-doomed-prince/

Students of History. (n.d.). *Ancient Egypt's Geography*. Retrieved April 10, 2022, from https://www.studentsofhistory.com/ancient-egypt-s-geography

Thompson, S. (2021, July 2). *Ten Facts on the Ancient Egyptian Pyramids*. Blog.bridgemanimages.com. https://blog.bridgemanimages.com/blog/ten-facts-on-the-ancient-egyptian-pyramids

Tikkanen, A. (2017). Great Sphinx of Giza | Description, History, & Facts. In *Encyclopædia Britannica*. https://www.britannica.com/topic/Great-Sphinx

UShistory. (2019). *Egyptian Social Structure [ushistory.org]*. https://www.ushistory.org/civ/3b.asp

Wendorf, M. (2019, April 23). *Ancient Egyptian Technology and Inventions*. Interestingengineering.com. https://interestingengineering.com/ancient-egyptian-technology-and-inventions#:~:text=The%20ancient%20Egyptians%20would%20come

WorldAtlas. (2016, October 5). *Ancient Egyptian Animals*. WorldAtlas. https://www.worldatlas.com/articles/animals-of-ancient-egypt.html

GREEK MYTHOLOGY FOR KIDS: EXPLORE TIMELESS TALES & BEDTIME STORIES FROM ANCIENT GREECE. MYTHS, HISTORY, FANTASY & ADVENTURES OF THE GODS, GODDESSES, TITANS, HEROES, MONSTERS & MORE

Adkins, A. W. H., & Richard, J. (2018). Greek mythology | gods, stories, & history. In *Encyclopædia Britannica*. https://www.britannica.com/topic/Greek-mythology

Cavendish, R. (1974). *Man, myth, & magic: An illustrated encyclopedia of the supernatural*. Marshall Cavendish.

Fry, S. (2019). *Mythos: The greek myths reimagined*. Chronicle Books.

Fry, S. (2020). *Heroes: The greek myths reimagined*. Chronicle Books.

Graves, R., & Guirand, F. (1968). *New Larousse encyclopedia of mythology*. Hamlyn.

Greek mythology. (2010). Greekmythology.com. https://www.greekmythology.com/

NORSE MYTHOLOGY FOR KIDS: LEGENDARY STORIES, QUESTS & TIMELESS TALES FROM NORSE FOLKLORE. THE MYTHS, SAGAS & EPICS OF THE GODS, IMMORTALS, MAGIC CREATURES, VIKINGS AND MORE

Alectryon (mythology). (2021, April 29). Wikipedia. https://en.wikipedia.org/wiki/Alectryon_(mythology)

Álfheimr. (2021). Religion Wiki. https://religion.wikia.org/wiki/%C3%81lfheimr

Arithharger. (2013, October 7). *Heimdall's Birth*. Whispers of Yggdrasi https://arithharger.wordpress.com/2013/10/07/heimdalls-birth/

B, V. (2018). Man holding rope. In
https://unsplash.com/photos/IYyvakvhi7I.

Branstock. (n.d.). Britannica Kids. Retrieved August 15,
2021, from
https://kids.britannica.com/students/article/Bransto
ck/310360

Cartwright, M. (2015, May 16). *Brahma*. World History
Encyclopedia.
https://www.worldhistory.org/Brahma/

Chidanand, A. (2017). Ocean moody waves. In *Image by
Aadya Chidanand from Pixabay*.

Climo, S., & Florczak, R. (2001). *The Persian Cinderella*.
Harpercollins.

Climo, S., & Heller, R. (1992). *The Egyptian Cinderella*.
Harpertrophy.

Eliot, T. S. (1971). *Four quartets*. Mariner Books, Houghton
Mifflin Harcourt, [201.

Furman, P. (2016). Person wearing red and white coat. In
Photo by Paweł Furman on Unsplash.

Girls, G. (2020). Reindeer Elk. In *Image by GypsyGirlS
from Pixabay*.

Hel (The Underworld) - Norse Mythology for Smart People.
(2012). Norse Mythology for Smart People.
https://norse-mythology.org/cosmology/the-nine-
worlds/helheim/

*How Frey Gained the Antlers of Saklauss | Thomas Hewitt's
Poetry*. (n.d.). Thomashewitt.org. Retrieved August
28, 2021, from https://thomashewitt.org/how-frey-
gained-the-antlers-of-saklauss/

Hrustall. (2021). Дмитрий Хрусталев-Григорьев. In *Photo
by Дмитрий Хрусталев-Григорьев on Unsplash*.

Keller, S. (2017). Fantasy landscape cave. In *Image by Stefan
Keller from Pixabay*.

Krause, W. (2010). Fantasy world. In *Image by Willgard Krause from Pixabay.*

Nilsson, O. (2017). Wind in the grey mane. In *Photo by Oscar Nilsson on Unsplash.*

NORSE GODS: MÁNI – Ýdalir. (2018). Ydalir.ca. http://ydalir.ca/norsegods/mani/

NORSE GODS: SÓL – Ýdalir. (n.d.). Ydalir.ca. http://ydalir.ca/norsegods/sol/

Northern Norway – where the sun never sets. (n.d.). Www.visitnorway.com. https://www.visitnorway.com/things-to-do/nature-attractions/midnight-sun/

Ragnarok | Encyclopedia.com. (2019). Encyclopedia.com. https://www.encyclopedia.com/literature-and-arts/classical-literature-mythology-and-folklore/folklore-and-mythology/ragnarok

Recap. (n.d.). Dictionary.cambridge.org. Retrieved August 20, 2021, from https://dictionary.cambridge.org/dictionary/english/recap

San, R. D. (1997). *Sootface : an Ojibwa Cinderella tale.* Bantam Doubleday Books For Young Readers.

Sigmund. (n.d.). Britannica Kids. Retrieved August 28, 2021, from https://kids.britannica.com/students/article/Sigmund/313536

Skjalden. (2018, July 30). *The Mead of Poetry - Nordic Culture - Norse mythology.* Nordic Culture. https://skjalden.com/mead-of-poetry/

Skjalden. (2020, September 19). *Yggdrasil - The World Tree - Norse Mythology.* Nordic Culture. https://skjalden.com/yggdrasil/

Skjalden. (2017, September 24). *Thor's Duel with Hrungnir - Norse Sagas - Norse Mythology*. Nordic Culture. https://skjalden.com/giant-hrungnir/

Skov Andersen, J. (2015, May 6). *Fashionable Vikings loved colours, fur, and silk*. Sciencenordic.com. https://sciencenordic.com/archaeology-history-denmark-society--culture/fashionable-vikings-loved-colours-fur-and-silk/1417589

Staff, History. com. (2018, August 29). *Was King Arthur a real person?* HISTORY. https://www.history.com/news/was-king-arthur-a-real-person

Stavrou, D., & Tchetchik, D. (2017, December 18). *In extraordinary photos: Sweden says a long goodbye to sunlight*. Haaretz.com. https://www.haaretz.com/world-news/MAGAZINE-in-extraordinary-photos-the-swedes-say-a-long-goodbye-to-sunlight-1.5628672

Survival International. (2018). *Sentinelese*. Survivalinternational.org. https://www.survivalinternational.org/tribes/sentinelese

Tanis, L. (2017). Pandora The World of Avatar. In *Photo by Luke Tanis on Unsplash*.

White, T. H., & Shadbolt, R. (1998). *The sword in the stone*. Harpercollins Children's Books.

Wikipedia Contributors. (2019, October 23). *Edda*. Wikipedia; Wikimedia Foundation. https://en.wikipedia.org/wiki/Edda

Wikipedia Contributors. (2020, January 9). *Ragnarök*. Wikipedia; Wikimedia Foundation. https://en.wikipedia.org/wiki/Ragnar%C3%B6k

Yantis, M. (2021). blue and brown ceramic vase. In *Photo by Michael Yantis on Unsplash*.

Zak, P. (2013, December 17). *How Stories Change the Brain*. Greater Good. https://greatergood.berkeley.edu/article/item/how_stories_change_brain

MYTHOLOGY FOR KIDS: EXPLORE THE GREATEST STORIES EVER TOLD BY THE EGYPTIAN, GREEKS, ROMANS, VIKINGS, AND CELTS

Apollodorus. (1921). *The library*. (J.G. Frazer, Trans.). Loeb Classical Library.

Bellows, H. A. (Trans.). (1936). *The poetic Edda*. Princeton University Press.

Britannica, T. Editors of Encyclopaedia (2017, April 27). *Cú Chulainn*. Encyclopedia Britannica. https://www.britannica.com/topic/Cu-Chulainn

Britannica, T. Editors of Encyclopaedia (2018, December 7). *Lugus*. Encyclopedia Britannica. https://www.britannica.com/topic/Lugus

Budge, W. (1912). *Legends of the gods*. Createspace Independent Publishing Platform.

Bulfinch, T. (1855). *The age of fable, or stories of the gods and heroes*. Sanborn, Carter, and Bazin.

Butler, S. (Trans.). (1898). *The Iliad of Homer*. Longmans, Green, & Co.

Colum, P. (1930). *Orpheus, myths of the world*. Macmillan.

Colum, P. (1920). *The children of Odin: The book of northern myths*. Macmillan.

Cross, T.P. & Slover, C.H. (Eds.). (1936). Bricriu's feast. *Ancient Irish tales* (pp. 254-280). (G. Henderson, Trans.). George G. Harraph & Co.

Curtin, J. (1890). *Myths and folk-lore of Ireland*. (1st American Edition). Little Brown.

Dillon, M. (1998, September 19). *Celtic religion*. Encyclopædia Britannica. https://www.britannica.com/topic/Celtic-religion.

Encyclopædia Britannica, inc. (1998, July 20). *Gaelic revival*. Encyclopædia Britannica. https://www.britannica.com/art/Gaelic-revival.

Encyclopædia Britannica, inc. (2012, March 2). *Irish literary renaissance*. Encyclopædia Britannica. https://www.britannica.com/event/Irish-literary-renaissance.

Encyclopædia Britannica, inc. (2020, November 26). *Viking*. Encyclopædia Britannica. https://www.britannica.com/topic/Viking-people.

Fry, S. (2017). *Mythos: A retelling of the myths of Ancient Greece*. Michael Joseph.

Gregory, Lady A. (1902). *Cuchulain of Muirthemne*. Alfred Nutt.

Gregory, Lady A. (1904). *Gods and fighting men: the story of the Tuatha de Danaan and of the Fianna of Ireland*. J. Murray.

Hesiod. (1936). *Hesiod. The Homeric hymns and Homerica*. (H. G. Evelyn-White, Trans.). (3rd rev. ed.). Loeb Classical Library.

Hornblower, S. (1999, July 26). *Alexander the Great*. Encyclopædia Britannica. https://www.britannica.com/place/ancient-Greece/Alexander-the-Great.

Jacobs, J., & Batten, J.D. (1968). *Celtic fairy tales*. Dover Publications.

Jordan, M. (1993). *Myths of the world*. Kyle Cathie.

Mercer, S. (Trans.). (1952). *The pyramid texts*. Longsmans, Green Co.

Meyer, K. (1904). The boyish exploits of Finn. *Eriu*, 1, 180-190. Royal Irish Academy. (Original work published 1881). http://www.jstor.org/stable/30007946.

Monaghan, P. (2004). *Encyclopedia of Celtic mythology and folklore*. (2nd ed.). Facts on File.

Morford, M., Lenardon, R. J., & Sham, M. (2019). *Myth summary chapter 8: Athena*. Oxford University Press. https://global.oup.com/us/companion.websites/9780199997329/student/materials/chapter8/summary/.

Murray, M.A. (1920). *Ancient Egyptian legends*. John Murray.

National Geographic Society. (2019, January 15). *Alexander the Great*. National Geographic Society. https://www.nationalgeographic.org/encyclopedia/alexander-great/.

Ovid. (2009). *Metamorphoses*. (A.D. Melville, Trans.). (Oxford World's Classics). Oxford University Press.

Persephone. Greek Mythology Wiki. (2009, May 17). https://greekmythology.wikia.org/wiki/Persephone.

Rank, O. (1914). *The myth of the birth of the hero*. (E. Robbins & S. Jelliffe, Trans.). (1st ed. in English). The Journal of Nervous and Mental Disease. (Original work published 1909).

Roman, M. & Roman, L. (2010). *Encyclopedia of Greek and Roman mythology*. Facts on File.

Sheppard, Norman. (2008, September 22). *Tyr*. The Norse Gods. https://thenorsegods.com/tyr/.

Sturluson, S. (1960). *The prose Edda*. (A. Brodeur, Trans.). American-Scandinavian Foundation. (Original work published 1916).

Turville-Petre, E. O. G. (1999, July 26). *Germanic religion and mythology*. Encyclopædia Britannica. https://www.britannica.com/topic/Germanic-religion-and-mythology.

Yeats, W.B. (1893). *The Celtic twilight*. Lawrence and Bullen.

OTHER BOOKS BY HISTORY BROUGHT ALIVE

- Ancient Egypt: Discover Fascinating History, Mythology, Gods, Goddesses, Pharaohs, Pyramids, and More from the Mysterious Ancient Egyptian Civilization.

Available now on Kindle, Paperback, Hardcover & Audio in all regions

- Greek Mythology: Explore The Timeless Tales Of Ancient Greece, The Myths, History & Legends of The Gods, Goddesses, Titans, Heroes, Monsters & More

Available now on Kindle, Paperback, Hardcover & Audio in all regions

- Mythology for Kids: Explore Timeless Tales, Characters, History, & Legendary Stories from Around the World. Norse, Celtic, Roman, Greek, Egypt & Many More

Available now on Kindle, Paperback, Hardcover & Audio in all regions

- Mythology of Mesopotamia: Fascinating Insights, Myths, Stories & History From The World's Most Ancient Civilization. Sumerian, Akkadian, Babylonian, Persian, Assyrian and More

Available now on Kindle, Paperback, Hardcover & Audio in all regions

- Norse Magic & Runes: A Guide To The Magic, Rituals, Spells & Meanings of Norse Magick, Mythology & Reading The Elder Futhark Runes

Available now on Kindle, Paperback, Hardcover & Audio in all regions

- Norse Mythology, Vikings, Magic & Runes: Stories, Legends & Timeless Tales From Norse & Viking Folklore + A Guide To The Rituals, Spells & Meanings of Norse Magick & The Elder Futhark Runes. (3 books in 1)

Available now on Kindle, Paperback, Hardcover & Audio in all regions

- Norse Mythology: Captivating Stories & Timeless Tales Of Norse Folklore. The Myths, Sagas & Legends of The Gods, Immortals, Magical Creatures, Vikings & More

Available now on Kindle, Paperback, Hardcover & Audio in all regions

- Norse Mythology for Kids: Legendary Stories, Quests & Timeless Tales from Norse Folklore. The Myths, Sagas & Epics of the Gods, Immortals, Magic Creatures, Vikings & More

Available now on Kindle, Paperback, Hardcover & Audio in all regions

- Roman Empire: Rise & The Fall. Explore The History, Mythology, Legends, Epic Battles & Lives Of The Emperors, Legions, Heroes, Gladiators & More

Available now on Kindle, Paperback, Hardcover & Audio in all regions

- The Vikings: Who Were The Vikings? Enter The Viking Age & Discover The Facts, Sagas, Norse Mythology, Legends, Battles & More

Available now on Kindle, Paperback, Hardcover & Audio in all regions

Made in the USA
Monee, IL
24 December 2022

a12f0341-adc5-4321-ba8c-99583aabb9caR01